STORY OF

A

STOLEN GIRL

PAT SPENCER

Copyright © by Patricia A. Spencer, 2018
Book Cover by Mike Spencer

Library of Congress Cataloging Publication Data
Names: Spencer, Pat, author
Title: Story of a Stolen Girl / Pat Spencer
Identifiers: LCCN 2018907581

ISBN 13:978-1721897179

Dedicated, worldwide, to all the stolen girls.

May they be found.

PAT SPENCER

CHAPTER ONE
Darby Richards - Day Two – Sunday, March 18

A door slammed and reverberated like a gunshot through a tunnel. Darby pulled her knees up, hugged them to her chest. When the vibration spent its energy and fell silent to the floor, she opened one eye, a tiny slit, to a room engulfed in darkness. She thought she called out, but no sound escaped her lips. In the distance, muffled voices…men…talking, laughing. She strained to hear what they were saying. They weren't speaking English. Their accent was familiar, not Spanish, maybe Middle Eastern, but she didn't comprehend a single word.

Struggling to turn toward the voices, her body convulsed. Darby couldn't tell whether from fear or cold. She covered her mouth as heavy footsteps moved her way. She prayed they wouldn't hear her whimper.

No…please no…

When Darby awoke again, the flutter of her heart accelerated into pounding. She pressed her palm against her chest, afraid the men might hear. She contracted her muscles to force her body still. The tension made her quiver even more.

Darby didn't know where she was but knew it wasn't by choice. Her breath came in raspy spurts. She swallowed the noisy gasps to quiet them and listened. Thoughts coming at the speed of sludge, she slipped her fingers through her tangled hair and massaged her head.

Where am I?

Every limb weighed heavy and awkward. She labored to roll over, but her shoulders wouldn't turn. With flailing arms, she probed for something on which to anchor. Darby pitched to her side, cringed when she rammed into a wall. Her fingers dug into its roughness until they found an edge. She told herself to pull harder. With all her strength, she clamped her finger onto the ridge and heaved herself upright. Pain knifed toward her elbow. She shrieked and lost her grip.

A warm thick liquid oozed from her hand. Even though Darby drew it to her face, she didn't understand what had happened. Her thoughts were as murky as the room. Pressure in her brain pushed against her eyes. Her vision blurred and blackened. As she crumpled to the cot, she whispered, "Mom…"

Darby couldn't tell how long she remained unconscious, and no one was there to care, yet she understood instinctively she was safer alone. As her senses cleared, she became aware of a pulsing throb. In the shadows, she felt more than saw two fingernails ripped and hanging loose. She picked at crusted blood, dried in rivulets down her arm.

Have to get out before the men come in…

Darby steeled herself and thrust from the bedframe to stand. On wobbly legs, she stepped to the far side of the boxlike room. Steadying herself against the wall, she staggered to the door. Darby ran her hand across the scaly metal and searched in the dim light until she touched the doorknob. When it turned, her anticipation soared but sank again as the mechanism clanked and froze.

I'm locked in?

Darby collapsed with her back against the door but pushed away when rusty slivers of metal cut through her blouse. Spots of blood rose warm on her back. She crumpled to the cot and whispered into the gloom. "Why am I here?"

Snippets of sounds and faces flitted as she rubbed her aching head. When a mental picture formed, Darby saw herself standing at the curb with her psychology professor, then looking around for her roommate, Esma.

Never get into a car with a stranger.

That was the most important thing her mother taught her before she allowed her to go out alone. Now that it happened, Darby knew she shouldn't have let it, but she couldn't remember how or why she did. A confused thought formed but evaporated before she grasped it. She pressed against her forehead and shook her head. The vision returned.

Her heart hammered against her chest, surging as it had when the black car screeched to the curb, and the driver jumped out and opened the door. She saw herself step back. The vision so real, she felt her professor grip her arm, his voice close as he whispered in her ear. "Do not worry, my dear. You will be fine." But she was miles and miles from fine.

Darby braced both hands against the dank wall, pushed away and rolled onto her side. The exertion caused her to suck down one deep breath. The reek of mold and urine from the mattress filled her lungs, and a grumble gurgled up from her gut. The contraction pushed bitter slime into her throat. Her nose curled at the smell of her own sour breath.

My head, my stomach, think I vomited. Was I poisoned?

Darby pushed against the soiled mattress and sat up. The walls swirled. She gripped the cot's metal rail. She tried to straighten her spine, but her head rolled forward, impossible to hold up. Warm tears pooled, cooling against her chilly skin. She called out.

"Help. Please… Someone help me. Anyone…" Her voice faded to a whisper when she realized it was a mistake to call them back to hurt her more.

CHAPTER TWO
Nina Richards - Day Two - Sunday Evening, March 18

The ringtone was a welcome break from the computer screen. Darby's mother rubbed her eyes and read the caller ID. Nina Richards sent her daughter's roommate a motherly smile even though Esma couldn't see it through the phone.

"Mrs. Richards? This is Esma Kulin. I must tell you something."

Nina pictured Esma at the other end of the line, brows furrowed, sable bangs partially covering one eye. The two girls, assigned as roommates at UCLA, grew to be fast friends even though they were as different as the cultures in which they were raised. Her daughter was strong, athletic with long blonde hair, sparkling eyes, and an instant smile. She reminded Nina of the American Girl doll Darby loved as a child. In perfect contrast, Esma was petite, dark, and exotic with cocoa-colored eyes that hinted they knew more than they revealed.

"Might be something bad. I am troubled."

The girls were young, having graduated from high school only a year ago at the age of seventeen, and Nina understood Esma well enough to realize she was a worrier. *First time in the United States, first year in college, living away from her parents and childhood friends, I'd worry too.*

"What is it, Esma?"

9

"Mrs. Richards, I am uncertain how to say this…" Nina waited in silence patiently, still not overly concerned. "Darby did not come home last night and hasn't called. We always let the other know."

"What do you mean she didn't come home?"

"Darby left without me. I have not heard from her all day. I do not know what to do."

"Did you call her? Text her?"

"Many times, Mrs. Richards. Every hour since ten this morning. I did not awaken until then. We stayed out late. When I went to wake Darby to study, she was not in her room."

"But you were together last night? Weren't you?"

"Yes, Mrs. Richards. But then we were not. We remained together most of the evening, but Darby did not come home with me. Then this morning, her room was the same as yesterday. She has not been here at all."

"Perhaps she just left for the gym? Or the Corner Bakery for rolls?"

"But she always makes the coffee. This morning, there was none."

Nina glanced at the desk clock. 9:14 p.m. This wasn't the only time she'd worried that her daughter, first time away from home, might lose her head over a young man. Could this be the first? Darby had several boyfriends in the last few years, but none who seemed too intense or caused Nina any concern. "Has she met someone, Esma?"

"What do you mean, Mrs. Richards?"

"Does she have a new boyfriend? Is it serious this time?" *An entire day has passed.* "Would she stay out all night?"

"No, no." Nina visualized Esma's earnest expression. "We met two nice boys at a fraternity party last week. We have a date to go out with them again, to dinner and the movies, but no, it is not like that at all."

Acid burnt its way up Nina's throat. "Where did you two go last night?"

CHAPTER THREE
Darby - Day One - Saturday Night, March 17

"**G**ambling club? You're kidding, right?" Darby was dumfounded by her roommate's proposal. Esma had shared tons about her sheltered childhood and restricted teens. Her vigilant father and brother monitored her behavior for compliance with cultural mores and religious teachings. Darby frowned as she tried to reconcile the disparities between all she knew of Esma's protected life in Turkey and what she now proposed. "You mean dance club, right? Not gambling club?"

"No, no, Darby." Esma drew the hair from her eyes. "The Belaruse is a private gambling club, members only. Except I have an invitation for tonight. My older brother belongs to one in Ankara. He says women are not permitted, but here in Los Angeles, this is not true. A college girl in Turkey will never experience this."

"Pretty sure the average college girl in the U.S. won't either." Darby experienced pangs of parental responsibility as she debated how she should react to this role reversal. Esma never owned a swimsuit, attended a beerfest, or dated without a chaperone. Since her thirteenth birthday, she always covered her hair with a scarf whenever going out. As a result of her culture and family upbringing, Esma was cautious, steady, rarely a risktaker. On the other hand, Darby led the life of a typical Southern California

12

beach girl, accustomed to going everywhere and seeing everything. During their first quarter at UCLA, the girls struggled with their differences, but Darby introduced Esma to American teenageism. By their second quarter, Darby believed they were more alike than different...until now.

"Esma, your brother will kill me if he finds out I let you go."

"Then he must never know..."

Esma interpreted Darby's silence as approval. With small jerky nods of excitement, she said, "You will come? A new experience for you also?"

"Don't know, Esma. Sounds scary. I'm certain private gambling clubs are illegal in California." Darby contemplated the pros and cons. "Not a great idea. What if it gets raided? And we get arrested?"

"I am confident it is safe."

"You are? How? I've gone to L.A. with my parents for theater, movies, family dinners and lately, a couple of hot dates, but this? I've never heard of a private gambling club except on crime shows. Who invited you?"

"Professor Balik invited me. And I invite you."

"Seriously, Esma?" Even though they agreed their psychology professor was hot, picturing him as a gangster gambler simply didn't compute. "The gambling clubs I've seen in the movies are sleazy, backdoor, down-a-dark-alley, where you give Guido the secret password to enter."

"Darby, do you not think that evilness is invented for the movies? If it was an okay place to play cards, well, that is not a good movie plot. Besides, Professor Balik invited us, not this Guido person of whom you speak."

"Good point, but wasn't Spider-Man arrested for private gambling?"

"What are you saying? I attended every Spider-Man movie. He does not gamble in any of them."

"No, no. Not Spider-Man. I mean Toby Maguire. Saw something online. Let's Google it." Darby scrolled down. "Here it is. No arrest, sued for the return of money he won in some guy's Ponzi scheme. Okay, Spider-Man's cleared, but Esma, I'm still not convinced this is a brilliant idea."

"Darby, Professor Balik would not involve himself in illegal activities. Of course, since this is my first time also, I do not truly know what it will be. But it cannot be the way you say, a sleazy backdoor place where Guido guards the door. I think I watched that movie, the one where innocent women are kidnapped and sold into prostitution."

Darby laughed. "That's the one."

"Professor Balik assured me the Belaruse is high-class, for wealthy people, their own little Monte Carlo. Will you go tonight? Professor Balik put me on the guest list and will be our host."

"Host? Does that mean he'll front us gambling money? I just bought my books for spring quarter. Loose change is all I have left."

From her purse, Esma removed a black business card printed in gold. "With this card and as Professor Balik's guests, we start with a courtesy allowance. However, Darby, I do have money. My parents established an emergency fund. We will stop at the ATM." Esma smiled and bobbed her head up and down. "This is not exactly an emergency, but it will be a new experience for us both. I think that qualifies."

14

"I'm still leery. Let's see if there's anything online about this place."

Darby typed "private gambling clubs." They found instructions for charity gambling, a Delaware bill for private gambling clubs, legalities on private gambling, and Wikipedia's site titled, *Gentlemen's club*.

"Esma, we won't find what we're searching for. This club is private. If it's illegal, it won't pop up. Let's type the name on the card, Belaruse."

As Darby scrolled down, Esma said, "There is nothing bad regarding Belaruse."

"Nothing good either. There's just nothing. Without the 'e' at the end, Belarus is a country in Europe."

"Please, Darby. Let us go tonight. Only for a short time. Quarter exams provide us with an acceptable excuse to withdraw early. Tomorrow morning, we cram. I am most behind in microbiology. The scientific terms, when I interpret them from English to Turkish and back again, by then I am confused." Esma shook her head in frustration.

"Okay, you win. I'll go, but promise we'll stay only an hour. Not even that if the place is the least bit seedy."

"Of course, Darby. Whatever you say. It will be your choice." A smile unfurled across Esma's face. "What will you wear?"

CHAPTER FOUR
Nina - Day Two - Later Sunday Night, March 18

Movie scenes reeled inside Nina's head. The cops always said, "Too early to get upset. We don't do missing persons reports until someone's gone twenty-four to forty-eight hours." *Was that true?* Her thoughts bounced like Mexican jumping beans. Her brain didn't even register that she'd thrown her phone down on the sofa.

Oh my God. Got to call the cops, LAPD, not campus police. As she patted each of her pockets, it occurred to her she should call her mom. *No...no need to worry her yet. Police first.* She reeled around in time to see her cell slide behind a cushion. She snatched it up and instinctively commanded, "Call Darby, mobile."

The phone rang, the same as it always did. Nina inhaled, heavy breath filling her with calm. The ring sounded perfectly normal. *Everything will be fine.* Darby would answer and say, "Hey, Mom," the way she always did. Nina would listen for a twinge of guilt in Darby's voice, speculating how her daughter might explain why she didn't tell Esma where she was going and then stayed out all night. A single ring, then the phone went straight to voicemail. Darby's voice, bright and clear, but not Darby. "Hi. You've reached Darby's cell. Leave a message and I'll call you back." In a state of confused shock, Nina froze. A sharp beep broke the silence. She snapped out of her speechlessness when the tinny automated voice said, "If you are happy with your message, press 1 or hang up to send your message. If not, rerecord now."

"Darby...Darby. Where are you? Call me immediately. Esma called and we're worried sick." Repressed panic in her voice, Nina continued, "Extremely worried, honey. Esma called the campus police. I'm calling LAPD as soon as I hang up. This is serious, honey. You've never done this. Stay out all night without telling anyone? Really? But we're not angry. Just call us now. Call Esma, call me. Just let us know..." The automated voice repeated. "If you are happy with your message, press 1 or hang up to send your message. If not, rerecord now."

Nina disconnected. *What number do I call? 911?* She flipped open her laptop and typed LA police department missing persons. There it was—LAPD Adult Missing Persons Unit. She scanned the page and spotted "877-ASK-LAPD."

She screamed at the website. "Are you kidding me? Unbelievable." She gritted her teeth and muttered, "It's a fricking emergency and you expect me to find the micro letters on this damn phone to dial the number? What the hell's the matter with you people?" Nina's index finger pounded the numbers. After the third ring, a robotic recording said, "Press one for English and two for Español." Infuriated, she disconnected and punched in 911. This time in only one ring, a woman's voice said, "San Clemente 911. What is the nature of your emergency?"

"My daughter's missing."

"How long has she been gone?"

"Since yesterday."

"How old is she?"

"Only eighteen."

"How did you discover that she's missing?"

"Her roommate called me. They're students at UCLA, live in Westwood."

Rapid fire, the 911 operator continued to shoot questions at Nina. "What is her name? What's your name?"

After Nina answered all her questions, the operator said, "Mrs. Richards, I'll give you the direct number of the LAPD Adult Missing Persons Unit. They'll help you. If you need anything else from me, call back."

"Okay, yes, thank you so much." Before Nina could tap the numbers, the phone rang in her hand.

"Mrs. Richards? This is Esma. I called the campus police. An officer is on the way. I'll call you back as soon as he leaves."

"Thank you, Esma. I'm calling LAPD." Nina sighed into the phone. "I just wish you'd told Darby to come home with you."

"I…I am so sorry, Mrs. Richards. I also wish that. But when Darby said Professor Balik had asked her to go for breakfast, I did not think a thing of it, except I was envious. I would be so flattered if he asked me." Esma's husky voice carried a twinge of embarrassment. "He is such a gentleman…and so handsome. But I should have been more…*sorumlu*…responsible. Darby is my best friend. We should not have separated. A terrible mistake. It's just that Professor Balik is so influential among the students, I could not show disrespect."

As Nina disconnected with Esma, she thought, *The professor…need to call him.* She opened to recent calls and tapped Esma's number. When she heard her recorded voice, a gust of despair blasted between Nina's lips. "Esma, do you know the professor's number? Call me back."

Then Nina punched in the number the 911 operator gave her. When the voice at the other end verified that she had reached the

LAPD's missing persons unit, Nina sighed with relief. However, "My name is Nina Richards. My daughter's missing," was all she could say before she was placed on hold. Nina glared at the receiver. "What the…" but she understood she had no choice other than to wait. She slowed her breathing and counted silently, *six…seven…eight…*while waiting for the voice to return. *Nine…ten…eleven…* An eternity seemed to pass before a smoke-damaged larynx boomed through the phone.

"Detective Max Wasden here. How can I help you?"

She repeated, "My name is Nina Richards, and my daughter's missing."

"How long?"

Nina braced herself, expecting him to explain she couldn't file a missing person's report until Darby was gone for forty-eight hours. But he didn't. He asked the same questions as the 911 operator. She answered in a staccato that matched the rhythm of his fingers banging on the keyboard.

When the typing stopped, he said, "Anything else I should know?" He interrupted only twice while she recounted everything Esma had told her.

"Somebody just dropped a note on my desk. UCLA campus police got a call and sent an officer to talk to an Esma Kulin. The roommate? Right?"

"Yes."

"Mrs. Richards, most women are taken by a present or former spouse or a significant other. Does your daughter have an admirer? Any chance she's with a boyfriend?"

"No, no romantic relationship right now."

"Any chance a relative took her?"

Nina explained they had no relatives, it was only the three of them now. "The last thing is what her roommate said, that Darby went to breakfast with her psychology teacher, Professor Balik."

"Do you know this Professor Balik, Mrs. Richards?"

"No, only what Esma told me."

"Can you see your daughter falling for this professor and taking off with him?"

"Honestly, I don't believe so. I guess it could happen, but it'd be strangely out of character. Besides, the professor invited Esma to the gambling club, not Darby. My daughter only went because of her."

"This club, do you have the address?"

"No. Esma does."

"Just got a text. The UCLA officer is talking to Ms. Kulin now. Two detectives will be at your place first thing in the morning, seven or so. They'll look around the house, your daughter's room. If you have anything that might be helpful, show it to them."

"Can't imagine anything here will help."

"Okay but give it some thought. Something may occur to you. You'd be amazed what sometimes helps." He faltered and coughed up the damage of a lifetime of unfiltered cigarettes. "I'll get there shortly after the investigators, around eight. Find two good full-face photos. If no one hears from her by morning, I'll put them out on the wire service. Other agencies may have leads."

"I'll email them now, her high school graduation picture and a casual photo in her Westwood apartment. Can't you send them out tonight? Please. Something's horribly wrong. Darby's not a party girl. She doesn't disappear."

Detective Wasden set down the phone and mumbled under his breath while looking for an old cigarette that might have sunk into a cranny in his desk drawer. "Oh, yeah, I can do it. Only been here twelve hours. Haven't had dinner yet. Wife's gonna be pissed if I miss it again." Nina was trying to decipher exactly what he had said when he picked the phone back up and said, "Sure, couple of things I can do tonight with the photos. I'll give you my personal email. Send in the next thirty minutes, and I'll post 'em on ABNet. Try to stay calm. Numbers are on our side. Most cases of missing women, there's no gun or other weapon involved."

"Gun? Oh my God. I didn't even consider a gun."

"Sorry, sorry. Shouldn't have said that. Slipped out of my big mouth." He shook his head, irritated at himself. When he spotted a bit of dry crumpled cigarette peeking out from under a box of paperclips, he snatched the stub and stuck it between his lips. "Listen, Mrs. Richards, what I mean is most victims are freed quickly and without injury. Anyway, we don't even know... She may call you anytime now."

Nina believed, in his own bungling way, he meant to comfort her. Unfortunately, the opposite was true. The instant she disconnected, her anger roared back. When Keith died three years ago, Nina suffered every one of the seven stages of grief. A textbook case, she was long past the third phase of anger, until now. Hot rage boiled up from her stomach, through her chest and pushed against the insides of her eyes. She pressed with her hands to hold it back. A scream tried to escape, but her throat constricted and crushed it into a moan. "Why did you leave? What do I do all by myself?" Her wailful cries melted into a whisper. "Please tell me what to do."

Almost as though Keith answered, it occurred to her. *Call the university. Find him yourself.* "Okay, Google now. Call UCLA."

After the first ring, a soft sweet voice answered. Nina thought she might be a student, the same as her Darby.

"Good Evening. University of California, Los Angeles. How may I direct your call?"

"Professor Balik, please." During the pause, Nina listened to the operator's fingers tap on a keyboard.

"Professor Balik isn't on campus this evening. He teaches Tuesdays and Thursdays. You may leave a message."

"This is an emergency. Can't wait 'til Tuesday. His home number, please."

"University policy does not allow me to provide home numbers. But, if you leave a message, our faculty members are prompt to return calls."

Nina listened to the operator transfer her and then a ring in the background. One ring…two…three. *What do I say? Everything?* Four rings…five…six. *Or only my name and number? What if I alert him and he runs?*

His voice sounded professorial, calm, and accommodating, so Nina left a message, first name and number only. Her finger moved toward the disconnect button, but she jerked the phone back to her mouth. "Please call me as soon as you receive this. It's important."

"What should I do now?" she said out loud, unsure if she was asking herself or her deceased husband, Keith.

Nina looked around as if the answer might lurk in the corners of the room. She sat, she stood, she paced in front of the sofa and agonized about her call to the LAPD. Detective Wasden had acted completely professional, even though somewhat of a bumbler, but clearly, she hadn't convinced him the problem was real. "Young people go places, stay out, and do things they don't tell their mothers or their roommates," he had said. *He thinks I'm a hysterical mother. Yes, I'm on the border of hysteria, but not a hysterical woman.*

During Keith's illness, Nina managed her grief by sleeping for hours, too exhausted to even cry, while her mother, Sally, had taken charge. Nina smiled when she remembered the documentary they had watched years before that explained the role of the female lion within its pride. With all the seriousness a seven-year-old could muster, Darby said, "That's you, Grandma Sally. You're our alpha female."

However, the tragic events of the last few years reversed their roles. After Nina's husband and father both died within a couple years of each other, she ascended to the alpha role. The first year, Nina remolded herself into what she believed her ageing mother and teenaged daughter needed. For hours she managed fine, then she'd lock the bathroom door and run the shower to drown out her sobs.

Nina's thoughts turned to how Darby worshipped her father, and he returned that devotion with affection and action. Keith taught his only daughter how to surf, do math, and play baseball the same as a boy. She taught him how to cry in sad movies, tie ribbons in her hair, and remove cookies from the oven while the centers were still gooey.

Pride swelled Nina's chest. Darby had grown into a strong and self-sufficient young woman, even though she occasionally reverted to a whining child from the stress of deciding on college and career as well as negotiating changes in her body, mind, and environment. Keith had been a good listener. Darby readily accepted his snippets of advice. Even though she never matched what Keith had been to Darby, Nina didn't resent it. She accepted that no matter how hard she tried, she simply wasn't as good at it.

In addition, Nina was often overwhelmed by her responsibilities as the newest partner in the firm, McGraw, Devine and Richards Architectural Designs. Pile on the home-front duties Keith had handled, and her responsibilities sucked up every free minute of her time. Each evening, she barely managed to remain awake long enough to brush her teeth and floss. Sometimes she skipped the floss.

Nina debated resigning her partnership. She could afford to, but quitting was against her nature. However, even when both her mother and daughter spoke against abandoning the work she loved, Nina still harbored doubts whether she was capable of keeping the three of them safe and healthy. Then it struck her.

Safe and healthy. Had she failed?

CHAPTER FIVE
Darby - Day One - Saturday Evening, March 17

Darby expected smoky and seamy, but the room reminded her of a small New England mansion. The immense chandelier that floated overhead first drew her attention. Distinctly different from the hundreds of almond shaped crystals that hung in grandmother's entryway, this one was hand-blown glass of contrasting shades of caramel and burgundy suspended by a thick cable of hammered gold. A work of art in itself.

Darby tried to catch Esma's eye, but she had turned toward the crackling sound. The massive fireplace was surrounded by doe-soft leather couches, arranged for intimate conversation. In the corner, a carved bookcase held hundreds of bound books waiting to be read. An antique buffet, laden with coffee, cold drinks, and trays of hors d'oeuvres, filled an entire wall.

Darby had thought they would walk in, take a quick look around. Then she'd grab Esma by the arm and scurry her back to safety. She even told the valet not to park her car, just hold it at the curb. Probably no more than ten minutes, she had said. But no way would Esma let her pull her out now. They were in, and they would stay in. Perhaps Esma was right. An awesome new experience for them both. A night they could brag about to all their friends, thanks to Professor Balik.

And there he stood, locked in conversation with a short muscular man sporting a devil's fork beard. Both men halted their conversation and looked directly toward her. Taken aback, the crimpy feeling of crepe fabric ran up Darby's neck.

Mom warned me about this feeling.

"We women have a sixth sense. When a person can't be trusted or something else is wrong, your skin will creep. You'll feel the tingle. Don't ignore it. Grab my hand, and we'll leave. I'll always be there for you," her mom had said.

Darby felt a tingle. *Maybe the air conditioner.* She drew her sweater around her neck as Esma said, "The room is chilly. I am glad I wore my jacket."

Professor Balik and the bearded man stepped toward them. "Esma, I am pleased you accepted my invitation. And you invited your classmate. Darby? You're also in my psychology class, correct? May I introduce my colleague, Durson Askoy." As they shook hands their professor asked, "Did you have any problems getting in?"

"No problems, Professor Balik. The card you gave to me commanded great respect. We were escorted here immediately."

"One problem," said Darby. "My car. I asked the valet not to park it until we decided…"

"It is nothing." Professor Balik raised his hand toward a tuxedoed man who stood near the fireplace. "It is done. Your car will be in the underground parking. Allow me to pour you a glass of champagne and show you around."

The girls glanced at each other and with a slight shake of their heads, declined his offer of a drink but followed their professor without question toward mahogany double doors. A good-looking man, his tux stretched tight across his muscled mass, opened the doors to a room filled with gaming tables. When Professor Balik cupped Darby's elbow, his touch stole her attention from the man at the door. She turned to make sure Esma followed behind, then scanned the room. Darby's comfort level increased when she realized the décor, mahogany tables with caramel-colored leather seats, looked similar to her family's favorite restaurant. *Nice,* she thought as her heels sank into the carpet.

A room-length gothic bar dwarfed the back wall. Darby speculated it had spent its former life as a church altar. *Thought there'd be gangsters bellied up to the bar, holding shots of whisky.* Darby admitted to herself she felt disappointed. The three men and two women at the bar appeared no different than her parents' friends. Nevertheless, she checked their attire for bulges that might accommodate a gun, then focused her attention on the people seated at the gaming tables. Muted chatter filled the air as players talked among themselves and with the dealers.

Professor Balik stepped close to a Middle Eastern man with charcoal wavy hair. "Russo, these girls are guests of Mr. Askoy. Please cover their chips." Darby speculated who Mr. Askoy might be, but not for long.

Both girls hesitated when their professor directed them to different tables. However, once seated, Darby's attention was pulled from Esma and the unknown Mr. Askoy. She was intrigued by the dealer's hands. He shuffled the cards and slid them toward each player as slick and silent as a magician. While he explained the rules of the game, she caught a glimpse of Professor Balik as he wrapped his arm around Esma's back and drew her close. Condemning herself for excessive worrying, Darby brushed off her discomfort and plunged into the excitement of the place and people. Esma had been right. They would never experience this adventure without the entre provided by Professor Balik.

Darby picked up a chip and turned it over in her hand. Grandpa Charlie had taught her to play poker with macaroni instead of money. She set the chip on the table in front of her. *Do these mean anything or are they simply for fun?*

Darby chewed her lower lip as she studied her cards. *Okay, let's see how many noodles I can win.* Her cards were weak. She motioned for another. *Good decision. Doubled my chips on the first hand.* A private smile teased at her lips as she glanced upward. *Thank you, Grandpa Charlie.*

Darby thought she would relax after a couple of hands, but her leg continued to bounce. *These people have money, real money.* Darby thought back to the TV show, "World Series of Poker." *Big difference. No one's wearing dark glasses, baseball caps, or tee-shirts printed with "I'm the Man."*

The players' conversations ebbed and flowed, but their real attention was on the cards. She glanced up from her hand to check on Esma. Professor Balik had left her side, but Esma didn't appear to miss him. A handsome young man with taffy-colored skin had captured her attention. Darby marveled at how relaxed her friend appeared while she still felt the tingle run up and down her spine. When the young man leaned into Esma and almost touched his face to hers, Darby sent her a full-on glare, but Esma didn't even look her way.

A committed people watcher, Darby also noticed the man called Russo appeared in charge, supervising everything. She picked up the new cards the dealer sent her way. Throughout the hand, she watched a small, yet sinewy man, slip in and out through a single door to her right. Every time he entered, he checked in with Russo. Few words were exchanged, and Russo never looked up as the man leaned in, seeming to communicate without moving his lips.

Darby glanced at her watch. More than an hour had passed, and the dread of final exams distracted her from her cards. *Fun, but I should get Esma.* Just as she convinced herself to stand, the woman next to her left the table and in slid a movie star. Anyway, she thought he might be one when his sapphire eyes, like those of a baby wolf, pierced through to her heart.

Perhaps a couple more hands.

"Hi, I'm Jason, Jason Coleman. Don't believe I've seen you here before."

Darby wanted to break the hold of his penetrating eyes, but she couldn't look away. "My friend and I are guests of Professor Balik."

Jason nodded. "Here we call him Doctor Taavi. How do you know him?"

"My roommate and I take his psychology class at UCLA."

As the cards came their way, they chatted about watching poker on TV. While playing, they compared shared experiences such as surfing the California coast and vacationing in Australia. He asked how she liked her classes. Darby confided how much the students respected Professor Balik and considered him the university's premier academic in psychology.

Darby paused when Jason chuckled. "I apologize for laughing. Taavi and I have been friends for years. He helped me with a business enterprise. I also respect him. However, I don't suppose he divulged to you students the meaning of his Turkish name?" When Darby did not respond, Jason continued. "Taavi Balik, first and last names put together, means adored fish."

"Seriously?" A small smile slid across Darby's lips. She wondered if Jason was telling the truth or simply rivaling for her attention.

After Darby lost several hands while Jason steadily won, he asked, "May I give you a few tips?"

"I probably need some. My grandfather taught me poker when I turned seven. Clearly, my skills haven't developed to the level played here. I'm in over my head."

Darby's handsome new friend said to the dealer, "Deal me out. I'll help this poor struggling student. She has books to buy, tuition to pay. Not polite to let her lose so much."

No one spoke as the dealer's manicured fingers deftly slid the cards in front of the four remaining players. Jason taught her to calculate the odds of which cards she might next be dealt. Swept away by his attention, when Darby checked her watch, another hour had ticked away.

She stood. "It's late. Esma and I…"

"Yusuf, deal me in. No further lessons or this beautiful woman might take all my money as well."

Darby sat back down. *Love a challenge. Chips might be worthless but bragging rights aren't.* Of the next three hands, she won twice. *Not bad. Getting the hang.* She flashed Jason a playful smile. "How shall we spend our millions?"

His reaction surprised her. He pulled back the intense attention she was enjoying and replaced it with a flat and impersonal response. "Need to make a call."

She watched his back until her professor slipped into the empty chair. "Did Jason show you the tricks of the trade?"

"Unbelievably, I've more chips than when I started. Since the chips are yours, I'm pleased to report, you made a profit."

"Not mine. Yours. The regulars drop plenty, enables the house to befriend guests." Balik tapped the table. "Deal me in."

They chatted comfortably as cards and chips traded places between the dealer and the players. Darby let her sweater drop off her shoulders, the tingle had disappeared.

"I know you're eager to study, my dear, but I am hungry. I would be honored if you would accompany me next door for breakfast. They serve the most delicious pesto scrambled eggs. May I tempt you?"

"I'm hungry, but Esma and I should head home. We planned to stay an hour. It's almost 2 a.m." Darby felt the tiredness growing, not to mention her guilt, but before she had a chance to speak, he stood.

"Finish this hand, my dear. I'll check on Esma, and then come back for you."

When Balik returned, Darby was still winning. However, she nudged her chips toward the dealer, preparing to go home. She frowned when her professor said, "Esma wants to stay. She's enjoying the company of my friend's son. They have much in common. Erhan is second generation Turkish. His father is Erem Solak, big in Turkish exports. I told Esma we might go next door for breakfast. Do you wish to speak with her first?"

Darby walked to Esma's table and whispered in her ear. "I think we should go. I'm exhausted."

With a covert glance toward the entrancing young man next to her, Esma said, "I am no longer tired. Please, have breakfast with Professor Balik, then return for me. Tomorrow we will commit ourselves one hundred percent to our studies."

As they walked toward the elevator, Professor Balik asked, "Did you enjoy the game?" Darby nodded, and he continued to

31

speak. "I also enjoyed it, but then, I enjoy the process of acquisition."

She thought that a strange way for him to say he enjoyed winning someone else's money. Something didn't feel quite right, but she wasn't sure if it was that. When he pushed the call button to go up instead of down to the ground floor, the move startled Darby, but her professor said, "It's cold outside. We will use the indoor entrance." Almost immediately, the elevator rose one floor and then glided to a smooth stop. Balik lightly touched the doors to prevent their closing. "Few have access to this private elevator." She balked again when he reached into his cashmere sports jacket. However, he nudged her forward as he removed his hand from the inner pocket. "Keycard."

Darby shrugged off her discomfort. When the elevator stopped, she stepped out into the restaurant. Her professor signaled the maître d' with one hand and with the other, pointed to a table in a secluded corner.

"Professor Balik, we're the only ones here?"

He nodded. "The restaurant is always slow at this hour, but one taste and you will agree the pesto scrambled eggs are worth the postponement of your studying. And please, call me Taavi. At the university I am Professor Balik. Here…Taavi."

Because she wore two-inch heels, they stood eye-to-eye. Darby held his gaze. His smile charmed and reassured her. *Nice man,* she thought.

They settled into a highbacked leather booth. Her professor ordered the eggs and a pot of tea. They chatted comfortably as they waited. "My mother introduced my brother and me to tea as boys. We were not allowed soda so we grew up drinking tea. She is more of an expert than I, but I have a few favorites."

"As a child, I was only allowed soda for special occasions. But tea, that's family tradition. Now it's only me, my mother, and Grandma Sally. When my dad died, our coming together for tea was a poultice for our wounds."

The intimacy of their conversation reminded Darby of those she shared with Esma. However, she warned herself he was still her professor, and she shouldn't confuse his skill as a psychologist with a budding friendship. They fell into a comfortable silence as the waiter served an Asian teapot painted with a fiery dragon and a mahogany chest filled with silk bags of loose teas.

"Since you are also a tea aficionada, will you try my favorite?" He reached into his jacket. "I carry a pocketsize sack of Gyokuro to enjoy with special people. I would love to receive your reaction to it." He pinched leaves from the delicate bag and gently packed them in the tea infuser. When he lifted the lid, steam rose from the dragon. "The bite is quite robust, especially if you are unaccustomed to its unique qualities. I will blend it with the restaurant's green tea. Their teas are good as well. Not the best, but good."

Darby watched him dangle the infuser by its metal chain and slowly bob it in the water. Mesmerized by the hypnotic motion, she looked away only when the heat of the dragon's raised red eye broke her attention. When the waiter reappeared carrying a tray, he lifted the silver cloche, then set in front of them gold-trimmed china laden with fluffy mounds of eggs surrounded by fresh strawberries, raspberries, and kiwi.

"For the best flavor, this tea must steep," said her professor. "These eggs are too good to wait. I'm eager to know your opinion of them."

At the first bite, Darby said, "I thought my mother made the best scrambled eggs, but these are incredible. Didn't realize I was so hungry."

"In regard to your quarter exams, you and Esma are worried? I cannot imagine either of you will struggle."

"The program's tough. The transition to UCLA is more difficult than we expected. In high school, we were at the top of our classes, but here at UCLA, that's true of all the students. The competition is at a whole new level. Of course, you know what I'm saying. Somebody still ends up in the middle and somebody at the bottom, but the range is so small. We worry about our position in the pack."

"The best in every discipline are at UCLA. Especially true in your chosen career. UCLA does not produce mediocre doctors." He lifted the dragon-covered teapot and poured steaming liquid into her cup. "I am eager to know your thoughts."

Darby brought the cup to her lips and nodded her approval. "I've also learned the freedom and independence I yearned for is more work than I expected. I didn't appreciate how much my mother did for me. I never worried about things such as toothpaste and shampoo. They were simply always there. The little details of life…"

"Ah, yes. And all this is magnified for Esma. It is exceptional for a young woman from her culture and country to leave home and attend an American university, even in a family as affluent as hers."

Darby closed her eyes and massaged her temples.

"Are you alright, my dear?"

"Whew. All of a sudden, I'm really tired." Darby rubbed the back of her neck. "The late night, the stress of upcoming exams…"

When she pulled her cell from her pocket, the screen lit up. "Have app for Uber. Too dizzy to drive." Balik watched as she tapped the icon to schedule her ride. Then Darby returned the phone to her bag and crossed her arms on the table. "Can Esma...?" she mumbled as her tired eyes closed and her head sunk to rest on her arms.

"Of course, my dear. Russo will have her meet us out front. You need a good night's sleep."

Barely intelligible, her words slurred together. "Marathon studying at the crack of dawn."

"Yes, the crack of dawn. Do not worry, my dear. You will be fine."

CHAPTER SIX
Nina - Day Three – Monday, March 19

Two detectives arrived early, precisely as Detective Wasdcn had said on the phone the night before. As Nina listened to them rummage through her house, the contents of her stomach rolled and twisted like wet towels in a dryer. She stood in the kitchen and gripped the counter as her knees buckled. Weak and shaky, she splashed cool water on her face, unable to fathom how this horrible thing could happen without her sensing something was wrong. Nina wet a dish towel and placed it on the back of her neck. A cramp bent her over. She vomited into the sink.

A mother should know…

She spun toward the bang of a drawer slamming shut. *What in the hell is he doing?* She marched to her home office doorway and opened her mouth to scream for him to stop. No sound came out. She couldn't even blink. The plainclothes detective didn't so much as look her way as he shuffled through her address book and notepads. When he chucked a blueprint on the floor, anger broke her trance.

"See this all the time in crime movies." Nina didn't realize the words seeped between her gritted teeth until the detective with the bloodhound face looked up.

"Pardon me?"

"Crime movies, drug movies, murder…"

"Pardon?"

"You see this in the movies, police tap the phones, take the computers, install hidden cameras." She wiped the back of her hand across her mouth. It smelled of vomit.

"Old technology, ma'am. We no longer physically install tapping devices. New technology secures info remotely, logs every call and text. Yours are programmed now. A monitor will listen and type up every word. Transcripts reviewed daily. Detective Wasden instructed the monitor to call him immediately if he hears anything concerning a ransom or threat. Anyway, I'm sure you'll let us know the instant you receive a call."

"So, if they call and want money, or threaten to harm my daughter, no police will be with me, here in my home?"

"No, that's only in the movies." His voice conveyed a hint of apology.

"I'll be here all alone when they call?"

"I'm sorry but yes, most likely. I mean, one of us might be here, but the odds are against it."

"Doesn't sound right. An officer should be here to help me, don't you think?"

"Sorry, ma'am. Doesn't work that way. More of that movie stuff. LAPD receives three thousand missing persons reports every year, and that doesn't count the ongoing, long-term cases."

"Just from this area? Three thousand missing?" Her stomach cramped as though a thick rubber band had pinched it into halves. The acidic slime crept up her throat. Her stomach was now empty, but she swallowed hard just in case.

"Afraid so, ma'am. We're working thousands of missing persons cases throughout L.A. County. Many missing for years and years."

"Years and years?" As her vision faded to gray, Nina braced herself against the desk chair.

The detective opened another drawer and removed an open box. They watched the drafting pencils slide to the floor. "Besides, we haven't confirmed that your daughter's missing. You might not even receive a call. We do everything we can. Not enough officers or even technicians to station one at each home."

Nina's shoulders slumped. She was overwhelmed by the responsibility of handling a ransom call alone but jerked her head up when the feeling accelerated to panic. "What do I say when the kidnappers call?" She felt like a child begging for help. "Do I ask questions? What kind?"

When he looked up, his bloodhound jowls dangled even lower, but instead of answering, he scowled at a pile of blueprints propped up in the corner.

"When they call, you'll know where they are, won't you, officer?"

He picked up the pencils, tossed them and the box onto her desk. "If someone calls, the monitoring will get us close. Not exactly on spot but to the cellular base station that serviced the call." His hand hovered as though he considered returning the pencils to their box. "It's a longshot, but possibly we can track the call." He opened the last drawer and after a hasty look, shoved it shut. "As I said though, a longshot. Criminals pay cash for burners. Destroy them as soon as they use them. Screws up our ability to track."

"How do I keep them on the line? And for how long, so you can track them?"

Under the barrage of questions, the detective finally made eye contact, then implemented his failproof plan for dealing with overexcited females. With no change of expression on his droopy face, he said, "My boss, Detective Wasden, is on his way. He'll explain everything."

In the awkward pause, they looked toward the ceiling as the second detective shuffled and clomped around in her daughter's room. *Heavy feet*, Nina thought. Her mother said the same thing about her. Nina's eyebrows flew up when a crash vibrated the ceiling overhead. The bloodhound simply shrugged.

"You realize she won't find leads up there, don't you?"

Staring at the mess he'd made, the bloodhound said again, "Pardon?"

Nina turned and trudged up the stairs to Darby's bedroom. She slumped as though a body lay across her shoulders. She could barely lift the weight, one step to the next.

"You know you won't find anything here, don't you?"

"Pardon me?" The female detective tugged at the front of her tight shirt as she glanced up from Darby's pink cosmetics case.

"Is it the gunshots?"

"Pardon me?" the detective said again.

Nina thought, *Gunshots, ear damage, are you all deaf?* Out loud she said, "Darby hasn't been home in three months. UCLA student. Lives in an apartment, Westwood Village. Not too far away but only comes home for quarter breaks. Lived at home all her life until then. First taste of independence, you know. Be home next week."

"You expect her next week?" asked the detective.

"Oh yes, spring break. She called last Monday, or was it Tuesday? Can't think. Bringing her roommate. UCLA is near the beach, but they've had no free time. They're only freshmen, program's intense. Esma, my daughter's roommate, she's from

Turkey…Ankara. I looked it up online. No beach in Ankara. Never been to San Clemente. New experience for Esma so they're both excited." Nina inhaled deeply, then forcibly expelled air through closed lips. *Dry weather, no beach. What's wrong with me?* Nina was chastising herself for chattering on as if this woman were her best friend when the detective spoke again.

"A detective is with the roommate again today, going through everything in their apartment. If there's anything helpful on the premises, he'll find it."

"He's good at his job?"

"Very good." She tapped her own badge as though to demonstrate that they all were good at what they do. "We'll check out the garage, then we're done."

"You're looking in the wrong places, doing the wrong things." Nina clenched and unclenched her fists. "Search where she disappeared from, not here. Especially not my damn garage, which she hasn't been in for months." Nina hardened her voice. "You're wasting precious time." She turned from the detective to Darby's belongings now piled in the middle of her room.

"Idiots."

"Mrs. Richards, you need to calm down. Do you have something you can take?"

Nina snapped her head toward the detective. "Take? I don't need to take anything. What I need is for you to get the hell out of my house and go find my daughter."

Nina stormed toward her own room and threw herself on the bed. *Need to rest. Just a moment.* As she lay crosswise at that twilight point before sleep descends, her mind replayed the time before when she lost Darby. Seven years old, working out her own personality, Darby had dressed herself for the shopping trip.

Ballerina skirt, denim jacket, and army boots, accessorized with plastic bracelets that clanked on her bird-like arm, Darby topped off the ensemble with Grandma Sally's floppy sunhat. In her half-dream, half-flashback, mother and daughter stood side-by-side while Nina lifted a pale blue scarf, tucked it in under the collar of her blouse, and knotted it in front. After she admired herself in the mirror, another in pink to purple neon shades caught her eye.

"Darby, this scarf's perfect for you." But when she reached to drape it on Darby's neck, the space beside her was empty. Two inches shorter than the display cabinets, Darby disappeared every time she stepped around a corner. Clutching the scarf, Nina hurried to the end of the counter. "Darby?" *Can't hear the bracelets.* She circled the counter. "Darby, come here." No response. *Where is she?* Nina spun in a tight circle, but the floppy sunhat was nowhere in sight.

"You've lost someone?" asked the woman behind the jewelry counter.

"My daughter, she's only seven. I picked out a scarf for her, but when I turned, she was gone."

"Let me help you look."

"I only took my eye off her for a second."

"Children do that. What's she wearing?"

After Nina described Darby, the clerk said, "We'll find her. Kids get bored in this department. Wander off."

They searched between every display case, then Nina jogged toward a rack of dresses. Her gut rolled, she could barely catch her breath. Within five minutes they had searched the entire first floor.

"Come with me. I'll call security to help us," the clerk gently said.

In less than a minute, he appeared. "Show me where you last saw her."

"Scarves...by the elevator."

"Could she have gone up by herself?" he asked.

Before Nina could explain that Darby was only seven and wouldn't do that alone, he said, "Let's go look." The elevator jerked and ground its way to the second floor. When the doors slid open, the security officer took charge. "Okay, let's spread out."

Moving swiftly, calling Darby's name, Nina swallowed hard to push down the panic in her voice. She covered the entire children's department in only moments. She could smell her own sweat. As she stepped from girls' dresses into the main aisle, she heard the officer in the distance. Nina spun in his direction and immediately recognized a familiar voice.

"Who are you? Why are you calling my name?"

Nina peered down a long row of coats and watched him reach for her daughter.

"Don't touch me. My mother will get you."

Darby's warning broke the dreamlike haze that now held Nina in her bed. The relief she felt then again warmed her heart but instantly dissipated and returned her to the cold reality of today.

It's different now...

The security officer had rapidly located Darby that day. Nina's worries hadn't even deteriorated to the nightmare happening now. Struggling to lift her head from the bed, she sensed a presence in her room. When she squinted, she could see the female detective's lips move.

"Mrs. Richards, are you alright?"

Nina rolled and flung her feet off the side of the bed. "I'm okay. Just needed a moment. What is it?"

"We're done for today. We'll let ourselves out."

If the detective could hear Nina's thoughts, she would have heard screaming. *You think you're done for the day? You haven't found my daughter.* But since she only saw Nina's slow nod, the detective shrugged and left the room. A wintry chill of silence filled the empty house.

Two hours passed before Detective Wasden arrived. He looked the same as his voice sounded on the phone, harried but forceful. The intensity with which he rolled an old cigarette between his finger and thumb as he interrogated her increased her anxiety. The creases in his forehead deepened as he spoke. With every change in his facial expressions, Nina's breath quickened.

I don't care how gruff he is as long as he brings Darby home.

By the time he finished, she felt confident he was the man to find her daughter. But the instant the door closed behind him, uncertainty overwhelmed her again. Nina scurried to her desk and dug for the notepads the bloodhound detective had thrown to the side. She wrote everything she could remember. As she reviewed her notes, she underlined important points and scribbled in missing words and thoughts. Within the hour, Nina had organized everything he told her. Next, she memorized and rehearsed Detective Wasden's instructions for what to say and do.

Assured she could handle a ransom call, Nina rose and walked into the living room. As she watched, the orange sun slipped toward the clear blue waterline. Darkness eclipsed the room in minutes. Still holding the notes, she headed upstairs to Darby's bedroom. When she stood inside, Darby didn't feel gone. The thick white comforter on Darby's bed looked wrinkled in such a way that she might have been there only moments ago, headset on, cell in her hands, snuggled into her pillow, feet up against the wall. Doing her thing. Nina blinked hard.

But Darby's gone...

Never so desperate, Nina stood in Darby's room, unable to move. *What can I do? Think. Can't miss a call. Need more phones.* She didn't keep a landline in her bedroom. Few calls came in on it, and none were important. Most regarded timeshare sales and Caribbean cruises she'd won.

She rummaged through the linen closet. *There's one here somewhere.* Out came old bath towels, no longer used, plastic bags of hotel shampoos and conditioners, four curling irons, two makeup bags, the first aid kit, and a variety of expired medicines. *When this is over, must clean this out.* She kept digging. Two pairs of frayed slippers, boxes of Band-Aids in every size and shape, an alarm clock, and an unopened bag of Mother's Chocolate Chip Cookies.

She didn't know whether to laugh or cry. Mother's Chocolate Chip Cookies were Keith's favorites. He loved to eat in bed and watch TV. She'd found his secret stash. The only smile of her day flit across her lips as she visualized Keith munching away while she worked downstairs to perfect an architectural design. Nina sat on the bed, opened the cookies, and crunched into one. *Crumbs between the sheets, crumbs everywhere.* Fat, slow-moving tears rolled down her cheeks. *Stale. Milk would help.* As she removed a second cookie, a memory flashed. *The garage. That's where we put the other landline.* Nina wiped her face on her sleeve, then headed to the garage.

As she stood before the cluttered dusty workbench, smells of gas and grease wafted up her nose. Another wave of loss hit, knocking her off balance. She steadied herself against the counter as she reached toward the top shelf. More tears welled and spilled from her eyes. Keith loved to dicker at his workbench. A fix-it guy. Anything that broke, he fixed it.

Oh my God, Keith, why aren't you here to fix this?

Spread out on an oily rag, his old Austin Healey radio lay in pieces waiting for him to come back. *It will have to stay there for now.* She opened the cupboard door. Behind a ragged cardboard box that overflowed with tangled electrical wires, she found the phone, then headed back upstairs.

Please let it work. Nina bent to plug the landline in behind the nightstand, then slid her cellphone from her back pocket and dialed its number. She jumped at the ring, sudden and sharp. She lifted the receiver and willed it to be the call she wanted. Met with empty silence, Nina replaced the receiver. Next, she plugged in her cell and stretched the recharging cord so it could rest on Keith's pillow beside her head.

Nina peeled off her tee-shirt and jeans, let them fall in a pile on the floor. She snuggled deep into the bed and pinched her eyes shut. As though spring loaded, she sat back up, picked up her cell and again called the landline. *Still works. Surely, I'll sleep now.*

Her mind flopped as much as her body as it searched for a comfortable position. *Darby would never stay away two days without calling. She's being held against her will. How will I find her if no one calls and asks for a ransom?* Nina slid closer to the phones.

Dear God, please make them call tonight.

Nina didn't consider herself rich, but she possessed resources. As a respected architect, her career flourished. Her clients, people for whom high-end custom homes were the norm, owned several in different states, often in foreign countries. In addition, Keith had provided for Darby and her. As a tight family, they prepared as best they could. His success as a pediatric surgeon provided security and luxuries. His medical training enabled them to understand the end as it was to be. Not early recognition of the disease, only an understanding of the inevitable.

Pancreatic cancer of any form produces fear. Celebrity deaths caused by this deadly disease made headlines—Patrick Swayze, Joan Crawford, Margaret Mead, Luciano Pavarotti. But the type of cancer that grew inside Keith, this rare and complicated form of pancreatic cancer, a neuroendocrine tumor, remained relatively unknown until it killed Steve Jobs. Even though Keith possessed the medical training and worked alongside the best physicians at a teaching hospital, he hadn't known until too late. As typical of this disease, there were no symptoms, nothing until the extreme abdominal distress. And it was extreme. They always teased Keith. A gastronomical lightweight, they called him. No spices, no red wine, never salsa. His stomach revolted with the slightest bit. Then, he died just like all the others.

Two sleepless hours crawled by. Nina meditated, expanded her chest and deliberately counted each inhalation. Sleep continued to elude her. So, she envisioned the three of them dozing in the toasty sun on the white sandy beach below their home, their problem-free zone, but the technique failed to bring sleep. Then she tried a method that worked even after the most hectic days, the wooden bucket. Mentally she watched it fill drop by drop and then empty in the same mind-numbing way. It never failed. Until now. Nina bolstered herself with the mound of virgin white pillows.

Okay, practice again what Detective Wasden said. When the call comes, I must get all the information. Make a deal to save Darby.

Nina lifted the cellphone to her ear and methodically repeated the questions in her most authoritative voice.

"Yes, this is Darby Richards' mother. Who is this?"

"Why should I believe you have my daughter?"

Nina placed her hand over her eyes to hold back the tears.

"Where are you keeping her?"

Her voice quaked.

"Why did you take my daughter?"

She pinched her eyes shut, but the tears broke free. Nina ignored the hot wetness that cascaded down her cheeks and neck, dampening her nightshirt.

"I must sp...speak to her if I am to believe you." Nina's voice skipped like an old phonograph record.

"No, I do not trust you have her just because you say you do."

She squared her shoulders and steadied her words. "I must speak to my daughter to know she is unharmed. Only then will I listen to your demands."

After practicing the final question twice more, Nina slid back under the covers, lifted the damp neck of her shirt, and wiped away the salty tears that stung her face. She used the remote to turn off the overhead bedroom light and whispered, "I need a clear head to help rescue Darby. Please let me sleep."

CHAPTER SEVEN
Darby - Day Three - Monday, March 19

When Darby awoke again, her eyes were crusted shut. She licked her fingers and wiped away the gunk. When the two ripped nails snagged on her cheek, she winced in pain. The one held only by a thin strip of skin, she took between her teeth and tore it off, gagging down a scream.

She blinked to hold back her tears. It was of no avail. They slipped out and dropped like rain upon her hand which lie limp and bleeding in her lap. When she raised her hand to wipe her face, a flash of pain tasered up her arm. Her body swayed, begging to lie back down. When Darby leaned against the cinderblock wall a surge of cold cut through her blouse. A shiver, so sharp that it paralyzed her, knifed up her spine. She inhaled rapid bursts of air and hugged herself. The only warmth was in the tears flowing down her cheeks. Rocking back and forth, she whispered, "Mom, I need you."

Unaccustomed to the gloomy darkness, she rubbed her eyes and squinted. Not even a chink of light was visible at the bottom of the door. In the shadow at the center of the ceiling hung a naked lightbulb. Her shoulders slumped as she realized the switch must be outside. Her only source of light was a missing cinderblock near the ceiling. Spellbound by the dusty microbes that floated in the yellow stream of light, she waited for something to happen.

A clammy wet towel of air descended and chilled her through her clothes. *What could've happened? Was it in the news? Renegade leaders flaunting nuclear power. Is this a bomb shelter? But I'm alone. Wouldn't there be others?*

Darby twisted her neck and peered into the dimness to inspect the room. *Need my phone to call Mom.*

Perched at the edge of the repulsive cot, her body swayed. Her eyelids drooped from the weight. *Stay awake. Someone will come.* No matter how hard she fought to stay alert, her mind still sank into the numbing murkiness. *No, no...don't pass out.*

Darby crumpled onto the cot. Pongs of dead skin and rancid hair oil kicked her gag reflex into action. Slimy remnants pitched from her stomach and caught in her throat. *Don't vomit.* Darby lifted her head and choked back the vile taste. Overcome by dizziness, she sat up and braced her head against the cold cinderblock. Her hair snagged on its roughness. A thought loitered just out of reach. When she closed her eyes, it came to her. *I was looking for my phone. Need to tell Mom where I am.*

Before the cancer, Darby's father was the one she always called. She could depend on him for anything, but Grandpa Charlie was the real family hero. Prisoner of War in Vietnam, it was his presence she felt in the dark.

Only a few years before his death, Grandpa Charlie began to share his experiences. As if working a giant jigsaw puzzle, Darby sorted through her drowsy thoughts to connect the pieces. Accounts of his months in solitary were captured in a corner of her heart.

Grandpa Charlie? It's Darby. I need you. Her body slumped forward. *Do you hear me, Grandpa? I'm alone in here...* Eyelids heavy, she drifted away.

When her body slid down the wall, she jerked herself upright. *Was I asleep? Is someone in here?* She held her breath, strained to catch the slightest sound. Met with clammy silence, her thoughts returned to the bits and pieces Grandpa Charlie told her of his time in prison camp. Even though jumbled in her mind, she sensed his stories were important now.

From an unearthly distance, Grandpa Charlie's voice filled her head. *"Starvation and torture were normal at the Hanoi Hilton, but isolation was the worst punishment of all."* Darby's pulse pounded in her temples as she remembered what he'd said. *"Howard spent two months in solitary because he gave his rations to a man weaker than he. That man was me. Howard saved my life. That's why he's the brother I never had."*

A crash followed by an echo yanked Darby from her thoughts. *A chair thrown outside the door?* Afraid the men might break in, Darby clung to the edge of the bed, prepared to kick and scream. She cocked her ear toward the door and listened until her head began to nod. She jerked it up, but it continued to weigh her down. When her head sunk onto the foul pillow, a fitful sleep reclaimed her thoughts, until the metal complained as the door broke loose. Like a door opening in a horror movie, it swung against the wall with a screech, scrape, and bang, frightening her into confused consciousness. Darby struggled to understand what was happening as the sound ended with a sharp click and silence.

Are they in here?

She looked from wall to wall, corner to corner.

Hold still. They might hurt you.

A violent shudder ran down her limp body. The metal cot shook and rattled. Focused on the possibility of another threat from outside, she struggled to remain conscious. However, the terror she felt was no match for the drugs.

Half of this world, half of another, she longed for the warmth of her own bed, either the apartment she shared with Esma or her mother's home in San Clemente. She visualized her snow-white comforter when in reality she drew a stiff gray sheet to her chin. Expecting the fragrance of lavender fabric softener, Darby gasped. To wash off the stench, she imagined a warm and pulsing shower. But when the effort became too much, she surrendered and let her eyes glide shut.

Hours later, Darby rolled over and blinked caked sleep from her eyes. She focused on a dark spot near the door. Everything else looked the same. She couldn't see anyone, but her cheek twitched for fear that the man was hidden in the shadows. Goosebumps tingled and warned her that while unconscious, someone had been inside the room. She ran her hands over her arms and legs, then her face and neck. She knew it was irrational. She would feel the pain if they had hurt her, but she did it anyway.

Darby swung her feet off the cot and wiggled her toes to warm them. Glancing side to side, she warily stepped toward the dark spot. She bent low to take a closer look but didn't touch it. A dented metal bowl held a spoon sunk into a gunky white. A sudden pang of hunger caught her by surprise. With a trembling hand, she picked up the bowl and removed the spoon. A glob of the lumpy stuff rolled off and plopped on the floor. She stooped to inspect the splat.

Her gut screamed. *Don't touch it. Could be poison.* Overriding the message, she refilled the spoon and sniffed. It didn't smell like anything. But as she drew it to her mouth, Darby cocked her head to listen to the mystery substance scream its warning.

"Put me down. Don't eat me."

She yanked the spoon away, but a speck took flight. *Oh my God. It's on me.* In her haste to brush it off, she lost her grip. The bowl clattered to the floor and propelled the gunk into the air.

What are you thinking? Drugs, poison... Could be anything.

Darby stumbled back to the cot. She steadied herself against the thin metal rail and swept the sour smelling sheet with her throbbing hand. *Where are my things? On the chair?* As her eyes adjusted to the gloomy dark, she scanned the tiny cellblock but saw no chair. *The floor?* Darby tightened her grip, lowered herself to her knees, and peered under the cot. When her hand slipped, she lost her balance. Her face skimmed the floor, allowing her a glimpse of her shoes. Apprehensive about what else her hand might touch, Darby cautiously stretched out one arm. She heaved a sigh of relief when her trembling hand found only the missing shoes.

Glad to find my shoes, but I need my phone to call 911.

Darby stood and tore the putrid sheets from the cot, waved them in the air, then dropped them into a greasy puddle on the floor. She lifted the limp thin mattress off its gunmetal frame and peered through the wire springs. Her stomach constricted at the acerbic smell of urine that emanated from the mattress. She dropped it back on the bedframe. The floor looked cleaner than the cot, but when she lowered herself, the concrete chilled her like a morgue. She grasped the metal rail, yanked with all her might, and heaved herself up from the floor.

A shuffling sound snatched Darby from her thoughts. She jumped and grabbed the filthy mattress back off the cot. With quivering hands, she positioned it between the noise and her body, her only protection from what might come. As if the missing cinderblock had blinked, the lone beam of light disappeared. She snapped her head toward the opening, but before she could focus, the light came back.

What was that?

Darby returned to the metal cot and balanced on its edge. *Calm yourself.* She wiped her nose on the corner of the bedsheet and counted quietly to slow her pulse. "One…two…three…" *What do I know?* "Four…five…six…" *Must've learned something, somewhere.*

There was that unexpected storm the summer she served as a camp counselor. Darby had led her group of children to escape a muddy torrent that blocked their path, threatening to wash them away. "Seven…eight…nine…" The slow breaths calmed her mind. *I was brave then. Got us out. I can do it again.*

Then hazy thoughts returned her to her high school years. The boy was a senior, older and stronger than either she or her friend. As they strolled to chemistry class, he grabbed Donna by the arm and jerked her into the boy's restroom. Darby had walked on for several steps before she noticed her friend was gone. She turned to see the bathroom door swish shut. When she pushed it open, her friend was pinned against the wall. Darby kicked Donna's captor in the back of his knees. She resisted the urge to jump on him as he fell. Instead, she looked down and snorted, "Puny sissy jerk." From that day forward, the boy stayed away.

The memory of her friend in peril shifted Darby's thoughts to Esma. *Best friends don't desert each other. She must be here somewhere.* So, she stood and softly called out. "Esma?" When she heard no response, Darby stretched as tall as she could toward the single opening in the wall and called out louder. "Esma, it's Darby. Are you there?"

Torn between determining if Esma was close by and alerting her captor she was awake, Darby slid down the wall, sat on her haunches and waited. After what seemed like hours, her legs cramped. She extended them and leaned against the cold wall.

Darby fought the urge to sleep, but she felt her body slip. No matter how hard she tried she couldn't stop the descent. Then a strong warm hand cradled her head, and a familiar voice whispered, *"Don't worry, baby. I've got you."*

CHAPTER EIGHT
Nina - Day Four - Tuesday, March 20

"**R**oll that back to before he opens the door." The two men watched the awkwardness of reversing human movement. On film, Darby rose from the seat and stepped backward out of the car. "There, stop. Play it again." Both men shifted their faces closer to the computer screen. "Again, Wally. Did you see that? Slow it down and play it again."

Their noses hovered inches from the screen. Neither man blinked. "Slower, Wally. As much as possible, then run it again." Detective Wasden cranked his head toward the technician. "Watch his right hand. He's opening the door with his left. She's getting in the car…and there…down into the seat. Watch this… When he leans toward her, up goes that right hand to his mouth. Like he's blowing her a kiss."

"That's no kiss, Wasden."

"Roll it one more time." Neither man spoke as they watched Professor Balik put his hand to Darby's elbow and nudge her into the backseat. She didn't turn, twitch, sniff, nothing. No reaction. The driver closed the car door.

"Zoom in on his right hand. Something's happening there." The driver peeled off a thin flesh-colored glove and got into the driver's seat. "Quick…get close. What's he doing?"

Wally reversed the surveillance tape again, adjusted the angle and focus, and zoomed in. Wasden asked, "What's that spot of white?" The men looked at each other, shrugged, and shook their heads. "Okay, try it again." This time Wally blew the picture up to its blurry maximum.

"He's wiping off something white. Wally, need frame by frame stills, magnified, eight by ten. How quick can you get it done?"

"Couple of hours. Maybe a little more."

"Call me...immediately." Needing to clear his thoughts and stretch his legs, Wasden bypassed the elevator and headed up the inner stairwell. He paused on the third floor, gasped, and then kept going. Doing double time, he sprinted up the last two floors then commanded his cellphone, "Call Navarro." Wasden struggled to catch his breath as Tony answered.

"Navarro here."

"Hey, Tony. It's your good buddy, Wasden. Need some info. Couldn't think of anyone better to call than my favorite narc."

"Don't have any good buddies, and nobody but Grandma Clair ever called me their favorite. You've got the wrong number. What's your buddy's name. I'll patch you through."

"Very funny, Navarro. Still mad about the hundred bucks I took off you? Not my fault your team tippy-toed around like a bunch of ballerinas."

"What the hell do you want, Wasden."

Wasden described what he and Wally, the police technician, had seen on the surveillance tape.

"Need to see it or the stills, but I'm guessing it's Devil's Breath. Yeah, could be Devil's Breath. How'd she act after that guy blew in her face?"

"Don't know. We didn't see any reaction on her part, and then the driver slammed the door behind her. So, what's this Devil's Breath? Another date-rape drug?"

"Could be used for that and much more. It's an old drug, a mainline crime drug in Columbia, but its introduction into the U.S. is relatively recent. A micro-amount of powder blown in the face or slipped in a drink renders the victim completely compliant to any suggestion."

"Why haven't I gotten wind of it?" asked Wasden.

"Because you're too busy writing parking tickets."

"Hilarious, Navarro. Side splitting. Last night I rolled over in bed and told your ex that you should've been a standup comedian. But right now, I don't have time for your entire comedy routine."

"Okay, hard-ass. This drug simply is not well known here. So new in the U.S. that most cops aren't tuned into it. In narcotics, we're only starting to recognize the signs of Devil's Breath. The more I learn, the more I'm convinced its popularity is growing. Since the victim doesn't remember anything that happens while under its influence, my theory is that Devil's Breath is used a lot more than we realize. Since it's an amnesiac, how would the victim know?"

"Good question, how would they know? Is it a pill, a powder?"

"Its application makes it doubly dangerous and hard to track. Devil's Breath is a very fine odorless powder, I mean really fine. Such a small amount does the job that it's unlikely the victim will see it. An overdose could kill in five to twenty minutes. Blow in the face and the vic could end up in a box without ever knowing what hit them."

Narcotics detective Tony Navarro continued, "Interestingly, the drug has positive uses such as treating Parkinson's disease and sea sickness, but that's not why its popularity is booming. Street name of Zombie Powder. A good name since the victim is completely controlled through verbal commands. They retain no recollection of who gave them the stuff or what they did while under its influence. And the kicker is that general toxicology testing will miss it."

"Tony, what kind of cases are associated with this Devil's Breath?"

"I have a new robbery case in which I'm sure it was used. This guy wakes up in his swanky high-rise condo to find the place ransacked. His safe's wide open, cleaned out…cash, gold certificates, passport, credit cards, two Patek Philippe watches, and list of passwords. Gone. Dude was wearing one of his cheaper watches, a 1970s Heuer Carrera and even it was missing off his arm. Wilshire Boulevard, no less. High rent district. This guy's no slummer, owns his own real estate brokerage. Says he wasn't out drinking or carousing, walked one block for one of those designer cups of coffee, and that's the last thing he remembers."

"No security at the door?"

"Yeah, Wasden. There's security, and on video we got this snappy guy dressed in his custom tailored Zenga suit accompanying our victim through the front door, up the elevator, and into the apartment. Slick. They walk in like best friends or maybe business acquaintances. No questions asked. Perp walks back out twenty minutes later, alone, looking like a million dollars, carrying a nice fat duffle bag."

Both men, deep in their own thoughts, were silent until Navarro spoke. "Hey, Wasden, one other thing. Several of the cartels formerly dealing only in drugs have refocused."

"Refocused? What do you mean? Reformed? Going straight?"

Navarro snorted, "Isn't that sweet…on the road to righteous redemption. No, you bonehead. Instead of selling drugs, they've switched their main product to trafficking women and children. Better business plan. Unlike drugs, the merchandise is sold more than once."

"Great. Listen, Tony, the tech's here, waving photos in my face. Gotta go. Thanks for the info."

"Wait a minute. If your perps are dealing in people, they're probably dealing in drugs as well. Put me on your team."

"Not a bad idea. Call you in a couple of hours. By the way, you playing poker again Sunday night? I'm a little short this week. Could stand to win another hundred or so of your money." When Wasden heard a snort, a click, and the line go dead, he mumbled, "Lousy loser."

Wally spread the enlarged photos out in front of Wasden. "Sorry to interrupt such an intimate call, but something's happening here. The driver is definitely blowing powder out of his hand."

"Thanks, Wally. Leave those here. I'll get back to you. Need to call the victim's mother right now, give her an update." As he lifted the receiver, Wasden mumbled, "Hate this part of the job."

Nina was making circles across the granite counter, slowly rubbing the damp sponge over the surface with no awareness of whether anything was becoming any cleaner. She had set her phone down on the kitchen table. When she spun to grab it on its first ring, the sponge flew from her hand.

Detective Wasden began to speak before Nina could get the phone to her ear. "Mrs. Richards, it appears you were correct in saying something's out of kilter with your daughter leaving her roommate at the club. You said she would never do that. And now we have surveillance tape indicating she probably did not leave of her own volition."

"Someone took her? Was she drugged? Or threatened? Is she hurt?"

"We think she was drugged with something that fairly recently hit the streets in the U.S., street name of Devil's Breath. Technical names of hyoscine and scopolamine. It's a strong amnesiac, causes memory loss."

"I picked up a lot of doctor talk from Keith at the dinner table. I've heard of scopolamine to relieve nausea, even vomiting caused by motion sickness. Also helps patients recover from anesthesia, things like that."

"You're correct on that, Mrs. Richards. The stuff has bona fide uses, but in the wrong forms and amounts, in the wrong hands, it's devastating."

"I didn't know it could cause memory loss. This Devil's Breath, is that all it does, make you lose your memory?"

"Unfortunately, no. Devil's Breath is a hallucinogenic. However, right now its power to strip the victim of self-will is the reason it's so wildly popular with organized crime. With only a small dose, the prey will do whatever they're told. Bad stuff. Not only does this drug make the victim totally compliant, it works on the brain to block memories from forming. Even after the drug wears off, the unsuspecting target has no memory of what happened."

Totally compliant. Darby won't be able to fight back. How will she get away? "Detective Wasden, we have to find her. She must be so afraid, all alone, wondering what might happen. Not knowing if we are coming for her."

She tried to keep him talking, but his tone let her know that he was ready to hang up. "Need to get back at it. Got leads to follow up on."

Nina continued to hold the receiver to her ear, willing him to come back. When he didn't, she hung up and mentally replayed everything he had told her. *Wasden said the surveillance tape indicated it happened around three in the morning.* Her skin crawled. Instantly Nina grasped the horrifying truth of what she had been doing while her daughter was being taken. She was working.

She remembered struggling with the blueprint. Luxury beach homes were her specialty, the Gebhardt project was her first mountain mansion. She needed the giant firs and the gorge below to merge as if a part of the room, yet they stood isolated outside the home. Her eyes burned from the computer glare. When she glanced away, her gaze had fixed on the scum at the bottom of her coffee cup. Turning back to the screen, she reshaped the wall-sized opening and framed it in rough-cut cedar, then modified it again. Nothing worked.

Out of ideas, she had put the computer to sleep and contemplated how she might do the same. Nights were invariably cold and damp this time of year, so Nina grabbed a winter coat. Wine in hand, she walked onto the deck. The breeze carried the sounds of invisible waves and the fishy stink of sea lions sleeping on the rocks below. Mist fogged the glass, but cleared her mind, counteracting her caffeine overdose.

Feeling lonely and still eluded by a solution for her design, Nina had considered calling Erika. But even her best friend wouldn't appreciate a 2:00 a.m. call. Instead, she sipped her chardonnay and settled into a pity party of one. When that proved untherapeutic, she went into the house and cuddled up with her favorite movie. After the teary-eyed blonde told her returning soldier she still wanted to marry him even though his wounds left him paralyzed for life, Nina turned off the television and heaved herself from the depths of her recliner to brew a cup of chamomile tea.

That's when Darby was taken. Nina's legs buckled. *How did I not know?* She gripped the counter. *I should have felt it.* She slid to the floor and leaned against the cupboard door. Everything had been so normal that night. Nina clawed her way up, collapsed over the kitchen sink, and vomited half-digested chunks of chicken tetrazzini afloat in a foul-tasting mucus.

I designed a window while...

She dreaded the next thing she must do, but it had to be done. *Call Mom.* Darby and her Grandma Sally were close, and that bond grew even stronger after Keith's death. But this? This would crush her. Her mother would experience everything she herself felt, excruciating heartbreak, fear that cut through every conscious thought, confusion, loss, anger, and worst of all, helplessness.

I need her here, need her strength. I've no one else.

Nina drew her cell to her mouth. "Call Mom." As it rang, she choked back her tears. Yet her voice revealed not so much as a quiver when Nina told her mother she'd pick her up in two hours. "Pack for several days."

"What's wrong."

"Sorry, Mom. Don't have time to talk now." Nina silently lost control of her tears. "I'll tell you everything when I come get you. Don't worry." As she disconnected, the last thing her mother said bounced inside Nina's head. "But, Nina, I am worried."

Nina slid the phone in her pocket and stared at the wall. She needed to know more regarding this drug, the Devil's Breath, so she sprinted to her office to do the only thing she could think to do. She tapped her fingers on her desk, impatient for the computer to wake up. Her hands quivered, she typed devil's breath four times before she got it right.

A barrage of listings lit up the screen. She scanned the titles, then returned to the top and clicked on the first posting. Labeling Devil's Breath as the most dangerous drug in the world, it told the story of a victim who emptied his bank accounts, then helped robbers strip his home. However, the second posting was the one that stopped her deathly still. Its description of abductors removing and selling their victims' organs on the black market made the drug more real and dangerous than the article before. Anyway, that posting most disturbed her until she opened one that stated, "Devil's Breath—the perfect drug for human traffickers." She read it once and then again until the tears swelled her eyes red and puffy. The words blurred on the screen.

Nina plucked a handful of tissues from the dispenser and pushed away from her desk. She wiped her eyes and nose, struggled to gain control. When her vision cleared, she pulled herself back up to her computer.

Nina read silently of Devil's Breath's long and illustrious past. "In ancient times, the drug was given to the mistresses of dead Colombian leaders -- they were told to enter their master's grave where they were buried alive."

Oh my God. What are they doing to my Darby?

This same posting also noted that during the Cold War, the CIA used Devil's Breath as a truth serum in interrogations. *There's no reason to drug Darby to make her talk. She doesn't know anything that would be of value to these creeps.*

The next post she opened described medical use in the early twentieth century. "Devil's Breath was used to ease the pain of childbirth, when in fact, the drug does not have that capacity. It simply blocked the memory."

As she scrolled down, up popped a photo of a tall green plant with pure white trumpet flowers gracefully hanging from its branches, the borrachero tree, commonly translated as the "get you drunk tree." *Wow, this is the plant? Is that the tree up the street in front of the white wooden cottage?* Nina continued to read. "In South America, the tree grows naturally in many villages. Mothers forbid their children to sit under the tree to avoid the temptation of taking a nap in the shade of the lush green tree decorated with giant white or yellow flowers known as Angel's Trumpets."

Next, she clicked on a YouTube clip that showed a man cracking open the pods to prepare his own batch of this terrible drug. As he crushed the seeds, he said, "This is the perfect criminal drug. You don't remember, so you don't report the crime committed upon you." As he lifted the pestle from the mortar bowl and tilted its contents toward the camera, he warned his viewers. "The flowers have a wonderful aroma but don't be tempted to sniff. An overdose is the nightmare from hell. Delusions, hallucinations, even cardiac arrest. There are reports of such strong anxiety and agitation that some commit suicide."

Nina rubbed her temples and propelled hot air out between her lips. *Unbelievable. Who would think that this beautiful flower is so horribly dangerous?* Nina glanced at her watch, still thirty minutes until she left to get her mom. *Time to call work.*

After four years as partners, their relationship was tight enough that she needed to explain what had happened. One partner, Louis McGraw was the closest thing Nina had to a man in the family. She slid her cell from her pocket and said, "Call office."

The voice of her assistant instilled Nina with a brief sense of normality. "Office of Nina Richards. How may I assist you?"

After Nina gave her an encapsulated account, Sherrill asked, "What can I do?"

Nina knew her partners would be in the regular Tuesday morning meeting of senior and junior partners. "Ask Louis to call when available."

Sherrill responded, "Stay on the line, Nina. Mr. McGraw will want to talk to you now. He'll blow a gasket if I don't connect you."

Nina twisted a strand of hair while she waited for Louis. Her nervousness related to the multiple forms their relationship had taken. Urgency, the drive to get going bubbled and boiled inside her. She was moving her finger toward the disconnect symbol when he spoke.

"Nina, Sherrill told me what happened. Darby's been missing four days? Why didn't you call me?"

Nina wasn't prepared to verbalize the reasons she hadn't called. The first day, when she considered the possibility Darby might had been swept away by love, she felt uncomfortable sharing her worries. But after Wasden's visit earlier that morning, she realized that both love and lust were preferable to other possibilities.

Then again, Nina might have called Louis sooner if it weren't for their affair. They'd become close during those late nights when he slighted his own family to help her achieve full partner. Louis was kind and compassionate during Keith's illness. While at her lowest, she warmed to his advances.

All the love and passion I enjoyed with Keith, I transferred to Louis. But it wasn't his to keep. So, she stopped.

"Truly, Louis, I'm sorry, should've called. I thought I was taking care of it. Thought the police were taking care of it, that they'd find Darby right away and bring her home. But they haven't. I'm making a public announcement later today."

"By yourself?"

"No, a detective named Wasden, the lead on Darby's case, is orchestrating everything. The time, the place, what I say, what I don't say. He'll be with me the entire time. And my mother."

"Do you want me there with you, Nina? I'll drop everything, come right over."

"Thanks. I appreciate the offer, but it's not necessary. We have this public announcement under control."

"Flyers?"

"Printed hundreds. Gave them to Darby's roommate with a credit card to continue printing. Esma organized a crew of fellow UCLA students who walk the streets posting flyers and asking people if they've seen Darby. Esma's a wiz at technology so she's also creating multimedia messages."

"Good. What can I do?"

His tone, so earnest and kind, warmed her as though she was, once again, curled up in his arms. "Louis, I need time away from the office and the Gebhardt project."

"Absolutely. Anything that comes up, I'll take care of it. Harry Gebhardt stopped by yesterday to see the blueprints. He's headed to China, a new business development. Won't be back for a couple of months. I'll tell him what's going on, but he's not the least bit concerned with the completion date. For him, another new house is small stuff."

Nina tried to chuckle, but she couldn't muster it. Her attempt dissolved into a whimper. "Nina," Louis hesitated, his voice uncertain. "I know your daughter almost as well as my own. She wouldn't run away. Do you think Darby was kidnapped?"

Nina whispered, "Yes, kidnapped." The sound caught in her eardrums and repeated like a dripping faucet. *Kidnapped, kidnapped, kidnapped...*

"The police are conducting a full investigation, but they haven't found her." *Kidnapped...kidnapped...* "Louis, I expected a ransom call, but no one called. Why else would anyone take her? Certainly, they realize I can pay."

"Nina, we have a resource to help you. Remember the first year you joined the firm? Ralph and I were flying back and forth to Dubai to close the deal on those four resorts? On our second trip, maybe you recall, we had a hairy moment. Almost got in the wrong limo. Two guys masquerading as the Shah's drivers drove up. Fortunately for us, Ralph left his sunglasses in baggage pickup, and he hightailed it back to retrieve them. Just then, the real guys who were supposed to pick us up, roared in behind the first limo. I'd already put my carry-on bag in the backseat and my butt hung half in, half out, as I watched Ralph waddle away. Then behind me a scuffle broke out, some pushing and shoving. I froze, didn't know what to do. This enormous man grabbed me and yanked me to the curb. Scared the hell out of me. However, it turned out he was the good guy. The fakes jumped back into their limo and squealed out. Lost my overnight bag in the excitement. Not that I minded losing my shaving kit and some dirty underwear. Least of my worries."

"I do remember that incident, Louis, and the discussion of how our international expansion came with the personal risk of traveling into unstable regions. But I need to hang up, keep the phoneline clear."

Louis continued as if Nina hadn't spoken. "After that incident, we contracted for another layer of protection. One new service is executive kidnapping insurance."

"Insurance? What good is that? Darby's gone."

"It covers funds for investigators and a ransom. Possibly more, don't quite recollect. Ralph can wrap up our meeting while I call our insurance agent. Don't worry, Nina. I'll get you help."

Her tone dropped low and husky. "Thank you, Louis." Unfailingly he'd been there for her, even when he shouldn't. Not that she didn't hold strong feelings for Louis. She did, the wrong feelings.

Nina turned back to her computer and clicked on another of the many postings. "One gram of powder costs forty to fifty pesos." *Pesos, what's a peso worth. Not much. Maybe a penny? Couple of cents?* "Okay Google now," Nina commanded her cellphone. "Convert one peso to American currency." The canned voice of Google replied, "Today's value for one peso is approximately five American cents."

So, two dollars and fifty cents buys a gram of this vile stuff? Oh my God.

Nina slid the cursor down the screen and clicked on "Prescription for Murder." This author described the drug as highly addictive and potentially deadly.

Not going to happen. We'll get Darby back before anything happens.

Nina scrolled to another posting that provided a historical perspective on Devil's Breath. She began reading how Joseph Mengle imported the drug to interrogate his subjects in the 1930s and '40s, but a quick look at her watch interrupted her thoughts. She grabbed her purse and headed out to pick up Mom.

Sally sat with tears pouring down her cheeks. Face chalky white, her breath came in shallow bursts. Nina had expected her mother to bombard her with questions, but she simply sat and cried. Nina wrapped her arms around her mom and pulled her close, but she was limp and cold in her arms. Only when Nina told her that they needed to leave to do the public announcement at UCLA did Sally revive.

Traffic was the normal L.A. chaotic mess, but Nina and her mother arrived at the university in plenty of time. They met Detective Wasden at the information desk.

"One warning before we do this," he said.

"Warning?"

"Some reporters will ask the same questions we asked you. Others will go for the dirt, try to make this their headline story. Shoot, I didn't mean that the way it came out. To you, and to us, your daughter's disappearance is the headline. We want it in the headlines, but for the press, a good story reads like a byline for an R-rated movie."

"They'll make Darby's disappearance into something it isn't?"

"Listen, they love sensationalizing the connection between local kidnappings and the Mexican drug war. None of us thinks that's a factor in your case, but such an assertion would jazz up their headlines. Some bonehead reporter trying to heat up the discussion may spring the question. Don't want you thinking reporters know stuff we kept from you. You know everything."

Nina nodded, and Detective Wasden continued, "It's common for a reporter to ask about a troubled homelife, you know, turn it into your fault she ran away. In their search for intrigue, the press often tilts questions to blame the boyfriend or a male relative, father, husband, but you don't have any of those." Wasden pressed his palm against his forehead and pushed back through his hair. "Mrs. Richards. I'm so sorry. I didn't mean that the way it sounded. The men in your family are deceased. I'm a real muttonhead. So wrapped up in the facts that I say what's on my mind before I think about people's feelings. Again, I'm sorry, but we have no control over what will come out of the mouths of the press. Be ready for anything."

"I'm ready."

The sun intermittently emerged and receded between low hanging clouds. Detective Wasden extended his strong, yet fleshy hand, and helped her up the steps to the lectern in front of the UCLA public information office. The press was pushing forward, but Wasden positioned his body to shield her. Nina surveyed the mix of people as he tapped the microphone to quiet the audience.

Ten, maybe twelve, were obviously reporters accompanied by their photographers. Esma stood in the center of the crowd holding a poster board with an enlarged photo of Darby. Large black print read, "Help Find Darby Richards." Two students to each side of Esma held stacks of colored flyers under one arm and smaller signs in the opposite hand. An additional thirty or so students and college staff had gathered.

When they planned the public announcement, Detective Wasden cautioned her of the remote chance someone involved in her daughter's disappearance might appear. "Not to worry," he assured her. "I've no problem detaining anyone whose behavior is questionable."

Nina recognized two detectives who work with Wasden even though they were now dressed casually in jeans and tee-shirts. The female investigator who was at her home the first day mingled with a group of three young men. Hair combed back in a ponytail, she wore a lime green tee-shirt that looked as if it had shrunk on her body. With a denim backpack hanging off one shoulder, she appeared to be just another student. Visible, yet unobtrusive, uniformed officers stood in the grass a few feet off the patio. Thinking back, she recalled the first day when she thought college police were not "real police." *Yet, here they are, armed and ready.*

In his most authoritative voice, Wasden revealed only the facts he thought would motivate the public to join the search for Darby. Then he introduced Nina and stepped back so she could move to the microphone.

"My daughter was last seen four days ago." Nina inhaled deeply to suppress the cracking in her voice. "Her name is Darby Richards. That's her on the signs you see in the audience. She's a freshman here at UCLA. Wants to become a doctor, to help others. The same as each of you students, she's working hard toward her goals. Also, like you, she was preparing for exams. However, she and her roommate took a night off and went to a card club. My daughter never came home. She was last seen, Friday night, getting into a late model black, four-door Lexus sedan on South Doheny Drive in Los Angeles. No one has seen or heard from her since. My daughter, Darby Richards, is five-foot-six, a hundred and thirty pounds, athletic build, long golden blonde hair, and was last seen wearing a black skirt and green blouse with a scooped back."

Nina gripped the sides of the wooden lectern. "Like all of you, she is not the type to run away. She's a serious student and a good daughter. Her credit cards have not been used, so we do not believe that she's the victim of a robbery. Information such as the year, model, and license plate of the car that took her away is printed on the flyers being distributed in the audience and is rolling on the bottom of your TV screen for those of you watching from home."

"Please," she caught herself as her voice quivered and broke, "please help me find my daughter. We've used social media to distribute information we expect to bring leads. I urge you to take flyers. Talk about my daughter with everyone you see. Please spread the word, widen the search. Help find Darby by discussing her disappearance with your friends and family. Each additional person who joins the search increases the chances of seeing her or overhearing someone say something about where she is."

Nina searched the crowd in hopes that someone would signal her that they knew something. When it didn't happen, she continued her plea. "LAPD and FBI are working every lead, but I beg you, anything you think might help, please call the number rolling on your screen right now or simply call 911. She's been gone too long. I need your help. Please." Only then did tears fill Nina's eyes.

Most of the follow-up questions were benign. Detective Wasden answered them quickly and succinctly. However, he lost his patience when the reporter he most disliked hollered out, "Mrs. Richards, what do you say in regard to reports that your daughter enjoys the drug culture?"

In his no-nonsense voice, stronger than Nina had ever heard, Wasden replied, "Whoever you're getting your information from is completely mistaken, so unless you're writing crime fiction, you should get better sources." With that he spun on his heel and escorted Nina off the stage, away from the public eye. "Go home, Mrs. Richards. I have work to do. Calls are probably already hitting my office."

"Do you think anyone will have seen Darby?"

"That's our expectation, but Mrs. Richards, I have to warn you. Calls will come from people who think they know or saw something, but we often find they are mistaken. Others will call with bad information. In every missing persons case that becomes public, a few people purposefully try to mislead authorities simply because they don't like us. Some are seeking their day in the public eye, a few are just plain malicious. Going through all the tips takes time, but rest assured, we will follow every credible lead. Typically, we also receive a call or two from a psychic. Not to say that resource has never provided good info, because it has, occasionally, but mostly not. Try to get some rest. I'll call you the minute I learn anything that's real."

Traffic from L.A. to San Clemente moved slowly and time crept. Her mother hadn't spoken since they finished the public announcement. Nina said to her car, "Play favorites." But she couldn't tolerate Adele bemoaning another lost romance, so she said, "Play Enya." Five minutes into *Dark Sky Island*, she thought, *Mind numbing. Won't stay awake long enough to get home.* "Open CBS Radio News." Half listening, she picked up that the traffic was bad and the weather was good. She was thinking *tell me something I don't know* when she heard the first report of her public announcement. The reporter presented Darby's background and known circumstances of the case, then Nina's plea for help.

"Mom, it's working."

Nina changed channels throughout the drive home. By the time she parked the car, two additional stations had broadcast the public announcement. Sally carried the takeout tacos they had stopped for into the living room. But before Nina joined her mother, she stepped onto the deck and watched the sun sink into the Pacific Ocean. Waves rolled peacefully, not a white cap in sight.

Idyllic childhood, incredible career, beautiful home, love-of-my-life husband... So very lucky, until...

In the distance, a dark fog floated toward Catalina, encapsulating the island. That same wet weight settled in Nina's bones. Slowly, she turned and joined Sally in the living room. Grease had congealed at the bottom of the cold taco shells. She couldn't bring herself to eat. Nina sat beside her mother on the couch, close, leaning in so their shoulders touched. She switched channels, stopping at every news broadcast. Some reports were short and direct, while others of greater depth. "Mom, this is good."

Sally left to retrieve her laptop. Upon returning, she said, "Have to email my book and bridge clubs. Both are at my house this week. Need one of the other ladies to host the meetings."

"Mom, how many contacts in your address book?"

"Over a hundred."

Nina's face lit with a flicker of hope. "That's good. Approximately two hundred in mine. Here's what we'll do." Nina snapped a photo of the flyer and emailed it to her mother. The two women sat side by side, not speaking, and worked their way through every contact. The messages asked each recipient to forward the flyer to everyone in their contact list.

A little after eleven, Sally said goodnight. An hour later, Nina headed upstairs. After a long hot shower, she felt ready to sleep. But it wasn't to be. "You flip and flop like a dying fish" was what her father had said when Nina was a child. But now, each time she felt sleep's drowsy approach, a flashback from the public announcement jolted her awake. She pinched her eyes shut to block the glare of flashbulbs in her face and shouts of reporters, so loud that they overpowered her plea for help. Nina thought she would have no relief, but finally fell into a troubled sleep.

CHAPTER NINE
Darby - Day Four – Tuesday, March 20

A miasma of airborne matter filled Darby's nostrils. She gasped herself awake. Her throat crackled like a dehydrated maple leaf. She ran her tongue around her mouth, outlined her teeth. Not a drop of saliva formed. Feeble and dazed, she didn't remember her earlier awakening in this bleak and unidentifiable place. Desperate for a breath of fresh air, she stood and paced each wall with three-foot strides.

One, two, three, and a half steps...maybe ten feet? Dank...smells haunted. She pivoted and counted her steps along the adjoining wall. *One, two, three, ouch, what's that?* Darby peered into the metal toilet, black mold grew at the water's edge, low inside. *I've seen this before. Movie? Crime shows? Americans in Mexican jails?*

Like a cat in a cage, Darby paced the room. The damp chill turned to fear. When chicken skin prickled up and down her body, she hugged herself. She looked toward the dark ceiling and prayed for a wormhole to the heavens. When none appeared, she closed her eyes. A memory from home filled her thoughts. She had stayed home from school, sick with a flu. While her parents worked, her grandfather spent the day with her. As Darby accepted the aspirin from his hand, Grandpa Charlie began a prison camp story of how he hid six tablets from the guards and slipped them to a fellow prisoner as he walked to the latrine.

Rather than give his chocolate bar to his captor, the determined soldier had gulped it down. With the butt of his rifle, the Viet Cong guard knocked him down and ground his filthy boot on his prisoner's hand. Shattered bones protruded through his skin. The swelling and pus that oozed from between the shards of broken bone left the man in agony.

Grandpa's voice had cracked. *"Darby, I couldn't let him suffer."* The same as his friend, Grandpa Charlie gave to another prisoner with need greater than his own. And as with his friend Howard, Grandpa Charlie's punishment was solitary confinement. *"Many days I prayed to die."*

As Grandpa Charlie's words faded, the familiar heaviness drug her down toward the mattress that smelled like an overcrowded elevator on a humid summer day. Darby tried to protect her face by resting against the headrail. The thin metal cut into her flesh. She pushed up and suspended her feet off the side of the cot. The concentration required to swing them back and forth helped clear her mind.

Need to get out now. But how?

Darby turned toward the missing cinderblock and stared at the lint filled yellow beacon overhead. *Someone's out there.* She followed the beam pooling on the dented metal bowl. *Who's bringing it?* She blinked to take a better look. *I won't turn away until they come.* Her eyes grew dry and scratchy. Against her will, her eyelids had just slid shut when the rusty door hinges creaked. She leapt forward as a second metal bowl careened across the floor. She grabbed at the door but stumbled and fell to the cement floor. Pain scorched through her neck. Before she could jump up, the door slammed shut.

Stunned, Darby lay on the floor. The chill inched toward the marrow of her bones. Too painful to endure, she rolled into a seated position and picked up the bowl. *White with specks of brown.* Her hands trembled when, with considerable doubt, she filled the spoon.

In her family, mashed potatoes were comfort food. Topped with homemade gravy, they were Grandma Sally's cure for anything that ailed you. When she cooked a special batch, you knew you were loved. However, even though these disgusting lumps looked as though mixed with dirty dishwater, Darby's worry extended far beyond their appearance.

"Grandpa, whatever they put in this could kill me."

"Darby, they wouldn't lock you up if they planned to kill you." His words hung in the damp air. She looked around the room expecting him to materialize. *"Eat what they give you, baby. Don't let them make you weak."*

"Okay, Grandpa Charlie." She lifted a morsel to her mouth. "You're right. Must want me alive, but why?" Her stomach cramped. The potato mush caught in her throat. To distract herself from gagging, Darby focused on another of Grandpa's reminiscences.

One Thanksgiving, when Darby threw a temper tantrum over the creamed spinach, he admonished her. *"In prison camp, I'd have done anything for creamed spinach. We only got a few boiled vegetables and soggy rice."* While grandpa's story had made her nose turn up, now she was resolved.

I'll eat it like he said.

Exhausted from the effort, Darby set the bowl on the floor. She leaned back and drew the threadbare sheet to her neck.

Several hours later, Darby sat up, shivering and dazed. *What day is it? I call Mom every Monday night.* She tried to count the times she'd fallen asleep but found it impossible to calculate. *How long have I been here? Is it Monday? Did I sleep all night? It might be Tuesday. Mom must be frantic.* Her eyelids hung halfway closed as she looked at the corroded door of her prison cell. *No, she must be coming.*

Darby's thoughts, slowed by drugs, remained in shambles. She was certain of only one thing, she would try to break free again, and this time, be more prepared.

When the door opens...

Hours seemed to pass. Anger festered and gnawed inside her chest. She stood, gripped the bedrail to bolster her unsteady legs, and shouted toward the dim stream of light.

"I never should've listened to you, Esma. You got me in here. You better get me out." Fists clenched, Darby screamed again. "This is all your fault."

Darby waited for someone to return her shouts. When that didn't happen, she pressed her ear to the corroded door. *Am I the only one?* She stepped up and balanced on the cot's wobbly frame. The metal cut into her feet. She ignored the pain, leaned against the wall, and stretched closer to the yellow light, high on the wall.

Esma must not be here. She'd call out...

The cot rattled when she jumped to the floor. Darby choked down her dread, tiptoed to the door, and tried to turn the knob. Her arm quivered, then stilled at the sound of a clicking, like spurs on cowboy boots, coming toward her from the other side of the door. She flattened against the wall and watched the doorknob grate and turn. When the rusted door scraped open, a long thin face emerged. Darby froze in fear of the piercing eyes and crooked nose, scarred from its tip to the scowling mouth below.

"What're you doing awake?" The snarling man slammed the door. The lock clanked and echoed into the dark.

I lost my chance. Darby spun face-on to the door, screamed and banged her fists until the pain became too great. "Come back. You can't keep me here. Let me out." Darby gagged on the lump in her throat. With each contraction, the dry skin seized and stuck together. "Please…a glass of water."

She tottered backward. When her legs hit the metal frame, she dropped to the center of the cot. Alone again in the darkness, adrenaline spent, her muscles relaxed. In her drowsiness, the oily sheets appeared inviting. When her eyelids slid closed, the apparition snuggled in, detaining her in this world. *"Stay awake, baby."* The ethereal voice levitated in the air. *"Can't sleep now, Darby. Time to think. Get ready."*

Her mind ordered her to stand, but her body didn't respond. "Grandpa Charlie, how long were you in isolation? I try but can't figure out how long I've been here."

"I know, baby. It's okay."

"Can you tell Mom where I am?"

"She's looking for you, baby."

"Grandpa, did they beat you? I ache all over. Do you know if they hit me?"

His warm hand lifted her chin. *"Get up, Darby."*

"I'm trying, Grandpa. It's so hard." Darby heaved up but a surge of dizziness crumpled her back down on the cot. But when he touched her again, she opened her eyes. Grandpa Charlie knelt in front of her, his face so close she could hear him breathe.

"It's hard, baby, but you can do it."

She reached her hands toward him but they slipped through the misty haze. She only wanted to curl up in his arms. There he sat, the same as he always appeared in her mind's eye. She smiled at the few remaining wisps of hair that stuck out from his head.

"Grandpa, I'll lean against my arm if that's okay." Darby slumped against the clammy cinderblocks and slid toward the mattress's sour smell.

"No, baby. Stay with me."

She doubled the worn-out pillow to pad the metal rail that cut into her head. "I'm with you, Grandpa Charlie," she whispered. "Just need to rest." In her dreamlike state, Darby rocked with her grandfather in the redwood swing that hung in his backyard. His arm rested protectively across her shoulders. Earlier, Grandpa had received a call telling him his best friend, Howard DeYoung, had died. The swing swayed lazily in the breeze, matching the pace of his words.

"One thing that got to Howard and me in prison camp was our conditions compared to American prisons, especially isolation. Jealous, I suppose, definitely resentful. You know, Darby, in U.S. prisons, you get an hour a day out of the box, but in Vietnam not one minute. Does a job on the spirit."

Darby gazed upward and whispered. "Now I understand."

"Baby, your chance will come."

"Always while I'm asleep, Grandpa. The door opens, the bowl comes in, and there goes my chance."

The relief of lying down erased all other intentions until a hypnic jerk shuttered her awake. Darby groaned softly as she rolled off the cot. She tugged at the sheet and folded it into layers to protect her knees from the concrete floor, then knelt and waited for the door to open. *When he brings the potatoes, I'll hit him in the legs, knock him down, and run for my life.*

Time crept. The throb in her knees marked every second. Her thigh bones burned as if steel rods pushed toward her pelvis. *I can do this. Ignore the pain. Only way out is through that door.* Darby massaged her thighs. *Much worse will happen if I don't get out.* She rocked back and forth, shifted from one aching knee to the other.

When her head began to nod, Darby leaned back to sit upon her legs. Bent awkwardly under her body, her right foot lit up with pin pricks. *Foot's sound asleep. Can't run.* She shifted onto her buttocks and wiggled her toes. When the numbness reverted to a mild tingling, she stood and tested it with her weight. *Okay, I got this.* Darby lifted the sheet and tried to fluff it, but there was nothing to fluff. *Stay calm.*

Her body jerked. *I fell asleep. Did I miss my chance?* She squinted into the darkness. Everything appeared the same. Darby couldn't risk nodding off again, so she slapped her cheeks and neck. Because the effort helped her stay alert, she kept at it until the rhythm of her slapping slowed unconsciously and her head twitched. Darby mumbled under her sleepy breath, "Help me, Grandpa. I'm dozing off."

Darby shook herself awake. The drowsiness transformed into terror as the clamor of men's voices rose above her thoughts. Muscles tense, she prepared to spring forward. But no one came. She held her position, didn't even blink until the air was again still and silent.

Just when she decided it was safe to rest, a scuffle in the distance changed her mind. Barely detectible, soft soled shoes lumbered along as if too cumbersome to lift. Darby stood beside the door. An old man's wheeze, a struggle for breath, grew louder the closer he got. She pressed her ear against the door as the drumming of her pulse threatened to drown the sound out.

Grab the doorknob. Yank him off balance.

Darby inhaled deeply to tame the fear surging through her veins. She braced her shoulder against the wall and seized the knob with both hands. When the door opened and the tiniest sliver of light shone through, she heaved with all her might. The momentum widened the opening, but only for a second. With the power of a monstrous rubber band, the door snapped back into its frame. Pain tore up her jaw from her chest, and her prison darkened again.

"The bitch is still fighting. Balik's a stupid ass. She'll never behave. Get more dust."

Darby's knees buckled, and she slid down the door. As if flattened in a vice, her heart stopped. She couldn't take a breath until she heard him shuffle away. But only minutes passed until he returned.

CHAPTER TEN
Nina - Day Five - Wednesday, March 21

During the early hours, the marine layer rolled in and engulfed Nina's home. The tropical ringtone cut through the fog in her head. She yawned and stretched toward the cellphone still resting on Keith's pillow.

Detective Wasden's raspy voice jolted her fully awake. "Have you heard from your daughter?" He didn't give her time to respond. "Didn't think so or you'd call me. On my way to your place. Be there in an hour, give or take, depends on traffic. Nothing definite yet, just stuff to discuss." The phone went dead.

"Are you still there?" Hearing no response, Nina reached for the washcloth she'd tossed on the floor during the night. It smelled stale, but was still cold and damp, so she plastered it across her forehead. The headaches were back. They started earlier this year with menopause. Sporadic and unpredictable. *No better remedy than a margarita on the rocks, but that can't happen now. A double dose of Advil and a fresh washcloth will have to do the job.* She wiped crusty sleep from her eyes and squinted at the clock. 5:48 a.m.

True to his word, Detective Wasden arrived within the hour. She wanted to say, "Alright, already, what do you know?" However, Nina understood there was no rushing this man.

"Coffee's brewing. Want a bagel? Doughy stuff, all my stomach can handle." Nina dropped the bagels into the toaster and leaned against the counter. She watched him sit at the kitchen table and flatten his hair with his palms as if to calm his short-clipped curls.

"Have you spoken to your daughter's roommate anymore?"

"Twice. She told me the detective who interviewed her had her repeat every detail several times. Said the way he asked questions helped her remember small things she hadn't realized might be important. Esma thinks he'll find my Darby."

Detective Wasden nodded. "She was thorough and consistent in her report. When you spoke, don't suppose she said anything new? Something previously left out?"

"No, not at all. Esma's smart, speaks several languages. Impressive memory. She described what people wore, how long they stayed, what they said and did. I wrote down everything."

Nina extracted her notes from the papers at the far end of the table. While they ate the bagels, he read silently, nodding from time to time. When he looked up, she asked, "Is any of that different from what Esma told the UCLA detective?"

"No, I'd like these though. Got a copy machine?"

As soon as Nina returned, Wasden said, "Spoke with that Professor Balik. His account of the evening is pretty close to Esma's. He told me things about the breakfast the roommate wouldn't know. Said Darby overdid the champagne so she called Uber. Balik also said he sent word to Esma that your daughter was headed home and had left the car for her. Then stated he escorted Darby to the Uber, watched the valet open the door and helped her into the backseat. After the car pulled away from the curb, Balik claims he went back up to the card club."

Nina rubbed her hand across her mouth. *Something's not right.* She searched Wasden's face. "Do you think the professor's telling the truth?"

"Couple of discrepancies. First, Balik said Darby had at least two drinks, maybe more. The roommate said Balik offered, and waiters served, while they played poker, but neither drank."

Nina thought back. Esma had told her the same thing. Not that Darby had never had a drink. On her seventeenth birthday, Nina allowed her daughter a few sips when Grandma Sally treated them to champagne breakfast on the Queen Mary. Then there was the time when the silly behavior, behind closed doors in Darby's room, led Nina to suspect her daughter had been drinking when she and her friends returned from a party.

"Detective Wasden, do you believe this Professor Balik?"

"Honestly, I'm not sure. The roommate swears they didn't drink. She described it as though they made a pact."

Nina rubbed her forehead. "Something's off kilter, makes me uneasy. Darby and Esma are close, like sisters. It's out of character for one to leave the other behind."

"Another thing, at the restaurant, the maître d' and the waiter thought your daughter looked fifteen, maybe sixteen. She piqued their interest, you know, young blonde girl, older Middle Eastern man, wee hours of the morning. But, staff saw nothing inappropriate. They ate those eggs the manager brags about and drank a cup of Balik's special tea. Then each made one phone call. Waiter said your daughter laid her head on the table, seemed to doze off. I asked if she appeared intoxicated. He said he didn't think so, just tired."

Wasden's hair crackled with static electricity as he rubbed his hands over his nappy curls. Nina sensed he had something else to say, so she waited silently.

"Would your daughter do that? Put her head down as if she's falling asleep, in a restaurant with a man she wants to impress?"

"No, she wouldn't."

"Just asking because my daughter wouldn't when she was that age. She'd go forty-eight hours straight before she crashed. Then sleep fourteen and wake up like a hungry bear, but she'd never fall asleep in public. Just didn't sound right. There's a bigger issue though. Balik maintains this place is a card club. Everyone we interviewed swore the chips are not backed by money, only credit for food, drinks, or prizes at the end of the year." Wasden shook his head. "That's bunk. We've known for a while that it's illegal gambling."

Nina frowned. "What will you do about it?"

"Mrs. Richards, I called in the FBI. Come to find out they've been watching this place for months."

"That's good. Right?"

"They have a guy who moves through the gambling scene throughout Southern California. He's in the game tonight, so we'll see what he finds out."

"Shouldn't you close down the club?"

"At this point, that's an FBI decision, but I don't think so. If the Belaruse had anything to do with your daughter's disappearance, we don't want to shut it down and have suspects run for cover. For now, we play along, pretend to believe their bull. Let them think we're dumb and slow like garden slugs. Leaves the door open so we can go back."

Nina nodded. She watched him pull that same old cigarette from his pocket and brush loose tobacco off into his hand.

"Could pull in this Professor Balik. By inviting the girls to an illegal gambling establishment, he's guilty of a misdemeanor. Not a good collar though. Conviction only gets him a fine of five hundred bucks or six months in the slammer. Best case scenario would be both. Balik's worth more to us free to do his evil deeds and lead us to your daughter. But there's something else." He stuffed the cigarette back in his pocket. "Shouldn't discuss it yet."

"Why?"

"Might have nothing to do with your daughter. Don't want to upset you unnecessarily."

"Saying that upsets me. Now you must tell me."

Wasden hesitated. "The FBI is more interested in his other activity. They've collected evidence of him prevailing upon women to visit the Belaruse, but not for gambling."

"For what?"

"Some talk, possibly, not positive, maybe prostitution."

"Oh my God."

Wasden retrieved the rumpled cigarette and studied it. "Again, and this will be hard for you to accept. The problem is, if we go in, we warn them. We could make a couple of arrests based on California gambling laws, but we might shake them enough that if they have Darby, they take her even deeper. Someplace we might never find her. Need to nail the head guy first."

"I don't care about the head guy. I want my daughter back."

"Yes, yes, I know, but it's not my decision. FBI…"

"Darby's just a child…"

"Mrs. Richards, I understand where you're coming from, but the FBI won't compromise their case. When the evidence is sufficient to shut the cartel down, that's what they'll do."

"When will an FBI agent come here and talk to me?"

"For now, I'm your connection. They prefer to work with you through me. Might change, but for now…"

Nina nodded, but didn't speak. He interpreted her silence as acceptance. "Mrs. Richards, my guys are getting the security camera surveillance footage for the forty-eight hours prior to Darby's disappearance. The tapes from the vantagepoint of the front of the building will show everyone who went in or out of the Belaruse." When his cell buzzed, Wasden turned away. Nina strained to catch what was said at the other end, but she couldn't hear over her own screaming thoughts. *Prostitution… He said prostitution.*

"All right, we've got that footage. Told the guys to review it. Sending text to Boutros, our FBI agent." When Wasden finished pounding on his phone, he looked up at Nina. "Interviewed a few other folks. Something else needs looking into. Valet confirms that Balik stayed at the curb and helped Darby into the car." Wasden paused and rubbed his forehead. "This is where it gets strange. A second Uber shows up moments after the first car pulls away with your daughter. Valet says he didn't think anything of it at the time, a simple error, two cars sent by mistake."

"So, he didn't report it?"

"No, says he didn't hear about Darby's disappearance until we started asking questions. Only then, when he hears she's missing, does he think it might be important. We're trying to contact the driver. Uber says they sent one car, and then their driver reported the passenger had already left. Something's not right there. My guys will call me when they're done watching the security surveillance tapes. FBI Special Agent Boutros is on his way to talk to the driver of the second car. As soon as I hear what he finds out, I'll move forward on our plan to find your daughter."

Nina studied Wasden's face, every line, every shadow. She searched for confidence but all she found was exhaustion. He lifted his cup. "Refill?" While she poured the coffee, he removed a small ringed notepad from the inside pocket of his jacket. "Also talked to the pit boss, a guy named Russo. My intuition tells me he's in charge of more than cards. Did the roommate mention him?"

"No, not at all."

"We haven't yet got the name of the woman at the table with Darby or the man who sat at Esma's side for so long. However, we tracked down the young man who befriended your daughter. Jason Coleman. Anyway, Mrs. Richards, that's where we're at. I'm gonna go." He stood and smoothed his wrinkled pantlegs. "Got a couple of people to question this afternoon. Know I don't need to remind you to call me if you come up with something that might help."

Wasden twisted a stray gray curl. As he checked his notes, a buzz alerted him to the arrival of another text. "Good news. We have the license plate number of the first Uber car. My guy will trace it."

Nina walked Detective Wasden to the front door but stopped in the entryway. "Amber Alert, do an Amber Alert."

"Can't, sorry. Criteria restrict them to children only. We're prohibited from using it for anyone older than seventeen."

"My Darby is one year too old? That's not right."

"I'm sorry, but we're putting out alerts to other agencies in every other possible way. Not to worry, Mrs. Richards." When he ended his update with, "We're utilizing every resource at our disposal," she scrutinized his face to see if he was spouting a canned PR response.

Nina closed the door behind him, trudged to the TV room, and collapsed in her favorite chair. Whenever a problem stuck in her head, she curled up in this chair and watched the waves roll in. Normally calming, there would be no comfort today. She grabbed a handful of hair and pulled it tight to release the vice that gripped her head.

Nina slipped the napkin from beneath an old cup of coffee that still sat on the end table. She wiped her face and then balanced her laptop on her knees. In an instant she was online. When she typed "missing persons," the upper left-hand corner read, "8,400,000 results." She couldn't pull her eyes from the number.

Narrow the search, she advised herself. Furiously, Nina pounded out "adult amber alert." The pressure in her head spread and a numbness leaked down her neck. The posts confirmed what Detective Wasden had said. *Amber alerts are not allowed for adults*.

Nina altered the search to "adult missing persons." When the tally didn't change much, she began at the top. The first listing had a national focus. The second provided a link to LAPD's website. Many postings originated in other states, so she added "CA" to the search title. The results soared to four million, nine hundred thousand.

Are you kidding me? Millions? I'll never get through them. Nina looked around the room as though help might be hidden in its corners. She whispered toward the ceiling, "Keith, what do I do? You know Darby can't wait that long."

Nina heaved herself out of her favorite chair and headed to her home office. Her mind whirled. She needed to keep her hands in action, so she straightened the mess the bloodhound detective had left behind. She stacked the papers into two piles, in no particular order then opened the top drawer. Pens, staple remover, rubber bands, note pads, all in the wrong places. As she crawled on the floor for the drafting pencils the detective had let roll off the desk, she listened to her mother shuffle down the stairs and turn on the TV. When the volume blasted across the hall, Nina dropped the box on the desk, ignored the pencils as they rolled back to the floor, and went to see what was happening.

Her mother stood frozen in front of the television, her arm suspended in the air, pointing the remote at the screen. Sirens wailed, police cars screeched, their emergency lights cut through the night. Rapid fire shots, people screamed, one deep voice rose above the chaos. "Run, run. Get behind that car."

The screen flashed faces, crying, calling out names. Two men hugged and then separated. Nina's eyes locked on the bloody handprints left behind on a white dress shirt. "Is this a movie, Mom? Doesn't look like a movie. What's happening?"

Before her mother could speak, the reporter said, "I suggest you remove children from the room. What you are about to see is cellphone video taken last night by a man who escaped the theater." The camera panned across bodies strewn on the ground, then zoomed in on a woman whose legs had twisted underneath her when she fell. Others, impossible to tell if they were dead or alive, were being carried away in the arms of police and friends.

"The footage is horrific. Twenty-six people hit by gunfire. At this time, we do not know if they are injured or dead. As you see, the scene is pandemonium."

Nina's mother clicked to Fox News as a reporter said, "The burning building behind me is the Pantages Theatre in Los Angeles. Earlier this week the controversial play, *The Other Side,* opened to a sold-out crowd and has continued to play to a full house every night." Nina watched smoke roll out the front doors, flames shoot through the roof. People, mostly young, bolted. Rapid fire gunshots ripped through the air. People fell. Their bodies blocked the doorway. The next wave of shrieking people, their exit blocked by fallen bodies, backed up into the burning building. From the corner of her eye, Nina watched her mother's body drop lifelessly into a chair.

Nina gently uncurled Sally's fingers from the remote and changed the channel. "FBI and police are looking into all connections, domestic and international. Two shooters have been identified. Abraham Rafiq is twenty-seven years old. American born, his parents and older sister were born in Syria and legally immigrated to the United States. The second shooter is Rasheed Mina. Both men worked at Cousin Ralph's Pizza Parlor in South Park, L.A. At this time, little else is known regarding the shooters."

Nina switched the channel to L.A. news. "Police Chief Helmer reported the LAPD is ramping up security at local theaters and other venues likely to draw large crowds." She lowered the volume but kept the channel on KTLA.

"They'll show our public announcement in this broadcast," Nina assured her mother.

"Okay, dear, I'll make us a bite to eat." Sally turned her back and mumbled her way into the kitchen. Nina caught only broken bits. "Be back on... They won't stop broadcasting. You'll see..."

Neither woman ate a single bite as the oatmeal cooled and solidified in the bottoms of the bowls. "Mom, there has to be more we can do."

"But what? You've done everything Detective Wasden recommended. What you said at the public announcement was very moving. People are actively looking for her now."

"But the public announcement is completely gone from the news. It's horrible. Poor people. But the terrorists, what they've done, it's taking all the broadcast time."

Sally picked up the bowls. As she headed to the kitchen, she turned her head and called out over her shoulder. "Detective Wasden will find that Uber car right away. License number, good solid lead."

Nina jumped at the abrupt ring of the phone setting beside her. Wasden called so often that greetings no longer mattered. "Bad news. The license plate is fake. The legal plate is registered to a seventy-eight-year-old man living in Yreka. Talked to a police sergeant up there. He sent an officer to the man's house. Plate's still attached to his 2014 Toyota Camry. Owner says he rarely drives it. Hasn't been out of the garage for weeks."

"Yreka? The real license plate is in Yreka? Are you saying the car can't be traced because the license plate is fake? It's useless?"

"Not quite useless. We'll still use it in alerts and bulletins. The owner said he and his wife will keep the car in their garage, use their other one until we notify them. So, if the car your daughter got in is still driving around with fake plates, it might be identified and called in."

"But in the movies, they always take the car to a chop shop and remove the license plate, paint the car, make it look different."

"Unfortunately, movies depict that pretty accurately. Little else is, but they got that right. In this case, these slugs don't even need to paint the car, just remove the plates, and it's a dead lead. But there's still a chance. Criminals make stupid mistakes. You never know, so we'll continue to put the license plate number out there. Somebody might see it."

"Detective Wasden, I'm reading about this Devil's Breath. Scary stuff. The posting I was looking at earlier…let me find it. Here it is. 'While under the influence, the victim is easily controlled by suggestions and verbal commands to perform unspeakable acts.' If that's what they used on Darby, they can make her do anything?"

"They could, but we've no proof of what was used on your daughter. The surveillance tape shows the suspicious movements of the driver, but we don't know for sure. We're looking at all possibilities. Mrs. Richards, FBI's on the other line. I'll call you back."

Nina set down the phone and called out to her mother who was still in the kitchen cleaning up the breakfast mess. "I'm going back online." Even before she sat, she was wiggling the mouse to wake her computer. Furiously typing "LAPD adult missing persons unit," the website opened immediately. Nina read out loud, "two hundred and fifty to three hundred reports per month." *Pretty much what the bloodhound detective had said.* She replayed his words in her head. "LAPD receives three thousand missing persons reports every year and that doesn't count the ongoing, long-term cases." Nina was overwhelmed but didn't let that stop her."

Possibilities came further down the website. *Now were getting somewhere.* The first recommendation was to call local area hospitals. *Okay, we'll do that.* The second was to check homeless shelters. *Doesn't fit. She'd just call me, but we'll do it anyway.* The third suggestion said to check the Los Angeles County Sheriff "Inmate Locator" website. *That's worse than the last recommendation. Doesn't apply to Darby.* But Nina kept reading. The fourth piece of advice snatched her breath away. "Check the Los Angeles County Coroner and morgue websites." *She's not dead.* Nina sat, her hand completely still on the keyboard until her mother entered the room.

Can't show Mom this. Then Nina's eye caught the next paragraph header, "Investigation." Nina read aloud. "Most missing persons cases are solved within a few days or weeks." She hesitated, letting the ramifications sink in. "Mom, this is day four. That's a few days. This says a few weeks? That's ridiculous. We're not waiting that long."

"What should we do?"

"LAPD website suggests calling local hospitals. Would you look up the numbers and call while I keep reading?" Sally nodded and removed her cell from her pocket. "Mom, here's something else. Suggests hiring a private investigator."

"But so many detectives, and now the FBI, are looking for Darby. Would a private investigator do anything different?"

"Don't know, but I'll find out. Perhaps a private investigator is part of the executive kidnapping insurance Louis is checking on." Nina glanced at the clock. It was only ten forty-five. "I'm expecting him to call this morning."

Right on cue, Nina's cell rang, but it wasn't Wasden. The caller said, "Any news? Do you have Darby back?"

When she heard her partner's voice, the old warm feelings of being safe and cared for unexpectedly washed over her, but only momentarily. Then it all went cold. "No, Louis, no we don't. Can't talk now. My detective is supposed to call me right back."

"Give me two seconds, Nina. Found out our insurance covers kidnap, ransom, and extortion, not only for us, but our families as well. Completely covered. Private investigators and negotiators will help you deal with the kidnappers, and they'll pay the ransom. It's complex, though. I need to hang up but let me tell you one more thing. A representative named Grady Prescott can be at your house this afternoon. Does that work for you?"

"Oh, yes. Thank you, Louis. Both Mom and I are here. Should I have our detective here also?"

"No, he wants to talk to you first, alone. Your mother's okay, but they don't want law enforcement at this first meeting. Some of their practices, such as negotiating with terrorists, conflict with U.S. policy. Prescott will get the information he needs from you to set up a crisis response team. You need to keep this line open, so I'll let you go. But these guys are good. They'll help you. I'll call again later tonight. Hang in there, honey. You know I'd do anything for you."

When Nina disconnected, Sally said, "Let's take the cells with us and go check the news."

The first reporter to appear on the TV screen was a striking, but plastic blonde, her face so paralyzed by Botox that only her lips and eyelids moved. "Forty people have now been taken to local hospitals. Dozens are being treated for smoke inhalation. As you see, emergency services set up triage to my right." The glare of the emergency lighting cast earie shadows as the camera panned between two fire trucks where victims huddled and medics scurried.

Nina changed the channel to CNN. The camera vantagepoint from the front of Cedars-Sinai Medical Center showed several police officers gathered on the steps. "LAPD and FBI agents are providing protection for victims transported to this hospital. At this time, the press is not allowed to enter. Hospital officials will provide us with victim updates within the hour."

Nina flipped back to Fox News. "Were victims' relatives informed?" a middle-aged reporter asked a man with FBI written on his jacket front. As the agent listed various methods they use to inform relatives, Nina lowered the volume.

Her voice cracked. "Mom, Darby's gone."

"I know, dear, but the police will find her. We'll get her back."

"No, Mom, I mean she's gone off the news. Her picture, her story, me talking about her, Detective Wasden giving contact information. All gone." As a child, her mother fixed everything that went wrong. Nina's eyes begged her to do it now.

Nina stood, her mother sat as they watched the horror unfold. Nina's mother gripped the arm of the chair until her fingers turned sickly white. Using all the strength she could muster, Sally pushed herself up and staggered into the kitchen. When she returned with two steaming cups, Nina still stood, stunned and dazed, in front of the television.

"Sit down, dear. Take this tea."

Nina shook her head. "Don't think I can swallow."

"Give it a try, dear. I know it's hard, but the tea will soothe your nerves. This afternoon could be big. The police still might find that first Uber car and get Darby back."

"Oh God, I hope so, Mom." Nina pointed the remote and clicked on the local cable news. "Marine layer until one this afternoon and then clearing with sunshine…" The suntanned reporter paused. "Hold on, folks. We're receiving live camera action of relatives arriving at the Pantages Theatre." A man with a close clipped beard and mustache scrunched his dark baseball cap down to meet his sunglasses and spoke into the camera. "We've allowed this kind of activity into our country. We must hit ISIS where it lives, deal with it overseas."

He looks like the man for the job, thought Nina. *I need someone like him.*

They sat in front of the television for more than an hour. Long after the tea had cooled, Nina took a sip, but mostly she lifted the cup and set it down again without drinking. Sally stood and stretched out her hand. "I'll put these in the dishwasher."

"Thank you, Mom. Then let's get back on line." Nina hoped her mother understood that she was thanking her for more than the tea.

They worked silently until Sally said, "So much of this has to do with children. It boggles my mind that Darby is one year too old for so many of these services. Especially the Amber Alert. I don't understand the cut off at seventeen years old. Seventeen, eighteen, what's the difference? She's still a child."

"I don't know. It's just not right. Look at this." Nina pointed to the listing at the bottom of the search page. Silently they read that the LAPD's website allows relatives to post information about a missing family member. "But you know, Mom, we probably won't need to do this. Wasden should call any time now." Nina spoke with confidence, "We could have Darby back tonight."

"Yes, dear, but just in case…"

Nina's mother had just begun to input Darby's information into the form when the security system chimed like a doorbell to signal someone was at the gate. Nina and Sally scurried to the entryway and looked up into the security camera screen to the imposing figure of a man. Gray streaked his sandy brown hair. His muscular frame was testing the limits of his expensive suit. The clock on the screen read 12:15 p.m. Grady Prescott was not due until two. Nina pressed the intercom button. "May I help you?"

The man raised one arm to hold open a small leather case with a driver's license on one side and a business card on the other. "I'm Grady Prescott. Your partner, Louis McGraw contacted the firm."

"Please come in. We need your help."

The force of his entrance filled the foyer, pushed them back. *Massive, even bigger than he looked on the security screen.* Nina nodded at her mother to indicate that this was good.

As he stuffed his hands in and out of his pockets, Nina thought, *He's nervous.* When she extended her hand to welcome him, she grasped him like a bulwark, the lifeline she so desperately needed. When she became aware that she was making him uncomfortable, Nina released her grip and introduced herself and her mother. He stuffed his hands back in his pockets as they proceeded into the living room and sat down.

Grady Prescott dwarfed the overstuffed chair in which he settled. When he spoke, his tone was deep and reassuring. "Mrs. Richards, I'm a senior consultant with Cox and Mason Executive Insurance. Briefly, let me tell you I've twenty-five years of experience in domestic and international hostage and kidnapping negotiations and investigations. Twenty of those years I served as a Special Agent of the FBI. I'm happy to further share my credentials and experience with you later, but for now, let's get to it. I understand there's a strong possibility your daughter was kidnapped."

In unison, Nina and Sally said, "Yes, she's been kidnapped."

"I spoke briefly with Detective Wasden. He's tracing the car that drove away with your daughter, but I can get a head start if you tell me what the police and FBI have shared with you. I'd like your prospective."

Nina picked up her note pad. "I've tracked everything we were told by everyone involved." Nina recounted events and conversations in chronological order. Her mother sat quietly. Her only movement was an occasional nod.

"Okay. If you don't mind, I need a room to make a private call or two. I'll create a team of professional response consultants. Need a couple of hours to do that. Also, I'll stay with you until they arrive." When he looked into Nina's eyes, everything else in the room faded from her consciousness. "Is that okay with you?"

"Yes. Yes. Thank you so much. I thought the police would be here with me in case the kidnapper called, or maybe the FBI would come, but they don't do that."

"Our service is different. We provide individualized and intense efforts to ensure return of your loved one. When I get my people here, I need you to talk us through the ordeal again. I apologize for the redundancy, but they need to hear everything in your words and ask their own questions. Then we'll build a response strategy."

Nina led Prescott into her office and set him up with everything he requested. She shut the door behind her as she exited but didn't walk away. She leaned into the door. Being near him gave her strength she couldn't muster up on her own. However, she decided it was not a good idea to be collapsed against the door when he opened it to come back out.

Walking toward the living room, a familiar scent wafted from the kitchen. She sniffed and thought, *Therapeutic mashed potatoes and gravy.* Every bad day, personal turmoil, and case of the flu was connected in Nina's mind to Sally's mashed potatoes and gravy, her mother's cure for whatever ails you.

Nina clicked on the Fox News. She flipped through the channels, but no one was talking about Darby. She rose and cat-walked back to the office door. Grady Prescott's cavernous voice blended into one monotone drone as he spoke into the phone, not a single word distinguishable. She left, headed to the TV room, and picked up her laptop.

Nina logged on to Darby's Twitter account. She flushed with appreciation at Esma's good work. Darby's account was populated with photos, contact names, and numbers for LAPD, FBI, and Cox and Mason, as well as her own. The account was alive with descriptions of search efforts, a video of Nina's plea for help and links to several news reports. The account now registered more than forty thousand followers. Nina was optimistic as she read the Tweets. A number of people tweeted about the importance of keeping watch for Darby, urging that everyone remain vigilant and continue to search until she is brought home. One Tweet was written by a UCLA student actively going door-to-door handing out flyers and talking to business owners and their customers. He closed his Tweet by writing, "If you were missing, how long would you want people to search for you? Forever? Yes, forever. Keep looking and keep Tweeting."

Nina used this opportunity to send her own message of encouragement and thanks to everyone contributing to the effort.

She also asked each Tweeter to hit the retweet button. "Please keep the momentum going. The more people, the more possibilities."

At a shuffling sound behind her, Nina looked up to see her mother with two cereal bowls so full of mashed potatoes that gravy hung precariously over one edge. A large dollop hit the white carpet.

Nina ignored the brown stain. She said, "Thanks, Mom," but thought, *Can't eat this.*

Nina's mom picked up the television remote. "Still nothing about Darby. I don't understand it. They deserted her so quickly." Sally cocked her head. "What if we call the stations and offer to do interviews?"

"Great idea, Mom. Let's see what Grady thinks."

Grady was just coming around the corner. "You've a question for me?" He nodded in agreement as he listened. "That's a good idea, but let's talk to the response team first. They're only a couple of miles out."

"No word from Wasden?"

Grady shook his head and headed back to the dining room but stopped when his phone buzzed. "My team's at the gate."

As they entered the front door, Grady introduced Lara Kensington, Willard Stolfus, and Ed Perez. "Let's go into the dining room." Once seated around the table, Grady turned to his team members. "I want each of you to share your areas of expertise as related to this case with Nina and her mother, Sally."

The scene was familiar. In her mind, Grady's face softened at its edges. Nina was still sitting at a rectangular table, but it was larger. The room was colder. Instead of Grady, it was Keith's voice she heard. *"These guys are the best. If anyone can cure this cancer, it's these guys."*

"Mrs. Richards? Are you alright?"

Keith's face receded. Nina blinked and shook her head. "Yes, sorry. I'm okay."

"As I was saying, I'd like Lara Kensington to tell you about herself first."

Way too young, thought Nina. *Could be a college student herself.* But when Lara spoke, it was with authority grounded in experience. Using few words, Lara clearly conveyed her expertise. She hit the highlights of her career, first as an undercover narcotics officer with the DEA and then her special assignment with the FBI before joining Cox and Mason Executive Insurance.

"You may recall the Buffet kidnapping and the Greenburg niece's disappearance. Not to vaunt myself, but I was head investigator and both cases were resolved with the victims' safe return. Cox and Mason cited these two cases as the reason they pursued me to join their team. So, for the previous five years, I've worked exclusively on kidnap and missing persons for their clients."

Lara directed her gaze toward the painting of an ornery pelican and made eye contact with no one else. Like the fog rolling in, her hesitation hung in the air. Nina sensed that she considered saying more. However, if she could have read Lara's mind, she would have known that her thoughts were shrouded in emotion as she relived her own tragedy, the loss of her young son, Gunner.

When Lara took an audible breath from some place deep within, her eyes broke away from the pelican. Grady seemed to know she was finished and nodded to Willard Stolfus.

"I've got twenty-five years of experience with the FBI, last ten devoted to human trafficking cases." Firm and strong for a man of his age, Stolfus softened his posture and leaned toward Nina. With a firm hand, blemished with age spots and scars, he pushed back the silver wire-rimmed glasses that kept sliding down his nose.

"In these cases, Mrs. Richards, there may or may not be a ransom demand. However, money is always an issue. I find law officials generally overcautious when it comes to hostage or kidnapping demands." Strength and determination palpable in his voice, he continued, "Without hesitation, Cox and Mason does whatever necessary. Without question, if information must be purchased or bribes offered, we get it done. God forbid, but if we discover that your daughter is a victim of human trafficking, we will not hesitate to purchase her freedom." Stolfus paused when the color drained from Nina and her mother's faces. "I apologize for alarming you. We don't know what we're dealing with yet. I'm just saying, we get the job done."

Ed Perez spoke last. Slighter than Grady and Willard, his body rather soft and spongy, Ed's eyes were those of a mother deer. "My specialty in the army was hostage negotiations and recovery during the war in Afghanistan." When he spoke, Nina marveled that such a plangent voice was housed in this small man. But in the manner of rolling waves, his voice calmed all within its carry. "I find the similarities striking, my military experience compared to civilian life. The dangers and complexity of securing safe passage in a hostage situation during the war were much the same as dealing with human traffickers and drug warlords today. They say I could talk a jackal out of the robin hanging from its mouth." Believing this to be true, Nina nodded gratefully.

Grady spoke when Ed fell silent. "First of all, I assure you that our mission is to quickly bring Darby home. Every situation is unique and requires a response designed specifically to address that uniqueness. Together, we will plan that response." He placed his hand atop Nina's. When her delicate Southern California tanned hand disappeared under his bearpaw, she felt his strength permeate up her arm. "Clearly, commonalities and generalities do exist in kidnapping cases. Nevertheless, the intricacies of each case drive a specific course of action, yet our plan must also be flexible and fluid in order to bring the victim home."

When he lifted his hand, Nina wanted to bring it back, but she held still and let him continue. "Our actions are guided by all these issues. However, it's important for everyone to understand their role and the process which will begin immediately. As we proceed, Nina and Sally, you may find our actions in conflict with procedures set out by LAPD or FBI. We are not bound by standard protocol. At this point, we have no conflict and will work cooperatively with law officials. However, we operate at a different level because we're a private organization. We maneuver in a realm of commerce and politics within the criminal world that the average person does not even know exists." Grady paused and looked from Nina to Sally and back again.

"I don't say this to frighten you, but those cases confined by U.S. and international laws don't always result in positive outcomes. Additionally, unlike the police and FBI assigned to your case, for the four of us, you are our sole interest. In contrast to these agencies, we're not assigned to multiple cases." Steady and intent, he met her eyes and held her gaze without so much as a blink. "All efforts will be dedicated to bringing your daughter home. I will not be distracted by any other endeavor."

Nina searched each face. They nodded their solemn agreement as Grady continued. "We will work as a team toward the best possible outcome, but as your response consultant, I hold the final vote on all decisions at every stage of this case. Once a decision is made, no one on the team will act outside the plan without consultation. Mrs. Richards, we need this same commitment from you and your mother."

Wide-eyed, Sally nodded the barest hint of agreement. Nina read awe on her mother's face. She shared her mother's admiration for the strength and unity of these people who live in a world of which she and her mother had only read or seen on television and in movies. Nina whispered, "Of course, Mr. Prescott."

"At some point, I may ask you not to share certain aspects with LAPD or FBI. Let me assure you again, we will work with them, but in instances in which we push or even overstep the boundaries of the law, I'm not so open with officials. We must be careful not to divulge any information or actions that might derail our operation. Now, Nina, Sally, if you will let us have the room, my team's ready to discuss strategies and develop a plan to return Darby safely back to you."

Two hours later Grady swung open the double doors and asked Nina and Sally to rejoin them. Fidgeting with the keys in his pocket, Grady explained that the first step they would implement was to place full-page advertisements in several L.A. newspapers. These ads would offer rewards for information that leads to arrest and conviction of the kidnappers. "Your insurance policy covers the cost of the ads and the reward. We'll start the reward at fifty thousand. That amount will attract media attention."

Sally asked, "Will that work? You know Nina and Detective Wasden did a public announcement. The news covered it for a few hours, but then the shooting at the Pantages consumed the airtime."

"You were simply overpowered by a terrorist attack. Given the frequency since 9/11, people throughout the world personally experience the effects of each new attack. People virtually transpose their everyday lives on top of such a tragedy. They think, I go to the theater, airports, restaurants… I work in a government office… Take my family to the park… This could happen to me, to my family. The consequence is that we must work harder to carve out media attention and public sympathy for our cause."

"Money commands attention," interjected Willard. "Most rewards for information begin at five, maybe ten thousand. An offer of this size will grab people's attention, distract them even from a terrorist attack. If fifty grand doesn't turn heads then we increase the amount. I repeat, we get the job done."

Lara spoke quietly, "Additionally, Mrs. Richards, I'll purchase spots on the most widely used search engines such as Google, Bing, and Yahoo. It's the new milk carton. A large part of my experience is victim recovery with drug cartels worldwide, working drug related kidnappings of a rival's child or relative. This is an extremely dangerous type of kidnapping because these folks are not interested in ransom. The victim is killed to teach the rival a lesson, to convey a message. At this point, we do not know who has your daughter or why she was taken. Drug use is quite rampant among college students, even at the best colleges such as UCLA."

"But my daughter is not a drug user."

Lara continued cautiously. "Our initial contacts with her friends indicate that's not quite true. Your daughter used recreational drugs at a couple of parties during her first semester on campus. Most students give it a try. I believe that's what we're dealing with."

"You know this about my daughter already? At the public announcement, a reporter asked that but I thought he was crazy."

"Don't let it get to you, Mrs. Richards. We don't yet know how the drugs were supplied to these parties. There's no indication that your daughter uses regularly or that she ever purchased drugs herself. Could be another student made a purchase on a Westwood street corner, you know, close to the student apartments. Maybe one even has a regular supplier. At this point, there's no direct connection with a drug cartel. Still, we need to follow this lead. I've learned that no matter how successful, many cartel members aren't particularly smart. We've identified a couple of UCLA students from warring cartel families. The point I'm trying to make is she could've been taken by mistake."

Ed shifted his body toward Nina. "Our goal is to negotiate favorable provisions for the safe return of your daughter. In one form or another, that's where our expertise lies. We will negotiate her release no matter who we are dealing with."

Nina looked toward Grady for confirmation. He simply nodded and said, "Our folks began reconnaissance the moment Mr. McGraw called our office. Let me just say, the lack of association with any known cartel is good in two ways. First, in the absence of cartel involvement most kidnappings do not result in death." When Nina gasped, Grady paused and turned her way, then continued. "Second, most often the victim is returned upon payment of a negotiated ransom. Right now, we want to get the word out that money is available."

"Having said that," added Grady, "given the time that has passed, it's the consensus of this group that your daughter was taken for some reason other than ransom. We have contacts in various underground economies and cartels. We've begun working our sources and listening to the chatter."

Lara continued, "We'll analyze all possible scenarios. No one in your family has a political or governmental role. No involvement in anything controversial. Your family does not have the kind of high profile that garners the interest of a terrorist group."

With one finger, Willard Stolfus pushed on the nose bridge of his glasses and added, "Your husband had no military connection and your father's experience was Vietnam. Too long ago to create a link. As Mr. Prescott explained, the U.S. policy is to not negotiate with anyone defined as a terrorist. This policy conflicts with our practices. If connection to a terrorist group is discovered, we will negotiate with anyone, under the auspice of any organization or country, to insure safe return of our clients or their family members...of your daughter."

Nina turned to Grady as he jingled the keys in his pocket. He held her gaze, then looked toward the door. "So, if you'll excuse us, we'll get to work."

Nina flipped the switch to open the glass accordion doors and walked out onto the deck. As she gazed down the steep stairs to the sandy beach below, she filled her lungs with the coastal breeze. Keith always claimed that whatever went wrong, salty air heals the soul. Only it wasn't working now, so she began her descent. She silently counted the wooden steps down to the shore. *Thirty, thirty-one, thirty-two...*

Her best friend, Erika, called her OCD...*thirty-three, thirty-four*. Nina liked to think of it as therapeutic. The same as counting sheep...*thirty-five, thirty-six, thirty-seven*. She sucked down the moist air...*thirty-eight, thirty-nine, forty*...and exhaled toxins with each breath...*forty-one, forty-two*. By the time she reached the final step, she'd be prepared to confront the atrocities ahead of her.

No matter the cost, she would save her daughter. However, she understood that they would both be forever changed.

Nina paused, one foot on the bottom step. A breaking wave crashed over buckets of plastic toys and a folding chair. As she stepped into the warm sand, the mouth of the wave gobbled everything. Further up the waterfront, a mother and her little girl screamed and dashed after their seaward belongings.

The unexpected, unfathomable... In that moment Nina understood, more than ever, that all the world expects the mothers to keep the children safe. And she had failed. Her heart sat like a boulder in her chest as she dug her toes into the warm sand. But rather than basking in the serenity that usually waited at the bottom of the stairs, Nina worried how she would claw her way back up to her normal life. With each wave that crashed into the shore, her thoughts became more concrete.

Later that night Nina flopped and twisted in bed. Even though so exhausted she couldn't lift her head from the pillow, she'd have no real sleep tonight. *Pills, I still have sleeping pills the doctor gave me after Keith died.* Nina rolled to her side and rummaged through the nightstand. She shook the brown container. *Ten, maybe fifteen.* After Keith's death, there were nights when she felt desperate and used the small white pills to take her into a fitful, mind-numbing slumber. But at least it was sleep.

Only a half. Need to hear the phone when it rings.

CHAPTER ELEVEN
Darby - Day Five - Wednesday, March 21

As Darby inspected every inch and shadow, the chamber grew darker. When the clammy walls slid toward her, shrinking the tiny room, she curled up as tight as possible. Just as they were about to smash her flat, she pushed away with all her might. Even though her hands slipped through the blackened mist, the walls moved back into place.

As the vapor cleared, so did her recollections of Grandpa Charlie's description of his sporadic awakenings and elusive hours lost. When he shared how disoriented he had become, the thought of losing time had perplexed her, but now she understood. Groggily, Darby sat cross-legged on the cot and rested against the cold cinderblock.

What is happening? Why can't I figure it out?

Then he spoke to her again. *"A prisoner of war is confined in solitary to break his will, so he'll weaken, give up vital information."*

But, Grandpa Charlie, that can't be why these men are keeping me. I don't know any secrets or anything of value. If they thought I did, they could just ask.

Darby sat, deep in speculation. *Has to be one big fat mistake. I'm the wrong person.* She decided she would tell the man who brought the bowls of mush. Feeling optimistic, she waited.

Certain hours had passed, Darby reconsidered. *If it wasn't a mistake, why else would they lock me in this cell? Even the worst criminals have due process. I should get to explain, tell them they're mistaken.* She shifted her weight. The metal springs cut through the thin oily mattress and left marks on the backs of her legs. *Did I do something I can't remember?* Darby looked around again at the revolting toilet, the dribble of light from the opening above her head.

I broke no laws. Don't deserve to be locked up.

Defeat steamrolled her body. Her shoulders rolled forward until her chin touched her chest. *This is not an American jail. The only answer is that I was kidnapped. But why?*

A shudder of fear wriggled down her spine. Then Darby felt more than saw movement. A glutinous material blocked the light as it oozed down the side of the wall. She pinched her eyes tight and willed it away. After three slow breaths, she peeked.

Where'd it go? How'd they pull it back? That's their strategy, make me small, coiled up in a corner to keep the slime from touching me. She squared her shoulders. *I'm sorry, but that won't work.*

Darby glared at the half empty metal bowl. It occurred to her that its beat up condition was a symbol. She knew it couldn't talk, yet still heard its voice. *You're damaged goods, unworthy of concern. You have nothing except what we give you, and neither you nor it is worth a damn.*

Darby laid her head on the pillow. Its meager padding was full of lumps. Her discomfort warded off sleep, but her mind did not clear. Each time a possibility formed, it disappeared into the greyness that swirled in her brain. A bolt of confidence that she could conquer the monster that kidnapped her jolted her upright.

But the heavy damp air pulled her back down. *Mom, where are you?*

It was the same when her father died. There were moments when her mother would lean on her for support, then unexpectedly banish her to the waiting room while she spoke privately with the doctors. The flux left Darby doubting her strengths and abilities. In time, she came to understand that her mother and the doctors were protecting her from the devastating truth. However, all she had wanted was to sit and hold her father's hand, comfort him, but also comfort herself. *But no one's trying to protect me now.*

Darby refocused on her escape plan. She took three steps and stood stick straight, plastered against the wall. *This time, as soon as the door cracks open, I'll reach through and grab whoever's there. I'll fling them toward the toilet and bomb out the door.* She stood, alert, poised to act.

The minutes crept. The dampness seeped from the cinderblock through her shirt. The exertion of shivering sapped the last of her endurance and pulled her thoughts from her singular task. Darby worried what her mother thought when she didn't call home on Monday night. *That I'm too busy for her? Don't need her anymore?* Darby's eyelids slid shut and her head bobbed forward. *Probably thinks I'm an ungrateful brat.*

When the doorknob clanked, Darby jerked alert. *Someone's coming.* She repositioned herself, ready to pounce. The door rattled. In the dim backlight, she saw twisted and calloused fingers on the knob. As the door creaked open, Darby rammed her hand through and grabbed the arm, but it wrenched free. The door slammed and bounced off her palm. She screamed, then slithered to the floor into a sobbing mass. "You broke my hand."

A shadow passed over the dusty yellow light. *What was that?* Darby looked up toward the opening. A soft puff of air tickled her face. She stepped away. Her knees weakened. She cradled her aching hand to protect it as she lost her balance.

"No," she screamed as she stumbled back up to her feet. "You can't do that to me anymore." The movement shot an electric bolt up her arm. "No, no, no. I will not go to sleep." But the Devil's Breath quieted her, overpowered her resolve. When the man's voice said, "Go to your bed and lie down," she complied. The drug had done its work.

As her mind retreated, in the instant before it abandoned her completely, Darby grasped one fleeting thought. *I have to stop them...*

Darby awoke to find herself lying on the metal cot, hot and damp, feverish, yet shivering. Her injured hand, throbbing like a broken heart, was wrapped in thick layers of gauze. She looked at the bandage, then around the room and whispered toward the yellow light.

"Thank you."

CHAPTER TWELVE
Nina - Day Six - Thursday, March 22

Nina lifted her cellphone from Keith's pillow and checked the time. Five a.m. She stretched the kinks from her body, grateful to sleep more than an hour at a time. Slipping into Keith's frayed terrycloth robe, she headed downstairs to brew a new pot. As she turned the corner, the fresh smell of coffee coaxed a smile to her lips. She expected to be met by her mother's kindly face, so she was surprised to find Lara Kensington leaned up against the counter, looking completely at home with a cup in one hand and the TV remote in the other.

On the tiny screen in the refrigerator door, a CNN reporter was saying, "Within the last month, the shooters legally purchased two Glocks and four AR-15 semi-automatic rifles. Police report they had previously detained the suspects, but their offense did not rise to a level that hindered purchase of these guns. LAPD stated the shooters allegedly threatened church-goers on Ash Wednesday at St. Timothy's Catholic Church. However, since church members declined to press charges, no arrests were made."

"We gotta get tougher," muttered Lara.

Nina jumped when the landline rang. "Nina Richards?" The voice was filtered, fuzzy, yet understandable.

"Yes, who's calling please?"

"I have your daughter. I want…"

"You have my daughter?"

Lara moved toward her and pointed at the phone to indicate Nina should put it on speaker mode.

"I want her back." Nina wanted to say, *I want her back you son-of-a-bitch bottom-dwelling lowlife,* but Wasden had been emphatic. She should do nothing to make a caller mad. His words cut through her fury. *"You want him on your side. Make him want to give her back."*

"Well, there's something I want too," said the deep voice.

Lara grabbed her phone from her belt and began tapping out a text message.

"Of course, you do." *You stinking sleazebag.* "But first, tell me…is she alright? Please don't hurt her."

Sally was rubbing her eyes as she entered the room. Confusion washed over her face, then she rushed to Nina's side. Nina slid her cell from her pocket. She hit the callback number for Detective Wasden and handed off the phone. Her mother knew what to do. Sally headed to the far side of the room so the man to which Nina was speaking could not hear.

Nina spoke slowly and methodically, asking the questions exactly the way Wasden had schooled her.

"Who are you?" *You bastard.* Her question was met with labored breathing.

"Let me talk to my daughter." *Or I'll rip your tongue out.* She hesitated after every question to extend his time on the line, waiting for answers that never came.

"I need to know she is unharmed." *Hurt her and I'll kill you with my bare hands.*

"Where are you?" *I'll find you and…*

"I said I want something too. Stop yakking and listen."

"I'm listening." But her head pounded so loudly it threatened to drown out his words. Then she remembered the last thing Wasden told her to do. *"Stall. Takes time to track the call."*

"Wait a minute. I need to sit down. Need to get a pencil and paper."

"You don't need anything. Trust me, you'll remember what I say."

"Trust you?" She whispered the words so faintly that she wasn't sure he had heard her.

"I need two million dollars. I'll call back and give you an account number where you will immediately wire transfer the money."

"Okay, okay."

"Okay?"

"Yes, I'll give you the money. How do I call you back as soon as I've arranged for the transfer?"

"You don't call me. I'll call you."

Wasden's voice echoed in her mind. *"Demand proof your daughter is alive."*

"I need to know my daughter is okay. Let me talk to her."

"Not possible."

"You get the money when I know she is unharmed."

"She's fine. As long as you do what I say, we're not gonna hurt her."

Nina looked around the room in panic. Lara mouthed, "Keep him talking."

"I must talk to her."

"Jesus, lady. Just a minute." The phone became so quiet she thought she'd lost him.

Then a sound, maybe a scratchy cloth, slid across the receiver. She snapped still and quiet. Faintly in the background, a woman begged, "Mom, help me. Please, Mom."

"Let me talk to my daughter now." Nina's command was met with silence. *Don't panic...stay calm.* Even though she could hear his ragged breath, she asked, "Are you still there?" *Don't hang up. Don't you dare.* Her mind churned. She tried to silence it as she strained to detect even the slightest noise or movement. *I should be able to feel her.* "I asked if you're still there. Do you hear me?" Her question hung in the dead air.

What do I do now? Nina realized she was holding her breath and gasped for air. *Wasden said to ask a question to which only Darby would know the answer.* "Okay, if you won't let her talk to me, ask her where Buddy is." Nina held her breath and waited for his response, but there was only silence at the other end of the line. "Hello, hello. Are you there?" She collapsed against the wall. "No...no. Come back you son-of-a-bitch." Nina's mother hurried over and handed her the cell.

"We got it, Mrs. Richards. The call was copied. Just hit my computer. My guys are locating it now. You did good. Your last question, who's Buddy?"

"Darby's first dog. Buddy died six years ago."

"Nice. Good question. Listen, I'll call you as soon as we do the analysis. Hold on a minute." Someone was talking in the background, but Nina couldn't decipher what was being said. She could tell Detective Wasden had pulled the phone from his mouth, but his squawk still made it through. "What? You've got to be kidding." Then in a clear professional voice, he said, "Gotta go, Mrs. Richards."

"Wait. Should I call the bank?"

"No, not yet. Something's not right about this. Generally, the kidnapper is ready to accept the funds, already knows where and how. I'll call you back. Won't be long."

Lara's cell vibrated in her hand. She glanced at the screen and said, "Grady's on his way."

Nina frowned and shook her head. "I'm not waiting for anyone. I'm getting the ransom money."

When Nina finished her discussion with the bank manager and looked up, the kitchen was empty. She hadn't seen Lara and her mother leave the room. The sharp sense of being alone in her decision, the responsibility of her action to secure the ransom money, left Nina dizzy. She was leaning against the counter, holding the edge to keep from fainting, when Grady barreled in.

"Tell me what demands the caller made."

His presence calmed her. Her heartbeat slowed, almost to normal, while she recounted every detail. He jotted notes in the leather notebook balanced on his knee.

"The caller demanded a two-million-dollar ransom. He wanted the money through a wire transfer. I've spoken to the bank, but the kidnapper didn't give me the account information. He said he would call back. But Mr. Prescott, Detective Wasden thinks something's wrong. Said it was uncharacteristic for the kidnapper not to be ready to accept the funds."

Grady nodded. "I have the same concern. My experience tells me that anyone asking for a ransom wants to get in and get out before we track them. Strange they weren't ready, not unheard of, but unusual. You're positive the female voice was your daughter's?"

"It was so quick. All she said was, 'Help me, Mom. Help me.' Her voice wasn't clear. A cloth, maybe a hand, covered the receiver, made it hard to be sure."

"That's not unusual. Did the man say when he'd call back?"

"He didn't. Detective Wasden said I should ask the kidnapper to have Darby answer a question for which only she would know the answer. But when I did, he hung up, like he was mad." Nina scanned Grady's face. "I was relieved when I got the ransom call, but now that's all gone away. I feel sick."

"Of course, you do, Mrs. Richards, but I'm here to bring your daughter home."

"But if Detective Wasden tracks the call, picks them up, none of this is necessary." Nina looked at Grady but he didn't say or do anything to demonstrate agreement. He just stood there looking back until he said, "Lara will stay with you, but I need to go meet Willard. He's got a lead. I'll be back soon."

Lara stayed in the kitchen making phone calls. Nina and her mother went to the living room, sunk into the couch, and stared out into the endless horizon. Any observer would have thought they were mesmerized by the rolling sea, the sparkling whitecaps reflecting the sunlight as waves crashed upon the beach. But neither woman saw any of that. Both were blinded by their own dismal thoughts until Nina's cellphone rang again. Caller ID read, "Detective Wasden." *This won't be good. Too much time has passed.*

"Mrs. Richards, I have bad news."

"Is Darby hurt?"

"It's not that. It's the ransom call. I hate telling you this, but it's not credible."

Lara entered the room, set down her coffee, then moved closer as Nina responded, "Not credible? What does that mean?"

Lara pointed to the phone and mouthed, "Speaker."

"You're the second Nina Richards to receive a ransom call," said Wasden.

"What on earth are you talking about? I'm Nina Richards. Darby's mother."

"Right, but there's another Nina Richards in Los Angeles. While you were on the phone with your professed kidnappers, she called 911 to report a ransom call. This woman was unaware of your daughter's disappearance. She has three sons, so she recognized the call as a hoax, but not the kind this guy should get away with. Said she'd read about people who received such calls, were asked for money because their child or grandchild was traveling or away at school and supposedly needed help. She didn't know if this was the same sort of scam or if someone had been kidnapped, so she called us. We confirmed that this woman is who she says, and, in the process, located another Nina Richards fairly close by."

"So that man, the caller, doesn't have Darby?"

"No. Listen, if he did, he'd have found you on the first call. He wouldn't go through the directory calling everyone with the same name. Apparently, he watched the public announcement on TV or read the newspaper reports, maybe did an online search. Located three Nina Richards within a viable distance. Since we stated that your daughter lived in Los Angeles, he figured the Nina Richards who was her mother also lived in L.A. So, of the three of you, he called this other woman first because that's where she lives. The third Nina Richards lives in Universal City but didn't receive a call. By a stroke of luck, this scammer called you second."

"Detective Wasden, you're sure this woman got a fake call? She's not making it up from what was on the news? Not simply looking for attention?"

"We're certain. Billing record details verify she received a call from the same number you did only thirty minutes earlier. We confirmed that both calls were from the same base station. Officers are closing in now."

"But the voice in the background? I heard her say, 'Mom, help me.'"

"Are you confident it was your daughter?"

"No, no. I'm not. As I said, it sounded as if the receiver was covered. The voice was faint. You'd think I'd recognize my own daughter, but it wasn't clear."

"Not necessarily, Mrs. Richards. With the stress you're under, sometimes the mind plays tricks, tries to give you what you want, like to hear your daughter's voice."

Nina drew a deep breath. "If it wasn't Darby, does that mean a woman is also involved?"

"Yeah, a man and woman duo. Virtual kidnapping is increasing throughout the state, more in L.A. than many other cities, but this type of extortion is increasing everywhere."

"Virtual kidnapping? I don't understand?"

"The callers try to convince a family member that someone was kidnapped. They often claim membership in a drug or crime cartel to scare the parents. We suspected early on that your call was fake because he didn't give you the info needed to complete a wire transfer. Successful abductors get their money before we have a chance to track them."

"But these virtual cases are all where the person actually isn't missing, correct?"

"Sometimes yes, sometimes no. These scammers use social media to find out a family member is away from home for school or business, or actually is missing, but it could be they're just on vacation. For example, in a previous case, virtual kidnappers used Facebook to identify potential victims. You know, posting of photos and verbiage where people announce they're in Timbuktu or floating down the Yangtze River? Bad stuff to post until after you're back home." Wasden paused. "You still there, Mrs. Richards?"

"Yes, yes. I'm just stunned, don't know what to think…or say."

"I understand. Do you mind if I tell you about a recent case?"

Nina shook her head, then realized he couldn't see her. Her voice was little more than a whisper when she said, "Okay."

"The son was in South Africa, working on a water project with folks from his church, out in the Savanna where communication's spotty. Call came in, parents wired money. These scammers said they'd call back to arrange for pickup of the son, but they didn't. Several hours passed. When the parents hadn't heard from their son or the alleged kidnappers, they notified LAPD."

"So, the young man wasn't kidnapped, but his parents paid because of a threat?"

"Exactly, except there wasn't any real threat. The boy was safe, totally unaware, but the demand for payment was immediate to avoid getting caught. In virtual kidnapping, a callback is not the normal M.O. The creep who phoned you is an amateur. Anyway, Mrs. Richards, you did a good job of keeping him on the line. Hold on a sec. Just got a text from my guys. They're outside their building. Listen, my other phone's ringing off the hook. I'll get back to you."

When the phone went silent, Nina turned to Lara. "What do we do now?"

Lara stepped forward, as if to hug Nina but then stopped. "I'm so sorry, but frankly, our team expected this. We haven't been sitting on our hands waiting for this ransom call to pan out. We have other leads. That's what I was about to tell you when Wasden called. I've got one to follow up on now, so I'll call you after I report to Grady."

Nina and Sally poured coffee and sat across from each other, not drinking, not talking, until Nina broke the silence. "Okay, it's back to us. We need to educate ourselves more. Back online."

Nina again typed in "adult missing persons." She scrolled and skipped the purple titles of those already viewed. She clicked on National Missing NS Unidentified Persons System and read aloud, "Welcome to NamUs Missing Persons. Mom, this looks promising. A six-minute video. Let's watch it first."

Nina clicked on *NamUs Behind the Scenes: How It Works. Why It Matters.* When another screen popped up, she opened the video. Debra Culberson, Carrie Culberson's mother, described how in the beginning she didn't know what to do to help find her daughter. Nina and her mother nodded as Carrie's mother spoke to them from the computer screen, "…there's nobody who wants to find your child, or your loved one, more than you do."

Mrs. Culberson explained the NamUs database was accessible to the public, and that family members and law enforcement may input and access data. She acknowledged her sense of helplessness but explained that by registering her daughter, she contributed to the search. However, when Carrie's mother said, "This has given me hope that I will eventually find my daughter's remains," Nina closed the video and the two women sat in stunned silence.

The screen turned black. Neither looked up until Nina said, "Mom, Darby's not dead."

"No, dear, of course she's not. This video's confusing." Sally touched the screen, and it lit up again. "This section is labeled resource center for missing person and unidentified decedent records. Darby's just missing, but we still should enter her info, a complete description. We must try everything."

Nina entered height, weight, eye and hair color, a description of the tiny tattoo on Darby's hip, every detail for which there was an input box. She posted the photos used for the posters. When Nina hit submit, their prayers were answered. No match in the death records.

Like the ocean tides outside her home, when Nina did something she thought might help find Darby, her spirits rose. However, the highs lasted only seconds, then retreated into lows. She'd spent hours sitting behind her computer and none of this research had led to Darby. *But I'm not giving up.* As she logged on to Facebook and typed Darby's password, Nina thought, *Glad I overruled Darby's protests. If I wasn't protective, obtrusive by her definition, I couldn't do this.*

Nina began to edit. She increased the font and wrote in caps. "HAVE YOU SEEN ME? HELP FIND ME! I AM MISSING!" Before closing, Nina added information on how to contact her, FBI, LAPD and Cox and Mason Executive Insurance.

Sally stood and read over Nina's shoulder. As her mother manipulated the knots in her daughter's neck, Nina said, "Darby has hundreds of friends. They'll spread the word. Someone has to have seen her."

Two hours later, Nina's cell rang. Detective Wasden blurted out, "Picked up the man and woman, confirmed this was a virtual kidnapping. So many of these cases, we barely keep up. Luck was with us on this one. Another piece of good news, these two aren't connected to a gang or other organized crime. This extortion was just boyfriend and girlfriend, not very bright I might add, who saw the news and thought they could make an easy couple of million. Scam's over. We're moving on."

"But you're sure they aren't holding Darby?"

"Absolutely. Never had her. The woman read postings of the search for your daughter on Facebook. Spur-of-the-moment opportunists, saw the publicity and thought they had a great idea. Now they're demanding a lawyer. Don't have enough money to hire one, so a public defender will be assigned. Probably two, one for each of them. So, we spend taxpayer dollars to catch these lying degenerates and then waste a bunch more to defend them."

Nina put the phone down and looked up at her mother. "Detective Wasden said those creeps used what we posted to scam us. And I just added more. What have I done?"

"You did what our research suggested, dear. There's more good people who want to help than filth like those two. If Darby's on the streets and can't figure out where she is or where to go, anyone who's read your posting might find her. Or what if she's drugged, can't escape, but someone saw her or overheard something?" Sally shrugged, but her expression was hopeful. "Maybe…just maybe."

"You're right, Mom. Will you check the police website? Perhaps someone posted a lead, a sighting."

The only sound in the room was Nina and Sally tapping on their keyboards. They both jumped at the chime that let them know someone was at the gate. The security camera screen filled with

Grady's face, brows pinched together above anxious eyes. "Mr. Prescott, Grady, I wasn't expecting you. You have news?"

"Yes, some."

Nina hit the button to open the electronic security gate and held the front door until he entered. She searched his face as they walked to the living room, but he adverted his gaze in an edgy, nervous way. "Some of the news is good, but the rest is Godawful. Let's sit." Grady expelled air between his teeth as he logged onto his tablet. "Your Darby is alive. We've seen her, well, not seen her, a clip of her on the extranet, the dark web."

"Darby's okay? She's alive. Thank God." Nina slumped against the couch. "She is? Right?"

"Yes, your daughter's alive. We don't have her physical location yet, but we're closer."

"Is that what's Godawful? That you don't know where she is?"

"Only part of it, Mrs. Richards."

"Is she okay, safe?"

"She appears okay for now but definitely not safe. I realize I'm confusing you. Let me explain. How are you with technology?"

"All my work's done on a computer. I design homes and create blueprints using specialized programs. My home's computerized." Nina's brows furrowed. "What's that got to do with bringing Darby home?"

"Mrs. Richards, we've gained access to a particular data room. Do you understand much about the dark web?"

"I've read a little, saw it on a TV series."

"The dark web's an extranet that houses all sorts of illegal business enterprises. Online data rooms can be found both on the worldwide and the dark web, for both legal and illegal purposes, to facilitate projects when the parties are physically distant from each other. Vendors store information and give confidential access to entities of their choice. Sound familiar?"

"Yes, as an architect, I have nothing to do with the data rooms, but my firm uses them on the projects in the United Arab Emirates."

"Same as those, the one I'm going to show you is restricted to individuals with a secure log-on. CIA tries to break into data rooms set up for criminal activity. One of Willard Stolfus' informant has had access to this one for several years. He stays out of the federal penitentiary by feeding the CIA and earns spending money by selling info to Cox and Mason when we inquire."

"Grady, please, just tell us."

"Okay but brace yourselves. There's no good way to say this." Grady faltered, then continued while trying to subdue his military voice. "The undercover identity of our guy is that of a wealthy business man who deals in human trafficking...trafficking of young women."

"No, please, no." Sally's chin quivered. "Please don't say they have Darby."

"Our guy logged in for an auction. Sort of by accident, he found your daughter on the dark web. We suspect Darby's no longer in the U.S., probably drugged and taken out of the country..."

"Show me." Nina turned to her mother. "Don't look. I'll tell you if it's her."

"Ladies, I can't show you here."

"I want to see my daughter."

"I don't have access to this data room. Our informant snapped a cellphone photo." Grady reached toward Nina, then dropped his hands to his side. "Our guy put himself at great risk to take this photo, but we pay him sufficiently to persuade him. Mrs. Richards, bear with me, let me explain. Briefly, when logging on, a technique called watermarking imprints unique info regarding whomever views or downloads each document, info such as the viewer's email address, IP information, a timestamp, or another identifying mark. Can't log on here because they'll know we're watching. We rely on our informant to get us what we need or take action in this data room. Dynamic watermarks are easily identifiable. Once we log on, they can't be stripped from the documents. Can't risk alerting them that we're watching. If someone outside our confidence gets a copy, our access will be compromised."

"We understand, but please, can we see the photo?"

"I dislike showing you this, but I must verify it's Darby." Grady paused then slid an eight by ten glossy out of his folder.

Nina's hand shook as she took the photo. "It's Darby. Mom, she's alive." Nina and Sally clung to each other until Nina broke the embrace and reached out to Grady. She collapsed against him. He curved his body into hers, then wrapped his massive hands around Nina's biceps and pushed her upright.

"Grady, let's go get her." Nina turned back to Sally, words tumbling out. "Thank God. Darby's safe." With the corner of her shirt, Nina wiped her tears.

"No, Mrs. Richards, your daughter's not safe. She's in the hands of extremely depraved people."

As if body slammed, Nina grabbed her chest. Then she knelt to retrieve the photo that had slipped from her fingers and fallen to the floor. She pointed to the faces. "These women, girls, all kidnapped?"

Grady didn't respond, but Nina knew it must be true. She studied each face, unsure what she expected to find in the women's expressions. The bottom edge of the photo was folded under. She flipped it open. "Babies? What? They do adoptions? I don't understand."

Grady looked at Sally as though he hoped she'd explain to her daughter why children were pictured.

Nina covered her mouth to hold back her stomach contents. "Grady, a four-month-old girl and five-year-old sister offered...offered for...?" The tone of her voice beseeched him to say she misunderstood.

Grady remained silent. He swallowed hard, his throat muscles contracted and stretched the skin. "They don't do adoptions."

Nina leaned over and put her head between her knees.

Grady rocked, one foot to the other, then dragged his hand through his hair. His eyes darted from Nina, folded over gagging, to Sally who had shriveled in place. He removed a hanky from his pocket and held it out to Sally, but she simply stared. Except for the tears pouring down her face, she had hardened into stone.

"Mrs. Richards, Sally, didn't mean for you to see that. I should have cut the bottom off the photo."

Nina swayed. Grady pulled her bent body to him and steadied her against his side.

Sally sobbed, "No, no, no."

Head still between her knees, Nina's arm flailed in the air as she reached for her mother, but Sally was gone. Without looking up, Nina asked, "Grady, you have more pictures?"

"Mrs. Richards, you've seen enough."

"I asked if you have more pictures."

"Please, Mrs. Richards, I don't want..."

She raised from her doubled over position and gripped his arm. "Grady. You do, don't you?"

"Yes, sorry no, not exactly. There's a video on the website. Haven't seen it yet. Our informant hasn't copied it. Too risky. Two-way camera watches every person who logs on."

"What's on the video? I need to know."

"I understand, but it's not a good idea." Grady pulled on his ear. He stuffed his hands deep. His pockets convulsed as if full of angry snakes as he clenched and released his fists.

If he doesn't stop, I'll scream.

"Mrs. Richards, seeing more will rip you to pieces. No reason to put yourself through it. Darby's alive. This photo was posted last night. We're in business now. I'll bring your daughter home."

"I must see her. Please, Grady. Certainly, you understand." Hot tears ran down her face. "Don't keep this from me."

He glanced sideways at the door. For an instant, Nina thought he would plunge toward it, but then he said, "Ok, Mrs. Richards, when our CI copies the video…"

Grady paused. He looked into space and pulled his ear again. "I get that you need to see your daughter, but it will change you."

"I'm already changed." Nina blinked to pinch back the flow of tears, but every movement forced them down her cheeks.

"Let me make a call." He headed into the kitchen and closed the door. Grady's baritone voice carried across the room. But even though Nina leaned against the door and pressed her ear to hear, she couldn't distinguish a single word. When he yanked it open, she tumbled through the doorway.

Grady's eyebrows shot up when Nina almost fell. He motioned for her to enter. The laptop sat on the kitchen table, but the screen was blank. Grady touched and it lit up. "This is against my better judgement, but the tech crew created a blind entry. Should be able to log in without them knowing who or where we are."

"Thank you, Grady," Nina whispered. "Thank you."

Sally tottered into the kitchen. Face as white as plaster, she clutched the table and crumpled into a chair. Grady looked at his handwritten notes, pounded on the keyboard, faltered, and backspaced. Nina stepped to her mother's side as Grady swore under his breath. "That's not it." He slowed his pace and typed more carefully, hesitated, then banged away. "Okay, we're in."

Nina braced herself against the table. She feared she might collapse at the sight of her only daughter in such a despicable place. But when the screen filled with photos of young women, what she felt was rage. "God damn bastards. I'll kill them myself."

"Mrs. Richards, there's something else. We identified someone from the Belaruse using this site. I got Lara invited to the club. She'll go undercover and identify this person. Get them to divulge the physical location of the women from the website. Then we'll know where Darby's being held."

"I'll go with her."

"With Lara?" Grady shook his head. "Sorry, Mrs. Richards. Can't happen."

"You can't stop me. This is my daughter we're talking about."

He placed his hands on her shoulders as if to soothe their shaking. "I understand, Mrs. Richards. If I were you, nothing on earth could stop me."

"That's why…"

"You must trust me on this. Lara's a professional."

Nina jutted out her chin.

"Lara's trained to infiltrate the scene and secure the needed information without raising suspicion."

Nina crossed her arms over her chest.

Grady looked to Nina's mother for support, but Sally lowered her gaze. "Nina, you were on TV. If these guys recognize you, you'll blow Lara's cover."

Nina's shoulders slumped and her hands fell to her sides. Her nod was almost imperceptible, but Grady interpreted it as his cue to exit. When she closed the door behind him, she recognized the familiar sense of loss, as if a piece of her were missing. When she spoke, her voice sounded far away.

"Mom, go sit on the deck. I'll bring you a glass of wine."

Neither Nina nor her mother had more to say, and it was just as well. The roar of the tide crashing would have swamped their conversation. Goblet in hand, Nina watched the seagulls ride the air currents without a single flap of their wings. But when her phone vibrated in her pocket, her thoughts retreated back to shore. To check caller ID required energy she didn't have, so she answered with no inkling who the caller might be.

The pounding sea almost overpowered his voice, but she recognized it anyway. "Nina, how are you?" Not waiting for her response, Louis continued, "I know Prescott's been over a few times. He reports to me. Do you want me to stay with you for a few days?"

"Thanks, Louis, but no. Mom's here. LAPD, FBI, Grady and other Cox and Mason staff are in and out at all hours."

"But I'm your best friend. I can comfort you better than anyone of them."

Louis sounded jealous. Nina thought she'd reassure him by saying, "Getting Grady was the best thing you could do for me." But, after she said the words, she realized she had pricked his ego. Nina simply shrugged because she no longer cared.

Later that night, Nina stood at her bedroom door and squinted down the hallway that led to where her daughter ought to be. The walls moved inward. The opening shrank until the carpeted path disappeared. "Same as the road to Darby," whispered Nina. "Could close forever." Nina stepped into her own room. She sat on the edge of the bed, ignored all other intruding thoughts, concentrated on only one. *Once inside the Belaruse, how will I get to Darby?*

Every idea struck her as irrational, implausible, but that wouldn't stop her. She walked to her dressing table and peered into the magnifying mirror. *Not bad for forty-one. Not good for under thirty.* Keith had said, "Throw that mirror in the garbage. No one sees you the way you see yourself in that thing. I'm telling you Nina, trash it and you'll be happier."

Now she didn't need her skin magnified to know it hung slack. The shadows under her gold-flecked eyes had spread as fast as Keith's cancer. "I've aged twenty years." Nina spoke to the mirror. "I have to do more than trash you to look younger than forty-one." She smoothed the skin at the corners of her eyes, but when she let go, the wrinkles crinkled back. Nina tried to force a smile, but it didn't work.

My face reads like the cover of a book, and it's not a happy story.

Six months earlier, under friendly duress from her longtime friend, Nina honored the appointment Erika made for her. In the four years she worked for cosmetic surgeon, Evan Winchester, Erika reversed her own aging process.

"Everything's so quick and easy," Erika had said. "Come for the free consultation. No obligation. Tell me what you think."

So, Nina went. A few hours in the clinic and she'd look thirtyish again. No down time. A little Boletaro here, a shot of Juvederm there, a considerable amount of Botox and then "Back to the Future." Nina had been tempted. Dr. Winchester's computer enhancements replicated the young woman in her own wedding photos.

While she agreed the result was striking, Nina couldn't work up the enthusiasm. Erika argued that her heart would heal faster if when she looked in the mirror, she saw her pre-sadness self. It was a good argument then, but now Nina deemed it a necessity.

I'll not let this forty-one-year-old face sabotage my plan.

Nina picked up her cell. When the familiar but groggy voice answered, Nina apologized, "Erika, I'm sorry to call so late. You were sleeping?"

"Is this about Darby? Did you find her? Is she okay?"

"We found her, but she's not okay. I need your help. Lunch tomorrow?" They decided to meet at their favorite downtown café. When they disconnected, Nina set the phone back on Keith's pillow, then slipped off her clothes and crawled into bed.

Erika will flip out when I tell her my plan. But she'll make it happen. Mothers stick together.

Nina's head sunk into the pillow. The vision of the NamUs video of the distraught mother describing her efforts to locate her missing daughter played in her mind. *Debra Culberson will never see her daughter alive again. I feel what she must have felt. But I've seen my Darby. As horrible as it was, she's alive.*

CHAPTER THIRTEEN
Darby - Day Six - Thursday, March 22

Darby tried to hold her breath and dodge the puff of air that stole her consciousness. It never worked. Every time she fought to break free, the men drugged her again. But she wouldn't stop. It wasn't that she didn't think about giving up. She did. But even though weak and tired, she couldn't wait any longer for someone else to rescue her.

Darby pushed upright and groaned as she bent to sit cross-legged on the floor. Gingerly, she massaged her upper arms, the skin so dehydrated she feared it would tear. When she rubbed her wrist, a burn radiated from it. *Bruised? A thumbprint?* Gently, she nestled her aching arm in the folds of the plush terrycloth in her lap. One small sigh of relief, then fear.

She slid her hand up her chest. *Who put this on me?* Darby leapt up and spun on the slick floor, expecting someone to jump out from a shadowy corner. Unconsciously, she tightened the belt hanging at her sides. *My clothes?* She peered under the cot. *Nothing.* Fear blistered through her veins like boiling oil.

She ripped off the robe and threw it to the floor. Darby stood naked and glared at the pile of terrycloth. Icy blades rose from the cement floor, pierced her feet. She quaked, almost fell, then lurched and grabbed the robe. Pulling it tight, Darby crumpled on the cot and rocked. She kneaded her cold cramped toes. *Hurts as if I was wearing high heels.*

Her intuition warned her to be prepared. She stood and braced herself against the stony wall. With a balled-up fist, she rubbed her itchy eyes. The crusty lumps that loosened scratched and burned. So, she spit on the corner of the robe, wiped her eyelids, and then squinted to inspect the black residue. *Mascara? Who did this?*

Darby shivered. Exhausted from the effort, she again lowered her shaking body onto the cot and hugged herself. The metal frame rattled against the wall, but her quaking wasn't caused by the frigid room. Like the first bits of sunlight cutting through fog, memories flashed in Darby's mind. A man was making her do things against her will…

Mom? She pinched her eyes shut to block the tears. *Are you coming?* Darby always thought of herself as brave, but she had lost confidence. The darkness of the room filled her mind, weighing her down. Unable to rally the strength to stand, she let her head rest against the pillow. Her wearied eyes drooped. She fought to keep them open but drifted into a restless sleep. In her dream, the tiny room was shrinking again, the walls threatened to crush her. Then a loud bump against the door startled her awake.

They're back.

She curled tight at the creak of the rusty door. A harsh male voice cut through the darkness. "Got food and clothes. Behave and you can have them."

Darby held her breath. She slid her hand to her mouth to stifle any sound. When he kicked the bedrail, she whimpered.

"Get up. I know you're awake."

Cautiously, Darby rolled upright and perched at the edge of the metal bedframe, prepared to fight. But when she made a fist, her bloated fingers shot excruciating pain up her arm.

"I won't hurt you. Got a bar of soap, a bowl of warm water." He set them on the floor. "Do what I say. Then I'll let you out of this hole."

"Okay," Darby whispered as she stood and positioned herself to run out the open door. The man was Arabian, muscular but not too big. When he turned to toss something on the bed, she saw her chance. Darby bolted toward the door but froze when a black and burly man filled the doorway. She backed away and smashed herself against the wall.

The Arabian snorted. "We'll be back."

Her knees buckled, and she slid to the floor as the door slammed behind them. The clang of the lock bounced from wall to wall. *I can't go with them. It could get even worse. They're not going to let me go.*

Darby crawled through the murkiness toward a pile of blue made by what the man had left behind. She grabbed one corner and a pair of jeans unrolled. Comforted by finding something so ordinary, she inspected the remaining items. She lifted a bra by the strap. She touched a silky fabric, but when she picked it up and realized that it was panties, she threw them to the opposite side of the room. Darby plopped on the edge of the cot and crossed her arms across her chest.

I'm not wearing that stuff. I won't let them take me anywhere.

She sat and waited. While the men didn't return, her misgivings did. *Should I go with them? Escape might be easier at this new place.* With a silent nod, she agreed with her new plan and stepped back to the pile in the middle of her cell.

139

Darby dipped the soap in the bowl while scolding herself for not washing before the water cooled. After slipping on the jeans and tee-shirt, she picked up the hairbrush. She doubted she was the only one to use it but set aside her repulsion. She winced when the bristles grabbed the knots and tangles but after a few strokes the brush slid through her oily hair.

The way Mom used to when I was little.

The repetitious movement soothed her nerves. For the first time since awakening in the cinderblock cell, she straightened her back and squared her shoulders. *I can do this. I'll stay quiet and calm, do as they ask. When I see my chance, I'll run, scream, whatever I need to do.* With each stroke of the brush, she became more resolute. *I'll know when to make a break…*

This time when the bolted door clanked, Darby stood and waited for their orders. When the Arabian man sneered, the yellow light from above stained his crooked teeth. He and the black man stood side-by-side to block the exit and glared with suspicion, braced for her fight.

Not this time, boys. Watch me obey.

"Okay, here's what will happen," said the Arabian. We'll go out this door, down the hall, up the stairs. Outside a car's waiting to take us to the airport. We'll board a plane and fly to our new destination."

"Where's that?"

"Quit being such a damn troublemaker and maybe I'll tell you."

An airport. People. Darby flushed at the opportunities, but her brain conjured one possible ruinous outcome after another as the Arabian shoved her through the door.

At the top of the steps, the alley was dark, no moon or starlight to help determine where she was. Nothing looked familiar. Dim light shone from two dirt caked windows on the opposite side of the street. She smelled the disheveled homeless man rolled tight in a shredded blanket, asleep in the doorway close to her feet. The black man kicked him aside. She pivoted toward the end of the alley where two guys hunkered toward each other. Darby tensed. She hoped these men might help her, but every expectation died when her eyes adjusted. Even in the feeble light, she recognized a drug deal when she saw it.

The Arabian man, gun handle bulging out the top of his pocket, motioned for her to sit in the backseat of a boxy black Land Rover with windows tinted so dark she couldn't see inside. Darby hesitated, and he nudged her from behind. When she sat, he slid in beside her. Another man, with scruffy two-day-old facial hair and his baseball cap turned backwards, sat in the driver's seat.

The car lurched from the curb. Familiar with the roads leading to the Los Angeles International Airport, Darby checked every street sign, certain she'd get her bearings. When she failed to recognize a single landmark, she regretted her decision to go with them. The car paused for the chain link gate to open, then stopped in front of a row of private airplane hangars. She feigned disinterest when nothing was further from the truth.

Where are the people? Airport employees? TSA? She froze when the driver yanked open the door. The Arabian slid out and hissed, "Out." When she didn't move, he reached in, gripped her elbow, and jerked her through the open door. Darby stumbled, flinching when his fingernails dug into her arm.

Private airport. I'm screwed. Darby scanned the area, barely moving her head. A man stood more than a football field away, his white jumpsuit lit by the runway lights. *Can't get on this plane. Don't know where they'll take me or what they'll do.*

The Arabian shoved her toward the boarding ramp of a small jet. When Darby's foot caught on the bottom stair, he lost his grip. She spun and bolted toward the white jumpsuit. She screamed, but the man didn't look up. Two steps…three steps and the driver took her down.

"Dumb ass," he growled at the Arabian who was now pointing his gun at Darby where she lay on the ground. "Told you she wasn't broken yet. But no, you said she'd be grateful because we let her out of the box. Now, if it's not too much for you, hold on to her. If you can't manage it, I'll get the guy who can."

The Arabian stuffed his gun back down his pants and shoved Darby up the boarding ramp, into a seat at the rear. "You'll pay for that." Then he clamped her wrists together and wrapped them in electrical tape. "I'd slap you silly if Solak didn't say your face was worth a million bucks." With that he called to a woman near the captain's cabin. "Kadira, get me a shot."

Darby examined the plane for an escape route as the woman handed the Arabian a small glass, half-filled with what looked like water. "Drink, sweetie," he sneered. Darby sucked her lips inside her mouth and bit the flesh to lock them from behind. "Drink," he repeated. "You don't have options here." Darby took the glass, tilted it to her lips and let the liquid run over her chin. "Cute," he snapped. "Think you're smart? Not to worry, you got plenty."

The engines broke into a steady moan. The force pressed Darby against the headrest, lulling her into a drugged and fitful sleep. In her dream, she was flying with Grandpa Charlie. The vibrations of his new Cessna tingled through her feet, up her legs, and settled in her heart. The wings dipped, and they began their descent. Wrapped in her grandfather's protective gaze, she felt safe. When his warm hand squeezed her arm, his lips didn't move, but she heard him anyway. *"Don't worry, baby. I gotcha."*

The hand tightened and shook her roughly. "Wake up," growled a familiar raspy voice. Darby struggled to open her eyes. The plane bounced once against the runway and rolled forward. Her vision of Grandpa Charlie splintered when the cruel voice said, "Listen to me." The Arabian knelt, his face close to hers. Darby recoiled at his stale cigarette breath, strong with the reek of evil. He cranked her head back until his gunmetal eyes bored into hers. "Listen, we'll do this one of two ways. One, I drug you again, and you'll do whatever I say. Or two, you get off this plane, keep your trap shut, and board the next plane without pulling anymore crap." He gave her a jerk to pull her face up to his, but Darby remained mute.

"Which is it? One or two?" The Arabian wrenched her arm tighter.

"Two."

"Smart decision, sister. About time you learned to obey." Darby flinched when he twisted her arm. "Don't get foolish. It's no problem to tape you up again and give you more of the Devil."

CHAPTER FOURTEEN
Nina - Day Seven - Friday, March 23

Nina and Sally picked up their purses and stopped in front of the television one last time before leaving for the second public announcement. The TV ran every waking hour. The two women called to each other whenever the news came on. They were on first name basis with the regular reporters such as gray haired, but still handsome, Sebastian Greyson who was now saying, "Tragedies comparable to this change social behavior. Society holds theater performance to a standard similar to the role of education. It's a place to critique the world, the people that populate it, the feelings they hold, and the behaviors they exhibit given the context of their lives."

Then he paused and pushed against his earpiece. "We're cutting away to speak with the parents of a twenty-four-year-old woman who died in the shooting." On screen a reporter, holding her shaggy blonde bangs out of her eyes, caught the young woman's parents as they slipped out of their backdoor into the car parked in their driveway. "Mr. and Mrs. Guetta, the police released an updated list of confirmed deaths. Your daughter and her friend, Cassidy Miller, are on that list. How are you feeling?" As the grief-stricken parents ducked their heads and slipped into their worn Honda Civic, the last question they ignored was, "Who do you hold responsible for the death of your daughter?"

They're stealing Darby's airtime. She's still alive. With the force of a Fourth of July firecracker, Nina's anger propelled itself from every pore until shame cooled her. *I know, I know. I feel horrible for those poor parents, but it's too late for them.*

As though her mother had read her thoughts, Nina tried to assuage her guilt. "I'm sorry they lost their daughter," she whispered, "but the press must help find Darby."

Sally pried the remote from her daughter's hand, pressed the off button, and placed it on the coffee table. "Come on, dear. Can't be late."

Los Angeles freeway traffic was not as sluggish as usual so Nina and Sally arrived at the L.A. Police Station an hour before the public announcement. Detective Wasden steered them to a quiet corner. "We need to talk, prepare you for what reporters might ask. You'll think the first public appearance was a walk in the park after this one. Our public information officer tells me that the reporter who got wind of the postings on the dark web is here. You'll see her right away, always in front, long auburn hair, good looking, name Elizabeth Rivera. When she brings up the connection between the gambling club and the photo of Darby, those reporters caught by surprise will go stupid on us."

"Stupid?"

"Seriously stupid. First, they'll accuse us of hiding information. Reporters are unhappy when their competition gets the scoop. Rivera, sure-fire, will bring up what we found on a dark web. The reporters outside this loop, they'll be caught off guard. You can bet the family inheritance the guy from The Daily Blast will go batshit and kickoff the descent into stupidity. Likely another obnoxious reporter will ask, 'Did you have any idea your daughter was interested in the escort business?' Or 'Did she have a gambling problem?' Some of them will ask anything to rev up the discussion."

Detective Wasden continued, "The hardest to bear will be those who say that unless a woman's tortured and beat within an inch of her life, she does this willingly."

"That's sick. Darby was kidnapped, forced…"

"I know, Mrs. Richards. I'm only warning you. Most people have no understanding of sex trafficking and the various ways women and girls are forced into prostitution. Hollywood hasn't helped. There's always one moron who thinks *The Girlfriend Experience* depicts everyday life, like the victims are entrepreneurs who chose this as their profession. It's possible some reporter might claim your daughter chose this for entree into the fastmoving life of the criminally rich and famous. Just want you prepared for anything said by folks who are no smarter than their last bad TV show. Sally, do you need to sit down?"

Detective Wasden reached out to hold Sally by the arm. When she shook her head, he continued. "Besides being plain stupid, there's the holier than thou character who maintains a woman would escape if she wanted. Not the reputable reporters, but there's always at least one ignoramus who's oblivious to the abject terror, abuse, and brainwashing these vile traffickers and their customers mete out on these women. People make incredibly stupid statements. So, all I'm saying is, be prepared."

Fortified with harsh but realistic expectations, Nina stepped onto the stage with Detective Wasden. She made eye contact with Grady and marveled how he subdued his presence as he moved through the crowd. When she began to speak, her remarks were similar to her first public announcement until her thoughts twisted.

Shouldn't need to do this a second time. FBI, LAPD, professional investigators, why hasn't one of them brought Darby home? A sharp jab in her temple made her aware she had quit speaking and was grinding her teeth.

A reporter shouted over the heads of the crowd. "Mrs. Richards. Your daughter is alive. Why do you think she hasn't contacted you?"

Wasden jumped in front of Nina and barked, "Because she was drugged and kidnapped, held against her will." He leaned back and muttered, "Idiot." Then he squared his shoulders and spoke into the microphone. "We do not know Darby's physical whereabouts. If anyone has information concerning this case, contact me, the FBI, or any local law enforcement officer. Call 911. You, the public, have helped us solve other such crimes. Now we need your help to bring Darby Richards home."

Twenty minutes later, Nina dropped off her protesting mother at the bookstore a block from where she would meet Erika. Grove Street Café held many carefree memories, old times when she met her friend for long lunches of delicate chicken salads drizzled with blackberry vinaigrette dressing, chilled glasses of chardonnay, the latest gossip, and lots of laughter. Today would be all business. Nina arrived first. She ordered a glass of wine for Erika but water for herself.

Eyes turned as Erika swooshed in the door. Swooshing best described Erika's entrance because she always wore clothes that flowed out and about as she floated through the room, a burst of summer breeze. Combine all that with Erika's luminescent complexion, the perks of working for a cosmetic surgeon, and she walked toward the table as if on angel wings. Nina counted on Erika to be her angel today and stood to embrace her friend.

When Erika said, "You're not looking any better," Nina unconsciously put her hands to her face as if to smooth the lines of worry. "What do you know, Nina? Have the detectives found out anything?"

"The private kidnapping company has located Darby, sort of."

"What does that mean? Is she safe?"

"No, not safe. She's in great danger, has undergone unbelievable horror. Things women don't even pray for protection from because it's so hideous, so unlikely to happen, that we aren't even afraid of it."

"Nina, what are you saying? You're scaring me."

Nina leaned forward, lowered her voice so their fellow diners couldn't overhear, and told her best friend everything. Erika's rosy cheeks turned ashy white.

"Nina, how can I help?"

"I have to rescue Darby myself. They found out that traffickers have her, but even the FBI has not located where they're holding her. Vile scum, now she's being sold…to men, monsters." Nina's voice cracked. "There are pictures, filthy business deals on the dark web, but not even the FBI has sent someone to get her. So, I'm going myself."

Erika's mouth hung slack. If it weren't for the Botox, her eyebrows would have shot up. "You mean… No, you can't mean… You'll…?"

"If I'm to infiltrate, I must look younger."

"Infiltrate? Holy crapola. You'll be in monumental danger. They'll kill you when they find out."

"Maybe but I've no other option. Wouldn't you go?" Nina hesitated, but Erika, mouth open, just stared. "The investigators are stymied. If I don't, I may never get her back."

"Nina, you asked for my help. What can I do?"

"Squeeze me in. I need the work done immediately. I backed out before because it wasn't important to me, but now I must. Will you do it?" Nina had hoped for an enthusiastic response, but Erika's face was blank, so she continued to present her case. "Everything should be in my file. Dr. Winchester showed me how in one afternoon he'd make me look ten years younger. I had an extensive medical exam in case the firm sends me to Egypt for the new project. Perfect health, inoculations for every conceivable disease. I'm ready."

"I'd have to tell Evan why this is so sudden."

"Please Erika, no. I don't want to involve him. He might feel obligated to contact the police. They'd try to stop me."

"How will I pull this off? Let me think. Lordy, it's unthinkable." Erika put her wine to her lips, almost took a sip, then slammed the glass down, sloshing wine over the edge. "A friend is coming in tomorrow for a similar procedure. She's had horrendous stuff to deal with. Facial work is part of remaking her life. Won't tell you about it now, but when she hears your story, she'll give up her time." Erika jumped to her feet. "Have to go." She lifted Nina's hand and gave it a light kiss. "I've got this." Erika spun and crashed into two befuddled seniors. At the door, she waved back at Nina and sprinted out of the café.

Sally hugged her sweater to herself as she stood at the corner outside the bookstore. She scurried into the car when Nina stopped alongside the curb. She gave her daughter a sideways glance but didn't speak.

The long drive home added another layer of tension atop doing the second public announcement and the stress of asking Erika for a favor that could cause trouble with her boss. Nina wanted to lay her head on the steering wheel and close her eyes. Her mother's pouting silence didn't help. Sally stared out the front window and waited for her daughter to speak. But Nina simply wasn't ready.

When they arrived at home, Nina plodded toward the kitchen. Sally, still punishing her daughter for leaving her at the bookstore while she met with Erika, turned and walked the opposite way. With one hand, Nina pulled out a chair while waking her computer with the other. She pounded in her password, began a new search, misspelled every word. *This is getting me nowhere.*

Nina slumped until her forehead rested on the backs of her hands. For only a moment, she felt Darby sitting beside her. She was pouring a glue and flour mixture into a bowl of shredded paper. Darby's first experience with papier Mache. The trunk dropped off her soggy elephant. Two flaxen ponytails, goo gobbed on her nose, Darby stretched out her hand. Her little mouth was moving. *Help me, Mama.* Nina jerked awake. Her hands slammed forward and sent the keyboard careening.

I must find my Darby. Lots of people trying, but nobody doing. It's up to me.

Nina's mind raced as she logged on to *Fox News* online. In the broadcast from the Grossman Burn Center in West Hills, the distraught face of eighty-six-year-old Angeline Wood filled the screen. "I should've died with my friends. We've lived our lives. A couple, maybe a husband and wife, fell at my feet. Shot dead when they ran from the fire caused by the bomb inside. Did they have children? I don't know. It's more than I can bear. I wake up crying for those killed by these insane terrorists. Shouldn't be me who's still alive."

You feel guilty? Nina projected her thoughts at the fragile, gray haired woman. *What if your daughter was kidnapped and sold to despicable men while you, the person who should keep her safe, sleep in your own bed and wait for someone else to do your job, to bring your child home. Now, that's a guilt you can't survive.*

"Nina, come here. Hurry." Nina bolted into the living room where her mother stood waving the remote in the air. "They announced that after the station break and the weather, then an update on Darby." When the broadcast returned, Sally sassed the weatherman. "It's spring, Southern California, for God's sake, the weather's always the same. Get to Darby."

Then the blonde botoxed reporter appeared. "Special Report Tonight. Human Trafficking: World's Fastest Growing Crime. Hosted at 9 p.m. by Victoria van der Waal, winner of the Bergmann Excellence in Criminal Justice Reporting Award. China allows more modern slavery to thrive within its borders than any other country. However, State Department statistics indicate that the numbers have grown in the USA."

The screen split and Victoria van der Waal's face appeared. "The U.S. Office of Human Trafficking reported twenty-seven million victims. Approximately eight hundred thousand people every year are trafficked across international borders with the count increasing between two and four million when those held within their country of origin are included. However, many cases go unreported, rendering accurate accounting impossible. The State Department report is damning but doesn't tell the entire story. Studies reveal that due to globalization, trafficking occurs on every continent from huge and bustling China to small and remote Iceland. One would expect these reports to stimulate efforts to stop this crime against humanity. I ask, will this knowledge make a difference?"

"They're not talking about Darby," Nina whispered.

Victoria van der Waal continued, "I hope this report and the commitment of President Brighton's daughter will result in action. Watch as we bring you a clip of her interview."

"While drug trafficking remains the largest form of organized crime in the world, human trafficking is tied in second place with the sale of illegal arms. Ending human trafficking is a priority for my mother. And on a personal level, as a mother myself, this is much more than a policy issue. It could happen to anyone of us. Of huge proportions, this crime which men perpetrate against women and children, must be stopped. You have my commitment. This is my highest priority."

The screen shifted from the President's daughter to Victoria van der Waals, then split again to show Nina at the public announcement earlier that day. "This woman's daughter, Darby Richards, has been kidnapped and trafficked. To support her and thousands of other victims, I urge you to back the President's daughter in her quest to end human trafficking. Personally, and professionally, I am eager to aid in this cause. The first thing I will do is separate fact from fiction regarding this heinous crime. The second is to keep the faces and stories of the victims before the public. Tonight, I am focusing on three ongoing California investigations."

Nina's face disappeared, and Darby's filled the screen. "UCLA student Darby Richards is the most recent victim. She is the only child of the woman we saw begging the world to come forth with information on her daughter."

"Thank you," murmured Nina. She held her mother's wrinkled hand. Neither woman looked away as Victoria van der Waals closed the hourlong show until Nina's cell rang. When she read the caller ID, she sighed with relief.

"You're in, tomorrow, one-thirty. Got to go. Doctor's calling for me." Erika disconnected before Nina even had a chance to say thank you.

CHAPTER FIFTEEN
Darby - Day 7 - Friday, March 23

Darby snuggled into the clean softness of the bed. A sleepy smile crossed her face as she rubbed her nose against the pillow and took a deep breath without gagging on the stench. She pinched her eyes closed, wanting to hold on to the fantasy. When she pulled a crisp clean sheet to her chest, she realized she was awake. Darby shuddered herself upright and scanned the room.

Where am I now?

Darby stood and held onto the headboard until her eyes stopped on a strip of sunlight. Drowsy from the drugs, the yellow path seemed to be an escape route, but when she stepped into it, her shadow let her know it was a mirage. She moved closer and squinted through the window's wooden slats. In the courtyard, coppery clay covered the ground. Stalks of purple buds clung to sundried brick walls. Flowers shriveled in the sun at the bases of large Magnolia trees. She twisted her neck. The upper floor of the building hung out past the room in which she found herself. In the shade of the overhang sat a mosaic bench designed of colored tiles.

Where on earth am I? In the desert? Not L.A. Maybe Palm Springs?

Darby placed her head against the warm glass and peered out from the corner. She could see a square white building. Its roof of four triangles met in a high point in the center.

Not American architecture. Mom would know.

Darby turned and leaned against the wall. A large white door beckoned. She chastised herself for wasting time at the window. Her arm jostled as she scurried. She ignored the pain and clutched the doorknob. It was locked.

Her hand settled into a rhythmic throb. She nestled it to her body as if it were a newborn. Only then did she realize her clothes had been changed. She now wore a long red dressing gown that pleated itself around her ankles. As Darby lifted her arms, large triangle sleeves unfurled and the front of the gown fell open. Underneath she wore a silk teddy. Puzzled, she picked at a seam.

Expensive...but wrong.

Vague images of airplanes floated in her memory, accompanied by a sense of running, screaming, falling to the ground. Darby shook her head and continued to study her surroundings. Her gaze settled on a settee, heavy gold brocade on a rich mahogany frame.

When her heavy eyelids slid shut, visions formed, much like a movie trailer in which she played a part. Darby saw a plane and felt the wind of its engines. As she climbed the boarding ramp, her knees buckled when she was shoved from behind. A man's face touched hers, then evaporated. Unconsciously, she wiped her mouth at the memory of the liquid she'd let run off her lips.

Darby worried her captors might lurk outside the door. She sat on the settee and waited until the room darkened. Her skin crawled at the thought of the men watching, so she continued watching back. At the foot of the bed stood a carved table with two chairs that matched the brocade settee. A copper tray covered the tabletop. In its center sat a pottery plate painted with pink tulips clustered among lush green vines. A glass pitcher held a milky liquid. She speculated whether it was safe while she fingered the curved handle. Her parched throat urged her to drink so she poured enough to barely cover the bottom of the glass.

Darby looked up and whispered, "Grandpa, should I?"

"Drink it, baby. If they wanted to poison you, they would've done it by now."

She turned on the bedside lamp, lifted the glass, and spun it in the light. She controlled the flow so that only drops crossed her lips. The licorice flavor surprised her. *Watery, same as the stuff that floats in a yogurt container. Only salty. One more sip, then I'll wait to see if I get sick...or pass out.*

A dark cloud of sadness settled in as she struggled to understand why no one had come to rescue her. But then, in a twisted way, her spirits rose. She was grateful the men hadn't returned to hurt her again. A noise, tiny as a mouse, caught her attention. The door opened. Except for her eyes growing larger, she didn't move a muscle. When a woman entered, Darby's sighed with relief.

She looks normal. Will she let me go?

Motionless, Darby waited as the woman strode toward her. A gun protruded from her pocket. While acting as if she hadn't seen it, Darby spread her fingers and prepared to grab, but the woman stopped too far away. Beneath the silky robe, Darby quivered, but neither woman moved.

Now or never.

Darby sprung forward but stumbled when the folds of the dressing gown wrapped around her ankles. As she fell, she reached out to grab the woman who ducked and shoved Darby down. The crack of her chin hitting the tile floor left her stunned.

"Berat. Quick. Grab the dust. She's still fighting."

The woman sat on Darby's buttocks and cranked her arms behind. Darby cried out. She kicked her feet, tried to knock the woman off. Face pressed against the cold tile, she felt and heard footsteps coming closer. Darby writhed like an angry snake. A man grabbed her hair and bent her neck to its breaking point. His face contorted into a menacing sneer. Dark and muscle-bound, he knelt so close that she inhaled his fetid breath.

"Not ready to behave? I've just the thing for you." As he lifted a latex gloved hand, Darby fought to break his grip. "Not so fast. You're feisty, but no match for me." His fingers touched her cheek. She recoiled as he appeared to blow her a kiss. But it wasn't a kiss that caressed Darby's face.

CHAPTER SIXTEEN
Nina - Day Eight - Saturday, March 24

With only four hours of broken sleep, Nina was irreparably exhausted. She got out of bed anyway. Once in the shower, even the weight of the water was too much, so she leaned against the granite wall. Finding no relief, she pushed away, leaving the imprint of her body in the moisture beads.

Nina opened the shower door. *Two hours until Wasden arrives. Go back to bed.* Fifteen minutes later, she gave up and crawled out from between the sheets. Her feet hit the floor with a thud. Voices wafted up the stairs. She recognized the 5 a.m. broadcaster.

Nina stopped in the living room and looked past the back of her mother's head to the television. "Any mention of Darby?" Her surge of hope met its demise when Sally shook her head.

A reporter who appeared too young to fly without parental supervision reviewed airport safety tips. "Be observant. Security experts ask that everyone report odd or suspicious behavior."

"Are you kidding, child? It's LAX. Odd and suspicious run rampant there." Sally continued to grouse about sending a child to do an adult's job, so Nina increased the volume to drown her out.

The young reporter shoved a microphone in the face of a uniformed man. "You've served fourteen years as Chief of Security and Public Safety at Los Angeles International Airport. Given the increase in extremist activities, how is LAX preparing for terrorist attacks such as the one last night at the Pantages Theatre?"

"Training and increased hiring of armed TSA officers. Also, 3-D bag screening and biometric fingerprint identification, but nothing guarantees there won't be another attack. Airports are vulnerable. Our country must take military grade weapons out of criminals' hands."

Sally turned to her daughter. "Sit, dear. You surf the channels while I make breakfast. You're not eating enough to keep up your strength."

As they finished their bowls of oatmeal, not a single reporter mentioned Darby or the previous night's episode of Victoria van der Waals's award-winning series, Criminal Intentions. Nina switched to broadcasts she'd recorded and fast forwarded through the commercials. She paused when the screen filled with a panoramic scan of the Pantages Theatre. Clusters of multicolored flowers were propped against the building. A ponytailed girl, maybe six years old, set a one-eyed teddy bear on the ground.

"Oh, Mom. I know how they feel. These people lost someone they loved. I get that. I hurt for them, but the news needs to focus on Darby."

As though the reporter heard Nina's lament, the vigil faded and Victoria van der Waals appeared. "LAPD and FBI report no advancement on locating Darby Richards, the kidnapped and trafficked UCLA student featured on my show last night. I pledged to the President's daughter to keep the topic alive until Darby is recovered. As part of that effort, I'm pleased to announce that a private donor matched the fifty-thousand-dollar reward offered for information leading to conviction of Darby Richards' abductors.

Please tune in for tonight's show. DEA Detective Tony Navarro will further discuss Devil's Breath, the drug used in the kidnap and murder of Alisa Methron, a new talent who had recently emerged on the Southern California art scene."

While Victoria reminded viewers of the broadcast time, Nina left the room and walked to the far edge of the deck. Mist clung to her face as she leaned over the railing. They had worried about erosion, her feet only inches from the drop off. However, since the Coastal Review Board denied their request to build a retaining wall on the bluff, it was in the hands of nature. Matching its cadence with crashing waves, Keith's words echoed in her mind. *"This place will fall off the cliff. Might be years. Could be the next raging storm and into the ocean we go."*

"Could be never," Nina had always countered.

For the moment, their home remained atop the bluff. Nina licked salt crystals from her lips. *If one disaster would negate another, I'd get a bulldozer and push it off myself.*

An alert from her cellphone broke through Nina's thoughts. The screen was lit with Wasden's harried face as he stood out front. She touched the icon to open the security gate as she stepped back in the house. When Nina opened the front door, there stood Wasden in his rumpled suit and scruffy beard. He looked as if he hadn't been home in days. "Come in, Detective. Please tell me you have good news."

His failure to respond filled her with foreboding. He maintained that silence until they joined Sally where she still sat, eyes locked on the television. He sank into the couch and rested his head in his broad hands. Everything about him seemed tired.

Sally squirmed and Nina clenched her teeth, impatient for him to speak. Wasden dug in his pocket for the frayed cigarette. He rolled it between his fleshy hands. "I have a lead. CDRs revealed a pattern of calls."

"CDRs? A branch of the FBI?"

"No, sorry, police jargon. Call Detail Records are phone company billing records. They show a pattern of calls to Durson Askoy, Professor Balik's colleague at the Belaruse. All from a known head of an international sex trafficking organization."

"The one that posted Darby's picture on the dark web?"

"Good chance. If not, they're connected in some other illegal activity. CDRs are stored for years. Looking back, there's considerable traffic coinciding with the disappearance of two other college girls, close to the time we discovered Alisa Methron's body. Remember hearing of her death?"

"More than that. The gallery owner's a friend of mine, Juliette Marchand. I was there, Alisa's first show. She didn't show up. Then later, after she was found, my friend's PR was broadcast over and over. Beautiful young woman, so full of life, and grateful to Juliette for hosting her first show."

Nina sucked in a ragged breath. "Forgive me. I'm rambling… Nerves."

"You're fine, Mrs. Richards, and you're right. That's her. We think she escaped the cartel run by Askoy, but they tracked her down, beat her, shot her up with a drug strong enough to drop a linebacker."

"These animals took Darby?"

"Not clear. And there's no hard proof just yet that this group murdered Alisa Methron. If it was them, can't figure why they'd leave her in an alley. But the billing records indicate a connection, so, we're working it with everything we've got." Wasden slipped a photo out of his notebook. "This is Jason Coleman, the guy I told

161

you attached himself to your daughter at the Belaruse. As a private citizen, no criminal record, we need a content warrant to look at his texts. Takes another twenty-four hours. Have you seen him?"

Nina shook her head and studied the photo, silent until she memorized every feature. At that point, she noticed sweat beading on her forehead so she wiped it with her sleeve. "What else?"

Wasden grimaced. "That may not seem like a lot, but it is. I'll get back to you as soon as I know more."

When Nina stood to walk him to the door, spots appeared inside her eyes and her vision obscured. She braced against the wall, fighting not to pass out.

"You okay?" Wasden's hand was heavy on her shoulder. "Listen, I handed this info over to Grady Prescott. Him and his team, they're good. Hang in there." He gave her shoulder a squeeze. "We're all giving it our best."

Nina closed the door and leaned against it to steady her legs until her mother called out. "Grady will be here soon. He'll tell us more."

When the security system chimed like a doorbell, alerting them to someone at the gate, Sally, two cups of coffee in hand, met Nina in the entryway. Nina ignored the coffee and hurried past her mother to open the door. She searched Grady's face, hoping to find comfort in his expression. Seeing none, she motioned for him to enter.

Sally lifted one cup. "Take this, Grady. I'll pour another." Grady followed the women to their usual workspace, the kitchen table.

"We're making headway but let me put it in context. Sex trafficking crimes are characterized by three phases. The first is

162

acquisition. The third phase is exploitation. As you're aware, we have proof your daughter is being exploited." He hesitated to gauge their reaction. Neither woman appeared to be breathing. He paused and then continued. "It's the second phase, movement, we're dealing with now. Eight days since your daughter's disappearance. FBI say Darby's no longer in L.A. Our informant says she's not in California, maybe not even in the U.S."

When Sally gasped, Nina and Grady snapped their heads in her direction. "But you're close to finding her, aren't you?"

Grady nodded. "We're narrowing in on the location. Cox and Mason have technology LAPD does not. Through it, we connected the virtual data room on which Darby's photo is posted to other women held in Turkey." His face filled with concern as Nina's hand shook and coffee splashed onto the table. "Should know who kidnapped your daughter after tonight."

"Then we go get her, right?"

"Can't promise that, Mrs. Richards. Not that simple. However, I'll either call or come by tomorrow."

As Nina closed the door behind Grady, multiple disjointed images bombarded her. *Detectives, FBI, all busy with clues and leads, but they're still here…and Darby's not.* Nina locked the door and sucked down a huge gulp of air. *The more they discover, the less they know.*

Barely able to lift her feet, Nina shuffled toward the stairs. *The longer Darby's gone, the less likely I'll ever get her back.* Nina raced upstairs, two steps at a time to retrieve her purse. She was ready for her appointment with Dr. Winchester and the first step of her plan. She contemplated slipping out without saying goodbye. Her stomach told her that her mother would catch her in her lie. She crept up behind Sally and watched her skip from one channel to the next.

Nina cleared her throat. "Mom, it's early, but I don't want to miss Esma. You never can predict L.A. traffic." She breathed a sigh of relief when Sally didn't question where she said she was going and only nodded without looking away from the TV screen.

As Nina rolled onto the I-5 Freeway, the traffic was flowing. She drove unimpeded all the way to Los Angeles. The dashboard clock showed that three hours remained until her appointment. Her thoughts strayed from the road ahead and drifted to the steel girders she had designed for a new multilevel condo. *Invisible bonds of support...the same way women support each other.*

Nina had told Wasden she'd be in L.A. that afternoon, but not why. So, she wasn't surprised when the car phone rang. "Got time to stop by?" He tried to sound casual, as if he were an old friend calling to chat, but he couldn't do soft and warm. His words were jagged. She pictured him with that same war-torn cigarette stuck between his lips.

Nina was mentally reviewing her rescue plan when she entered the police station. She removed her cell from her bag and set them both in the tray to be scanned. Her belt buckle set off the security alarm, distracting her from her thoughts. Turning toward a bedlam of pushing and shoving, she ignored the officer who outlined her body with the wand.

Nina marched past the scuffle toward the office where Wasden said he'd meet her. When she started to speak to the desk sergeant, a skinny bedraggled man tripped on the beat cop's foot, hurtled across the floor, and stopped at her feet. The fracas held her attention, but when she looked up, the sergeant glared, sending her a message that she'd better not be the next disruption in his chaotic day. She wrenched her lips into a smile. "Nina Richards, here for Detective Wasden." Feeling like a second in a cop reality show, she sidestepped two thuggish guys in dark hoodies, hands cuffed behind their backs, being helped toward an exit door.

"Yes, Mrs. Richards. Wasden just thundered out, said to wait in that office." The sergeant jerked his thumb to the left. "Said he'd be back shortly, but with Wasden, ya never know."

For the next fifteen minutes, Nina people watched, and there were interesting characters ripe for observation. A woman wearing a tiny skirt sat opposite a dodgy-looking man scooching down to get a better look. An elderly couple waited at a gray metal desk. The man, scrutinized the assorted characters, then pulled his wife's sweater up over her shoulder as if to protect her from the other occupants of the room.

Nina assumed she'd be there a while, so she pulled out her cell and checked the tweets for news of Darby until the desk sergeant's edgy voice captured her attention. "Miss Paige Vickers. It is, indeed, a pleasure to see your lovely face again. Detective Wasden will be genuinely sorry to have missed you. But you're no stranger to his methods. You know his return might be anywhere from thirty seconds to three days. How may I assist you?"

"Find Wasden. Get him to call me. Left multiple messages. The word is they're moving the other UCLA student to the same place as Methron."

"I'll tell him. Anything else I may do for you, Miss Vickers?"

"Yeah, my expense account's late. Tuition's overdue. I can't stay undercover if I'm not enrolled. Can't buy books, can't sign up for classes…"

"No idea why he's not returning your calls, but your payment, I'll fix that." The sergeant punched the intercom and barked, "Garrison. My desk. Now."

Then he tossed her a pen and notepad. "Second thought, I'm off in two hours." He motioned with his thumb. "Leave your message for Wasden on that desk."

"Yeah, right, leave another message." The woman named Paige walked in where Nina sat. As she dropped the note on the battered metal desk, the man leaning to sneak a peek up the short skirt rolled out of his chair and thumped to the floor. Laughter erupted. With all eyes on the disruption, Nina scrambled to open the camera on her cell and snap a photo. The purple streak in the woman's blond hair covered most of her face.

With a flourish, Paige slipped the sergeant's pen in her bag, rolled her eyes, and stormed out. The note lay half open, but strain as she might, Nina couldn't read it. She was barely able to restrain herself from grabbing the note. Then everyone turned toward two cops dragging three cussing and swearing men, so under the influence that they tripped over their own feet.

In slow motion, Nina opened the note, snapped its photo, and headed out the door. As she scurried past the sergeant, she called out over her shoulder. "Out of time. Tell Detective Wasden I waited as long as I could." Nina jogged down the hall and out of the police department trying to catch the woman. She scanned the parking lot but was too late.

Nina pulled up the photo of the note. She remembered the name. Both Grady and Wasden had mentioned it as a person of interest at the Belaruse. She smiled at her good fortune as she enlarged the picture. Scribbled at the bottom was "Paige" followed by a phone number. She debated what action to take. A quick time check on her cell verified she was late and didn't have time to call. Nina sprinted to her car, dug for her keys as she ran. *Can't miss this appointment.* Nina cringed as her back tires jumped the curb and spun on grass. *Need to get to Winchester's office fast, but don't need a ticket, especially in the LAPD parking lot.*

When Nina's procedures were complete, Erika drew her aside and hugged her. "Be safe."

Before she opened the car door, Nina squinted in the sideview mirror and rubbed the numb spot between her eyebrows. She tried to frown. Nothing moved except her eyelids. She touched the tiny bruise forming under her eye. *Hurt more than he said. Doctors lie.*

As Nina turned the key in the ignition, she gave herself an approving glance in the rearview mirror. The filler had flowed like hot melted plastic, but her lips were plump and firm. She wouldn't miss the droop that had formed at the corners of her mouth during Keith's illness. Intrigued, she took another glimpse in the mirror as she backed out of her parking space. *Am I fooling myself? What if my face looks paralyzed like the blonde on Fox News?* As she drove out of the underground garage, she couldn't resist another hurried look. *This will do the job.*

The traffic was the normal six o'clock mess complicated by her inability to synchronize her speed with the street lights. While she waited in line at her eighth red light, Nina took one final peek. *The miracle of Botox. Brain screwed up in a scowl yet my face is oblivious.* As she merged into the freeway traffic, a twinge of anxiety pinched at her neck. Now the hard part...telling Mom the truth.

As Nina inched the car through the gated entrance of her beachfront home, she whispered into empty air. "We're a family of strong smart women, unbroken by anything life has hurled at us." She almost finished with "until now."

Nina straightened her shoulders, stiffened her resolve and marched into the kitchen, prepared to drop the bombshell. Sally greeted her daughter. "Dinner's ready. Keeping it warm for… What did you do?"

Nina started to give her well-rehearsed justification, but her mother cut her off. "I mean it's good. The same as your wedding photos. But how? The bags? I'm sorry Nina but the dark circles under your eyes, the frown. Oh my, sounds as if I thought you looked awful. That's not it at all. You're always beautiful but losing your father, then Keith, took a toll. And now Darby, every horror and uncertainty was imprinted on your face. So, what did you do? And why?"

"I've lots to tell you, Mom, but let's eat first."

"I have something to tell you too. Gossip." Nina watched her mother's expression change. That certain way she lifted her brows and looked down her nose always preceded scandalous information.

"Okay, Mom, let's hear it."

"Been a busy day, telephone-wise. In addition to the onslaught of reporters, Louis called again."

"And?"

"He acted nice, concerned, asked if he could come over and bring dinner." I told him I'd check with you and call him back. Louis said the firm hired an intern, Cal Poly, Pomona. He prattled on and on…how enchanted she is with the '50s architecture, the Spanish influence in San Clemente. Said he's eager for you to train her."

Nina reflected on how attentive Louis had been to her. The hours he'd spent working with her, grooming her to become the firm's only female partner. When Keith died, Louis was there for her, taking from his family time, until it became inappropriate. Nina pulled herself from her thoughts. When she looked up, her mother still wore her "I've got a secret" face.

"There's more?"

"Oh, yes. Louis was so thoughtful. I even considered changing my opinion of him, which you know I rarely do."

Nina hoped her mother wouldn't mention the affair. Balanced on the far edge of her patience, she opened her mouth to change the subject when Sally spoke again. "Thirty minutes later, your secretary called." Her mother paused, with the skill of Helen Mirren, waiting for the tension to mount. "Sherrill also had a few things to say about the new intern." Sally lowered her voice. "Louis is boinking her." She searched her daughter's face for a reaction but found no clue of what Nina was thinking.

Textbook. He cheated on his wife with me and now…

"She's twenty-three."

"Five years older than Darby? Young enough to be my daughter?"

Sally watched Nina closely, expecting a blowup. It was happening, but only in Nina's mind.

My white knight. Ha. Son-of-a-bitch.

Sally continued to scrutinize her daughter's face, but it couldn't hold less expression. Disappointed, Sally reacted for her. "Slimy, rat-assed, dick-brained prick."

Nina smiled in agreement.

Nina and her mother spent the evening in front of the television, scouring the news for mention of Darby. The second public announcement only garnered twenty-four hours of airtime. Once again, Darby's disappearance was filler news.

After more pushing of the food around the plate than eating it, Sally broke the silence. "Okay, let's hear it. What's happening?"

Nina inhaled, filled her chest to strengthen her resolve. "I have a plan to rescue Darby. While I was driving, Wasden called, but by the time I arrived, he'd left."

"A wasted trip?"

"No, not at all. This woman came in, maybe an informant, maybe a plain clothes officer. She's undercover as a student. She told the desk sergeant that the other UCLA student was being moved to the same place as Methron."

"The other UCLA student? Darby?"

"Yes, I'm sure. The woman put a note on Wasden's desk. Said it was a name he's looking for. So, I snapped a picture of the note."

"You got the name?"

Nina nodded. "It's someone Grady mentioned as associated with the Belaruse. He arranged for Lara Kensington to go undercover tonight. I'm going with her."

"He won't let you."

"Lara's got a way of getting what she wants from him. If Wasden calls tonight, don't say a word. He'll throw a conniption fit, lock me up to stop me from going."

"Oh, Nina, what if they hurt you? I can't lose you both."

Nina picked up her mother's hand and traced the puffy veins the way Darby did as a child. "I need to go. Wasden, Grady, FBI, no one's brought Darby back. It's up to me."

"You're hoping they'll kidnap you too?"

Nina looked away. She couldn't bear to watch the moisture pool in the corners of her mother's eyes. "The woman's name is Paige Vickers. She put her phone number on the note. I'll see how it goes tonight with Lara, then call Paige tomorrow. Gives them twenty-four hours to bring Darby home. Wasden with the info from the note and Grady with whatever Lara learns tonight. If not, I'll call Paige Vickers and make something happen."

"But all that work on your face today?" Sally blinked to restrain her tears. "You must be exhausted. You should rest."

"Mom, every moment that passes means more abuse for Darby." Nina met her mother's gaze. "I understand you're confused, unsure who you should protect, your daughter or your granddaughter. It's horrible, but you know I have to do this."

"I do." Sally used her napkin to wipe the tears streaming down her face. "But if I lose you both…"

"I'll be fine, Mom. I know what I'm facing." *I wish that were true.* "But, you're right. I'm tired. Think I'll shower and take a nap. Wake me when van der Waals comes on. Lara's picking me up at nine-thirty. I can watch for a while."

Nothing she could say would stop her mother's tears, so Nina left and climbed the stairs to her room. She felt her mother's heart shatter, a new shard with her every step. But she didn't turn around.

As Nina emerged from the shower, exhaustion overcame her. "Please," she whispered, "just thirty minutes of sleep." She lay atop the thick duvet and sank into a bottomless slumber until Sally broke the spell.

"Ten minutes 'til Victoria's show."

Nina swirled her hair into a knot and loosened strands to fall around her face and neck. She smoothed on the makeup sample

Erika gave her. Her skin was as flawless as alabaster. She rubbed sultry gray shadow onto her eyelids. The mirror reflected the image of a youthful woman, but it gave her no pleasure.

Her cell lay on the dressing table. *Call Paige now?* Nina's hand quivered as she layered on the mascara. *Don't be stupid. Give Wasden and Grady the twenty-four hours.* She filled the makeup brush with coral blush and dusted her cheekbones. *Twenty-four hours is a long time.* Darby's copper sheath shimmered in the light as Nina lifted it off the bed. *First decision's always the best.* The dress slid over her head like silk and clung like butter. *Work the plan.* She took the strappy sandals from their box. *But what might happen to Darby in twenty-four hours?* Nina picked at a scuff on the matching bag. She held her own gaze in the mirror and said, "Wait the twenty-four hours." With that, she picked up her phone and called Paige Vickers. While it rang, Nina rehearsed. The ringing stopped and a recorded voice said, "Leave a message."

"I'm, uh, Nina Richards, Darby Richards' mother. Please call me. I saw you today, this morning at the police department. Need to talk to you. Please…" Nina repeated her callback number and disconnected.

Victoria's TV voice met Nina halfway as she descended the stairs. "Devil's Breath is the topic of tonight's show. This horrific drug is made of seeds found inside the flowers of the borrachero tree. So beautiful that a large specimen lives in the Bogota Botanical Garden." The picture of the ominous tree faded and was replaced by Victoria's face.

"Consider selling your soul to the devil and relinquishing self-will. As if an eager puppy, you obey. Whether asked to bake cookies or provide sexual favors, one puff of Devil's Breath and you comply. Unlike a hypnotic state, no memories survive. Your

172

mind is wiped clean regardless of how catastrophic your actions might be. Scary? You bet it is."

On the television, the faces of two men replaced Victoria's. "My guests tonight are DEA Detective Tony Navarro and LAPD Detective Max Wasden. Welcome, gentlemen."

"Detective Navarro, you have evidence that Devil's Breath played a role in the death of Alisa Methron. Our viewers may remember Ms. Methron, the innovative artist who disappeared before her first L.A. showing." Victoria turned toward Navarro. "You believe she was drugged and trafficked before her body was found near her Westwood apartment?"

"Yes, Victoria. Originally, Devil's Breath was not suspected. However, new evidence led to retesting. A specific screening, not included in our standard battery of tests, is needed to detect it. Increased use of this drug in the U.S. is demanding that we alter our testing practices."

"At what point did you come to believe this drug was used on Darby Richards?"

"When we reviewed the security video taken outside the Belaruse. The driver blew something into her face, most likely Devil's Breath," said Navarro. "Victoria, Detective Wasden will explain what we are seeing."

A blurry six second clip of a man wearing a latex glove blowing across his hand into Darby's face played on the screen.

"Let's see that again," Victoria requested of her producer.

As the film replayed, Detective Wasden described key movements, concluding with Darby sinking into the backseat of a large black car. "Darby Richards was unaware and unable to fend off this assault. Even if she had recognized the danger and covered her mouth and nose, it would not have helped. Devil's Breath penetrates through surgical masks. The drug is maniacal. A few grains sprinkled on your hand, then you rub your eyes or mouth, prepare food or take a drink, and you are defenseless. The perpetrator only has to wait a moment for the drug to breach the body's natural defense systems."

As the tape ended and Detective Navarro reappeared on the screen, Victoria asked, "You said this drug is now more prevalent."

"Yes. Not only right here in L.A. but across the world, Devil's Breath is growing in popularity with trafficking cartels. Years past, mystery writers often used chloroform as the knockout drug in kidnapping stories. Devil's Breath is the current day chloroform. In both crime novels and real life, kidnappers get better results."

Navarro leaned closer to Victoria. "Devil's Breath has been an immense problem in Columbia for many years, recently in Africa and China. INTERPOL reports its use in a current rash of Paris street robberies. Given we are experiencing growth in the number of cases in the Greater Los Angeles area, I have recommendations for your viewers." Navarro turned to face the camera.

"First, if you think you've been dosed while out in public, alert people that the drug still may be in the air. Ask bystanders to call 911. If you're alone, try calling yourself. Devil's Breath works fast, but you may stay conscious long enough to punch in three numbers. Try to get away. You've only seconds, but you might get yourself into the hands of friends or family, best case scenario, a medical professional."

"Given what you describe, it seems unlikely that I would know if Devil's Breath was blown or sprinkled on me."

The camera shifted to a closeup of Wasden. "Exactly, Victoria. The perpetrator takes control without the victim knowing anything happened. Uncharacteristic behavior provides the first clue. The victim finds their circumstances drastically changed yet is clueless how it happened. A case last week in Hollywood, homeowner wakes up in the morning. He's surrounded by drawers pulled out, clothes on the floor. He goes to his home safe, finds it open and empty. Calls police, reports a burglary. Security footage shows the guy ransacking his own bedroom and carrying a canvas bag downstairs. He heads to the front door and there in the entryway, is another man. The owner hands over the bag. We're watching the tape, but nobody realizes that the homeowner is the victim. He appears to be an accomplice. Maybe for the insurance? Since he remembers nothing, he's one befuddled suspect. Anyway, his behavior got us thinking, and he agreed to a drug test. Sure enough, Devil's Breath."

As Detective Navarro spoke, the cameraman drew back to include all three in the screen. "Similar to that case, the behavior we saw in the video of Darby Richards alerted us to the possibility she was drugged."

"Detective Wasden, is the Devil's Breath always inflicted in powder form?" asked Victoria.

"It's equally effective in paste, tablet, or capsule. But powder is the most prevalent form used by criminals and dealers, easiest to administer, generally undetectable. For example, a stranger posing as a tourist or lost person might ask you for directions. Let's say he hands you an address on a piece of paper. When you put the note close to your face to read it, they've got you."

When Wasden paused, Detective Navarro said, "Columbian police are sharing plenty of examples of what they're dealing with.

For example, they report strippers dosing people by slipping Devil's Breath into drinks or swiping it across a customer's face during a lap dance. The victim's unaware, not in the market for a drug of any type. But now the prey is compliant, and the stripper simply asks for his money and credit cards, or keys to his car."

"Detectives, let's revisit the connection between Darby Richards, Alisa Methron, and Isabella Costa. I understand photos on the dark web provided the link."

"That's true. A confidential informer alerted us to a site of human trafficking. We now hold irrefutable evidence in the death of Ms. Methron," said Detective Wasden. "However, the circumstances of Ms. Costa's death are different. While both tested positive for Devil's Breath, and both women were victims of the cartel, evidence indicates that Ms. Costa committed suicide. Given the ongoing investigation, we cannot divulge more at this point."

"Detective Wasden, the connection between Isabella Costa and Darby Richards is they were both UCLA students. Does Isabella's suicide weaken her connection to Alisa Methron?"

"No, Victoria. An overdose of Devil's Breath can lead to suicide. Additionally, studies show seventy percent of trafficked victims exhibit suicidal tendencies or thoughts."

"Are you confident you'll apprehend the responsible parties?"

Both detectives nodded and Navarro said, "We will apprehend with overwhelming evidence to convict in a court of law."

"Detective Wasden, what are the consequences for the leaders and participants of the cartel?"

"In addition to murder and drugging, we have evidence of fraud, abduction, and recruitment for prostitution and slavery as well as forced transfer across state and international borders. The law's clear and the penalties are severe. I expect a minimum sentence of life imprisonment." Wasden looked down and paused. When he turned back to Victoria, he said, "There's one more point I'd like to make. When consumers quit purchasing any given product, it ceases to exist. In my mind, consumers of human trafficking should be prosecuted to the same level as the traffickers."

As the doorbell chimed, announcing Lara's arrival, Victoria wrapped up the interview. "The viewing public will rest easier when you have shut down this cartel."

Moments later, Nina closed the car door behind her. Lara wasted no time laying out the rules for the evening as she backed out of Nina's driveway. "Okay listen, Grady changed his mind. Told me not to bring you. Says it's too dangerous. I respect Grady more than anyone. There's only one reason I'm willing to be insubordinate."

Nina froze. She wanted to know the reason but feared asking might give Lara cause to turn around the car. Just as Nina decided she would hear no explanation, Lara cleared her throat. "My son was kidnapped. Six years old, big green eyes, crooked smile, trusted everyone. Happy kid. In a raid, I took out the son of Ramón Oliviera. He didn't take it well that I killed his eldest son, his *capobastone*, heir to his role as mafia boss. My actions did not go unpunished. DEA, FBI, they gave me protection, but the one afternoon I asked my neighbor to pick up Gunner at school, two mobsters forced her off the road, crashed her into a brick wall. Held a gun to her daughter's head. Took Gunner…"

"Lara, I'm sorry, so very, very sorry."

Lara's distress was raw and penetrating. Nina thought she would say no more, but her shaky whisper broke the silence. "I never saw him alive again. Gone ten months, six days, and four hours. When we finally found him, cigarette burns covered his little chest. I held him. He was so cold. I couldn't warm him."

"You must be dying inside."

"Grady and my partners, these guys get things done, but they haven't lived it. So, while my gut's screaming I'll get fired for bringing you, my heart doesn't give a shit. That being said, bottom line, we're doing this my way, exactly my way. Understood?"

"Yes, I understand."

"I'll do everything in my power to bring your daughter back, but we're going to be careful. Mafia, showed me…"

"I swear I'll do as you say. I won't be a problem. Lara, I'm grateful."

For the next forty minutes, they rode in silence as both women fought to control their emotions. When Lara dug herself up from the dark place inside, her voice was hushed, yet absolute. "Tonight, we're guests of Russo. He knows me by my undercover persona. Not a streetwalker, but not an A-lister either. As escorts go, he thinks I'm an independent middleclass escort. I asked him to get me in on the premise that I want to work in a foreign country. I told Russo you're not a working girl, just interested in kicking your income up a notch."

"He believed you?"

"It appears, but Nina, I can't impress upon you enough how dangerous what we're doing is. Your presence ups the danger quotient at least fivefold."

As they drove closer to the Belaruse, Lara described how she would work the people and the scene while Nina played cards, looking gorgeous and vulnerable. "The only other thing you'll do is keep your eyes and ears open."

For the first time, Nina felt fear in a measure that equaled the risk. However, as the valet opened the car door, Lara's final comment brought a faint smile to Nina's face. "By the way, you look great. I want your doctor's number."

Nina followed Lara into the Belaruse and through the double doors to the cardroom. The room and its occupants puzzled Nina. *Must be the wrong place.* She paid little attention to the men who tended the doors even though they wore tuxedos, but now she scrutinized the dealers.

I watch too many movies. Nina had expected leggy showgirls with shimmering tops cut to the navel leaning low to deal cards. Instead, the dealers were men wearing black slacks, white tuxedo shirts, and tailored vests. The players looked professional, like doctors, attorneys, and business people. *Way too many movies. Not a thug or sleazy chick in sight.*

Across the room, Lara sashayed up to a Eurasian man with ebony hair. While not tall, his stature emanated benevolent confidence, a king overseeing his lands. *His suit? A Kiton, maybe Brioni? On a professor's salary?* Nina squirmed. *What happened to rumpled camel-colored wool jackets and wide wale cords, standard wear for professors of my college years?*

The security video Wasden had shown her was dark, but when Nina stepped a little closer, she recognized him as the man who took Darby by the arm and helped her into the car. Nina's eyes narrowed. She wanted to sink her nails into his neck and claw him to the ground. Instead, she clenched her fists and set her face into a flirtatious smile. As if a cat stalking its prey, she moved toward them. Lara seemed to chat like an old friend with the professor.

Their lips moved, but Nina couldn't hear what they were saying. The room had gone silent. She stopped and tried unsuccessfully to read his lips.

Nina forced a smile and joined them. When Balik stretched his hand toward her, she recoiled. She searched Lara's face for a clue as the sounds of the room reemerged. *Lara must have introduced us.* At the thought of touching him, slimy balls of food roiled up toward her throat. Nina swallowed and extended her hand to meet his. The way he encased it and held the embrace too long discharged a chill along her spine. But she didn't pull back. Nina cocked her head and held his gaze without a blink. He leaned in, his noxious odor burned her nostrils. When Balik spoke, his voice was as slick as oil.

"Call me Taavi. I am pleased you will spend the evening with us."

It took all her willpower not to writhe away. A slow burn moved through her body, seared every nerve. The only person she ever wanted to kill spoke to her with the intimacy of a prospective lover. Her jaws locked, but she managed to speak. "I'm also pleased."

With that, Balik pivoted and nodded to the man Lara had identified as her connection to the Belaruse. Russo stepped outside the center of the poker tables. "Welcome. Allow me to start you in a game."

From that moment on, Nina felt Russo's scrutiny. Whenever she looked up, he was looking back. His omnificent smile disrupted her concentration on her cards. The hair stood on her arms. With her palm, she smashed them flat as a young man settled in next to her. She leaned away so as not to touch him.

"Erhan Solak. We've not met." He extended a smooth olive-skinned hand. "My father is Erem Solak, a dealer of original Turkish art and part owner of the Belaruse."

Nina recalled his name as the young man who attached to Esma, her daughter's roommate. Her heart thundered like a herd of wild mustangs. She worried he could hear it as she fought the urge to scream, *What have you done with my daughter?* However, she willed herself calm. To keep from slapping him, she rearranged her cards.

Don't blow it. Do as Lara said.

Conscious of his eyes following the skirt of her daughter's dress as it crept higher on her thigh, Nina extended her right hand. "Glad to meet you. I'm Kristi Barker."

"Welcome, Kristi Barker," cooed Erhan as smooth as liquid silk. Goosebumps rose to agonizing peaks when his hand brushed across her shoulder. "Tell me about yourself, Kristi. What do you do besides play poker?"

Nina rolled out the personality she and Lara had created for Kristi Barker during the drive. "Not much right now, but I need to find work."

"Why is that?" Erhan leaned closer. "Do you need money? Or just looking for adventure?"

Lara's directive rang in her memory. "Tell the truth whenever possible. These guys are experienced at beating it out of people. Stray too far and they'll know."

Nina's problem was that not a lot was true. Nevertheless, she looked straight into his eyes and told Kristi Barker's story. "Money's the issue. My husband died and the finances took a nose dive. Haven't worked since part time in college, so I have no résumé. Still some medical bills not covered by insurance. House, car... Can't survive on minimum wage."

"I understand. Let me consider who among my colleagues might help. In fact, I will move to the gentlemen at the bar and start the discussion. You never know..."

Erhan traced the dimple of her elbow as he slid out of his chair. *Sleek and silent, like the snake he is.* Intent on watching him approach the three men, Nina jumped when a new deep voice whispered close to her ear.

"I noticed you lost the last two hands. The owners of the Belaruse have more money than they need."

When Nina turned, she recognized him from the photo Wasden had shown her. Jason Coleman, the young man who paid attention to Darby at the tables seven days ago. Nina clasped the rim of her seat to restrain from grabbing his face. A vision flashed in her mind. She had knocked him to the floor and was pounding him as she screamed. *"Where is she? You son of a bitch, I want her back."*

If he were more observant, Jason would have noticed Nina's eyes narrow like a rabid dog ready to pounce. But he didn't. He was too busy preening. "May I offer you a few tips?"

Oblivious to the fury welling up high in Nina's chest, Jason sat next to her and exuded charm. "No cards for me now," he said to the dealer, "but give me a tall stack on the house. My new friend, Kristi, needs my help. This stunning lady will never return to our Belaruse if she loses all her chips tonight."

When it registered that he called her by name even though she hadn't told it to him, she braced herself. Her anger was so hot that her cards stuck to her sweaty hands. *He's moving in. Doing his job.* As she laid her cards down, a sinister smile formed on her lips. *I can play my part too.*

Nina recalled her college days, the bantering and flirting. *Hated it then. Want to vomit now.* After an hour of personal attention, Jason excused himself to join Balik at the bar. She tried to cool the scorching waves of adrenaline melting her self-control.

Lara had been clear. "Act out, and you're out."

Nina played her cards and played innocent with each man who approached. From under heavily mascaraed eyelashes, she watched Lara work the room.

By three in the morning, they hadn't seen or heard anything that could lead them to Darby, but Lara continued playacting. With one eye on Balik and Russo, who were deep in hushed conversation, she walked toward Nina and spoke in a voice intended to carry to the men.

"Kristi, unlike you, I work tomorrow. Let's head out."

Nina tensed in anticipation as she glanced over Lara's shoulder. Both men stopped talking and looked in their direction. But nothing happened, so the two women stood and sauntered toward the elevator.

The drive home passed in disappointed silence. Neither cared to discuss their regret for what did not occur that evening. As Lara dropped Nina off at the gates of her home, she simply said, "I'll call you."

CHAPTER SEVENTEEN
Darby - Day Eight - Saturday, March 24

Darby pitched in her sleep. In her vision, she was spinning, swirling on her tiptoes in stiletto sandals. The flesh colored dress floated up midthigh as she spun. A bright light caught the organza's crystal sparkle. She wanted to stop, run, hide. She looked in the direction of the men's voices. Blurry figures moved at the edges of the light.

She hated them for looking at her. A skinny mustached man, a film camera in his hands, stepped closer, then squatted on the floor. Darby tried to hold the billowing skirt against her legs. An older man, Shar-Pei wrinkles rolling down his arms and chest, trudged toward her. She sniffed at his odor, similar to the skatole smell of the cadaver in her anatomy class. When he stretched out his sweaty palms, she woke herself screaming.

"No, no… Don't touch me."

With a shiver, Darby reached for the sheet pooled at the side of the bed and drew it to her neck. When it slithered against her body, she realized she was naked. She wrapped the sheet around her, tucked the corners under her armpits and held stone still in a fetal position to listen for any noise. Her muscles ached, so she untangled herself and walked to the window. In the hazy glow of dawn, dew drops formed on the latticework, then fell, slow motion to the ground.

No movement outside. No sound inside. Time to get out of here.
Darby decided to try the obvious. She scurried to the first of two doors. With a gentle grip, she turned the doorknob so no one would hear. It spun, half an inch in both directions but didn't budge after that. She hurried to the second door. *Bet it's locked as well.* Her hopes soared when the knob turned, until it clanked and stopped.

Darby slid her feet along the cool tiles, silent as a mouse, toward the fireplace. She crouched and stuck her head up the chimney. The oversized cedar mantle created the illusion that the opening would be large, but the throat narrowed as it rose, too small to provide a way out.

She expected to find a strong piece of wood in the firebox. When she undid the latch and lifted the cumbersome lid, it was empty. She looked for other options but lost her balance when the sheet tangled around her knees. To keep from falling, Darby clutched the edge of the carved table.

The omnipresent creepiness of being watched stiffened the muscles in her neck. A tingle ran the length of her jaw. Darby tiptoed to the door and placed her ear against it. The only sound was her sigh of relief. She walked to the window and stood tiptoed to see if a camera was concealed in the drapes. Seeing nothing, she moved back to the table. She lifted the vase of artificial flowers, turned it over and shook. Only flowers fell out. Darby put it back and proceeded to the huge mirror on the wall. The frame, carved in graceful leaf patterns, showed no signs of a camera. Then she stepped toward the dresser and traced its ornate carving with her hands. The sense of eyes boring into her back send a chill down her spine. She clutched the sheet tighter.

Darby was doubtful she'd find the clothes she wanted but looked in the closet anyway. It was filled with slinky dresses, miniskirts, and low-cut flowy things. She rifled through them, surprised to find what she had hoped for. She removed a tee-shirt and a pair of jeans, but then recoiled. Her thoughts disarranged, and the image of an airplane returned and obscured her view. When she blinked, the plane disappeared.

Darby took the jeans and shirt and went to the dresser. She casually opened each drawer to show whoever might be watching that the contents were only of mild interest. She pulled out panties and a cami, stepped into the closet, and closed the door. As she slipped into the jeans, her fingers quaked, making impossible the snap above the zipper.

Again, Darby strolled to the window, trying to appear nonchalant. She inspected it, then shook her head in dismay. It was thick, solid, the same as storefront glass. It wouldn't open, but she thought she could break it. A beam of sunlight bounced off the copper tray covering the table top.

Heavy. Might work. She clenched the tray and rammed it hard. The force knocked her off her feet. The noise of it hitting the window was huge. She stood and gripped the tray, ready to use it as a weapon. Legs braced, she waited, but no one came. So, she stood and ran her finger over the glass. The effect of the chip was negligible. Darby reared back and slammed the tray into the same spot. But before the noise subsided, a man yanked her backward and pinned her to the ground. She kicked and screamed but couldn't break free from his brutal grasp. She spun her face away, repulsed by the welts scalded down his face. When he spoke, his snarl exposed hyena teeth. "Done screwing with you, you ungrateful bitch. Like you're some kind of princess." He jammed her head to the side. "Berat, give it to her again."

Darby tore one arm loose and made a fist. Her knuckles caught his ear. The man flinched but held on. He sat on her stomach and pinned her arms to the floor. Her face contorted in horror as Berat pulled a latex glove and a plastic baggie from his back pocket. His movements were jerky, like an old silent movie. He dusted his gloved hand with powder and blew into her face.

"Now get up and sit your ass in that chair."

For a single conscious moment, Darby's fear and rebellion evaporated. Her muscles relaxed as if dissolving. From a distance, far away, she heard her own voice drift in. "Yes, sir."

CHAPTER EIGHTEEN
Nina - Day Nine - Sunday, March 25

Nina awoke to sunlit reflections of the ocean dancing on her bedroom ceiling. While shocked she'd slept until after sunrise, given the lateness of their departure from the Belaruse, she calculated she only slept the three restless hours that had become the norm. She sniffed the air. Fragrant scents of coffee beans wafted up to her room, enticing her to ignore her headache and shuffle to the bottom of the stairs.

She was only a few steps from the kitchen when her cell rang. Louis's name appeared on the screen. Nina hit "Ignore" before the second ring. She mumbled, "Piece of shit," as she rounded the corner and came face-to-face with her mother.

"Good morning, dear. Feeling alright? Your day yesterday, and last night…"

"I'm okay, just disappointed."

"You didn't learn anything about Darby?"

"Nothing. Lara said she knows what to do next but wouldn't tell me what she plans." Nina leaned against the counter and watched the last drop of coffee fall into the pot. "I met the professor. Smooth, reminded me of a mafia kingpin. Quietly scary. And the young man Wasden thinks set up Darby. Slimy. Tried to act as if he were my protector. Gave me complementary chips, helped me win, the same as I imagine he did to Darby. I wanted to kill them both, but Lara was clear that I could blow the entire operation, so, I did as she ordered. Played poker, acted defenseless, and flirted…"

"Flirted?"

"I know, Mom. Sounds horrid but Lara thought someone might slip and say something that might turn into a lead."

"No one did?"

"No. I expected either Balik or Jason to put a move on me, but they didn't. I won four hundred and thirty-two dollars. When the cashier handed me the cash, I wanted to throw it in his face. So disappointing. No one approached me in the way I hoped."

"You mean offer you a job or kidnap you too?"

"Mom, you're appalled, I understand. But I'm crushed to the bone. Nothing happened that got me any closer to Darby. I failed."

"Will Lara call or come by today?"

"Don't know if I'll hear from anyone. Could be a long day."

"Nina, I have a premonition. Something good will happen. Take this cup. It's your favorite, hazelnut. Go rest in the living room. Watch the news. I'll bring you a bite to eat."

Nina's shoulders collapsed as she took the coffee in both hands. A ghost of her normal self, she slumped away.

Carrying a tray of poached eggs and toast, Sally paused at the doorway. Nina was in her favorite chair, but her body had curled in upon itself. She rocked back and forth as if sobbing but didn't emit a sound. Sally placed the tiny breakfast on the coffee table then knelt in front of her daughter and took her hand. "Just like when Keith died." Nina looked in her mother's eyes as if in a trance and nodded only once.

Nina stared at the food, then lifted her fork to her down-turned mouth. When her cell rang, she jumped to answer it and the fork flew from her hand. "Hello?" Nina waited. No one answered, so she repeated, "Hello?" She signaled for her mother to reduce the TV's volume and waited for a response.

"Nina Richards?"

"Yes." She recognized Paige Vickers' voice from the preceding day. "Thanks for calling back."

"Wasn't going to. Wasden's not gonna be happy, but I saw you speak at the public announcement. I also have only one daughter. Raised her on my own since she turned five. Husband disappeared. You know, same old tale."

"I am so sorry…"

"It's okay. I'm good with it. That's not your situation. Your husband died and your daughter's older, but I felt a connection. You know, our similarities, having to be both mother and father."

"Paige, will you meet me? Today? Lunch?" The hush that followed was as still and quiet as a tomb. "Are you still there?" The silence unnerved Nina, but she wasn't afraid to beg. "Please? I need your help." She grasped at thoughts, struggled to come up with words that might persuade Paige. "Please, I'll meet you anywhere."

"One o'clock. Crusty Crab Sandwich Shack, Ports O' Call Village, San Pedro."

Nina's "Thank you," came out so faint she wasn't sure Paige heard it. Then a click.

"Can't eat, Mom. Got to shower, get dressed. Paige Vickers will meet with me. This could be our opportunity."

Grateful as Nina was to Paige for driving south from Los Angeles to meet her, the trip up I-5 to the 405 was brutal. She glanced at her GPS as the entire route changed from orange to red. *No problem. I have time.*

Nina had just settled into the stop-and-go rhythm when a bearded man driving a battered white pickup truck with a "Baby on Board" bumper sticker in the window veered into her lane and slammed on his brakes. Even though he couldn't hear her, screaming at his bald head relieved her stress.

The rest of the trip was uneventful. Nina arrived at the Crusty Crab with twenty minutes to spare. She walked to the water's edge and watched two cargo ships inch their way out to sea. Overcome by their enormity, she felt diminished.

Unfamiliar with the Crusty Crab, Nina had looked it up online. Their website described seaside dining in a relaxed atmosphere. As she waited for Paige at a rickety wooden table adjacent the fresh fish display, she felt anything but relaxed. Her gaze deadlocked, eye-to-eye, with a swordfish resting in his coffin of ice, his pointy nose pink where his sword had been chopped off. Unable to pull her eyes away, she jumped when Paige plopped herself in the vacant chair.

"Paige, thanks for coming."

"I'll catch holy hell when Wasden finds out, but as I mentioned, I get your story, what it means to be a single parent in crisis. Anyway, he'll be madder than a jilted wife if he discovers I went behind his back, but when I saw your pitiful face, all stymied and sad, I couldn't sit by and watch anymore."

"I'm grateful."

"There's another reason. My mother's younger sister disappeared, never found. Fourteen years later and no clue what happened or if she's still alive. Your case hit home."

"I'm so sorry, Paige. It's impossible for anyone to comprehend until it happens. People living their ordinary lives, the way I once did. Oblivious."

Paige fingered the paper menu but didn't read. "Mrs. Richards, I'm not much for chitchat. What do you want?"

"For you to take me to the Belaruse."

Paige snorted. "That's not going to happen. What else might you want?"

"I understand your hesitancy, but…"

"I'm not hesitant. My answer is no, flat no."

"I was there last night."

"No, you weren't. Wasden wouldn't allow it."

"He didn't know. Lara Kensington took me." Desperate to bring Paige to her side, Nina spoke rapidly. "My firm has executive kidnapping insurance. Lara's with Cox and Mason. Only problem, they aren't bringing Darby home. Nobody is. Lara said no at first, but I talked her into it." Nina read Paige's reaction as total disbelief. "I wanted this Professor Balik to kidnap me as well, but Lara wasn't having any of that."

"Well, I'm not having any of that either." Paige locked her jaw, ready for an argument. "Mrs. Richards, do you realize what they might do to you?"

"Yes, the same thing they're doing to Darby while we sit in this quaint little restaurant. My daughter's a slave. You think I don't get that? The police, FBI, Cox and Mason, all claim they're getting closer, but not fast enough. Every day these monsters hold Darby, the more she's abused. God only knows…"

Paige sucked in her upper lip and bit down.

"You know what they're doing to her. You know exactly…"

Paige squirmed. Again, she appeared to study the menu. When she looked up, she recognized the agony on Nina's face, the same imprint as on her own mother's after her sister vanished. "This is so against my better judgment, but I'll pick you up at six. Wasden's staking the place out tonight. We've got to get there before he and the boys."

"Thank you, Paige."

"I must be certifiable. Wasden will kick my ass so far out of the department, I won't even be able to pay my parking tickets."

"Thank you, thank you." Nina jumped up and stretched her arms out to her new ally.

Paige ducked and blocked Nina's embrace. "Don't thank me, don't hug me. Don't even touch me. I'm gonna get fired."

Drained after hours of fighting freeway traffic, Nina's nerves were frayed by the time she arrived home. She walked into the living room and said, "Mom, I need to rest. Wake me up an hour before Victoria's program."

Once upstairs, instead of turning into her bedroom, Nina continued down the hall. Skipper, her daughter's threadbare dolphin, peeked out of the basket beside Darby's bed. When she lifted him from between Darby's less favorite creatures and hugged him tight, she could visualize the dolphin cuddled under her daughter's arm as she snuggled in for the night. Nina dropped to the bed, rolled herself and Skipper into a ball. She pulled Darby's pillow to her face. The lingering scents of her daughter released an onslaught of tears. "Skipper, I'm so very sorry. But don't worry. I'll bring her back to you."

With a gentle touch, she stuffed the padding back in Skipper's formerly white belly and tucked him under the covers. His head

193

rested on Darby's pillow. "Wait here," she whispered, then stepped to the other side of the room and opened her daughter's closet door.

Need to attract attention tonight, something more daring. Ah, here it is. Perfect.

Nina lifted the hanger and admired the stretchy black skirt. A brief smile formed as she replayed Keith's objection in her head. *"Way too short, Darby. Get in the car. We're taking it back."* Nina pushed hangers across the rack but the right top wasn't there. *My closet, the gold gossamer backless...*

With a final glance toward Skippy, Nina carried the skirt to her own room. She found the gossamer blouse in the far corner of her closet. When she hung it on the doorknob with the miniskirt, her hand froze in place. She shook off the paralysis, stretched across the bed, closed her eyes, and sucked down long labored breaths. *One...two...three...* Her thoughts returned to the moment when the department store security officer had found her lost little Darby. As she drifted off to sleep, Nina whispered, "Come, baby. Mommy's taking you home." Like a wisp of summer breeze, a hint of that same relief flitted across her face.

Nina dozed so lightly that she sensed her mother's presence before she spoke. When she sat up, she realized Sally wasn't looking at her. She was staring at the clothes hanging on the doorknob.

"Please tell me you're not going back again."

"I am, Mom, with Paige Vickers."

Sally's chin jutted out and her shoulders stiffened. Nina braced for her mother's protest, but it didn't come.

Sally's voice cracked. "Van der Waals in one hour." She turned and left the room.

Nina groaned as she rolled off the bed, then walked to the bathroom to shower. Wiping the condensation off the mirror, she inspected her new face. She massaged the numbness between her Botoxed eyebrows and applied coverup where the dark circles used to be. *Don't really need it now.* She scrunched and sprayed to replicate soap-opera hair. *How can I look so good when I feel so bad?*

After a final inspection in the magnifying mirror, Nina hurried downstairs to the living room. She ignored her mother's penetrating stare while waiting for Victoria van der Waals to appear.

"Good evening. Tonight, we continue discussing the Columbian drug, Devil's Breath, with Drug Enforcement Agency Detective Tony Navarro. Widely used in South America, this narcotic is relatively unknown in the United States. Tragically, a new victim, identified earlier today, is a woman who recently turned twenty-one, old enough to make her own decisions." The cameraman zoomed in to fill the screen with Victoria's face as her mouth pinched together with concern. "And wouldn't you know, the most important decision this young woman ever made turned out to be her worst. Two days ago, authorities discovered her bruised and battered body in a trash bag on the backstreets of West L.A. Stay tuned for the harrowing details."

Nina swayed as her world tilted another ten degrees off axis. Deep inside her gut she sensed that the death of this woman was in some way related to Darby's disappearance.

When the station logo faded, Victoria returned. "The story behind this cellphone video is shocking. We watch in horror as the coroner places this stunningly exotic woman into a black body bag. A closeup shows her face, scraped and swollen, clothes drenched in blood. You may ask, how I know she was stunning? Her older brother recognized his sister in the video and provided us with the family photo now on the screen. Her name was Qudsia Ghafoor. She lived with her mother, father, and four brothers in Zaranj, southwestern Afghanistan. Once successful importers, the entire family of Qudsia Ghafoor lost their wealth and personal belongings as a result of terrorist activities. The family left everything behind when Qudsia's uncle was massacred in the town market, a casualty of one of several suicide bombers.

Qudsia's name means angelic or celestial, but her life was neither. Believing their daughter was in the most danger, her parents spent their savings to secret her away to the United States through underground channels, to be delivered to an aunt living in Baltimore. However, she never arrived. Last week Qudsia was found dead.

The brother requested we not divulge his identity. His safety is still at risk. Authorities revealed little, but one detective reported commonalities in the murders of Qudsia Ghafoor and artist Alisa Methron." The TV screen filled with side-by-side photos of the two women. As it faded, Victoria said, "So alike in their natural beauty, now alike in death."

She shifted toward Detective Navarro. "If circumstances connect these two murders to the suicide of Isabella Costa, and photos of both Alisa Methron and Darby Richards are posted on the same dark website, what are the chances you will find Darby a murder victim as well?"

"Intel indicates Ms. Richards is alive. The LAPD is committed to bringing her home."

"Detective Navarro, is trafficking increasing or do we simply hear more due to media coverage?"

"First, let me be clear, the media fails at reporting human trafficking. Second, no point in history exists when it did not occur. Current statistics are unbelievable. Last year, approximately six to eight hundred thousand men, women, and children were bought and sold across international borders for commercial sex or forced labor. When including victims not transported across borders, estimates rise to between two and four million. Most abhorrent, fifty percent are children."

"Detective Navarro, research suggests the average American thinks trafficking and slavery are not issues in the United States. The prevailing assumption is that it's an issue in poorer, undeveloped countries."

"Victoria, a growing number of economies, including the U.S., cannot sustain a minimum standard of living. Worldwide population increases compound this problem. Deficits in education and resources leave people vulnerable to domination by the powerful, and power does not equate to good. Destitution can warp into a sinister trap for the weak and unsuspecting."

"Detective, to prepare for tonight's program, I read of trafficking in India. I found this unsettling given India's history. Many still consider India a society of nonviolence. Mahatma Gandhi, Mother Teresa, the Dalai Lama, Hinduism…"

"While unable to provide details, I'll talk in general terms of a case in which Indian women, themselves trafficked, under threat and coercion, use personal relationships to recruit girls. Many of these minors are forced into slavery in places you might never expect. Maine, Rhode Island, New Mexico, New York, South Dakota, and West Virginia."

"You claim the individual best able to warn a potential victim instigated the exploitation?"

"Yes, and while this happens worldwide, the U.S. is a major consumer."

"Detective Navarro, the public does not want to know this. It's more comfortable to hide their collective heads in the sand."

"That's understandable. A normal reaction. As a detective, I'd heard stuff. Didn't pay enough attention because my ambition was to bring down drug cartels."

"Noble goal. Our communities are safer because of officers such as you."

"Thanks, Victoria. What I didn't realize is that the illegal drug trade interfaces with human trafficking. Most disturbing is familial trafficking. I've worked cases in which a cartel purchased a child from a family member in exchange for drugs, cars, a multitude of desired goods. Innocent children are sold into servitude and sexually exploited for the price of a small baggie of white powder or even a television set."

"A television? Detective Navarro, please say you're not serious."

"Dead serious." He cleared his throat. "Familial trafficking, more prevalent in underdeveloped countries, is challenging to uncover and expose because the victim often has a degree of freedom. For example, the child may still attend school. In such cases, two different psychologies prevail. First, the victim has no way out, no way to care for his or herself. The family uses that weakness. Second, victimized children are often so young and innocent they don't know their treatment is abnormal, that they're being abused. Their living condition is their only experience, their normal. No understanding of how another child's circumstance is wildly different."

"Don't the children talk among themselves?"

"Not usually. They interact with friends, teachers, often attend church, but never speak of the atrocities, some from fear, others unaware that their condition needs discussing."

"Is this similar to the Stockholm Syndrome?"

"Yes, Victoria. The same in that the captor, the perpetrator, professes to love or need the victim, tells them they're important and valued. The Stockholm Syndrome works on adults, so you understand how a child is susceptible."

Victoria requested the audience stay tuned until after the commercial announcements. Nina hoped to slip out of the room unnoticed, but she felt her mother's eyes drilling between her shoulder blades. Nina untied her bathrobe as she scurried upstairs. One last makeup check. She worried it was too much. Ignoring her unease, she wriggled into Darby's miniskirt. The blouse slid over her head, as soft and clingy as a second layer of skin. She pivoted and considered her image in the full-length mirror. Folds of shimmering gossamer draped low on her bare back. Nina nodded, acknowledging she looked the way she needed to even though she felt dirty.

Slowly she descended the stairs to watch the final minutes of Victoria van der Waals' program. Her cell rang where she had left it on the coffee table. Nina bounded down the last few steps and snatched it up. Before she could utter a sound, the voice at the other end ordered, "Come on out," and disconnected. Nina sensed her mother's heart begging her not to leave. Without speaking, she picked up her purse and strode toward the door then paused and hurried back. Still no words came. When the dampness pooled in the crinkles of her mother's eyes, Nina collapsed against her. Then she pushed her mother away and headed out the door.

The instant Nina's bottom touched the car seat, even before she closed the door, Paige started the interrogation. "You said nothing happened last night. How did Lara keep you under control? She must've laid down the law."

"She did. Made it absolutely clear I'd be excluded in the future if I did anything other than chat, play cards, and play dumb."

"Let me be equally clear. Tonight's rules are the same. Further, I'm wired, so don't say a word to me once I signal you. When I turn it on, I'll flip my hair twice. From that time on, Wasden can hear everything you say. Neither of us wants that. Do you understand?"

Nina nodded silently.

"I didn't hear you."

"Yes, Paige. I understand."

"And you'll comply?"

The pause lasted long enough that Paige repeated, "And you will…"

"Yes, Paige, I will."

"Okay, we've got agreement. Now tell me every detail."

Nina began her description of the evening by saying, "My alias was Kristi Barker."

"You don't look like a Kristi Barker."

Nina shrugged and described the specifics of everything said and done. Paige listened while weaving in and out of traffic, swerving in front of drivers that irritated her and lurching at the ones not keeping her pace until she jerked the car to a stop at the curb of the Belaruse.

"That was quite a ride, Detective Vickers."

Paige shot her a warning look. Nina pretended not to notice. When the valet opened Paige's door, Nina opened hers without comment. But before she swung her legs out, Paige issued a final under-the-breath command. "This is not the army. Do not enlist."

In a replay of the prior night, the valet accompanied them to the door and used the intercom to approve their admission. As they entered the Belaruse, actions and scenes replayed for Nina as if she were watching the same movie two nights in a row. *Only one difference. Tonight, I know what I'm doing.*

Russo closed in on Paige and Nina. "Kristi...Kristi Barker, correct? How nice to have you here again. You were successful at the tables. I hope your luck continues." Nina looked into his opaque brown eyes for a sign he'd discovered her true identity. Seeing none, she bore Russo's gaze with confidence. "And you brought a friend. Paige Vickers, I presume?"

"I thank ya'll for having me."

Nina turned to see where the southern accent had come from. Russo said, "Ah, a southern belle. Taavi mentioned you might join us tonight. He has a soft spot for the South. I'll show you to a table."

Nina suppressed a smirk when Russo seated her next to Paige. *Strength in numbers. Thought he'd separate us the way he did Darby and Esma.*

Russo introduced them to the dealer. "Jerry, give these enchanting ladies each a healthy stack of chips. Put it on my tab."

"Very generous." Nina forced a smile his way.

Russo shrugged. He stood behind them as the cards flew across the table. Nina feigned deep deliberation, and he glided away, silently as a misty aberration. Before Nina completed her first hand, Erhan Solak, son of the Turkish exporter, slithered up to Paige, the same as he had with Lara. *They stick with the plan.* Nina mouthed his words as he spoke. "Welcome, Paige Vickers. Please, come sit with me."

Same as last night, slick as a politician. Nina cringed when his arm brushed her back but sighed with relief when Paige followed him to another table. Out of the corner of her eye she watched Paige flip her hair as she sauntered away. *Good. Wasden can't hear me with you over there.* Nina scooted to the edge of her seat, poised for action, yet she didn't make her move. Continue as is, she told herself while adding three white chips to the two in front of her.

Nina glanced up when another known performer entered the scene. "Kristi, I'm pleased to see you again. Had you told me, I would have greeted you when you arrived."

Nina nervously fingered her chips. She ordered herself to stop. "Professor Balik, a pleasure to see you as well." Forcing herself not to flinch, she returned his smile.

When Nina turned back to her cards, she caught Paige's piercing glare. Only then did she realize her voice was too loud. Over the top of her hand, she watched Paige use her covert skills on the young man she suspected of transporting more than art. During the drive, Paige had shared her strategy to elicit details of the family enterprise and the countries in which they do business without her prey knowing what was happening.

Nina surveyed the room. Her eyebrows shot up when Paige grabbed her chest as if in pain. *The tape holding the wire must have ripped lose.* Nina swallowed a chuckle as Paige wiggled in her chair in a clandestine attempt to reattach the wire, then shifted her full attention back to Erhan.

After an hour of applying her charm to the son of the half-owner of the Belaruse, Paige was losing patience. She cocked her head to listen for Nina's voice over the hum of the room. Given the parameters she'd laid out, Paige was not concerned. But as she looked around, pausing on each player, her warning system went on alert. She scanned the dealers. She locked eyes with Russo, felt herself flush, and turned away. When it registered that she couldn't place when it was she last heard Nina's voice, Paige's pulse quickened.

The valet opened the double doors for a couple to enter, offering Paige a straight line of vision to the far wall. Cautiously, so no one would notice, she leaned to the right and gained full view of the couches. A man and woman, heads together, were engrossed in conversation. Paige sighed in relief. But when the woman rose, it wasn't Nina. Paige leaned off the edge of her chair. Two men stood beside the fireplace. One handed a cigar to the other. But still no Nina. A cop's premonition rippled through her as she wiped her forehead.

"Excuse me, Erhan. I'll be back. Need a moment." She sauntered to the bar. When the bartender replied she hadn't seen her friend, Paige left the cardroom as rapidly as she could without drawing attention to herself. Resisting the urge to sprint to the women's restroom stretched the limits of her self-control. Once inside, she spun full circle. White marble, gold spigots, enormous mirrored walls, but no Nina.

Paige squatted and peered under the doors. "Damn. No feet." She called out. "Kristi? Are you in here? You better not have…" When she realized she'd forgotten to switch off the wire, Paige sucked the words back down her throat.

The bathroom door swung open. Paige propelled herself into the closest stall. As she closed the door, the reflection of the statuesque dark-haired bartender bounced from mirror to mirror. Paige leaned against the door. She inhaled one choppy gasp, then spun so her feet pointed out as if she were using the toilet.

Paige dug in her bra for the microphone that had sunk beneath her breast, clicked it off, and listened. The room was silent. As she flushed the toilet with her foot, her cell vibrated against her thigh. Seeing Wasden's name, she declined the call and stuffed the phone deep in her pocket.

She waited for the sounds of the bartender entering a stall. Met with silence, Paige peered out. Her angle was good. The bartender ambled to the counter and removed a lipstick from her pocket.

With a grin plastered on her face, Paige stepped to the sink. She waited for the water to warm before she washed her hands. In the mirror reflection, the bartender looked her up and down. In a race to accomplish nothing, both women continued at their slowest possible rate. At the moment Paige decided she couldn't bluff any longer, the bartender returned the lipstick to her pocket and pivoted to leave. A tiny smile, perhaps a snarl, swept her lips. "See you out there."

The door had barely closed when again Paige's cell vibrated. She heard Wasden growl before she even raised it to her ear. "What the hell's going on in there?"

"I can't find her."

"Who?"

"Mrs. Richards."

"What are you talking about?"

"She's gone."

"Son-of-a... You took her in there?" Wasden didn't wait for her response. "When I get my hands..."

"I understand. I'm sorry."

"You'll be more than sorry. Where is she?"

"Don't know," whispered Paige. "I was deep in working Solak's son when I became aware I couldn't hear her anymore."

"You have no idea where she went?"

"No sir, but I'm going back in and find out."

"Who was in the bathroom with you?"

"Female bartender. Think they sent her in to watch me."

"I'm coming in."

"Don't," she said with as much authority as her whisper could convey. "You'll blow everything..."

"Vickers, you've already blown it."

"Five minutes, just give me five. I'll find her. Then we're out of here."

Paige straightened her skirt, turned the wire back on, and stowed it inside her blouse. She faked a smile, then hurried out of the bathroom. She knew it wouldn't happen. Nevertheless, she acted as if Nina would be exactly where she left her. Scanning the area, Paige glanced again to the couches by the fireplace, then returned to her table. She slid her palm across Erhan's shoulder as she sat down.

"Erhan, darling, where is my friend? It's way past our bedtime. Time for us to go. We'll come back another evening."

"Kristi? Did she not speak to you when she left?"

Paige glared at him. He'd parked himself beside her the entire evening until she took off for the restroom. He knew Nina had not spoken to her. She licked her lips. "You know where she went?"

"To breakfast with Taavi Balik."

"Where?"

"Not certain, but I assume next door. He's always going on and on about their scrambled eggs. Shall I escort you there?"

As Paige pondered whether to go with Erhan or wait for Wasden's direction, her cell vibrated again. "Excuse me. Must be Kristi." Stepping aside, she lifted the phone to her ear.

"Heard everything. Sending Navarro in as Nina's jealous boyfriend to break up this cozy little breakfast." Without shifting the phone away from his mouth, Wasden squawked at Navarro's back. "Take off the vest," then he mumbled under his breath, "Overpaid idiot." To Paige he said, "Get out now. Meet me at the station."

An hour later Paige still sat in a dilapidated desk chair waiting for Wasden. She was tempted to call but knew he wouldn't appreciate it. In fact, he'd rip her to shreds the way her dog does the clothes he pulls from the hamper when left home alone.

Her watch read 4:23 a.m. She rubbed her dry eyes. As they closed, her arm jerked and plunged off the armrest. Paige shook herself awake. The sagging couch in the booking area looked better with every passing minute. Even with its worn plastic cover, it beckoned until an officer entered and plunked down a bearded drunk. The drunk rolled into a fetal position as he snored like a hibernating bear, spraying the couch with spit. Paige settled back into the rickety chair.

Her head bobbed toward her chest. Against her better judgment, she crossed her arms atop the dusty desk and lowered her head. Paige was doing some snoring of her own when Wasden slammed his fist, causing the desk to shake and rattle. "All worn out? You poor thing."

Paige leapt out of the chair. "Now that I've got your attention, Sleeping Beauty, can you explain how you fell asleep on the job tonight?"

Navarro and FBI Agent Henry Boutros leaned against the wall. She met their smug smiles with a snarky look. Wasden put his hands on his hips and scowled as though she were just another lowlife criminal.

"Okay, Vickers. Let's hear it."

Every muscle tensed when he used her last name again. It was not a sign of respect. Far from it. *So far down the shit hole, I'll never breathe fresh air again.* No excuse she could muster would improve her situation, but she tried anyway. "I was digging information out of Erhan Solak, son of Erem Solak, you know, the Turkish art exporter, part owner of the Belaruse."

"I know *what* you were doing. Remember? You were wired." Wasden shook his finger in her face. "It's *what you didn't do* that's the problem. Like following protocol. Like protecting civilians from harm. What was she doing in there?"

"I screwed up…"

"Understatement of the century, possibly of your career. What's left of it…"

"I'm really sorry. She promised me…"

"I don't care what she promised. You disobeyed orders."

"Please don't take me off the case."

"Vickers, I'm about to take you off the planet. Are you telling me you were so enchanted you couldn't even keep track of one small civilian who wasn't supposed to be there in the first place?"

"I was intent, squeezing some good stuff out of young Solak. That's when I could no longer hear Nina's voice mixed in with the background noise. You heard everything after that."

207

"No, we didn't. Our receiver cut out."

"He bragged that his father's trade is big in Ankara, Turkey."

"Okay, Vickers, I'm listening," snarled Wasden.

"They're exporting more than art."

Paige recounted every action observed and every word that might have gone unheard during the time period when the receiver in the stakeout van had failed. After she finished, they listened to the recording from the wire she'd worn, straining to pick up any clues that might have gone undetected. When the recording ended, all four listeners shook their heads.

"Didn't hear a thing that might help. Anyone?" When it became evident blank stares were the only response he would receive, Wasden expelled stale coffee breath. "Useless…you're all useless." He hollered out the door to the desk sergeant, "Call tech to come down to pick this up for analysis." Then he turned away from Paige and toward Navarro and Boutros. "Maybe Wally will lift something from the background, something besides Vickers falling asleep on the job."

The transaction the detectives expected to hear occurred too far away for Paige's wire to pick it up. Numerous hands of poker were won and lost prior to Paige noticing Nina's voice had gone silent. Taavi Balik had placed his cards face down and said, "Kristi, I am hungry. Will you join me next door for breakfast? They are renowned for their pesto scrambled eggs."

As they walked to the restaurant, Nina thought she would pass out from the warped sickness of it all. *Every move's the same. How many times has each role been played out, woman after woman?*

The waiter set a teapot in the center of the table. When Balik lifted its lid, the escaping steam formed a small dark cloud. He opened the box of loose teas and said something about the flavor. He moved the box aside, slipped a pouch of tea from his inner pocket, and filled the metal infuser with his personal blend. His words receded into the background as her thoughts screamed inside her head. *Say something before it's too late.*

She found it difficult to push her first bite of eggs past the fear wedged in her throat. *Say something... Now.* Nina gagged, then covered her mouth with the white linen napkin. "Taavi, I know of your business."

"Psychology? Teaching the best and brightest? Students more interested in factual principles and formulae with no respect for how the mind affects behavior within these contexts?"

"No, your other business."

His hand stopped midair. The infuser swung hypnotically. "Pardon me?"

"I'm interested."

"In teaching? What is your discipline?"

"No, your other business."

He dropped the infuser into the dragon teapot and bobbed it several times. "May I ask, Kristi, what is it that interests you?"

"I have experience..." The dragon's eye, raised and red, bored through to the center of her lie. Her voice quivered when it occurred to her the professor might also know. "I want to increase my income. To be precise, I'd like international work."

He returned the lid to the pot. "Let us talk while the tea steeps." But neither spoke until he removed the infuser and filled her cup. "In which foreign country do you prefer to work?"

"Where you took the others."

"Kristi, I do not understand what you mean."

"The women who offer services…"

"My dear, you misunderstand. My organization assists women such as Halina, the bartender at the Belaruse. All are rescued from horrible life experiences. Some are victims of indescribable family abuse. Others homeless and starving, living on the streets, often as a result of the ravages of wars occurring in their communities."

Nina toyed with the knife at the side of her plate. The only thing that stopped her from stabbing him in the eye to repay him for his lie was that she needed him to get to Darby.

"Taavi, some of your folks talk."

"I saved Halina from certain death. Pledged to marry at age thirteen, her new husband claimed she was not a virgin. Her father stoned her, and the family left her in the street to die."

"Taavi, they say women are compensated handsomely in the business you run with Solak and Askoy." Nina searched his face for a sign that he would acknowledge what she said was true. As he stirred his tea, his silence absorbed every noise in the room.

"Okay, Kristi. Let's say I have employment opportunities, we need to be clear. If I understand correctly, you want to provide escort services to a high echelon clientele in a foreign country? Is that the essence of what you propose?"

"Yes."

"Russo indicated your friend was interested but said nothing about you. She already has similar work. I don't think you understand…"

"I understand."

"And still want…"

"Yes."

"If you are serious, there is an additional layer. We report to another man. However, I can make the connection."

Balik's expression conveyed uneasiness. She placed a hand atop his arm. It fell to the side when he raised his cup as in a toast. "Drink the last of your tea, my dear."

Nina's eyelids grew heavy. When she leaned against the booth, she felt herself shrink. She attributed the sensation to stress and sipped the last of the warm fragrant tea. Balik brought his cup to his mouth, but her eyelids were sinking shut so she didn't see that he did not drink.

"We will go now, if that is what you want?"

"Yes, I'd like that."

"Do you not have someone you need to call?"

"I have no one."

"Well, now you have me, my dear. My car is in the underground parking. Rather than calling the valet, we shall use the private elevator. I will take you to the person who needs to approve your request."

As they exited the elevator, Nina's knees buckled. Balik reached out as though he had expected her to stumble. When he gripped her arm, she wanted to push it away. Instead, she clung tight. Balik wrapped his arm around her waist and steered her toward the car. Once seated, he handed her a black sleep mask. "Please understand, I cannot disclose our location."

Nina slipped the mask over her eyes and tried to position it so she could peek out. It fit too tight. She resorted to tracking the trip by turns and sounds. When they stopped and waited for a train to pass, she lost consciousness, but when the car surged forward, the force woke her up. As it veered right, she sensed they were merging onto a freeway. Moving in and out of awareness, Nina fought to stay awake. The drone of the road anesthetized her mind.

When the car made a sweeping arc, her body pressed against the door. She recognized the curve as an offramp. She listened for the sounds of a city but heard only muffled engine noises until the vehicle stopped. Disoriented, she jerked her head away when a rough hand tugged at the mask.

"Okay, okay. Remove it yourself."

The skies were dark and cloudy, but Nina recognized the shape of the buildings and the trail of lights as a private airport. She assumed she'd be taken to LAX, but nothing in the surroundings was familiar. When she saw the plane, she knew it was wrong. *Darby's in a foreign country. That plane can't cross an ocean.*

When Balik opened the car door, Nina stepped out and scanned the horizon. He moved toward a small white plane, but Nina froze. *I could end up anywhere, even farther from Darby.*

"Kristi, what is wrong?"

"This plane… It's the wrong plane."

"Rest assured, my dear, this is the correct airplane."

"No." Nina ducked as though dodging a firing squad. Balik seized her arm and pushed her toward the boarding ramp. Head still spinning from the tea, she slipped on the first step and fell flat on the tarmac. When her chin hit the ground, she thought the crack that reverberated inside her head was a gunshot. She curled tight to protect herself. Blackness descended, compromised her vision, but she remained conscious long enough to cower away from the hulking black man clanging down the metal steps. With little effort, he lifted Nina and carried her onto the plane. Her final conscious thought was to turn away when he wheezed alcohol breath across her face.

At the police station, Wasden still sat in his office fuming. "Any bright ideas?"

Paige grasped at possibilities to appease him. "Maybe she went home? We should call her mother."

"Brilliant, Vickers. Exceptional detective work. You're proposing Mrs. Richards simply got up and went home without telling you? Or without us seeing her go out the front door?" He slapped himself in the forehead. "Why didn't I think of that?"

"We need to rule out any possibility that we...I...just lost track of her, and the first step is to call."

"And give her mother a heart attack? Nice, Vickers. Boutros and Navarro, how about you two lunkheads just standing there..." The two agents looked at each other, then shuffled their feet. "Any chance, between the two of you, you've come up with one decent idea?"

Paige stepped back. She expected Wasden to rip into whoever spoke first. Navarro glared back at her, then turned expectantly to Boutros. Paige rolled her eyes to let Navarro know she wasn't fooled by him holding his silence in fake deference to the FBI agent. But when it became clear neither Boutros nor Vickers would break the silence, Navarro took a chance. "I'll retrieve the security tapes from the street and garage."

"Okay. How about you, Boutros?"

"I'll sniff around, downtown. Listen for scuttlebutt on the streets. Too early to check the dark web where we found the other women, but in twenty-four hours, maybe..."

"Okay, that's a start. I'll head down to shift change and release a BOLO. And Paige..." The relief she felt when Wasden used her first name again floated and popped as if it were a soap bubble when she heard her orders. "You drew the short straw. You inform the grandmother."

"Vickers gets stuck with grandma?" Heads snapped toward Navarro. "But you take the lovely Mrs. Richards for yourself? What's going on Wasden?"

Paige's mouth dropped open, and Boutros stepped back out of the line of fire.

"Nothing's going on, asshole. As soon as I figure out why the captain hired you in the first place, I might assign someone to you too." Then Wasden shifted his vitriol from Navarro to Paige. Through gritted teeth, he said, "Call the grandma. Now."

"No sir. I mean yes sir, but not on the phone. I'll tell her. But face-to-face."

"Go but get your carcass back by 6 a.m. Got it?"

It sounded as though she said, "Yes sir," but he wasn't sure because she'd already spun on one foot and was sprinting past the outer office.

CHAPTER NINETEEN
Darby - Day Nine - Sunday, March 25

When Darby awoke, she felt as though she hadn't slept at all. The only thing she knew for certain was that she had a jaw-clenching headache. At first, she thought the wisps of consciousness flitting in and out were dreams. But when she pushed the sheet away, the scratchiness of the sequined gown that snagged her skin was real. Memories drifted just beyond her grasp. As they congealed, she recognized them as the aftereffects of Devil's Breath and the champagne they ordered her to drink.

Darby saw herself standing in a room with three people, two of which she'd never seen before. A striking redhead wearing a scant burgundy dress leaned in close and whispered to the man she most feared. When Berat shook his head and straightened up, Darby turned toward the old man, his military uniform bearing medals so heavy they caused the wool to sag. Deathly parched, his lax skin lay pleated below piercing onyx eyes.

Darby didn't understand what was happening. But as the alcohol and drugs diminished, she sensed the evening had been choreographed, and with the exception of herself, all the actors knew their roles. She had to decide. Continue to kick and scream or join the others by playing a prescribed part which she couldn't yet define.

Darby lifted her hand. It held a delicate crystal flute. She spun the glass between her fingers, mesmerized by the colored light that bounced from its carved sides. As the Devil's Breath released her thoughts to once again be completely hers, she studied the people who watched her back. Sounds amplified in her ears. Every breath roared. One after another, the hair raised like a caterpillar creeping up her arm.

They're waiting for me to say something, do something.

She shuddered when Berat broke the silence. "General Takahashi is here to meet you. He's quite taken with your video."

Darby did not respond. She turned her head, refused to acknowledge anyone.

"Darby, this is an opportunity for you. If you want to take advantage of it, you must speak."

Her silence hung heavy in the room.

"Do you hear me?"

She tightened her grip on the glass.

"Many girls work without drugs. You've not been particularly cooperative. In fact, you're a royal pain in the ass. However, those in charge think you're more desirable un-drugged. Even though I advised against it, they're offering you the opportunity. Tonight's your first chance to accept."

Darby focused on the hard-straight line of his grimaced lips.

"Are you listening?"

She shifted her glare to the inflamed blotch on the side of Berat's neck. It pulsed faster, turning redder.

"General Takahashi is spending the evening with you. Would you like to do that without being drugged?"

Darby's fingers constricted around the crystal stem. General Takahashi reached out for Darby. She slapped his hand with the delicate glass. When shards cut blood points in his palm, he shouted in Japanese.

Berat lifted her off the ground. "What is wrong with you, woman?" As easily as containing an unruly child, he carried her out the double doors and down the hall to her own room. He threw her to the floor, slammed the door, and nearly ripped the head off the key as he locked it behind him. When he gave the door a thunderous kick, Darby stifled a shriek.

Choking on her sobs, she crawled on her hands and knees, pulled herself into bed and hid under the covers. Sometimes, even in the dank cinderblock cell, the darkness had comforted her. Now she quaked with fear. Before tonight, Darby had struggled to separate reality from hallucination. Now there was no question.

CHAPTER TWENTY
Nina - Day Ten - Monday, March 26

As Nina regained consciousness, engines droning filled her ears. Afraid to move, she feigned sleep and listened. The harder she tried to hold still, the more anxiety pricked at her nerves. Unable to resist, she opened one eye. Her first thought was that she had ended up exactly where she wanted to be. This plane was larger than the one she remembered. This one could fly across the sea.

Even though the seat was large, she hugged the pillow and curled into a small tight ball. A blanket lay folded on the seat beside her. She reached across the arm rest and grasped one corner. Nina drew the blanket to her face and peeked out over its edge. Bending her head toward male voices, she strained to figure out what they said, but the engine noises camouflaged their words.

A woman flounced down the aisle, hips swaying like an open invitation. Her tailored blue uniform, gold trim around the cuffs, smelled of wool, long stored away. Possibly the flight attendant, except the micro-mini skirt and stiletto heels weren't quite right for the job. The woman stopped. Nina slowly closed her eyes as though sleep had overtaken her. She exhaled an inaudible sigh when the footsteps moved toward the front of the plane.

That was close.

Nina drew the blanket back up so only her eyes were visible. Her mind churned. However, before she developed a plan, a deep male voice rose above the vibration. "Thank you, Kadira. I'll check in a moment."

Check what. Check me? Oh my God, what do I do? Nina quivered. The movement rippled down the blanket. She sank her head back against the headrest and pretended to be unconscious.

At the same time, but on solid ground, Paige returned to Wasden's office. Her cell read 5:30 a.m. Under strict orders to get "her carcass back" for the six o'clock meeting, she'd had no time to go home after leaving Grandma Richards in San Clemente. No way a warm shower and change of clothes was worth incurring more of Wasden's wrath. So, she stopped in the ladies' room. Without waiting for the water to warm, she leaned forward and splashed her face. Water trickled down her neck and blouse. "You look like shit," she told her image. Her attempt to scrape off last night's mascara with department issue brown paper towels left her eyes red and burning. As the final step of personal hygiene, she stuffed a wet wad up her blouse and worked on her armpits. "At least you smell better," she said to the unresponsive mirror.

Paige slunk into the detectives' bay. Neither Wasden nor the other detectives had returned. She sat at his desk, in the side chair typically reserved for suspects. When she covered her burning eyes with hands still cold from the bathroom water, her eyelids slid shut.

"Well, if it isn't Sleeping Beauty."

Paige jumped. Her elbow banged the corner of his desk, shooting lightning up her arm.

"How'd the grandmother take it? She okay?"

"No, she's not okay. First her granddaughter, and now her daughter, disappears. It's only the three of them. She's devastated.

I came close to calling a medic. Collapsed against me, didn't utter a peep. Heftier than she looks, almost knocked me down. I thought she was unconscious. Laid her down, then she sucked down a giant gasp and started sobbing."

"But she's okay now? She's at home?"

"Like I said, she's not okay. Tried talking her into going to Emergency, but she refused. Said she'd call her own doctor in the morning. Also said she'd call a friend to come stay. Pulled out pills from when her husband died. Years past the expiration. Swallowed them anyway. She was eerily calm when I left. I'm kind of worried…"

"Yeah, well if you hadn't lost her daughter, she wouldn't…" Pounding feet, as if the cavalry approached, halted Wasden from again launching full force into his tirade. "Here come the boys. Let's see what they found out."

Navarro spoke first. Paige shot him a disgusted look and imagined him wagging his tail as if he were a dog eager to impress his owner. "Here's what I know…"

Not to be upstaged by a simpleminded cop, FBI Agent Boutros cut Navarro short. "Security tapes from the underground parking show Mrs. Richards and Balik getting into a metallic tan Jaguar SUV. She stumbled once, and he took her arm, but she didn't appear to be under the influence. Gets in of her own volition. He doesn't force her. She even opens the door for herself." Boutros shrugged. "Beats the hell out of me."

Weary of watching the two men vie for top billing, Paige summed up the longwinded Boutros. "Boss, I think she volunteered." Paige squared her shoulders and watched all three men turn and roll their eyes.

"This better be good, Vickers."

"Driving to the Belaruse, Nina told me she's totally dissatisfied with how things worked out the previous night, you know, when she went with Lara from Cox and Mason. Anyway, I had a feeling that Nina planned to volunteer. During the drive I told her explicitly why that couldn't happen. Last thing I said, "This is not the army—do not enlist. Do you understand me?"

Navarro shrugged. "Apparently she didn't understand…"

"Oh, she understood. She did it anyway," Wasden growled. "Vickers, this is all your fault." Paige opened her mouth to respond, but his glare stopped her. "What else do we know?"

"I checked the Sugar House website," offered Boutros. "No new women. For the moment, I'm taking it as a good thing that there's no picture of Mrs. Richards."

"Are you highly trained FBI guys unable to track time? You think three or four hours gives them time to transport her and post her on their scummy website?" As Wasden turned away, he grumbled to himself. None of the other three could distinguish what he said until he swerved back.

"Nothing else? That's all you got? Next to nothing? Can't tell you how unimpressed I am. And you, Vickers, even your mother's unimpressed right now." Wasden glared, face-on with each detective, giving them one final chance to redeem themselves. Paige squirmed and the two men rocked from foot-to-foot. Wasden dragged the dried cigarette out of his pocket. When it broke in two, tobacco fluttered to the floor.

"Idiots." Tossing the remains in the metal trashcan, Wasden directed his scowl toward Paige. "Vickers, you're back to the Belaruse tonight, but not alone. I'm pulling in Ramirez. She'll go with you."

"I don't need…"

"Yes, you do, Vickers. Nothing I'd like better than to put you on a bus back to your mother, but I don't want to lose you in the Belaruse. Got other plans."

Paige opened her mouth to protest but closed it again when Wasden's eyebrow shot up.

"Okay, all of you back here at 8 p.m. Vickers, you and Ramirez wear wires. Wasden glared at Navarro. "We'll stakeout in a van again, but not the same van as last night. Get another one. And maybe you can manage to get a receiver that doesn't cut out every time something important happens. Then get back on the Sugar House website, scout around on the dark web for new activity. And you, Boutros, you're FBI. Go do whatever it is FBI do."

Nobody moved a muscle until Wasden threw his hands up in the air. "What are you waiting for?"

CHAPTER TWENTY-ONE
Darby - Day Ten - Monday, March 26

Each time Berat entered her room, heat rose to Darby's face. She stood and braced herself for what would happen. At least twice a day, he brought her food. Every other time he entered, his evil sneer morphed into a smile when he forced her from her room.

He looked different this morning. He carried no food and the snarl was gone. She leaned forward, prepared to bolt. But when Berat closed the door behind him, he leaned back against it and blocked any opportunity to escape. Darby's eyes darted around the room as though some other route might magically appear.

"Sit. Don't even think about it."

She ignored his command and balled her hands into fists. She watched for him to drop his guard.

"I've got good news for you."

Darby cringed. Nothing good ever came from this man. She put her hands behind her, ready to push off if he moved even one step from the door.

"You're going to have a roommate."

She scrutinized his face for signs he was lying, playing another of his cruel jokes. When Darby spoke, she said only one word. "Why?"

"Beats the hell out of me. You don't deserve it. Told them, bad idea. Like putting a kitten in with an alley cat." With that he spun

223

on the heel of his boot, stepped out the door and slammed it hard enough to vibrate it on its hinges.

It's a trick…but why? Darby walked to the window and peered through the lattice covering. *To spy on me?* The sun shone brightly into the courtyard. *Makes no sense. They watch me all the time.* She leaned against the window frame and whispered to the Magnolia trees in full bloom. "Don't you know this place is ugly?"

The word roommate repeated in her head. She'd only had one before, at college, and that was Esma. She flushed with excitement to think, perhaps they would be reunited. But in the next instant she whimpered at the thought of what that would mean for her best friend.

A clank at the door interrupted her thoughts. She pressed herself against the wall as Berat leaned in and held the door open. A short round woman shuffled in carrying a tray of breakfast foods. Her movements reminded Darby of Grandma Sally. When Darby reached out, the diminutive woman held tight to the tray. Her kindly smile brought tears to Darby's eyes.

"Seda, old woman…" Berat motioned toward the door. "Get out."

Darby watched Seda back out of the room. As Berat walked out the door, Darby called out, "The roommate…what's her name?" Berat poked his head back in, snarled with superiority, and slammed the door.

Alone once again, Darby sat and bit into the ring-shaped bread. It was warm and sugary. While it reminded her of Grandma Sally's homemade bread, it brought her no comfort. The only thing she could focus on was the possibility of a roommate. She held the bread in her mouth, forgot to chew. It swelled into a large gummy wad that she spat into her napkin.

Darby poured a cup of the strong Turkish tea. *Maybe they're being nicer so I'll cooperate.* As she dipped a silver spoon into a ceramic pot of honey, her own voice startled her. "Don't be a fool." The honey melted as she swirled the spoon. *I wonder if we'll share my room? Or go to another?*

Too excited to eat or drink, Darby stepped to the window. She pressed her face against the warm glass and looked for a gate. *Maybe she's allowed in the courtyard, then we could escape.*

In the far corner, she noticed a dark shadow that hadn't been there before. Squinting, she determined it was a stack of wooden boxes. Something green hung over the top. *Vegetables?* She saw patches of red that looked as if they could be radishes. She pressed her face flatter. Asparagus spears filled the far side of the box. She thought perhaps she'd found an outside entrance to the kitchen. The notion of people coming and going with groceries sent a tingle down her spine. The activity of food being delivered could create the commotion she needed to escape.

Darby watched the boxes for movement until her mind began to wander. *What if she doesn't want to leave?* Looking up, she sent a message. *Grandpa, it's Darby. Do you hear me? At least I won't be alone.*

Darby conjured a vision of the girl she eagerly waited to meet. *Young? Older? Probably older. I'm too young to be here. Will she be grateful to be with me? Or angry at my bad behavior?* Darby abandoned her lookout at the window and sat down to the tray of food.

She tore off a second hunk of bread, smashed creamy butter into its pores, then dipped it in her tea. Her eyes misted as she wondered whether her new friend had been there longer than she.

Darby shuddered when it occurred to her that the girl Berat would bring must have also been kidnapped, drugged, and…

As Darby lifted the teacup to her mouth, her hand quivered. Hot liquid sloshed over the rim. She wiped the dribbles from her lap, then the tears from her face. But when the tears escalated into sobs and the quivers into tremors, she threw the cup across the room. Then Darby flung herself into her bed and pulled the blanket over her head.

Maybe being drugged is better. Then I don't know… Don't feel it.

Eventually exhaustion slowed her moans, and she tumbled into a troubled sleep. Dreams played in her head as if they were news clips. She was with Esma. The warm sun baked their shoulders as they strolled along the beach. Then in another flash, they shopped at the San Clemente Outlet mall.

Darby sat up and shook her head, but the effort to shake off the sadness failed. Gloom permeated the air. As she sat in the chair by the window, she thought about how normally its luxurious fabric and thick padding would have provided comfort. She counted the stars visible at one corner of the window. Minutes turned into hours, and no one came.

Lies. They think they can break me. Make me be a good little girl.

Time passed and still no one came. By sunset, she knew they were punishing her again. As doubts filled her mind, her resolve to fight sank like a rock in a muddy pond. She decided to stop kicking and screaming and earn the freedom to go in the courtyard. The last rays of sun bounced off a large Magnolia flower, seeming to turn it into gold. She imagined inhaling its thick sweet perfume.

"Snap out of it, you fool," she said out loud. "You know that's what they want." Darby nodded to herself and recommitted her energy to the fight.

They'll get sick of me, turn me loose…or kill me.

When Darby began to tremble, she heard his voice. *"Shake it off, baby."*

"Hi, Grandpa Charlie. I'm glad your back."

"Find something to hold onto, baby. Might not be the roommate, maybe they did lie, but you're tough. Just like me."

Darby sat, still and silent, absorbing the strength of her grandfather's presence until a sound startled her. A clink came from behind the door at the side of her room, a door she had never seen open. In the doorway stood a young woman, motionless, until Berat shoved her from behind. When she stumbled, Darby jumped up and caught her. She expected to read fear on the new girl's face. Instead her head lolled to the side. Pupils enlarged, eyes void of reaction, the girl had been drugged.

"Here you go, ladies. As long as you behave, this door will remain open a few hours each day. Give me any crap, and I lock it. Got that?"

The girl in the doorway was too drugged to respond. Darby's attention was on the wobbly girl who was now clinging to her arm.

"I said, have you got that?"

Darby jutted out her chin and answered through locked teeth. "We understand."

Berat raised his hand toward her face. "You'd better or…"

Darby bottled up her own retort as he slammed the door behind him. When the key was yanked from the lock, she put her arm around the girl. "Are you okay?" Her only response was a blank stare. Darby held the girl by the elbow and helped her sit in a chair.

"They drugged me," she whispered.

"The powder? Probably the tea. Me too. Not always, usually the tea's fine. Other times… Maybe you should lie down."

She helped the limp and dazed girl to the bed in the adjoining room. Every few minutes, Darby peeked around the door. After an hour, she tiptoed in and the girl stirred. Darby rushed back to her own room to pour a glass of water. When she returned, the girl had propped herself up with pillows, but her eyes were still closed. Darby stood silently and studied her face until the dark-haired girl opened her eyes. She handed her the glass but didn't let go until she was sure the girl was steady enough to hold it. Then Darby sat at her side.

"Are you okay? I was worried. They gave you something. You were in bad shape, completely out of it."

"I am better." Between sips, the dark-haired girl said, "My head is clearing, but I am so tired."

"I waited and waited for you, and then I thought you weren't coming. I mean, they said I'd have a roommate, but when they didn't bring you I thought it was my punishment for fighting, trying to break free."

The girl looked around the room as if she thought someone might be listening. "They told me also that I would have someone to share a room again."

"They gave us hope and then stalled so we'd think it wouldn't happen. Another of their tricks to show their power, make us grateful. But we're together now. That's what matters. My name is Darby Richards."

"I am called Amira. My family name is Farooqi. I have two brothers and sisters, but I have not seen my family for a long time."

"Me neither. I miss them so much. I know they're worried sick. I'm American, a student at UCLA. Do you know where that is?"

"I know of Los Angeles and the university. My first roommate attended UCLA as an international student. Her name was Isabella. She..." Amira's voice cracked. She pushed back the covers, rolled out of bed to stand on wobbly legs, then silently walked to the bathroom. Darby stared at the closed door.

After a few minutes, Darby began to fret. She tiptoed over and leaned in to hear what was happening on the other side of the door. The soft flow of water was all she could detect. She debated calling out to Amira or tapping lightly on the door but did neither. She stood outside for another moment, then sat on the foot of the bed. When the door finally opened, a red-eyed Amira emerged, then hesitated to steady herself on the door frame. Darby went to her and held her arm. The girls slowly walked to the table and sat in silence.

After a few moments, Amira spoke and continued the conversation as if she had never left the room. "I am from Pakistan. Since a child, I dreamed of traveling to America to attend one of their great schools. In my hometown, Islamabad, great gender inequality exists. I yearned to become an independent woman, but now, I am not even in the United States."

Again, sensing they were being watched, Darby scooted her chair closer to Amira. "Where do you think we are?"

"I think I was flown from Istanbul to the Esenboğa Airport."

Darby tipped her head to the side. "I don't understand."

"Turkey, Darby. In the car, I awoke and lifted a corner of the mask they put over my head. I saw a sign for the Ankara American Consulate."

"The American Consulate? The embassy? Are you sure?"

"The sign pointed to a large official building, surrounded by a tall cinderblock wall, painted red at the top. The only opening was a large black iron gate. A huge American flag was in the yard."

"Is it far?"

"Less than ten minutes away, so I am sure we are still in Ankara, Turkey. Do you hear the airplanes at night? The Esenboğa Airport is in Ankara. Convenient for shipping us wherever they want." Amira rubbed her temples. "Also, Darby, the flowers and trees in the courtyard are native to Turkey. Outside your window, can you see the pointed roof? Classic Turkish architecture."

"You've been here before?"

"No, I was enrolled in International Studies before I ran away. My plan was to flee to a country where I could be free."

"Free? Free from what? Did something happen at school?"

"I did not run away from school. I lived at home."

Darby sat in silence and considered the implications of Amira's statement.

"Darby, I've never told anyone, but with you, I can confide. I feel a strong connection between us." Amira looked down and wrung her hands. "When I turned twelve, my father began molesting me."

"No one helped you?"

"My older sisters knew, but they had no influence on my father. They were busy preparing for their weddings, eager to escape."

"But your brothers?"

"My brothers knew, but they respected my father above all else, placed him even higher than God. I prayed to Allah to command my brothers to stop him, but my prayers went unanswered."

Amira's cocoa eyes turned black from the tears. Darby blinked to hold back her own. "What about your mother?"

230

"I tried to tell her. She slapped me, told me never to speak of it again."

"Amira, I'm so sorry. My mother is my rock. I can't imagine…"

"Even if my mother reported him, it is unlikely my father would be punished. The men protect each other and the laws protect the men over all others. Unlike America, divorce is not easy in Pakistan. My father would have to desert her for four or more years or fail to financially support the family for two or more. Or not have intimate relations with my mother for at least three years. These crimes he did not commit."

"He can treat you both however he wants?"

"I learned in school, Pakistan is the third most dangerous country for women. My counselor said close to seventy percent are psychologically or physically abused. Many are disfigured, maimed. Law enforcement does not consider such treatment by a husband to be a crime."

"Wasn't there any place you could go for help?"

"Very few shelters exist in Pakistan."

As Darby searched for words of solace, Amira continued as though they'd been confidants for years. "My father moved us to another city. This isolated my mother from her friends and family or anyone who might help her. If she had reported him, he would have thrown her out and not allowed her to see me or my brothers and sisters ever again. He beat both my mother and I at the smallest provocation. I feared he would kill her if she stood up to him. I prayed she would protect me, but it was too much to ask."

Amira removed a small linen hanky from her pocket and dabbed her eyes. "My name, Amira, means princess, but I was not treated as one. It is hard to confess, but I turned to evil. I prayed

Allah would compel my mother to poison my father. I thought, if she loved me, she would secretly kill him."

Darby cradled Amira's hands in her own. "How did you get away?"

"I sold the gold jewelry I inherited from my great grandmother. I paid the money to an underground immigration agent. He pretended to help but did not. He sold me and three other girls."

"The men that bought you, did they take you to Los Angeles?"

"Darby, how did you know? They drugged me and put a mask over my face. I don't remember everything, but I was in a prison for days. Cold and damp, a mole hole in the ground." Amira pulled her hands from Darby's and twisted the hem of her blouse. "Then one day, the men said we were going to an airport, but they would not drug me if I obeyed. The drive was long and slow. One of the men said he hated the L.A. traffic. I think he recognized his mistake because he never said another word until they dragged me from the car."

"And did you do what they said?"

Amira looked down. "I was afraid."

"How long were you locked in the cinderblock cell?"

"At least twenty days. I lost count. At times I thought I was unconscious for only a few hours. Others it seemed like more than a day and night." Amira met Darby's eyes. "At first, I fought to escape."

"Oh, Amira, me too." A cloudy vision of Grandpa Charlie formed in Darby's mind. "My grandfather said they use isolation to break our will, make us grateful for the tiniest scrap of kindness so we'll do anything they want."

Amira looked away again. "I was never grateful, but for a while, I gave up fighting. I wanted to kill myself rather than let them do what they wanted. I searched for a way, but there was nothing in my cell. Then I decided that they were not worthy of my death and began fighting again."

Darby and Amira turned as Berat opened the door. Grandmotherly Seda pushed a rolling serving table into the room. With an expression of pride, she uncovered a large pewter tray and revealed a variety of steaming plates. Darby and Amira sniffed, but neither touched the food until they were alone again.

"It's so late, I didn't think they were going to feed us any dinner. Another punishment…"

"Darby, this looks amazing, but what if they put something in it?"

"If they wanted to poison us, they would've done it by now."

"Could be drugs?"

"But that comes in the powder they blow on us. I think this food is okay. But I haven't been given anything this exotic before. Have you?"

"Sometimes, when I am obedient." Amira lifted a skewer from the tray. "Smell the kabobs. Darby, the triangles are manti, stuffed with minced meat. This drink is ayran, made from yogurt. My favorite part is the foam."

"Reminds me of a milkshake."

"Not that delicious." The girls shared their first laugh. Amira pointed to tiny off-white bricks lined up on a rectangular dish. "That is qurut. I do not care for it. Perhaps you will find it pleasing."

When Darby plopped one small cube into her mouth and ran her tongue around it, her upper lip curled. "Or not," she said.

For the next few minutes, the girls nibbled at the food, each deep in thought until Amira broke their silence. "That horrible white mess in the metal bowls…"

"You too? That's all they gave me. Did they ever bring you real food?"

"After many days had passed, during a period in which I had given up fighting, a man brought a steak and warm bread. They did not give me a knife with which to cut this meat, so I picked it up and took a bite. It tasted wonderful. But I thought, if I am able to take a bite out of that meat, I can bite the man who brings the food."

"You bit him?"

Amira nodded. "But he shoved me into the wall."

"Were you hurt?" When Amira shook her head, Darby continued. "He smashed my hand in the door."

"Why?"

"I tried to push past him to escape."

"Did he beat you?"

"No, he blew the powder in my face. I was out for a long time, but someone bandaged my hand while I was unconscious."

"On my last day, he drugged me so much that I hallucinated, thought I had killed my sisters. I saw my parents loving them, buying new dresses, gold jewelry, everything they wanted. I became jealous. I grabbed a machete and chopped them. I swear, I saw blood pulse from their bodies. I woke up screaming, afraid to see their dismembered bodies on my floor. I expected my hands to be dripping with my sisters' blood. I was wet and sticky, but it was only sweat." Amira looked away from Darby. "After that, I did whatever the men told me."

Darby looked around the room as the creepy feeling of being watched returned. She leaned forward to hug her new friend and whispered in her ear. "We are so screwed."

The door swung open, hitting the wall behind it. Berat snarled and ordered Amira to her room. The girls clung to each other. He grabbed Amira's arm and jerked her from the chair, breaking the hold the girls had on each other. Amira leaned away from Berat, pulled toward Darby but couldn't break his grip. He grasped Amira by the wrists and pulled her toward him. She cried out as her legs gave way beneath her. Darby jumped up. She reached out for Amira but took a step back when Berat swung and barely missed her face. One hand outstretched, Darby followed as Berat dragged Amira out.

When he slammed the door behind him, Darby banged with her fists. "No...no. Please bring her back." She listened at the door, heard Berat say something, then the room went quiet. She fell back on her chair, pulled her legs up against her chest, and cowered.

I'll be next.

CHAPTER TWENTY-TWO
Nina - Day Eleven - Tuesday, March 27

Sally awakened at three and listened to the motionless that always meant the house was empty. At the foot of the bluff, waves crashed upon the beach. Normally comforting, this morning the roar was unnerving. She strained to hear a single sound that would assure her Nina was safe at home. In its absence, she grabbed her aching back and rolled out of bed.

Sally realized it was useless, but she went to look anyway. Nina's bed was untouched. She told herself it wasn't too late. At any minute, her daughter might be back. Sally returned to the guest bedroom, pulled the covers tight, and descended into a restless dream. Her deceased husband, Charlie, was saying something about Darby. His voice was too muted to understand. The vision shattered when her phone rang. Anxious when the cell lit up with Unidentified Caller, Sally smiled when the woman identified herself as Detective Paige Vickers.

"I'm out front. May I come in?"

Sally entered the code to open the security gate, scrambled downstairs, and waited eagerly at the door. When she saw Paige's expression, she knew she'd been mistaken. The news would not be good. Before Detective Vickers completed a single sentence, Sally understood that Nina was not coming home. When Paige left, Sally closed the door and crumpled to the floor. Her sobs echoed off the entryway ceiling. Her lament, "I should've stopped you," pounded against her skull.

When her crying subsided into gasping and the burn in her eyes and throb of her head were more than she could endure, Sally heaved herself upright, trudged to the bar, and lifted the bottle of Glenfiddich Special Old Reserve. She poured two fingers worth into a leaded crystal glass. She raised it and watched the light bounce off its surface, then poured another finger of the rich amber liquid. With a giant swig, she choked down four Ibuprofen. Then she leaned against the bar and sipped the rest while hoping for relief.

Before either the scotch or headache medicine could kick in, Sally had devised a plan. The clock read 5:49 a.m., but after forty years of friendship and five years of sharing a wall at the Monarch Cliff Condos, she knew Teresa would be awake. Breakfast service began at six at the senior complex, but their social group didn't meet in the dining hall until seven-thirty, so Sally picked up her cell and tapped the tiny photo of Teresa's face.

Teresa took no time for a pointless greeting. "Did they find Darby? Do you know where she is? When will..."

To stop the questions shot-gunning out of her friend's mouth, Sally interrupted. "No, Teresa. Neither the police nor the FBI have rescued her, and now it's even worse. Nina's gone."

"Gone? Gone where?"

Sixty seconds into the explanation, Teresa said, "I'll be right there. I'm walking into the bedroom to pack a bag. Text me the address."

"Thank you, Teresa. I can't do this alone. I'm lost without my girls..."

"I'll be there as fast as these old legs will carry me."

The landline rang before Sally even touched the disconnect icon on her cell. A female voice said, "Hi, this is Rhyan Pickard from the San Diego Tribune. Is this Nina Richards' mother? Darby Richards' grandmother?" Not waiting for a response, the reporter's questions barreled through. "What did the police tell you? I understand your daughter's also gone. What can you tell me?"

"Nothing," answered Sally patiently. "I have nothing to say." She hung up, and the landline rang again. A man thundered, "Walter Cathro, L.A. Times. Any news on your granddaughter? How about your daughter? Was she kidnapped too? What do you know?"

"I'm sorry. I know nothing. Check with LAPD." Sally jumped when the cell she still held in her other hand rang again. The next two calls were from numbers her phone didn't recognize, so she tapped the red circle to ignore. After that, she let them all go to voicemail as she poured just one more finger of Glenfiddich Special.

Scotch in hand, Sally walked into the kitchen and organized the notes and articles she and Nina had collected in their research. She labeled each pile with a sticky note. Satisfied, she used a yellow legal pad to record everything Nina had told her related to Lara and Paige. She wrote until she could think of nothing else.

As she awaited Teresa's arrival, Sally sat in the living room, staring into the remnants of her Glenfiddich. Accustomed to discussing every aspect with Nina, she resorted to mumbling to herself. "Why doesn't someone call me. Wasden? Lara? Certainly, Grady. Never hear from that FBI guy, Boutros. Just made a pile for him. Detective Vickers, she's the only one, except for Nina's partner, that slimy Louis McGraw." Sally glared at her cell, willing it to ring. Then she picked up the television remote and directed her simmering dissatisfaction at the blank screen. "Thought he had some good qualities, except that he's married. Now we know he's a slimeball."

When she clicked the on button, a familiar face appeared. Sally continued mumbling as though Nina sat beside her. "There's our Botox reporter. Can't remember her name. Suppose it's because her little face is paralyzed, her personality's gone." Raising her voice and speaking to the reporter's image, Sally confided in her TV friend. "My Nina, she's pretty beat up. Last five years, really tough, and now this. She could use a good unmarried man to keep her and Darby safe. Maybe Grady? When he brings my girls home..."

The screen split and the Botox reporter was joined by correspondent Sebastian Greyson, his eyes crinkled around the edges, hair shining as if it were sterling silver. "Or maybe you? You look like a man who would help."

Greyson cut short Sally's mutterings when he began his report. "Members of President Alice Brighton's Cabinet used the services of a sex trafficking cartel based in Los Angeles and Ankara, Turkey. An anonymous source leaked photos of Vice President Jackson Connors and Secretary of Defense Frank Mortensen, known as Morty to his close friends, as they entered the Belaruse. This tipster revealed that three women who were identified as sex trafficking victims were also guests of this private gambling club in Los Angeles. Further, the Secret Service agent identified as the anonymous source indicated that security video recorded the now missing mother of Darby Richards entering and leaving the Belaruse. Stay tuned for the complete story."

"No, no, no. Come back here." Sally hit the record button. Then she sat, cold and still as ice, holding her breath. When he returned to the screen, she sucked down a huge gulp of air, then a small sip of Glenfiddich.

"In earlier broadcasts we covered the horrific finds of two women in back alleys of Los Angeles. Security tapes show Alisa Methron, the murdered artist, and Isabella Costa, a UCLA psychology major believed to have committed suicide, entering the Belaruse. Not together, but about a week apart. In addition, our own Victoria van der Waals reported on the death of Qudsia Ghafoor in her series on the South American drug, Devil's Breath. No clear evidence has come forth linking Ms. Ghafoor to the Belaruse. However, police report Methron, Costa, Ghafoor, and now Darby Richards are all victims of the Devil's Breath."

Sally placed her hand to her chest. The anxiety pills, still sitting in their brown plastic bottle, expiration date boldly printed, seemed to warn her off. Nevertheless, she removed the cap, poured a tiny white pill into her hand, and washed it down with a sip of Glenfiddich.

Sally gasped as her granddaughter's face filled the TV screen. "Darby Richards is the third young woman identified in security footage as she entered the Belaruse. Within days of this, her photo appeared on the dark web, the same website that showed photos of Ms. Methron and Ms. Costa. It is unknown if Darby Richards' mother, Nina Richards, has also been taken by the same human trafficking cartel."

Sally poured out a second anxiety pill, used her tongue to pick it out of her palm. She swallowed it with the final swig of Glenfiddich as the handsome reporter said, "And now, Autumn Wright will bring you the weather."

"Don't you dare, Greyson. Nobody needs a weather report. Look out the window."

Sally sat flipping one channel to another, when she received a text from Teresa. "We're turning onto your street."

Sally disconnected and muttered to herself, "We? Who's we? I hope she didn't bring that clingy Marvin."

A second text popped up. "We're here. Better come get us. Hordes of reporters. They'll crash the gate."

Sally scurried out but all she could see was people, cameras, and news vans. Only when she stepped up onto the rails could she get a peek of Teresa's car stopped in the middle of the pack. Sally opened the walking gate enough to wedge her body through but slammed it shut before any reporters slipped in. They swarmed and shoved microphones into her face as she forced her way toward Teresa's car.

"Do you know where your daughter is?" Sally kept her eyes glued to her feet and didn't utter a single word as reporters flung questions at her. "Was she kidnapped as well?" A skinny reporter with slick brown hair shoved a microphone toward her mouth. "Is your daughter an escort? Same as your granddaughter?" Sally clamped her jaws shut and swallowed the curses she wanted to hurl. Others called out, "Have you heard from either of them? What are the police doing to bring them back? How are you feeling?"

Sally snapped. "How the hell do you think I'm feeling?" When she reached the car and peered in, she did a doubletake. Recognizing the orange frizzy hair, Sally put her hand over her mouth to cover her complaint. "Great, just what I need. Ditzy Gaby." By the time Teresa opened the window, Sally regained her composure and greeted her friends. "Thank goodness, you're here.

Drive up to the gate, and I'll open it. Go through quick while I block their way."

As Sally expected, the mass of reporters crushed in and tried to squeeze through. She mustered up her brashest and most authoritative voice. "This is private property." Sally held her cellphone high. "If anyone enters, I'll call 911."

Teresa stopped her ten-year-old Mercury Grand Marquis just inside the gate. When it closed behind her, Sally climbed in the backseat. "Sorry about the mob. They've been lurking around the house all morning, but I didn't realize there were so many. And the phone...rings and rings. Never stops."

"Don't give it a thought. We're here to help." When Sally closed the garage door behind Teresa's car, the three women exhaled a collective sigh of relief.

As they unloaded their suitcases, Sally said, "I don't know how to handle reporters. We're not the kind of people who are in the news. It's a relief to have you here." As the elevator ascended from the garage to the entryway, the women embraced in a three-way hug.

Sally led her friends to the guest rooms. "When you're settled, come to the kitchen. I'll make a chicken salad. We'll eat while I tell you everything."

"I trust a martini's coming with that salad. It's five o'clock somewhere, and after that entrance, it ought to be five o'clock here." Gaby shot a look at Teresa, daring her to challenge the appropriateness of her suggestion.

Sally said, "I've already had my one drink for today." Teresa's eyebrows shot up as she checked her watch, but she held her thoughts as Sally turned toward the kitchen and mumbled, "Oh what the hell."

As the friends nibbled the salads and sipped martinis, on the opposite side of the continent, the President of the United States became involved in Darby's case. Alice Brighton sat behind her desk, still fuming at the senator from Maine even though he'd left the Oval Office ten minutes prior. "Where do you get off trying to kill my bill? You think Maine has no energy crisis? Let's turn off your electricity and see how much your constituency loves you then."

When Jeff Sanders opened the door, President Brighton stopped grumbling. The steady demeanor of the White House Press Secretary generally calmed her, except for today.

"Good morning, Madam President. I apologize for interrupting."

"Our regular meeting was only an hour ago?"

"I apologize, but you won't want me to wait on this one. It's hot. Hit the news, no heads-up. My sources failed me this time."

"Okay, Jeff. Give it to me. Does this have to do with Congress bashing my social security revision bill?"

"I wish it did, Madam President."

"Ten minutes until I leave to address Congress. What is it?

"As you know, there's still lots of news coverage of the terrorist attack at the Pantages."

"Now I have nine minutes. Then I'm out the door."

"Madam President, a new scandal just hit the news, and the wire service picked it up."

"What now?"

"Remember yesterday when we discussed Victoria van der Waals' series on the Columbian drug, Devil's Breath?"

"Yes, Jeff. What's that got to do with this office? Do we have staff using it? Selling it?" The President chuckled, hoping she had made a joke.

"No, that's not quite it…"

"Not quite it? What exactly *is it*?" She set her pen on the desk as her impatience approached the boiling point.

"We're following reports connecting the drug to the women found dead in trash bags in L.A."

"And?"

"And to Darby Richards, the UCLA student reportedly drugged and kidnapped, possibly by an elite sex trafficking cartel."

"Jeff, do I need to get plyers and wrench this out of you."

"I thought we had some time." He braced for her reaction to what he would say next. "But there's talk that one of your Secret Service detail leaked evidence of a connection to your Cabinet."

"Talk? Is that all it is? Talk?"

"No, Madam President, it's more than talk. I know you've been tied up in meetings, unable to watch the news, but only thirty minutes ago, it hit every news channel…"

"Please tell me this is just another sabotaging political rumor."

"Sorry, Madam President. I don't think that at all. At least one cabinet member, with the tag name of Cocoon, is using a V-room to select women…"

"Cocoon? Women? Back the firetruck up, Jeff. What in blazes is a V-room?"

"Madam President, V-rooms provide platforms for virtual transactions. Only subscribed users have access. We use one to sell military surplus to approved countries. Sort of an eBay for military sales, but we limit access to allies interested in purchasing our surplus. We're the only ones who can identify the members of these V-rooms. Confidential and guarded, allows complete anonymity from the other V-room members."

"Are you telling me someone in my Cabinet, who knows how this works legally within our own country, is now a member of a sex trafficking V-room?"

"Yes, Madam President. Before coming to you, I talked with the director of the CIA. Jeannette says this is not a baseless rumor and not a onetime incident."

"Which cabinet member are we talking about? I expect it's the one we love to hate."

"Ah, no, Ma'am. It's one of your favorites and his buddy."

"You're trying to ease me into this aren't you."

"Yes, Ma'am."

"Afraid I'll kill the messenger?"

"No, Ma'am. You don't kill messengers."

"Jeff, you're irritating me enough I may reconsider..."

"I'm sorry, Madam President, but..."

"It's Jackson Connors, isn't it? That's why you're doling this out with such caution. No. Jeff, please tell me it's not Jackson. My vice president? How could he?" Seething, she asked, "Who else?"

In his calmest voice, Jeff said, "CIA has evidence that both Secretary of Defense Frank Mortensen and Vice President Connors are members of this V-room and have purchased services."

"Morty? Morty's got four girls of his own. How could he?"

When Jeff didn't utter a word, didn't move a muscle, she understood that he spoke the truth. Glaring at the hard copy of her calendar that lay beside her coffee cup, President Brighton asked, "Is Vice President Connors available to confer with us after my address to Congress?"

"No, I don't think so, Madam President."

"You don't think he's available? He better get available."

"No, Madam President, not what I meant. I meant, no, I don't think you should talk to him. I'm recommending someone else talk to him first. Legal recommends that CIA present him with the evidence."

"Legal weighed in on this? Am I the last to know? Let me express how thankful I am you all finally decided to share this with me."

"We need to prepare a response to this before you address Congress. Give me two minutes and I'll add it to your speech." An ominous silence descended upon the room. Having seen this look on the President's face numerous times, Jeff braced himself while he waited. But when she spoke, he didn't understand the request. "Pardon me, Madam President?"

She repeated herself with a measured tone of impatience. "Ask Roberta to sharpen my scissors."

"What are you going to do?"

"Cut his balls off."

"Yes, Madam President," said Jeff without batting an eye, "but first, let me step out and locate Vice President Connors."

She returned to the bill on her desk, trying to make sense of the political jargon. Rage made it impossible to concentrate on a single phrase. She looked up from rereading the introduction when Jeff slipped back in. "Bad news, Madam President."

"How can it get any worse?"

"Vice President Connors isn't here."

"Not here? Send Special Services to retrieve him. *Now.* Where is he?"

"Madam President, he's in Turkey." He read her expression and watched to see if she would hold back the volley of curse words when he added, "Morty is MIA as well."

Her voice was cold and calm. "Get Jeannette Johnson up here."

As Jeff closed the door behind himself, he said to Rosa, "Call the director of the CIA. The President wants her now. Tell her to drop everything."

Seven thousand miles and fourteen hours of flight time away, Nina emerged from her drug induced oblivion. She resisted her body's urge to fight. Collapsed against the car door, she suppressed her need to gasp for air and maintained her sleeplike breathing pattern in an attempt to slow her racing heart.

We're stopping. Traffic light? When the car rolled forward and turned sharply, Nina used the momentum to straighten her neck and peek out the window. *Nothing familiar.* As they slowed, she tried to read the signs on the buildings. They were foreign. She didn't recognize the language.

The car crept through the downtown maze. *Strange accent marks. Çanhaya. What's the tail on the c?* As her thoughts cleared, she searched for other clues. Two women wearing gathered print skirts and white blouses shopped in an open market. Multicolored scarves covered their heads. Middle-aged women sat in an outdoor café, dressed in jeans and tee-shirts. Their hair flowed in the breeze. The street bustled with life. Most of the men wore either khaki slacks and pastel shirts or American suits. However, as the car swerved, they passed five older men clustered on the corner. Their vests were vibrant red, orange, and blue, trimmed with gold braid. Their loose-fitting pants tapered at their ankles. Sharp-edged skullcaps were perched atop their short haircuts. Nina held still, peered out through the one eye smashed against the backseat windowpane, and smiled.

Could be Turkey. I think I did it.

The driver hit the brakes. The passengers lurched. The automatic reflexes that caused Nina to grab the seat to steady herself did not go unnoticed. "She's awake."

"Bag her," commanded a cavernous voice from the driver's seat. Before Nina could react, her world darkened again. But she didn't panic, didn't fight. She congratulated herself because the American flag was the last thing she saw before they pulled the cloth bag over her head. It stood large and fluttered in the breeze. She closed her eyes and concentrated on the imposing wall of gray concrete cinderblocks, the top row painted red. It felt like a piece of home. She sensed it would be important later.

CHAPTER TWENTY-THREE
Darby - Day Eleven - Tuesday, March 27

"**P**lease don't go." The sound of her own voice woke Darby from a vivid dream. A fuzzy vision remained in her mind. Almost able to see the red curly hair and freckled nose of her childhood companion, the loss was as real as the day Jessie's parents backed their SUV down the driveway and moved the family to New Jersey. Darby remembered standing in the yard, waving until the car was gone. Now she pushed the covers back and rose from the bed.

My new friend, is she still here?

Darby scurried toward the connecting door, too distraught to put on her robe. She turned the doorknob and burst into the adjoining room.

Startled, Amira looked up and smiled. "Good morning, Darby. I checked on you earlier. I am glad you are now awake."

The girls hugged like long separated sisters. "I dreamt of a childhood friend," whispered Darby. "When I awoke, I hurt the same as when Jessie's family moved away. I panicked, thought you'd be gone too."

"Darby, I also worried Berat might take you away. I tiptoed into your room several times to reassure myself he had not. Please, sit." Amira filled the infuser with loose tea and bobbed the metal ball in the steaming water. The herbal fragrance filled the air.

"Amira, you must be very sad to think you may never again see your family."

"At first, I was overwhelmed. I wept until I could shed no more tears. My mother is weak, but I love her. My brothers... I held faith they would come to understand how wrong they were to let our father abuse me. After days of darkness, I understood that I am less than nothing to my brothers. That is why they chose not to come."

"You've lost so much."

"Your mother, she will come?"

A tingle spread across the back of Darby's neck and crept up behind her ears. She looked around the room, then leaned forward and whispered as if someone was listening. "Mom will try, but how will she find me?"

"At least she is coming. My family deemed me of no value."

"Surely your mother still loves you."

"Darby, I feel confused. These men who treat me so badly have placed me in this beautiful room. Our home was nice, but I was of no value to my family. Now that bowl of fruit, the apricots and sweet figs, holds a greater significance than simply being food. I held the golden pear-like fruit and marveled at its uniqueness but could not eat it. The fruit became a symbol of my worth."

"I understand, Amira." Darby hugged her legs to her chest. Amira leaned forward and lifted the brightly colored pottery teapot to fill their cups. The soothing scent filled their nostrils. The girls sat soaking in the warmth of their new friendship until the outer door opened and banged against the wall.

"Okay, girls. Sorry to break up this little tea party." Berat pointed at Darby. "Back to your own side." As Darby slowly walked to her room, she heard Berat ask Amira, "What's it going to be? Care to cooperate or shall I blow the Devil's Breath your way?" Berat turned and snarled at Darby. "Shut the door."

Darby still clutched the doorknob when he rammed the key to the back of the lock. She pressed her ear against the closed door. Even though she strained to catch her friend's response, she only heard a whimper.

CHAPTER TWENTY-FOUR
Nina - Day Twelve - Wednesday, March 28

After Keith's death, the doctor prescribed pills, the kind that create shadowy, bottomless pits of sleep. Nina's dreams were so ragged and disturbing, she'd wake and ask herself, "Where am I?" Something in this awakening told her this was no dream, yet nothing looked familiar. A nagging uneasiness urged her to pretend to still be asleep, but Nina ignored it and sat up to find herself in an enormous bed with feather pillows and sheets as soft as a kitten's belly. She fought the exhaustion that cried for her body to lie back down and sleep. As she rubbed her head, Nina remembered that when the car had stopped, the man blew something in her face. On the verge of recalling what happened next, but before the vision could form, the aftermath of the drug dragged her back into a dark nothingness.

Several hours later, Nina awoke again, thoughts thick and groggy. She rolled to a seated position and hung her legs off the bed. She inspected her bare arms and legs, found no bruises. The men hadn't hurt her. Confused, she tried to pull facts from her hazy dream.

Who were those men on the plane? Tough, in charge, like that new corporate crime series. But when she realized it wasn't a dream, rage simmered in her gut. *They drugged me when it wasn't necessary. I volunteered.* Nina's legs wobbled. She gripped the headboard and studied the room. She let go to lift a delicate clock off the night stand. Its gold trim caught the rays of sun streaming in the window. Carefully returning it, she shuffled toward an ornately carved table in the center of the room.

Curiosity overcame her hesitancy. She placed her hands on the sides of a large coffee pot, decorated with serpents slithering among green vines. From its warmth, she knew someone had been in the room while she was unconscious. She lifted one of the delicate cups and filled it with the brown liquid. The spicy smell of cardamom tickled her nose, enticing her to drink. She debated the consequences, then drew the porcelain cup to her lips. The first sip warmed her. Tension flowed down and out her body. Nina wiggled her toes and took a second sip. Then she sat in the brocade chair, crossed her legs, and waited for them to come.

Across the sea, Nina's mother's best friend also waited. However, her mood was far from calm and expectant. Teresa was impatient. She considered banging down bedroom doors, then she heard the shuffle of feet. "I thought you'd never wake up."

Sally cocked her head toward Gaby and defended them both. "It's 6 a.m."

"Okay, whatever. Listen girls. I have an idea. Couldn't sleep, up most of the night, worrying about what Gaby and I can do to help." Gaby raised her chin in pride. "So, here's my idea. Well, it's not exactly my idea. Got it watching American Greed reruns until three. I've been crawling with ants since then, anxious for you to wake up."

Sally wrinkled her nose at Teresa. Her expression conveyed a substantial dose of skepticism. "Okay, let's hear it."

"So, in the show, on the black web, dark web, whatever you call it, there's a drug site for buying illegal drugs. Anonymously."

"And that helps us find Darby how?" Gaby's voice oozed with cynicism.

But Sally understood where Teresa was going with her story. "We can buy back Darby."

"And Nina as well, if that's where she's gone," said Teresa.

Gaby was stunned into silence, but not Sally. She grabbed Teresa and spun her around.

"Put me down. You'll break my brittle bones."

Sally returned her friend to solid ground. "Sorry, Teresa. Just excited. I'd almost lost hope. The place where I saw Darby's picture, I don't know where it is or how to go there to rescue my girls. But now, we can buy Darby back."

"Let's get started."

Sally lifted a stack of papers from the kitchen table. "When Grady, you know, from the kidnapping insurance company, showed us Darby's picture on the dark web, I wrote down how he did it." She shuffled through her notes. "He said there's an app to access the dark web but told us not to do it."

"If he told you not to, then we shouldn't. It's probably illegal. We might get arrested."

"Really, Gaby?" Teresa asked, "Do you think the police will arrest three little old ladies for browsing the dark web?"

"Girls, girls. Logging on is not a crime." Sally continued, "It's what you do on the dark web that gets you in trouble. You know, like buying drugs or contraband."

"Or people?"

"Good grief, Gaby. We're the good guys, trying to buy Darby to save her."

"We would be the heroes?"

Teresa rolled her eyes, "My dear, we don't give a twit about being heroes. We merely need to bring Sally's girls back to her." She picked up the directions. "Step one. Open a Bitcoin account."

"Why don't we use real money?"

"Gaby, Bitcoin is real money, a digital currency used online. It says right here," Teresa read with authority, "commerce on the dark web requires Bitcoins."

"How do we get them?" asked Gaby.

"First, we open an account. The instructions don't appear too hard."

"If we can't do it, I'll call my grandson."

"Excellent, Gaby. You're a good resource," said Teresa to smooth over her earlier scoffing of her friend. "It says we need to install the Bitcoin wallet on a computer."

"Do it on my laptop," said Sally, "so I can take it wherever I go, like on an airplane."

Less complicated than the women expected, the installation was complete within a few moments. Teresa checked step one off with a red pen. "After we install the wallet, we create a Bitcoin account with a Bitcoin exchange service."

"Don't tell me you have a clue what that means," said Gaby.

"Honestly," said Teresa, "I don't, but we have step-by-step directions."

"Oh, that builds my confidence."

"Don't start, Gaby."

"Girls, no more snarking," said Sally. "If we can't figure it out, we'll call Gaby's grandson."

"Sally, we've argued so long your laptop went to sleep. Rev it up. I'll read the next step."

Sally plugged the laptop into the wall and Teresa said, "Okay, here we go. Open the Bitcoin site and click on *Get Started with Bitcoin.*"

"Teresa, my hands are shaking."

"I know, sweetie, but we can do this."

Sally squealed as she clicked the green bar that read, *Done.* "Wahoo. We have a Bitcoin wallet."

"Ladies, it says we link the wallet with our exchange account. Then we can conduct transactions."

"Do either of you understand what this exchange account is?"

"Gaby, why do you do that?"

"Don't get your knickers in a snit, Teresa. I'm simply pointing out the obvious."

"If it's obvious, why are you compelled to point it out?"

"Girls, girls. Enough squabbling. Let's do this."

Progress was smooth until the prompt required Sally to enter their country, and Gaby panicked. "Those dirtbags will know it's us. God only knows what they'll do."

Teresa turned to Gaby. "Rest assured, we are not the only U.S. citizens doing business with these dirtbags. The news is full of creeps who…who…you know."

After calming Gaby, they made steady progress until an email address was required. Again, Gaby went berserk. "Email address? They'll trace it and send some goon to get us."

"Hush. We're almost done," said Teresa.

"It wants your phone number next? Great, they can call and make sure we're here."

"Gaby, you'd be more helpful in the other room, watching the news. Let us know if anything happens."

"You want me out of your hair."

"Exactly, dear," Teresa cooed and returned to reading the directions out loud. "Answer your phone when it rings. They'll send a number that you type into the verification box."

On cue, Sally's cell rang, and Gaby screamed from the living room. "Is that them? We better get out of here."

Sally and Teresa made eye contact, and in that one look, agreed to ignore Gaby until they finished. However, the final step befuddled the two friends. They were on the verge of calling Gaby's grandson when it fell into place.

"Now we buy the coins?" When Teresa nodded, both women called out to Gaby. The response was a resounding thud that vibrated the ceiling above their heads.

"I thought she was monitoring the news?"

"Lord only knows what she's doing. I'll go find out." Teresa scurried up the stairs. When she entered the room, Gaby was lifting her suitcase off the floor. She looked up to Teresa's piercing glare. "Put that down. We need your help downstairs."

Entering the kitchen, Gaby beamed. "You need my help?"

"We're ready to fill our wallet with Bitcoins."

"I only have dollars. Do we need to go to the bank?"

Teresa groaned and rolled her eyes. "Don't you ever read the financial page?"

"You know I don't. Entertainment, comics…"

"Don't get offended," said Sally. "We want your help."

"And your money," added Teresa. "How much is in your checking account?"

"Thirteen thousand, four hundred, twelve dollars and fifty-eight cents."

"How'd I guess you'd know the exact amount? Never mind," said Teresa. "We'll take the thirteen four and leave you the twelve fifty-eight." Gaby's eyes shrank to slits and her eyebrows twisted, but she didn't utter a word of protest.

"Twenty thousand in my checking," said Sally. "And I can transfer another fifty from my savings. But, I can only do it every twenty-four hours. Keith set that up before he died, so I wouldn't get scammed."

"Not to worry. That's plenty. I sold my Starbucks stock, got thirty-five thousand." Teresa sat down at the computer and quickly made the transfers.

When the screen lit up with "You have purchased eight Bitcoins," Gaby screamed. "They stole our money. Ripped us off."

Downtown L.A., Detective Paige Vickers waited impatiently in the reception area for Wasden to return. When the elevator opened, and she saw his distracted expression, Paige walked toward him lest he get away again. "Look boss, Darby Richards' grandmother's looking for you. She's called every hour on the hour since yesterday. For the last two hours, she's called every thirty minutes to find out if I've seen you. She's upset because you haven't called her back."

"Upset? I'm working my ass off. Does she think I'm sitting around at the doughnut shop waiting for her daughter and granddaughter to reappear?"

"No, boss. It's just that you were there for her and Nina when it was only Darby missing. Now she thinks you've deserted her. Asked if you left on vacation."

"Yeah, right. Haven't had one in years."

"I know, boss. She said maybe you were too busy with the Pantages. I keep telling her you're working like a dog. Anyway, she has an interview on Fox News tomorrow morning. I'm thinking we don't want Grandma Sally going on TV saying the lead detective on her case is on vacation."

"Vickers, what'd I tell you about Grandma Sally?"

"Boss, you told me to handle her, but there's a new twist. She has two friends at the house. They have some sort of rescue plan."

"Three grandmas with a rescue plan? What the hell? I can't deal with them. You lost her daughter, so you're the official babysitter for all the grandmas. Got it, Vickers?"

Without another word, Paige stormed out to her car and headed toward San Clemente.

Back on the other side of the world, Nina's day passed slowly. She spent her first hour worrying about her mother. *She'll know what I've done and be absolutely frantic. Makes me feel really bad. But when I bring Darby home, she'll be okay.*

Finding the door to her room locked from the outside, Nina showered and then ate a few bites of fruit from the tray. She lifted a slice of an unfamiliar bread, but when she put it in her mouth, she couldn't swallow. Her plan hadn't included being held prisoner. Confident she'd find the door still locked, she stood up and tried it just in case. Doubts bit at her like African bees.

Maybe I'm in the wrong place. What if I screwed up?

Nina pushed against her stomach as it cramped and rolled. *What if I'm not even in Turkey? What if I am, but Darby's not?* When the door opened, her gut seized. Nina stepped back as a dark muscular man entered. Her nostrils filled with the smell of evil.

"I'm Berat. Your go-to-guy. I'll let you know when you have a date. My job is to get you what you need. Food, clothes, whatever. I'll also be your banker of sorts, keep your tips safe for you."

Goosebumps puckered Nina's skin. The obvious pleasure he derived from this power left Nina feeling dirty, but she met his piercing eyes and smiled. "When will I get to go out? I want to see the area, the culture, you know, do a bit of touristing."

"Not a chance." Nina cringed away from Berat's sneer. "You don't make a move without my permission."

"I volunteered. I want exotic work but didn't sign up to be a prisoner." Heat rose from Nina's chest and reddened her neck and face.

Berat looked down his nose. "Dress up. I'll be back for you. One hour."

The consequences of where she had put herself and what was about to happen pelted her like a rockslide. Nina stood, still and quiet, until he left the room and locked the door. Then she did what women throughout the world do every day in a universe of different contexts. She walked to the closet and decided what to wear.

The clothes hung in categories, dresses, blouses, and pants. Nina spoke to each outfit as she slid it across the bar. "Stupid, stupid. Doesn't matter what you wear. Nothing matters except finding Darby." She grabbed the first dress she had touched and threw it on the bed. Then she did as he told her. She dressed up.

Nina showered, curled her hair to drape over one shoulder, and applied the cosmetics she found in the bathroom. She brought her face close to the mirror. "You look like the walking dead." She picked up a large makeup brush, tapped it in the coppery blush, and used the color to bring herself to life. Then she sat down to wait.

Nina spun the gold band she had shifted from her left ring finger to her right. She didn't need to remove the ring and read the inside to remember what the inscription said. "For Better or Worse." *Keith, my darling, you have no idea how much worse.*

For her, time crept, but in actuality only one hour passed before Berat returned. Nina approached the door, fearful, but ready to do whatever necessary to find her daughter. When Berat said, "Let's go," she stepped forward but jerked back when he raised one latex gloved hand and blew into her face.

Her last conscious act was her own cry of alarm. "No, no drugs. He promised…"

PAT SPENCER

CHAPTER TWENTY-FIVE
Darby - Day Twelve - Wednesday, March 28

Darby's morning began the same as the previous one. As soon as she awoke, she rolled out of bed and hurried to the adjoining door. This morning when she touched the knob, it spun, and the door pulled away. When the girls came face-to-face, Darby's apprehension dissolved. Every time Berat took Amira away, she died a little, more afraid for Amira's fate than her own. When reunited, Darby felt like a lost family member had returned from a dark place. She clutched her friend as if to never let go again.

But when they broke the embrace, the girls returned to a routine of sorts, the only moments of normalcy they would enjoy. The same as the day before, Amira brewed tea. While sipping the Turkish blend, they shared their hopes and fears, bolstered each other's resolve to rise above whatever might happen.

"Darby, I could not go on without our time together."

"I feel the same. We've known each other only two days, but we're sisters." Darby moved her chair close to Amira so their knees touched. "We must escape. I couldn't hear your answer to Berat's question, but when I thought of what he might do to you, drugged or not…"

"Darby, what did they do to you after Berat took me away?"

"Nothing. I was in my room the entire day. Seda brought a tray filled with a ton of food. At first, I didn't understand." Darby

262

shrugged her shoulders. "Seemed weird but turned out to be the only food I got. Never saw another human being. Hours and hours, I tried to wait up for you, but I got so tired. Every time I fell asleep, I jerked awake." Darby took Amira's hands in hers. The friends sat, each softly praying in her native voice. When they finished, Darby said, "Amira, no one knows where we are. If we're going to get out, we must do it ourselves."

"How? Every room to which they take us, they lock us in. We can't even walk the hall alone. The only possibility is what Berat said. If he didn't have to drug us, we would earn a little freedom."

"Yesterday, how did you answer Berat?" Amira cowered. Darby tried to lift her friend's chin, but she wouldn't look up. "Will you tell me what they did to you?" She watched Amira bite her bottom lip and stare into her lap. "It's okay, my friend. You don't have to say."

"It is difficult to speak of. Very shameful. The thing I escaped from in my family, it happens here."

Darby swallowed twice in an anxious effort to dissolve the lump forming in her throat. When she looked into Amira's eyes, they were filled with tears. Darby wrapped her arms around her friend's shoulders, and the two girls cried together.

After a few moments, Amira caught her breath. "Yesterday, I declined the drug."

"Oh, Amira, so you were aware…" Darby shoulders shuddered when a chill ran down her back. "It kills me when I think how I stayed safe while you were being hurt. I should protect you."

"Darby, you have no way to protect me, nor I you. What you said earlier is our only prospect. We must break out."

"Amira, you were brave."

"No, I was not. I trembled the entire time, but how else will I search for possibilities?

"Did you find a way out?"

Amira nodded. "Perhaps, at least something we have not seen before."

"What? Tell me."

Amira scrutinized the room as though someone might sneak in to listen. "There is a reception area where the men enter. As Berat and I walked by, the door to the outside opened. I tripped myself and stumbled. Berat yanked my arm." Amira rubbed her shoulder. "He ripped it half out of its joint, but it was worth it."

"What did you see?"

"A concrete path leading to an outer gate. I saw the blue sky above it."

"A gate to the outside? The doors are probably locked to keep people out of the compound, but maybe it's not locked from inside. If we could get back there, do you think we could escape?"

"Berat knows I saw it. He raised his hand to slap me, but when I cried out, he held back."

"When he took you from your room, which way did you turn?" After Amira described the route, the girls sat deep in their own thoughts. And then, Darby asked again, "Amira, please tell me what they did to you so I'll be prepared."

Amira dug her nails into her palms. "Darby, they put me in another room, even more richly decorated than ours. Larger with huge couches, a bar, and…"

"No more, Amira, I don't need to know. I understand."

"We were prisoners in the dank cinderblock cells. Now, even though we are in lavish rooms, we are worse than prisoners. We are their slaves. Sometimes at night, I feel so dark and alone…

Darby, several times before you came, I thought I might kill myself."

"No, my friend. You can't do that. I wouldn't survive without you." Tears rolled down Darby's cheeks. "Today, when Berat takes me out, I'm going to watch for that door. So, I've decided not to be drugged."

"Oh, Darby. It is horrible and will be worse for you. I knew what to expect, I mean, my father…" Amira whispered, "You will remember everything…"

"I know, but we need to memorize the route, find flaws in how Berat handles us. Look for a weakness. It's the only way to develop an escape plan."

"But you are…" Amira stopped midsentence when interrupted by the clink of the outer door unlocking. In strutted the man they most dreaded.

"Good morning, ladies. I hope you slept well." Darby's nose flared at his vile voice. "Wear whatever you want. I'm bored with picking for you. Just make yourselves beautiful." Berat spun and walked away, then paused and sent the girls a nasty glare. "So, tell me ladies, how do you want it? Drugs or compliance?"

When both responded, "No drugs," his brows rose with amazement.

"I'll be back."

Darby and Amira dressed. Then Darby brushed her friend's long thick hair and French braided it so it hung down her back.

"I love it, Darby." Then she pointed to the closet. "Do the women at your college wear clothes such as those?"

"Heavens no. Only a few wear outfits this revealing, but they're not the quality of these. Student budgets, you know." Darby drew the lowcut V-neck up to her chin. "Less scanty and these could be gorgeous party clothes."

Their playacting broke apart when Berat reentered the room. "Change of plans. Amira, it's only you today."

Desperation covered their faces as Darby asked, "Why?"

Berat sneered. "Blondie, apparently you have a special admirer. Bought an exclusive with you. Only he hasn't appeared yet. Crazy. But you will stay in this room until we hear from him."

CHAPTER TWENTY-SIX
Nina - Day Thirteen - Thursday, March 29

Nina awakened multiple times during the night. Each time, unable to lie still, she rose, walked to the lattice covered window and peered into the courtyard. She searched for a sign to confirm she was closer to her daughter. But the scene never changed.

Shortly after sunrise, Nina's body recovered from the effects of the drugs. She awoke with a clear head, clear enough to realize what had happened. Not the details. But every woman recognizes the signs of intercourse even when she has no memory of the act. Her strongest urge was for a shower, hot and steamy. But no matter how hard she scrubbed, she still felt dirty deep within her pores. So, she filled the large jetted bathtub with scalding water and poured in liquid hand soap until it bubbled over the top. Lowering her aching body, the water burned away the revulsion but not the desperation.

I won't find Darby by sitting in this tub. Got to get out and look for her.

Certain they drugged her with Devil's Breath, Nina knew she'd acted like a mindless robot. Every time this happened, she would do their bidding but remember little, maybe nothing. If she was to rescue her daughter, she must stop the drugging.

Nina fretted over how long it would be until someone returned for her. Confident Berat wasn't aware she was there of her own

267

freewill, she wanted to explain. She needed to earn Berat's trust so he would allow her to move around without being scrutinized or drugged. A clear mind was necessary to find Darby.

Nina stood, walked to the closet and opened the door. *Hooker dresses.* She snarled at each outfit as she pushed it across the clothes bar. "Red hooker dress. Blue hooker dress." The third, a silver sheath dress was less revealing. *Nice, but a bit much for the breakfast hour.*

Next, she slid a flesh-colored top across the bar. Short in front, it would reveal a strip of her stomach but at least it was longer in the back to cover her hips. Nina removed the blouse and matching leggings from the hanger. *Not bad. I can pull this off. Now makeup.* She brushed gold shadow on her eyelids, followed by a layer of muted mauve. Then she blew her hair dry, slick and smooth. Nina assessed the effect in the full-length mirror. *Okay, you monster. Come back. I'm ready for you.*

When the key spun in the lock, remnants of the few bites of steak she'd been able to eat the night before rose in her throat. She choked it down and waited. But when Berat entered, his expression was so different it disarmed her. He appeared sheepish, like a boy doing wrong.

"I apologize. Screwed up, blowing the stuff in your face. Thought you were a different girl. Caught holy hell. Won't happen again."

"It better not." Nina relished this opportunity to put him on the defensive. "What's wrong with you? I'm not your prisoner. I'm here to work."

"Yeah, yeah, I know. Let's start over. I'll show you the compound. None of the girls are allowed in the restricted areas. But the longer you're here, the more freedom you'll earn. For now, let me know what you want. Chances are I'll be able to get it. There's a courtyard where the girls can go out, but only this side of the wall. You can eat meals in the dining room with the other girls. Or Seda, the old lady cook, will bring you food. Come now, I'll walk you around."

Berat escorted her down a long hall. As they walked, Nina paid close attention to her surroundings. Ceramic tiles with bright geometrical patterns reflected the clicking of their heels. They passed several doors with gold doorknobs and came to a huge carved door. When she paused, he told her that room was off limits. Further along the hall, a heavy white door opened into a large dining room.

Three women sat at a hand carved pecan table at least twelve feet long. Surrounded by a dozen chairs with insets of hunter green suede, it reminded Nina of the majestic dining room from the *Beauty and the Beast*. Uncertain what her next move should be, Nina searched each woman's face for a sign. Then with a graceful wave, the one with wavy cocoa-colored hair motioned for Nina to sit beside her. As soon as she pulled out the chair, the young woman introduced herself.

"My Afghani name is Palwasha. It means fresh grass. My father picked it because he loved the native grasses that flourished on our farm. Now they call me Alexa. Said my name must be sexy." Glints of gold sparkled in her brown eyes, matching the richness of the mass of hair piled atop her head.

Nina looked from one to the other. The women were striking. With platinum hair and high cheekbones, Vanessa was a true Norwegian beauty. Lin Su's dark almond-shaped eyes contrasted with her delicate porcelain complexion. Her hair flowed to her waist, the overhead light reflected off it as if it were polished onyx. After each introduced themselves, they compared backgrounds.

Vanessa told her story of a survival existence. She left her country after working the streets when her drug addicted parents kicked her out. While she expressed gratitude for her current position, Nina thought that given different circumstances, Vanessa might have had a career as a high fashion model.

Lin Su's voice grew mournful as she talked of her childhood in China. "When our father fell ill, his second wife banned my younger sister and I from our home. She very powerful, very mean. Everyone afraid of her. No other relative would take us in. We slept in a doorway, summer and winter. We ate what we could afford to buy but were always hungry. Once we almost got arrested for stealing fruit. We ran. Then, when I turned fifteen and my sister was only thirteen, a man offered the opportunity to get off the streets. He promised we would live in a large house with our own rooms and eat fresh food, wear nice clothes, work as housekeepers."

Nina sensed the ache Lin Su harbored in her soul. "I think you are very brave, caring for your sister. You did the best you could. From what we hear in the U.S., you might've died in prison just for stealing small amounts of food, even though you were starving."

"Yes, but we would have been together in our suffering and in our death." Tears flooded Lin Su's eyes. "She was so delicate, her spirit crushed from the shame…"

"Your sister? She's not with you?"

With a visible force of strength, Lin Su said, "They have forbidden me to speak of it, so I should not tell you this. I could be punished, lose privileges. My father named my sister Chunhua because she was born when the spring flowers bloom. Here they made her be called Connie. My precious sister," Lin Su lowered her gaze, "committed suicide after only one year, two days before her fourteenth birthday. Now I cry every time I see flowers, cut and placed in a bowl."

"I am so very, very sorry, Lin Su." The knot in Nina's throat grew as hard as a rock. "Every day must be so hard for you. And to keep going on, I don't know how you do it."

The women fell silent when a Turkish woman, shrunken and bent from age, entered and set before Nina a plate filled with fruit, crusty rolls, and American style scrambled eggs. Bile rose in Nina's throat at the thought of Balik's pesto eggs. Her hunger evaporated. She nudged her eggs to the side of the plate, then speared a melon ball with her fork but didn't eat.

When the woman returned with a fresh cup of coffee for Nina, Palwasha introduced her. "Nina, this is *Büyükanne* Seda. *Büyükanne* is Turkish for grandmother. We honor Seda with that title because she cares for us as if we are her family." The stooped woman tucked her head in deference.

Vanessa rolled her eyes. "That old bitty isn't my grandmother, and she's not yours. She's the cook."

Seda never looked up as she turned and left the room. "Vanessa, shut mouth. *Büyükanne* Seda is kind. Loves us, the way we love her."

Even though the door had closed, Nina doubted it protected Seda from Vanessa's hurtful words. "Lin Su, you're such a sap. Seda's a servant. I don't love her, and she doesn't love me."

"No one love you, Vanessa."

Nina broke the uncomfortable silence that followed. "Palwasha, how did you learn English? Your accent makes our language more interesting than how it is spoken in the United States."

"You are very kind, Nina." Her lips formed a bashful smile. "I studied hard in the schools of my home town of Rodat. My family was not poor before the war. We were farm people, but my father was successful. I attended classes until the Taliban bombed our town, destroyed all the schools. After that, parents feared more bombing and did not allow the children to gather to learn."

Vanessa let out an impatient sigh, but Palwasha ignored her and continued. "In Afghanistan, my family died in the bombing. I am the only one who survived. I stood out in the field, herding the goats, when terrorists drove by. The blast propelled me into a ravine, burned my arm, sprained my foot. Most of our family home, a two-story farmhouse, crumbled. The bedrooms on the second floor fell into the kitchen and burned. I hauled water from the well to stop the fire. The pain in my foot made me slow. Most of the house was destroyed. Our barn burned to the ground. Home to my crippled grandmother, my father, mother, two sisters and our animals, our farm was reduced to ruins. Our cats, cows, and horses, we even owned a herd of sheep and two border collies…all dead. The cluster of Afghan Fig trees that protected our home from the summer heat stood blackened by the fire. Fields of onion that once provided my family with a good income now made rows of soot."

Intent on Palwasha's story, Nina didn't notice when Lin Su smacked a metal nail file out of the bored Vanessa's hands until it skipped and clanked on the tile floor. The women glanced toward the noise, then ignored it.

Sorrow and guilt overcame Nina as she compared her privileged life to that of this young woman who lost her home and family, only to live in terror. "How did you survive?"

"With great amazement, I found canned goods that survived the blast by being thrown twenty yards into our burned garden. A blessing, but they did not last long. One morning, several days after I ate everything, I tried to walk to town, but the pain was too great. I was a few yards from the road when a man and woman drove by. They stopped and asked my name. I had a bad feeling about these people, so I told them my name was Louise. I don't think they believed me, so I was surprised when they helped me. They said they were going to town to deliver Red Cross supplies. They left me with a small box of food and bottled water. The woman said they would return the next day, bring medical supplies for my burns and swollen foot to the farmhouse, but they did not. Three, maybe four more days passed." Palwasha's voice cracked.

"When they returned, the man said there were no more boxes, but he gave me one water bottle and a pack of army rations. The woman used half the water to remove gravel and dirt from my burns. She wrapped my wounds in large bandages. I was grateful. Again, she said they would return, but they did not. I was starving, so thirsty my lips were split and infected. I lost much weight. My skirt kept slipping off one hip. But the swelling left my foot, so I decided to try to walk to town. My father had made a walking stick, carved it by hand. I dug through the rubble but still hadn't found it when the man and woman returned. This time, they brought no supplies, but offered to drive me to where they said the Red Cross had set up a waystation in town. I hesitated. I feared I could not trust them, but temptation weakened me. Perhaps I could get to my uncle's home in Kabul, one hundred and eighty kilometers away. I had nothing, no home, no family, not even a blanket. I ate everything I could find, but when gone, their promise became too much to resist."

Palwasha described how she climbed into the backseat of the jeep, believing the couple would take her to the bus station. "I cursed my own stupidity when the man left the road and drove into the desert. I asked to get out, said I could walk. He ignored me and drove more rapidly over the sandy path. I tried to open the door, but the handle had been removed. I put all my weight against it, hoping it would give way, but of course, it did not. When the sky darkened, the man stopped in the middle of the desert and ripped me from the car. The woman only sat there. I called to her to help me, but she looked away. Then two men stepped from another car that I didn't notice at first. Its lights were off, it was almost invisible in the starless night. I kicked and screamed. The larger man held me and the other blew something in my face. I remember nothing else until awakening here."

When Palwasha finished speaking, the room fell silent. Nina wanted to comfort her, but everything she thought to say felt trite. She dipped a corner of the bread into yogurt and took a bite but remained too distracted to chew. Nina's thoughts swirled and collided with each other, leaving her lightheaded. The bread became soggy in her mouth. It caught in her throat.

Seeing Nina struggle, Palwasha asked, "Are you alright?"

Nina lifted the napkin to wipe her mouth. "Your story... The world is so messed up." She raised her coffee cup and then set it back down. "Then I think of Lin Su's story, her sister... My only daughter's been stolen from me. Having you both confide in me as though we're family, I'm overwhelmed."

Lin Su's brown eyes filled with sadness. "Nina. I am sorry for your loss. Your pain is great. In life and in death, I am connected to my sister, but you and your daughter, she is part of you."

The women were silent as each one grappled with their emotions. After a few moments Nina said, "Palwasha, are most of the women here of their own freewill or forced the way you were?"

Before Palwasha responded, Vanessa laughed. "Not all sign up for this hitch, like the new girl, the one they have to drug all the time. You know, the screaming and kicking surfer blonde…"

"That's my…" Her words caught in her throat when Lin Su dug her nails deep into Nina's thigh. When she raised her head, Palwasha was pointing her fork tongs at Vanessa.

As Vanessa pushed away from the table, she snarled. "Enough of these touching family stories. I'm out of here."

The three remaining women sat in silence until Palwasha stood, walked to the door in the back of the room, and knocked. "*Büyükanne* Seda, may we have more of your wonderful Turkish coffee?"

Nina stared at the door. Her new friend had not even tried to open it. Nina understood this meant the door was always locked and not a possible escape route. Confirming her suspicion, the key made a clinking noise in the lock seconds before the door swung open and the elderly woman appeared in the doorway.

"Thank you, *Büyükanne* Seda. Will you read our coffee grounds?" asked Lin Su. The old woman poured thick black coffee into each cup, gasping when residue from the bottom of the pot splattered onto Nina's saucer. Then smiling at the spill, Seda rubbed Nina's shoulder with her free hand.

Lin Su had never seen Seda touch any of the women. "*Büyükanne*, what happened?"

The corners of Seda's eyes crinkled, the wrinkles sinking even deeper. "Good fortune. Troubles go soon." The women watched the old woman's back as Seda returned to the kitchen. The clang of the door locking rang in Nina's ears.

Then Lin Su leaned in and spoke in a hushed voice. "I dig my nails in to stop you. You about to say, the kicking and screaming girl, you think she is your daughter?"

"I do."

Palwasha's eyes grew large. "Nina, you came here to rescue her?"

"Of course, she did," said Lin Su. "They are one. We will help you."

"Help? Lin Su, you are a crazy person. We would get caught. You know what could happen." Palwasha looked from Lin Su to Nina. Not hearing the agreement she expected, Palwasha let out a groan. "Okay, what can I do?"

"I am Thelma," said Lin Su. "You are Louise. We blow this place." They threw their heads back and laughed, sealing their conspiracy pact. But the smiles disappeared when Berat walked in the door and motioned for Palwasha to come with him.

In the U.S., Detective Paige Vickers vowed not to rest until Nina and her daughter were safe. But once again, she made herself comfortable behind Wasden's desk and violated protocol by shuffling through his papers until she came to a photo of two Middle Eastern men. The name, Durson Askoy, was written below the face of one. She recognized him from the Belaruse. Below the second, Berat Çoban. Intent on memorizing the features of the men, Paige jumped out of the chair as Wasden caught his sleeve on the doorknob and plowed into the wall.

"Hey, Boss. Did Boutros track you down? Says he texted twice. Since you didn't get back to him, he called here. They gave him to me because he's dead set on talking to someone on the Richards case."

"Because you just happened to be sleeping at my desk again?"

"Boss, we've got an issue. Where have you been that's so all fired important?"

"Pantages. We caught the shooters."

"No one around here said a thing."

"Word's not out yet. Happening right now. SWAT team has them surrounded in a rat shack near the post office. Only got a sec."

Paige watched him assess the rearrangement of documents on his desk. Braced for another upbraiding, she was taken aback when he spoke civilly. "What's your issue?"

"It's our favorite grandma. Boutros said they traced one, and only one, IP address on the Sugar House website. Guess who it belongs to?"

"Vickers, you got to be shitting me."

"No, boss, wouldn't do that. They opened an account, purchased more than a hundred and eighteen thousand dollars-worth of Bitcoin."

"They? Whose they? I thought you meant Darby's grandma."

"Sally and her accomplices, the two friends I told you about. The ones that moved in after Nina disappeared. Anyway, the three of them downloaded the program to access the dark web. Sally dug up enough info to find Sugar House. I'm telling you, boss, these aren't your average grandmas. Here's the part that might go either good or bad, depending upon what happens next."

"Vickers, what could be worse than three grandmas on the dark web meddling in our case?"

"They spent every coin they put in their wallet."

"Spent it? What'd they buy?"

"Time… They bought time with Darby."

"Holy shit, Vickers."

"The good part is that for the days they purchased, Darby's safe. The part that could go bad is when no one shows up, or arranges transport, to use the purchased time."

"If the FBI traced their IP address, the Sugar House website manager can do it as well. Do these old gals realize this isn't eBay they're messing with?"

"Don't know, Boss. What are you gonna do?"

"What am *I going to do?*" He spat out his words between his clenched teeth. "Vickers, I'll tell you what I'm going to do. Nothing. A big fat nothing. I told you, the three grandmas are yours." As he pivoted on his heel and left the office, he muttered, "Do I need to put it in writing for you?"

Across the ocean, after Berat took Palwasha away, Nina and Lin Su still sat in the dining room. Neither woman said a word as they sunk into private thoughts of what was happening to their friend. Nina locked onto the snippet of blue sky she could see through the lattice work that covered every window. She pulled her gaze away when Lin Su spoke, her voice low and secretive. "If the girl Vanessa talked about is your daughter, it will be difficult for us to get to her. The children are behind the wall."

"There must be a way," whispered Nina.

"We will find it, but very dangerous. Our secret. No talk in front of anyone but Palwasha, especially not backstabber Vanessa.

Cannot trust her." Lin Su glanced around the room and raised her voice to normal. "We go into the courtyard. Enjoy a little contentment."

Nina started to say she couldn't imagine contentment while her daughter remained imprisoned but swallowed her words. There was no need to say what Lin Su already understood.

In the courtyard, they paced the wall that separated them from the rest of the world. Lin Su softly said, "I was brought here two years ago."

Nina shook her head. "No more. We'll all escape."

"I learned to appreciate the freedom in this courtyard and not despair. I accept my fate. For you, we look for a door left open, a weakness in the wall…" Nina's eye's widened. Reading her mind, Lin Su said, "Razor wire. No one climbs. We find another way."

CHAPTER TWENTY-SEVEN
Darby - Day Thirteen - Thursday, March 29

The sun shining through the window awakened Darby. She slipped into her robe and hurried to the adjoining door. The spicy fragrance of herbal tea filled her lungs. Amira greeted Darby with a warm smile and poured the steaming tea into two cups. As new best friends, they treasured their time to talk and share.

This morning, however, Darby was agitated. She shook with rage. She had to hold the cup with both hands to keep it from spilling. "Why did they kidnap me? I'm nothing but trouble. I fight them on everything. Why me?"

Amira looked up at Darby with sad brown eyes but continued to sit in silence.

"I don't want the drugs, but then I scream, kick and hit, try to run. Then they drug me again. I hate being helpless."

"Darby, truly, you do not want to know what happens. The drug saves you from..."

"But I have no control..." Darby licked the salty tears cascading on her cheeks. "I can't bear it." She choked on noisy sobs. When she slammed her cup down with a bang, the tea jumped straight up and leapt over the edge. "We'll break out, escape together."

"Darby, the men watch every minute, especially you. They will never let you get away."

Darby stood and paced back and forth. "Why do they want me? I'll never cooperate."

"They drug you, so you will. You are valuable."

"Why?"

"Do you not understand?" When Darby shook her head, Amira continued. "Look at you. The rest of us are shades of dark…eyes, hair, skin. You are golden, pale skin and sun-bleached hair, eyes the color of a summer sky."

"But you're all beautiful, exotic…"

"However, we are more the same than different. You are the gold in a basket filled with silver."

"Amira, this is so wrong. We're slaves. If we could talk privately to the other women, we could join forces."

"Darby, not all are angry."

"How can that be true? What could be worse than this?"

"Perhaps living in the streets, constantly in fear?" Amira looked away. "Or being used by your father or him selling you to his friends? Some are grateful to be alive, fed, not tortured. For others, our past lives, we…" Remorse filled her eyes. "I foresaw freedom, a home and family, maybe a career. Now, I don't know what will become of me. I have given up." Amira's eyes reddened. "I no longer pray for a husband to cherish me, and children…"

"No, no. Don't give up. There has to be a way." But even though Darby encouraged Amira to stay strong, she recognized elements of truth in Amira's words.

"My first roommate, Isabella Costa, kindness of an angel. She lived a rich life as a student at your University of California in Los Angeles before being kidnapped and brought here." Darby's eyebrows rose as Amira continued. "All possibilities for an amazing future."

"I may have crossed her path, even shared a class. Is she still here?"

"No, Darby. That is the great sadness. Isabella said suicide is a mortal sin within the teachings of her religion, but that this hell is greater than what she would face in death." A tear rolled down Amira's face. "She was taken to the United States for a week with a very rich man. She never returned. I believe Isabella may have taken her own life."

Darby swallowed the lump in her throat. "Amira, you wouldn't, would you? Kill yourself?"

"Many days I feel as though I have already died a hundred times, but perhaps, I still have a glimmer of hope?"

"Amira, someone will rescue me."

"Who?"

"My mom won't leave me here."

"It is true women in America are bestowed more power than in the Middle East. But still, your mother is only a woman."

"But she's smart, ferocious. We have resources, money. She'll call the FBI, CIA, hire someone. She'll come. And when she does, you'll come with me. I won't leave you behind."

CHAPTER TWENTY-EIGHT
Nina - Day Fourteen - Friday, March 30

Nina lay awake reliving the long and ugly evening. *I'll do anything to free Darby, but what I'm doing is not working.* As much as she appreciated Palwasha and Lin Su, they were in the same powerless position. Nina chided herself for wasting time walking the wall.

Ridiculous. Did you expect a hole to appear where we'll slip right out?

From the bed, Nina peered into the night. *Wretched, endless darkness.* She pushed the covers off, then yanked them back up. Her eyes grew dry and heavy as she waited to join her new friends for breakfast. Finally, when a glimmer of sun peeked through the corner of the window, she rolled out of bed and dressed.

As she entered the dining room, even the weight of all her worry didn't keep a smile from forming when she saw Lin Su squirm like a happy puppy. Nina turned to Palwasha for a hint, but she was busy stirring her coffee. However, Nina didn't have to wait long for the news. The instant she sat, Lin Su babbled under her breath. "Man from America come tonight. Not first visit. Vanessa say he is vice president of something important. Brag because he requested her again. But you need to be with him. We bribe Vanessa. She wench, do anything for money." Lin Su nodded toward Palwasha. "We give her lots so she will play sick.

Stick finger down throat and vomit when he arrives. He likes blonde ladies, so we think they will pick you next."

"But what if they don't?"

"Not many blondes here. Only Vanessa and you."

"And my daughter…"

Nina opened her mouth to ask another question, but when two new and younger women entered, an unexpected sadness silenced her. It hadn't occurred to her she wouldn't be the last to be abducted. Too distraught to wait for introductions, Nina returned to her bedroom. *Those poor girls, and their mothers. Where are their mothers? What are they thinking?* Nina closed her puffy eyes and pressed her hands to her face. *I know what they're feeling.* Her eyes filled with tears. She blinked and scolded herself. *No time for that. Doesn't help. Think…think.*

She allowed herself a tiny smile and a nugget of hope. *Maybe Lin Su is right.* Nina stood and walked to the window. The sun looked brighter, the sky clearer. She whispered, "This is my chance."

Perhaps he's vice president of a large corporation, with connections, funds to buy Darby away from these animals. Nina returned to sit in the chair. *Or maybe I can convince him to contact the American Embassy, or the CIA.*

Nina watched the seconds, then minutes tick by on the gold clock while she decided what to do next. In the scenario Lin Su described, the decision to replace Vanessa would occur at the last minute. She'd be prepared, makeup, hair, ready for her chance.

As she smoothed blush across her cheeks, Nina decided that she needed to gain his sympathy, make him want to help her. While patting on shimmering eyeshadow, she couldn't fathom how she could make this happen.

Vice president or not, this man's still a perverted scumbag.

As Nina wound the final blonde strand around the curling iron, she concluded bribing him was her best option. While she pondered how she might access her bank account, smoke rose off the curl. She yanked the hair from the iron and tucked the burnt strand under the other curls. But when she stood to check her appearance in the full-length mirror, she was repulsed. She swallowed the acid rising from her throat. *How can I tell what kind of man he really is?* Nina moved closer to the mirror, searched her own face for a clue. *I can't even see the kind of woman I thought I was.*

Nina closed her eyes to hold back the tears. When she opened them, she watched the scorching sun sink behind the courtyard wall. Hours passed, but she didn't give up. She sat, careful not to smudge her makeup or muss her hair. Occasionally her head bobbed and her eyelids flickered closed, but she jerked herself awake and waited until the blackness faded into a morning haze. *No one came for me. Did they take another blonde? The only other blonde...*

Only then did Nina despair. She couldn't even cry.

CHAPTER TWENTY-NINE
Darby - Day Fourteen - Friday, March 30

The head of his Secret Service detail held the door open, but the man he was paid to protect didn't even acknowledge him. And he continued to ignore Roger when he said, "I'll be outside this door." But when Jackson Connors, the American vice president, stepped through the doorway, he paused. She was more than Russo promised, more beautiful than the others, but her innocence made him uneasy.

When first invited to the Belaruse, he declined, well aware it would cause him nothing but trouble given his position. But Morty, his friend and secretary of defense, wouldn't shut up about the place so he'd said just one time. He always enjoyed a good hand of high stakes poker. The money, the risk, it excited him, so the vice president kept going back. When Russo told him of the other services available, Jackson turned him down. However, when Russo learned he and Monty traveled to Turkey several times a year, he upped the enticements, and they succumbed. He knew they shouldn't. The potential to ruin their lives was great, but in the end, they were weak.

From where she stood near the window, violet and copper rays of the setting sun framed her body. Her hair cascaded down her back in a waterfall of gold. He shifted from one foot to the other.

Unease crept through his body, even greater than the first time, but he couldn't put a name to why.

She looked in his general direction, careful to avoid his eyes. He expected her to come to him, but except for a small tremble of her shoulders, she didn't move. "You seem afraid of me?" When she turned away, he said, "Of all the guys, I'm not the one you should fear."

She raised her eyes but still did not look at his face. He lowered his voice. "Belle, I'm Jackson." When she didn't respond, he put his hands in his pockets and fidgeted with his keys. "Call me Jack. My friends do, and I think we'll be good friends." He waited, but she still didn't even glance his way. "Belle is a pretty name." He jangled his keys, then stopped. "Like the princess in *Beauty and the Beast*. I took my daughter when…"

"My name isn't Belle. It's Darby… My name is Darby."

"I apologize. Berat said Belle."

"He makes me say Belle, but I'm Darby Richards."

"Darby, it is. I prefer that name. Has a certain strength. Darby Richards, may I offer you a glass of champagne or wine?" He studied the plate of sugared figs and chocolate covered strawberries, then lifted a decanter from the ice. "I can tell you're nervous."

When she backed up a step, he rolled his shoulders forward. He was accustomed to trying to lean down to the height of others. His eyes crinkled at the corners. People usually reacted warmly to his lopsided smile, but he could see the fear on her face. And his hand quivered ever so slightly as he ran it through the gray at his temples.

He selected strawberries and light crispy wafers, placed them on two small plates. He felt her eyes on his back as he walked to the coffee table and set them down. Her eyes never left him as he returned to the bar. He stood unmoving, with his back to her. His voice was rumbly, like a summer storm. "I'll pour the champagne." Jack lifted the glasses and tilted one toward the couch. "Please, let's sit and get to know each other."

Darby complied with his request to sit but remained as silent as a cold and starless night. She turned toward the strawberries while watching his every move from the corner of her eye. He fidgeted with his glass, then sat beside her. When his shoulder brushed against hers, she pulled away.

"You're not Turkish. Where are you from?"

"California."

The thought of something familiar, something he'd heard, niggled in the back of his mind. Unable to identify the cause of his unease, he continued. "Have you worked here long?"

"No."

His palms were sweaty. When he smoothed his khaki pants legs, his hands left damp prints.

"Am I your first client?"

"I don't think so."

At a loss as how to respond, he shook his head and sat silent for a few moments.

"May I ask how old you are?"

"Eighteen."

"No. You can't be. My daughter's eighteen. You look different in your photos."

"I haven't seen any photos. Do you have one?"

"No, on the website. I thought you were older. Maybe ten years older?"

Darby shivered.

Jack started to take a drink but set the glass back down. *What am I doing here with this young girl?*

They sat in silence. He folded his napkin into small squares as she stared into her lap. "Will you tell me about yourself?" She looked up, and then back at her hands, clenched in her lap. He was still chastising himself, but when she finally spoke, he turned and focused on her face.

"A fuzzy memory. Parts are missing. I think I was an actress wearing an evening dress, short with a full skirt. An older man made me spin, faster and faster. The skirt swirled too high." Darby still didn't look up from her hands, balled into fists in her lap. "When I woke up, someone had put me back in my room, in bed, but I was naked. The men must've taken my clothes, the ones I had on before…"

Jack's baritone voice diminished to a whisper. "What do you mean, when you woke up?"

"You know, they drugged me."

"Are you sure?" *If she's telling the truth, I'm even a bigger scum than I thought.*

Jack ran his hands through his hair. He no longer tried to look her in the eyes, but Darby continued to tell her story. "They drug me because I fight to escape. In the cell, every time they opened the door, I tried to break out."

"Cell? What cell? The rooms here are the quality of a five-star hotel."

She looked around the room. When she spoke, her voice was so soft that he had to lean toward her. His shoulders slumped, as Darby described the hours of drugged confusion, in and out of consciousness, never knowing how long the men kept her captive in the cinderblock prison. He hung his head, winced, and looked away as she described the moldy toilet and how dirty she felt because she had no way to clean herself. When she described the mashed potatoes she'd been given while locked in the cell, he picked up a strawberry with a napkin and awkwardly held it out to her. She refused to take it. "Berat wants me to be grateful."

When Darby quit talking, he looked at her, kind but questioning. "Are you telling the truth? Russo said the women are here of their own volition. The money, clothes, parties…"

"I only know one other girl. Amira ran from an abusive father. Then the man she paid to help her escape to the U.S., he sold her. I was kidnapped, stolen away from my mother, my life…"

"Oh my God. What have I done? Sugar House promotes itself as an escort service, but kidnapping and drugging?"

"They call this place Sugar House? That's disgusting."

"The whole thing is disgusting. My colleagues and I have used Sugar House when we travel in the Middle East, on business. We were told, oh my God, it doesn't matter what we were told…"

Darby finally looked up and met his gaze. "Your daughter is eighteen? Like me?"

"All I can think of is what if this happened to her? It happened to you. It could happen to any young woman."

"Your daughter's mother? Where is she?"

His brow furrowed. "She died five years ago. Car crash…"

"My father died of cancer. He'd never have let this happen." She trembled. Silent tears outlined her cheeks. "I need my dad."

He put his arm around Darby's shoulder. "Of course, you do."

"I want to tell you something." She bit her lip. "I know…" Her chest expanded when she took a deep breath. "I know who you are."

The blood drained from his face.

290

"I watched television, read online news before…"

"You know who I am?"

She nodded.

"Darby, we must get you out of here, back to the United States, to your family."

She nodded weakly. Her head seemed to wobble, then she sunk back against the couch.

"Darby, are you okay? We're out of time. Berat will come back any minute. Go in the bedroom and stay there. I have to figure out what to do." She stood and straightened herself to full height. He thought she was trying to look stronger, braver.

"You're going to leave me here, aren't you?" Her lower lip quivered.

"No, no, I promise. I can't walk out with you right now, today. I need a plan, but I'll return for you."

He reached out to comfort her, but she recoiled. Feeling the weight of his guilt, he pushed himself up from the couch and watched her march into the bedroom and shut the door.

She thinks I've cast her aside.

CHAPTER THIRTY
Nina - Day Fifteen - Saturday, March 31

At the thought of food, acid reflux burned its way up Nina's throat. She gagged it back and headed to the dining room. The last thing she wanted to do this morning was eat, but her discomfort was nothing compared to her need to get to Lin Su. Her friend would know why she was not taken to the American man. Nina's thoughts gave life to her worst fear. *As the only other American blonde, Darby must have been chosen instead.*

When she entered the dining room, every sound amplified in her ears. In what seemed like slow motion, everyone looked her way. An unfamiliar woman smiled. Nina couldn't bring herself to smile back. Lin Su lifted a cup of dark Turkish coffee and nodded for Nina to sit beside her.

In an uncharacteristic moment of friendliness, Vanessa introduced the new woman. Lin Su's eyes rolled as Vanessa gushed over the party she and Zoya attended two nights before. Zoya bragged that the rugged men were as handsome as movie stars. When she described the excitement of the drugs, alcohol, and money, Nina clasped her hand over her own mouth. She wanted to take Zoya aside to talk about the things her mother should have taught her.

When Vanessa launched into an even more vivid description of their night, Nina looked from one woman to the next while waiting for Vanessa to shut up. Lin Su's face forecasted important news, and for Nina, the conclusion of Venessa's story couldn't come fast enough.

"Zoya, enough of this chatter. Another big night tonight." Vanessa stood and winked at Lin Su. "Since I was sick last night, now I need to sleep the day away."

The moment Vanessa and Zoya were out of view, Lin Su spoke in a hushed tone. "I found out…"

Palwasha interrupted with a cheerful greeting. "*Büyükanne* Seda, you brought more of your amazing coffee. You are our darling grandmother."

The old woman smiled but remained silent. Steam rose off the cups as she filled them with coffee. Seda stopped and placed her hand, knobby from arthritis, in the center of Nina's back. Lin Su faked a pout. "Seda, grandmother to us all, you love Nina better than the rest of us."

Tiny Seda stood eye-to-eye with the seated women. When she leaned in, her well-cushioned body folded around Nina's shoulder, her lips at Nina's ear. In her strong Turkish accent, she whispered, "And love your daughter as well."

Nina fought waves of dizziness as Seda slipped away toward the kitchen. She shook her head to clear her thoughts, then called out to Seda's retreating back. "Do you know something?" Nina gripped the table to stop the room from spinning. She braced herself to stand, then scurried to the kitchen door but was too late. The knob wouldn't turn. She tapped, but the door remained closed and locked.

Lin Su motioned to Nina to sit between her and Palwasha. "Come back. I have the scoop." The three pulled their chairs to face each other in a tight circle. "I know why you were not chosen." Nina nodded as Lin Su's words confirmed her fears. "Last night, they pick your daughter."

Palwasha covered her mouth to stifle a gasp. Nina's jaw twitched. The movement rippled down her body until she shook with rage.

"No, no. Not such a bad thing," said Lin Su. "Two things good. First, big blow up last night. Berat in deep trouble. Big boss say Darby must stay in her room." Lin Su lowered her voice. "Also it is good because this important American man she with, I find out he is the one we always wonder why he receives better treatment than the rest, and with the most secrecy. He is Vice President of the United States of America."

"Lin Su, that's impossible. Our leaders don't travel alone. A Secret Service detail escorts them everywhere. They're watched every minute."

"He does not come alone. A very big man, I mean really big, dressed in a black suit, is always with the vice president. He checks the halls, the rooms, everything. Very serious."

"Lin Su, that can't be true. Just a rumor." Nina shook her head. "Our vice president would never come to a place like this."

Palwasha whispered, "Maybe he will help her."

Nina smiled kindly at her friends. *If only they were right.*

"Maybe she told him who she is," said Lin Su.

"I don't think so," said Palwasha. "Berat drugs her because she fights. She wouldn't be able to tell him."

Nina interrupted. "I'm telling you, it's not him. Must be vice president of something else. Perhaps a corporation?"

The three friends sat in dismal silence, searching each other's faces, hoping the other would come forth with an idea. Then a smile lit Lin Su's face. "Word is out he thinks Vanessa still sick, from upchuck, you know. So, we only need to figure out a way for you to be with him tonight, not your daughter. Then you tell him. When he knows, he must help."

Lin Su lifted her cup and swirled the thick muddy sediment. "Make your wishes, ladies. Of course, we all wish the same thing." In solidarity, the women swallowed their last sips and turned the cups upside down.

"Okay, flip cups up." Lin Su squinted. "No need Seda to read these grinds. Everyone gets their wish. All grinds created favorable patterns." Lin Su pushed away from the table. "Except you, Palwasha. Grinds on side of your cup…negative." Scurrying like a tiny mouse, Lin Su stopped at the door. "Maybe you have bad hair day." Lin Su ignored the glare Palwasha shot down her nose. "I go now to visit my sources. Will bring you important information soon." Lin Su disappeared into the hall.

"Do not worry. I do not know how, but she always finds out."

Nina could not tolerate the wait. Rather than returning to her own room, she broke the rules. She wandered the halls, feigning aimlessness as she scrutinized every window and door. Everything looked the same. As Nina again drew close to the dining room, she hesitated. Amid scraping and thumping noises emerged hushed voices of men speaking Turkish.

Willing herself invisible, she hugged the wall as she turned in. At the far end of the room, the kitchen door stood open providing Nina with a clear line of sight to the street. A delivery truck pulled up and parked at the curb. Two men unloaded boxes and placed them on a metal dolly. The younger man tipped it back, grunted, and heaved it over the single step. Nina's hopes soared when no one closed the door behind him.

Seda's gentle voice deepened into commands as she directed the process. The boxes of fruits and vegetables being delivered held everyone's attention. After the men stacked the boxes on the kitchen counters, one pushed the dolly back to the truck and filled it again with larger crates.

Transfixed by the open door, Nina watched the men roll the loaded dolly through the kitchen, in her direction. She waited even though she knew she shouldn't. But when the old woman followed the burley men into the dining room, Seda's scowl sent Nina rushing out.

Nina darted through the hall and turned sharply at the exit to the courtyard. She closed the door behind her and leaned against it. Her heart pounded as though it would break free from her chest. Nina sucked air, not from the run, but from fear Seda would report her snooping. As her heartbeat slowed, and no one broke through the door, Nina sighed with relief. However, she moved gingerly, aware someone might still burst through and grab her. As she paced at the base of the wall, for the first time she noticed a difference. No razor wire tangled in the vines. *Why is this part less secure?*

As Nina inspected it, she remembered Lin Su had said the children were held on the opposite side of the compound. *Could it be that easy? Just over this wall?* At both corners, the wire created an insurmountable barrier, but in between were only spikes to prevent the birds from nesting.

Nina stretched every muscle and tendon in an effort to reach the top. She wasn't even close. She walked the length of the wall again and searched for a toehold, any imperfection in the plaster to help her climb. Pretending to appreciate the flowers and shrubs, Nina shrugged off the creepy feeling of being secretly observed.

And then she saw two black boxes that could hold cameras tucked under the rooftop eaves. She stopped and waited, but no one came.

Still worried that someone watched, Nina strolled to a large potted plant and rubbed a leaf between two fingers. She acted casual as she compared the size of the pot to the height of the wall. She judged it sufficient. If she stood on it, she could reach the top. After a final covert look, she clamped on and put her back into pulling the pot toward the inner wall. It didn't move. She shifted to the other side. In the stance of an NFL linebacker, she grunted as her body hit the pot. Her arms held strong, but it still didn't budge. She put her shoulder against it and shoved until her thighs cramped, and she fell to her knees.

Nina pushed away from the pot to stand. She brushed grains of concrete from her hands but froze as a baby's cry floated over the wall. Then it was gone. She bowed her head at the memory of the five-year-old girl and her baby sister pictured on the same dark website as Darby. Her chin quivered, a tear escaped her eye. Shoulders slumped, Nina turned and left the courtyard.

She walked to her room, down the middle of the hall, with no concern for who might see her. Her thoughts, like L.A. smog, hung foul in her mind, ready to lay the blame. *Who allowed the world to go so bad?*

With no memory of how, Nina arrived at her room. With heavy feet and heart, she lumbered to the chair. She collapsed and sat, appalled by the ways she'd come up short. Exhausted and heavy with guilt, Nina struggled to hold her eyes open. Just before drifting off to sleep, she whispered. "I've failed you, Darby. I'm so very sorry."

When her neck relaxed and her head fell toward her chest, Nina awoke with a jerk. One glance at the gold clock cleared her mind. It was time to go back and meet Lin Su and Palwasha for lunch.

Nina headed down the hall, unsure if what she felt was excitement or dread. Engrossed in her thoughts, she jumped when Lin Su popped out from a side door.

"Sh." Lin Su put her finger to her lips. "Keep walking. Too quiet here. Can't hide what I must tell to you."

Nina's heart thumped against her ribcage as they made a sharp left into the dining room.

"Good, only Palwasha here. Not snotty Vanessa. I told you our tea leaves are positive this morning."

Lin Su led the way to the serving table covered with traditional Turkish foods. Nina waited as Palwasha filled her bowl with red lentil soup. She fidgeted when Lin Su paused in front of the baklava and kadayif. In a raised voice, Lin Su said, "Our *Büyükanne* Seda, she made us special desserts. She love us a lot." Then ever so quietly, Lin Su turned to Nina. "Big news. My source say your daughter…" Lin Su whispered even softer. "Many hours purchased. No one know who or when they are coming, but tonight, Darby is safe. Stay in her room."

"Thank God. We must rescue her before they come. How long do we have?"

"Not sure. Two days? Maybe more? More than one hundred thousand dollars paid."

"Is this normal?"

"No, no. Never normal. The boss upset about not knowing the buyer. But your daughter, she is safe for a while. Coffee grinds never wrong. Positive outcomes for our wishes."

When the tremor of Nina's hands increased, her plate clattered to the table. As her vision filled with spots of light, her knees weakened, and she swayed backwards. Palwasha reached out to steady her. As the two friends lowered her into a chair, Lin Su took advantage of their closeness to whisper in Nina's ear.

"Second good wish come true. Powerful American, I right, you say I am wrong. I tell you he is Vice President of the United States of America."

Nina squinted at Lin Su, still disbelieving.

"Yes, Nina. I am correct." Lin Su nodded happily. "You with him tonight, with Vice President of America. He asked for your daughter again, but Darby is protected. Everyone crazy because of it, the purchase of her time. It scare them because no one contacted them about coming here. No one say to deliver your daughter somewhere else. Big chaos, so they keep her in her room."

"She's in her room? Safe?"

Lin Su's head bobbled excitedly. "Yes, Nina. Especially because Berat screw up the night before, they are afraid to not have her available in case big money guy shows up unannounced. So, vice president is not going with Vanessa because of upchuck. Too embarrassing. You with him. You tell him. He will help save your daughter."

The women fell silent. Sweat beaded on Nina's forehead and upper lip. Palwasha dipped a white linen napkin into the water pitcher. She gently wiped Nina's face until a creak from the kitchen door commanded their attention. The fragrance of fresh roasted coffee beans preceded Seda into the room. Mimicking the star of her favorite spy movie, Lin Su watched her every move. She waited for Seda to leave and close the door behind her before speaking. "Nina, you go to room. Rest, prepare. I bring you fresh lunch in one hour."

Once back in her bedroom, Nina worried that the nights of troubled sleep had affected her ability to think. She tried to nap. Sleep evaded her. Her mind churned with possibilities, good and bad. As she sank into the haze of a troubled dream, a light tap startled her. Before she rose to answer, Lin Su slipped inside.

"Lunch for you, Nina. You must eat, be ready for anything that happen."

Nina walked to the table where Lin Su placed the silver sini holding small dishes of Turkish meats and cheeses. Before Nina could object, Lin Su said, "You have no appetite. No matter, eat anyway."

From the tray, Lin Su picked up a narrow glass with a fluted ridge and held it up to the light. "This special. *Büyükanne* Seda say only for you." As Lin Su lifted the milky liquid to Nina's lips, she pulled away. "Do not worry. *Büyükanne* say you not able to rest, so she send you raki. Lion's Milk. Eat a few bites, drink milk, then take a small sleep. Be ready for tonight."

Nina sipped. It tasted similar to unsweetened licorice. She never liked the flavor, but she drank it because Seda wanted her to.

"Good girl. You rest now. When you wake, you get ready. My source say vice president, he come early today. Very unusual, no one know why. I will set the alarm so you have time to be pretty."

Nina emptied the glass and laid across the bed. As her head came to rest upon the pillow, the knots in her neck dissolved. Her fingers relaxed, releasing the fists she hadn't even realized she'd made. A foggy sleep shut down her brain.

When the alarm sounded, the hot yellow sun hung low in the sky, about to descend behind the courtyard wall. Lin Su's words flooded back to her. The room was warm, she was feverish. *A cool shower will take care of this.*

Nina's hands trembled as she slid the curling iron through her hair. But by the time she put the finishing touches on her makeup, her nerves had steadied, and she was ready. She stood before the full-length mirror. Hair, makeup, even the dress, everything looked perfect, yet her image repulsed her. She turned away, sat in the brocade chair and waited for Berat. The clock ticked passed eight. "Doesn't mean something is wrong," she told herself. She calmed her nerves by blaming Lin Su for being wrong about the time.

Nina walked to the mirror. She smoothed the clingy dress and checked her hair and makeup for a second time. Careful not to undo the look she'd achieved, she remained standing in the center of the room until darkness covered the entire courtyard. *Something's wrong. Lin Su was positive he'd come early.*

Nina was about to sit down when she heard the familiar clink of the lock. Berat leaned around the half open door. "Follow me. Now."

She scurried to keep up. A few steps down the hall she noticed one tiny corner of a plastic bag protruding from his back pocket. *I've seen him with those before. And the man in the car took one out of his shirt pocket, right before I blacked out.* Nina threw her body forward. Her shoulder hit Berat in the back hard enough to bend him over.

"What the hell?"

As Nina fell to her knees, she jabbed one hand between his legs and grabbed the inside of his upper thigh. *That ought to distract him.* With her other hand, she snagged the protruding plastic bag. She slipped the baggie through the slit in her skirt and tucked it in her panty leg. He whirled, then clenched her upper arm in his enormous hand. When Berat yanked her to her feet, a second small bag hanging over the edge of his pocket fell to the floor, but he didn't notice. He was intent on dragging Nina to their destination. Opening the door, he shoved her toward a man standing stiff and alert, as if at attention, in the center of the room. Berat stepped out and slammed the door behind him. When it quit vibrating, Nina and the man stared at each other in confusion.

"I don't think you are the right girl."

"You're not the man I'm supposed to be with tonight." Nina peered into his face. "But you look familiar. I've seen you before."

"No, I don't think so." Shoulders back, spine erect, he tried to appear taller than his five feet, ten-inch frame.

"Oh yes, I have. On TV. The news, at home."

"Where's home?"

"Can't you tell? We have the same accent."

"Okay, look, I don't have a lot of time."

Assuming the man meant he was in a hurry to get what he paid for, Nina stiffened and stepped back toward the door. What he did next caused her to drop her guard. His shoulders slumped and his voice softened like a little boy's. "I'm in trouble. Big trouble."

"You're Mortensen, our secretary of defense." She watched as he returned to his full height and stature. "You've been on the news, advising President Brighton. You and the press secretary tried to persuade reporters you were disposing of old warheads rather than giving them to South Korea. Not very effective. Nobody believed you."

The secretary of defense shuffled his feet. "Okay, you got me, but that's not important right now. Listen, I need to find a particular girl. Let her know we'll either come back or send someone for her. Expected her, not you. The VP called her the golden-haired princess."

Vocal chords frozen, Nina stood in silence as Mortensen continued. "VP calls his daughter princess. The girls here, they're not princesses. Sorry, didn't mean you, but something about this girl yanked his chain. He made promises he can't keep."

Nina's voice cracked. "How old is this girl?"

"He said eighteen. I think that's what put him over the edge. His daughter's eighteen."

"That's…that's my daughter."

"Your daughter? Mother and daughter? Here?" Mortensen snorted incredulously, then reconsidered. He motioned to the sofa. "Okay, tell me what's going on."

Nina began with Darby's disappearance, worked toward her night at the Belaruse, being drugged and transported. He interrupted. "Now I remember. I saw you on TV, searching for your daughter. Then the Pantages. Your story got pushed off the front page after the shootings, but since they caught the shooters, you and your daughter are the top story again."

"We are? Thank God. Someone will rescue us."

"Honestly, Mrs. Richards, nobody's coming for you."

"Nobody? Not the LAPD?" When he shook his head, she continued. "No, I guess they couldn't leave the country. Certainly, the FBI can't leave us here."

"But they are. That's what I'm trying to explain. International incident mumbo jumbo. Now the CIA got Jack and they're after me…"

"What about Cox and Mason? Grady won't let this happen."

"Don't know anything about any Cox and Mason, or this Grady. Anyway, it's up to me to get you out."

"I don't understand. No one's going to rescue us? And the other women stolen from their homes and countries?"

Mortensen stood, started to walk away, then reversed direction and sat back down. "President Brighton called Vice President Connors home. Ordered, not requested, but she softened it by saying things could go better if we came voluntarily. The VP told her he wouldn't leave without your daughter."

"Won't you lose your job if you don't go back tonight?"

"I'll lose my job whether I go or stay. I've already lost my job." Mortensen hung his head. "I deserve it. This morning, crack of dawn, the President sent Special Services to pick us up. Best of the best. Trained in extradition."

"But you're here?"

"This morning when I heard people in the hall, trying to not make any noise, I had a bad feeling. Right before they busted Jack's door, I grabbed my bag, crawled out the window onto the fire escape."

"They didn't see you?"

"No. America's finest didn't even look out the window. These are the guys who supposedly protect us from the really bad guys, and they didn't even look out the window. Only a matter of time though. They'll find me."

"Perhaps they let you go to lead them here?"

"Don't think so. Maybe, I guess, nah." He shook his head. "Couldn't be the plan. They know where this place is."

"I don't understand. Why don't they want to rescue us? And the other women? Wouldn't that make them heroes?"

"No. For so many reasons, no." Sweat beaded on his forehead. "A political nightmare for the public to know the vice president and secretary of defense are involved with a drug and sex trafficking cartel. Would annihilate any trust the American people hold in the current administration. Casts a wide shadow of guilt by association, not on just the President's Cabinet, but the President herself. Would obliterate her political career."

"Career? Careers are more important than…"

"Jack tried. Honest. Said he requested the President deploy a team to Sugar House, shut it down, and rescue all the girls."

"They're coming?"

He pulled a hanky from his pocket and wiped the sweat from his forehead. "Why in the hell did I ever come here?" Then he rubbed the back of his neck. "Sorry, no. No one's coming to rescue you." When he looked back at Nina, the blood had drained from her face. "They're looking for me, but it's not a rescue effort. I stomped on my phone and threw it over a wall before I caught a cab back here. They may deduce where I am but won't storm in. They'll watch. Nab me on the streets."

"But our president? She's a mother, has a daughter. How can she leave us here?"

"They…she…the President made a political decision. They deemed the U.S./Turkey relationship too delicate to risk an international incident. Most of the women aren't even American. Can't express how sorry I am."

"Two American women, kidnapped and trafficked into sex slavery are not worth an incident?"

"One woman." he said under his breath.

"One?"

"You volunteered, came of your own volition. Right? That's what they're saying?"

When Nina didn't respond, Mortensen continued. "Turkish government officials don't want this becoming public. Sugar House isn't the only such enterprise here. The current administration is proud of the recent trade and security accords they parented with Turkey. The U.S. prefers Jackson Connors and I cease to exist rather than allow our antics to taint all that." He lumbered to the bar, poured a healthy shot of whisky and gulped. Then he lifted the glass toward Nina, but she shook her head. He gave the glass a regretful glare, left it on the bar and sat back down.

"Any rescue attempt could be fatal to everyone here at Sugar House. The cartel won't allow anyone to get out. The news is full of the three dead women, two murdered, one suicide, all linked to the Belaruse, but they haven't made the connection to this place. A lot more people would disappear before the cartel let their existence become publicly known."

Nina straightened her shoulders and patted her hip to check that the Devil's Breath remained in place. "You think I should give up?"

"No, no, it's not that. If they catch me, they'll bury me. But, I have connections to the press. I promise, one way or the other, the public will know you and your daughter are here. That'll force them to come for you."

"So, we wait while the drugging, the rape..." Nina's words caught in her throat. She swallowed the lump. "While these monsters continue to sell my daughter? We wait and hope some unknown entity demands our rescue?" The tears that had dammed behind her eyelids gushed as she waited for the answer he couldn't offer.

"God, I can't believe we were so stupid. Sank so low. What we've done…"

Even though she hated him, a shred of sympathy led her to touch his arm.

Mortensen stared at her hand, then pulled away. "Mrs. Richards, you're correct. No telling what the cartel will do. Might move you both, maybe to another country. We'd never find you then, or they might…" He looked at his feet and rung his hands. "No, we must do this right. I can't go back to my hotel. You can bet those boys caught hell for letting me slip out the window. They won't let that happen again. They'll have eyes on the hotel and this place. CIA, Special Services…everywhere. I'm a dead man walking, but you and your daughter, got to get you to the American Consulate, the embassy. Nobody will want it to happen that way, but it's our best chance."

"American Consulate? How?"

"Not sure yet. First, I'll draw you a map to the embassy. You'll be surprised how close it is. All in the same neighborhood." Mortensen shook his head. "The world is so screwed up."

CHAPTER THIRTY-ONE
Darby - Day Fifteen - Saturday, March 31

The previous night, when Darby returned from being with Vice President Jackson Connors, she hadn't gone into Amira's room. She knew her friend would be gone all night but expected her to have returned by this morning. Now eager to tell Amira that the vice president would help them escape that very night, Darby scurried to the adjoining door. She swung it open but halted in the doorway, her hand frozen to the doorknob. Amira's dresser drawers gaped open, clothes strewn across the floor.

Darby's mind imagined the worst possible scenario until she read the note. Her hand shook so hard she could barely read what it said. In another life, in other circumstances, a week in the Aegean Sea, basking in the sun, breathing salt air while sailing from island to island, might be the trip of a lifetime. But not this time. Amira had been taken away just when they had their opportunity to escape. The note slipped from Darby's fingers, floated to the floor.

She returned to her room, crawled in bed, and drew the covers over her head. Huddled in the dark, she tried to convince herself that when she told the world Amira's story, they'd come for her. She settled in and planned the rescue of her friend. *They'll come for everyone once they know.*

With every passing hour, Darby's spirits sank lower. Cowering in the bed, she felt weak, like she had given in, so she rose and walked to the chair. There she sat and waited for someone to come and tell her when she would be taken to the vice president. Her head nodded. Her eyelids slid shut. In her dream, the vice president, followed by soldiers with their guns, broke down her door. The crash jolted her awake. But instead of rescuers, it was Berat who slammed the door against the wall.

Darby clung to the edge of the chair, undecided whether to fight or bolt. Berat tossed a plate of food on the table, knocking her tea cup to the floor. *He must know the vice president is going to rescue me. That's why he's so mad.*

She started to ask when she'd be taken but changed her mind. Berat was clearly on the edge of violence, and she didn't want to provoke him. She told herself she had plenty of time. *Surely escape will happen after sunset.*

As the light outside faded, Darby defended every imaginable delay. She prepared for the moment, sustained herself with expectancy. Five hours later, when no one came, the heat of anger burned at her skin.

Liar. He never planned to come back for me... Her thoughts were interrupted as the door swung open, and Berat walked in. Again, he brought her a plate of Turkish cuisine, but this time he set it on the table, minus the fit of anger. As if in the eye of a storm, she felt brave enough to speak.

"Will I be going soon?"

"You're not going anywhere tonight."

"But I was supposed to see the same man as last night."

"Don't tell me now you're eager to go?"

"No, no. It's not that. I was just expecting..."

"Well, expect away, but you're not going anywhere. Your time is taken by someone else."

"But who? I was supposed…"

"Another blonde is already with him. What's it to you?"

Darby held back her disappointment until he left and closed the door. But when the key turned in the lock, a torrent of tears poured over her cheeks, down her neck. She cried until the neck of her shirt was wet and cold.

He didn't come for me. Darby's chest heaved. *Can't do this anymore. I'd rather be dead.*

She stared toward where Amira ought to be. Through her swollen eyelids, the half open door way seemed to be closing up, preparing to disappear. Struggling to lift her feet, Darby stumbled toward the dark opening and entered Amira's room. She stood in the center and looked around.

How can I do it?

She walked to the buffet behind Amira's table.

Thought I saw a fruit knife?

She yanked the drawer with such force it fell to the floor. Snatching up its contents, one handful at a time, she threw napkins, forks and serving spoons against the wall. Darby kicked at a pile of clothes on the floor then moved to the dresser and searched the open drawers. The leather belt she remembered being there was now gone.

Shoulders slumped, Darby turned away. The nightlight in the bathroom seemed to be a sign. She walked in and opened the medicine cabinet.

Drugs everywhere, except when I need them.

She collapsed on the side of the bathtub and held her head in her hands. She thought about filling the tub and sliding under. The effort was too much. She grasped the shower curtain to pull herself up. It gave way, and they both fell to the cold tile floor. Darby willed herself to get up. She staggered to Amira's bed and laid down. Her eyes burned, raw from the salty tears, but she cried no more. Her eyelids fluttered shut. Free-falling into unconsciousness, a solution formed in the hazy memories of a novel assigned in English class. *Tie the sheets together.*

CHAPTER THIRTY-TWO
Nina - Day Sixteen - Sunday, April 1

When Nina awoke from a few hours of broken sleep, she looked at the clock sitting on the nightstand. Her vision blurred until she couldn't read the time. Anger welled in her throat. "I hate you. Delicate and gold, you don't fool me. You're ugly, same as the monsters who own you." She flung her arm, knocking the clock to the floor, but it continued to tick.

Three hours 'til breakfast. Too long...

Head and muscles aching, she padded to the bathroom and splashed cold water on her blotchy face. She resisted the urge to leave and find her friends' rooms. As she blotted dry, Nina cautioned herself to stay calm. *Can't roam the halls, draw attention.* She tried to take a deep breath, but her lungs constricted. Nina bent over and coughed until phlegm sprayed the sink.

Seda would have the buffet set up by now, but it was too early for her to go. Breaking their routine might attract unwanted scrutiny. Nina dressed and settled into the chair to wait until ten. The tempo of her pulse increased, pounded against her temples. She leaned her head back against the chair and counted to calm herself. *One...two...three...*

Satisfaction swelled her chest when she remembered the plastic baggie she stole from Berat. She picked up her makeup bag. The baggie lay tucked inside. When she touched it, she felt a surge of power. *I'll dose him with his own poison.*

Nina's eyes darted around the room, looking for a safer location to hide the drug. She carried her precious cargo to the dresser and buried the baggie in her underwear drawer. She patted the pile of panties until they appeared undisturbed. "There you go. You're safe."

The ticking of the gold clock rose to a crescendo in her head. Nina picked it up off the floor. As she placed it back on the nightstand, she decided the dresser drawer was too obvious. So, she retrieved the baggie, returned to the bathroom, and pulled out a box of tampons. She tilted the box until the contents fell on the counter, then shoved the baggie to the bottom and stacked tampons on top. A smile spread across her lips. *Perfect. The male aversion will keep him out.*

As she slipped the tampon box into its hiding place, the ticking in the other room amplified and bounced off the walls. Nina turned and glared at the clock, then sat beside it and fidgeted. Time seemed to have slowed to a snail's pace, so she walked around the room. When 9:55 a.m. finally arrived, she left. Worried anyone who looked at her would know what she'd done, she stayed close to the wall and slunk toward the dining room.

When she arrived, Vanessa and Zoya sat next to each other at the table. Nina assumed she'd receive a halfhearted "good morning," but neither woman glanced her way. With a shrug, Nina waited for her friends. She only looked up when the kitchen door creaked. Seda entered carrying a steaming cup of Turkish coffee. The old woman put the cup down, and as had become her habit, patted Nina's shoulder before she returned to the kitchen. Nina raised the cup to her lips, then cocked her head toward the hushed voices in the hall.

"And you know what happen then…" Palwasha and Lin Su fell silent when they turned the corner and found Zoya and Vanessa seated across from Nina. Trying to appear unconcerned, they took their time to fill their plates. When they sat, one on each side of Nina, Lin Su and Palwasha gave each other sidelong glances but didn't speak.

Everyone looked toward Lin Su, expecting her to break the uncomfortable silence. "Most interesting night…" When she paused as if to wait for someone to request the details, Nina smiled at Lin Su's ploy to annoy Vanessa and Zoya.

Lin Su wriggled in delight when Vanessa rolled her eyes and stood in a huff. "Zoya and I entertain exclusive clients tonight. We don't have time to listen to your childish stories."

Lin Su continued to squirm in her seat, eager for Vanessa and Zoya to leave. The instant they were out of sight, she whispered, "Nina, very happy you are here. You will love to hear this. Berat in huge trouble. He lost drugs."

Nina opened her mouth to confess, but Lin Su cut her off. "Last night, somewhere, he dropped two tiny bags of the big stuff, the powder they call the Devil's Breath." Lin Su lit up, a smile engulfed her entire face. "Big boss found a bag in hallway. One still missing. Berat in serious trouble. We so happy…"

When the blood drained from Nina's face, left her looking as if she'd been electrocuted, both Lin Su and Palwasha stopped giggling. Nina tried to speak but only managed a quick jerky shake of her head.

Lin Su frowned. "What? You not like Lin Su's big news? So disappointed. Thought you would be very happy."

Nina focused on her bowl and pretended to be intent on scooping up a spoonful of yogurt. But before she put it into her mouth, she whispered to her friend. "Oh, I like it, Lin Su. I like it a lot. But don't react when I tell you…"

"Tell us what?"

"Shush, Lin Su. I have what he lost."

Nina's friends' eyes bulged, but neither uttered a word.

"I'll get out of here with Darby. Tonight."

"How will you do that with drugs? You need more than Devil's Breath. Can't drug everyone."

"I need keys for the other side, to free Darby from her room. The only ones I've seen are Berat's."

Palwasha's lips turned down, and she shrugged. However, the mischievous elf, Lin Su was not without a solution. "I get gun. You shoot Berat and take the keys."

Yogurt spewed from Palwasha's mouth, flew across her plate of fruit, and splatted against the water pitcher in the center of the table. "Oh, yes. Great idea, Lin Su. Where will Nina hide a gun?" One hand over her mouth, Palwasha laughed and lifted two fingers to the air. "Better get two." She motioned as though to slide her hands inside her bra. "She could put one in each side." But the laughter froze on her face when neither of her friends laughed back. "Lin Su, you are a crazy China woman. Berat will kill Nina if he finds her with a gun. Maybe us too."

Nina cut their bantering short. "I don't need a gun. Quiet. Listen, Lin Su." The familiar feeling of being watched was like a damp rag on her neck. Nina looked over her shoulder and lowered her voice. "I wasn't with the American vice president last night." The intrigue on her friends' faces reverted to disappointment. "But it's okay," Nina whispered. "The other man's name is Mortensen.

He's the secretary of defense, a member of our President's Cabinet, vital to the country." A smile brushed across Nina's lips when Lin Su wiggled with anticipation. "He's coming back today to help Darby and me escape." Lin Su and Palwasha both gasped. "He didn't say what time, but he promised."

"I find out for you. Do not worry, Nina. I got this. I will have time by lunch. Promise. Someone owes me a big favor."

"Thank you, Lin Su. The problem is how to find Darby before the secretary of defense comes back. Yesterday I inspected the courtyard wall, where we think the younger girls are held on the other side. I tried to climb over. Couldn't do it. Tried to push a pot to the wall. It wouldn't budge. How will we get to her?"

The three women each fell into their own thoughtful silence. When it became obvious no ideas would bubble up, Nina pushed back her chair. But before she could stand, Seda entered carrying a large cup of coffee. As was her habit, she rested her arthritic hand on Nina's shoulder, but this time with force, holding her in her chair. The bent old woman spoke directly into Nina's face. "Take this with you to drink. Alone. Only for you. Bring good luck."

When Nina raised the cup to her lips, Seda dug her knobby fingers into Nina's shoulder. "No, no. Take it to your room. Don't kill good luck."

As Seda retreated to the kitchen, the friends sat speechless and watched the door swing shut behind the old woman. Then Lin Su shrugged and broke their silence. "I work my people. We meet for lunch."

As Nina plodded to her room, she hesitated at every door hoping to overhear something useful. The harder she tried not to spill the coffee, the more her hand shook. When the warm liquid sloshed over the rim, she lifted it to take a sip but then remembered Seda's words. *"Don't kill good luck."*

Nina set the coffee cup on the table and stood for several moments without breaking her gaze. *Good luck in a cup. I need a planeload. One cup won't do the job.* She walked away and left the cup sitting alone. At the window, she looked out to the Magnolia trees. Soft white flowers fluttered in the breeze. She refocused on the lush green vine clinging to the courtyard wall. When Nina realized her answers weren't hiding in the plants, she turned away.

The ceramic cup that had been sitting small and ignored on the table grew in size and proportion. *Pathetic. I'm so desperate that I think it might be true.* Nevertheless, the cup lured her to it. She brought it to her lips and drank the dark liquid until something clanked against her teeth. Startled, she jerked her head back and peered into the bottom of the cup. There, half covered by soggy coffee grounds, lay her luck. An old-fashioned brass key.

Could it be? Like a disobedient child who thinks someone is watching from some secret location, Nina glanced over her shoulder. But no one crashed in to take it from her, so she hurried to the bathroom door and inserted the key. The familiar clink told her the door had locked. Nina tried to turn the knob. It didn't move. Unlocking it again, she scurried to her own outer door. Blood pounded against her temples as the key turned. *A master key?*

The key slipped from her trembling hand and clattered on the tile floor. When she bent to retrieve it, her shoulder banged into the door. The rattle resounded down the hall. She feared the noise would alert everyone to what Seda had given her. Nina flinched but didn't hesitate. She snatched the key and crammed it into her pocket. Then she braced herself against the closed door to stop Berat from crashing through.

But once again, no one came. After a few moments, she sat and breathed deeply, but her scrambled thoughts failed to settle. The time ticked by, measured by the gold clock, yet Nina was no closer to a plan. She berated herself because her only thought was to find Lin Su. Nina ran her hand over the key to reassure herself it still hid in her pocket. She worried someone would notice its outline, so she removed it and clasped it in her hand.

In the bathroom, she dug to the back of the cupboard for the tampon box. Again, Nina poured its contents onto the counter, including the plastic baggie she'd hid there before. Then she pressed the key and the tiny bag of Devil's Breath to the bottom, stacked the tampons on top, and whispered, "You're safe in there." She tucked the box away, intending to return to the hallway. But when she reached the bedroom, she thought, *What if I need to unlock a door?*

Nina dashed back and removed the key from the tampon box. This time she wrapped it in tissue, but when she stuffed it into her pocket, it made an uncomfortable lump. She pulled out, wound the tissue tighter, and slipped it deep into her bra. A quick check in the mirror left her satisfied with the results.

However, her confidence degenerated the moment she walked out. Her hand trembled as she slid it over her breast. Reassured the key remained invisible, she straightened her shoulders and continued to the dining room to find Lin Su and Palwasha.

When Nina arrived, the door was locked. Perplexed, she looked around. She was still standing there, debating whether to pull out the key when Lin Su's high-pitched voice bounced along the hall. The familiar giggle floated around the corner an instant before

Nina saw her friend. But when they made eye contact, Lin Su froze in place and waved Nina off. Trusting her friend's instincts, Nina pivoted on one foot and jogged back to her room. She closed the door behind her and fell against it to support her quivering legs.

Lin Su must know something. I can't just sit here and wait to meet her at lunch...

Nina's instincts told her to run back. Their demands so great, her muscles cramped from denying them. But she stayed quiet and leaned heavily against the door because she had no alternative. Then a tap, so faint she thought she imagined it until it happened again.

Berat knows. He's coming. Her urge was to run and hide, but she stayed her position and held the door closed. She barely heard the childlike voice over her own heavy breath.

"Nina? Nina, are you in there?"

She recognized the whisper but remained cautious. She opened the door just a crack. When Nina peeked around its edge, she came face-to-face with Lin Su.

"I have news."

Nina seized Lin Su's arm and hauled her in. Spinning to face her friend, Nina again put the weight of her body against the door to protect them from anyone who might try to force their way in.

"Thank God, you're here. I have news as well. I have a key."

"What you mean you have key?"

"The coffee, this morning, *Büyükanne* put a key in it. A master key."

"That is big news. Now you will be really thankful for mine. You girls, no more calling me gossip hound. Lin Su have the most important news."

"Tell me."

319

Lin Su leaned in. "I know where room is."

"Darby's room? You found Darby's room?"

Maintaining hcr covert ops demeanor, Lin Su looked over her shoulder and deepened her voice. "Of course, I have."

"Show me."

"Not now. Need a plan first. Here is what I think. Important man, secretary of whatever you said, we will make escape happen when he is here. You said he is coming with his plan, so we only need to have Darby ready. Not hard. Palwasha and I will do it."

Nina pushed against her temples to contain the pulse threatening to break out. "I can't give you the key. I'm sorry, but I can't let it out of my sight. Could be Darby's only chance."

"Okay, tell you what. You keep. Bring with the little bag of magic when you go to Mr. Secretary. I…and Palwasha, we will be by the dining room. Then you slip me the key. We will get Darby. Bring her to room where you meet Mr. Secretary."

"Okay, might work."

"Will work. He is important man. He knows what to do."

"Lin Su. How will I ever thank you?"

"No need to thank. Right thing to do."

"Come with us, you and Palwasha."

"No, no. More people, more chance of failure. Besides, Lin Su's legs too short to run fast. Can't keep up with long-legged Americans." When Nina protested, Lin Su said, "All will be okay. When you are free, come back for us. We will go live with you in America."

Nina wrapped her arms around Lin Su and held her tight. "I'll be back. I promise. As soon as my daughter's safe."

"Go make yourself pretty. Wear good shoes so you can run and hide. Now, act normal."

"But, Lin Su, I don't know what time he's coming."

"Of course, I know that also. Early this time, six o'clock. When you slip me the key, Palwasha and I will bring Darby to you." Nina watched Lin Su jut out her chin and straighten her spine to make herself as tall as her frame would stretch. Nina thought her friend acted more confident than she felt when she said, "Our plan will work."

Once back in her room, Nina dressed for flight. She chose flared pants to cover the tennis shoes. She stuffed the precious plastic bag into her bra on the side opposite the master key, then sat and waited. Nina stared at the clock. She pressed against her leg to stop the bouncing. It wouldn't hold still so she stood and paced in a circle. The third time past the door, she stopped to peer down the empty hall, then slipped around the corner and flattened herself against the wall. She tried to convince herself no one would notice. Her gut was alive with warnings, telling her she was wrong.

Nina slunk toward the dining room. *Stop. Follow the plan.* She turned and headed back to her room. *Can't blow it. No second chances.* When the door closed behind her, she recoiled as though slapped. Through the lattice covering of the window, a thin beam of sunlight glinted off the gold lettering of the book on the nightstand. Her hands trembled as she lifted the Qur'an. *Stupid, stupid.* She fanned its pages. In slow motion, a folded white paper fluttered to the floor. *How could I forget?*

She picked up the map the secretary of defense had drawn and stuffed it into her pants pocket. To ensure they were still safe, Nina again tapped the spots where she hid the key and plastic baggie. She walked to the door and pressed her ear against it, expecting to hear the forceful steps of Berat's boots. Instead, only silence. Dread filled her, but she didn't have long to wait. A door slammed, vibrating the walls of the hall. She cocked her head toward the sounds of people running.

Nina opened her door just enough to slip out. She cringed and braced for what might come. When no one came her way, she pressed her back against the wall and slithered toward the dining room. She stopped when she heard men's voices and scuffling noises coming from beyond a door she had never seen open before. Leaning forward, she could see into what looked like a reception area.

Monty caught her eye and jerked his head in warning. "Down. Get down."

The doorway was blocked by a large man holding a rifle across his chest, but behind him, was a strip of clear blue sky. When she looked back to the secretary of defense, he had raised his hands up behind his head. Men in military flak jackets stood at his sides. Hopelessness ran through her veins when she realized that Monty also was now a prisoner.

Fear and defeat defined his face. She wanted to help him, but knew she wasn't strong enough. She shook her head in apology. Then the soldier from behind rammed his rifle butt into Monty's back as if he were a common criminal. Nina clamped her hand over her mouth to strangle down a scream. No one even glanced in her direction. She reached out to Monty as he struggled to his feet. When he regained his balance and looked up, shame covered his face. As the two soldiers at his side yanked him backward and dragged him out the front door of Sugar House, she read his lips.

"I'm sorry."

Beads of sweat ran down her forehead, yet she shivered with fear. *It's up to me now.* Nina pushed off the wall and sprinted the last steps to the dining room. Then she saw them coming single file, cowering to hide from the enemy. Tiny but fierce, Lin Su led the brigade. Palwasha followed an armlength behind, one hand resting on Lin Su's shoulder. But it was the movement beyond Palwasha that captured Nina's attention. Golden strands of hair created a wild halo in the electrified air. Nina ran toward the human chain. A third person was hunkered behind the two shorter women.

Then everyone stopped. Berat, with his mass of muscle and sinew, stepped in front of Lin Su. It appeared she would stop, but Lin Su stormed forward like a miniature bulldozer. She rolled her shoulders in and clamped her fingers into ironclad fists. With the force of a cannonball, she plowed into Berat. Her head crashed into his gut while her hands pounded, working their way down to his crotch. Losing his balance and rolling to the floor, Berat jerked his knees up to protect his vitals from further onslaught, but Lin Su did not relent. As she pummeled him, her voice rose to a glass-shattering octave. *"Bíráng. Wǒ shā nǐ."* No one understood her battle cry, but it didn't matter. She repeated it in English. "Get out of way. I kill you."

Palwasha shoved Darby away from the fight. An enormous man barreled around the corner and grabbed Lin Su by the waist. Nina crouched, plunged against the man, trying to knock him off Lin Su. With one massive arm, he flung Nina against the wall. Then as if peeling a banana, he tore Lin Su down Berat's body, toward his ankles, but couldn't break her grip. Lin Su's skirt slid up her thigh to reveal short but musclebound legs. Still clutching Berat, she swung her leg with the accuracy of a Karate master. Her high-heeled foot found purchase in the hulking man's jaw. The crack of bone breaking came only an instant before his howl.

Palwasha shoved Darby past the thrashing bodies toward her mother. Nina wanted to hug her tight and kiss her face, but she couldn't take the time. She seized her daughter with one arm and with the other, flung open the dining room door. With the clutch of a gorilla, she heaved Darby through and slammed it behind them. The door rattled as if hit with a bomb blast.

"Go Darby." Nina pointed. "The backdoor. Run." Nina reached for a chair and shoved it up under the doorknob. As she spun, she tripped on her own feet and stumbled to the floor. Leaning against the wall, she crawled back up and shot forward.

Darby slid on the slick tiles and banged into the white wooden door on the opposite wall. She cranked the doorknob, but it didn't move. When she looked back, her mother's face was contorted with confusion and terror. Darby hesitated. Then she tugged with full force, but the door stood strong.

Nina dug for the master key, now sunk to the bottom of her bra. Frenzied, she grappled with the underwire. The key clanked to the floor and bounced under the table. Darby dove for it then jumped back to the knob. Her hand trembled. She stabbed at the lock several times, then the key slid in. But before she could open the door to the kitchen, her nose curled at the rank scent that closed in from behind. Darby whirled and saw the enormous man charging toward her like an out-of-control army tank. Only steps behind, a laboring Berat dragged Lin Su along, her arms clamped to his leg like the tentacles of a mad octopus.

Darby begged, "Please... Please, open." And in that instant, it did. She held the door for her mother, but Nina propelled her daughter forward, then slammed it shut behind them. "That way.

Out. Go, go." They leaped forward, but Nina caught her hip on a drawer's metal handle. The force spun her. Grappling to regain her balance, she hit a large copper kettle. It shot across the counter and clanged to the floor. As Nina steadied herself, the door behind them swung open.

Nina thrust her fingers deep into the other side of her bra until she grasped the plastic baggie. An inner calm flooded her mind, her movements slowed. She opened the baggie and emptied the white powder into her palm. Berat stretched out to grab her. She filled her lungs and blew the Devil's Breath from her hand. His eyes widened with recognition, and he threw his body backwards. The tank of a man crashed into Berat. They slipped and thudded to the floor.

Nina didn't know if the drug had reached him, but she couldn't wait to find out. At the least, it bought them a few seconds of time. Aware the minutest particle could stop her just as she hoped it would stop the men, Nina wiped her hand on her pants leg as Darby reached the next door.

"The key, Darby. Quick."

This time Darby knew what to do. With a steady hand, she inserted the key and wrenched the door open. Nina looked out over her daughter's shoulder. The first thing she saw was a snippet of powder blue sky. Next to hit her senses was the music of engines roaring, brakes screeching, and people shouting. Darby and her mother darted, slamming the kitchen door behind them. Nina threw herself against a stack of wooden crates. They wavered, then fell across the steps, blocking the doorway.

"Left...left." Nina seized Darby's hand and pulled her along the path. The roadway was congested with trucks and lorries that honked and lurched as pedestrians stepped from between parked cars into the busy street. A taxi screeched to a halt at Darby's feet. She banged on the window and screamed. "Let us in." But the driver cringed and drove away. Nina gagged on the rotten egg fumes from his exhaust, then seized Darby's arm and pulled her forward. Two men carrying a large wooden crate in the middle of the street blocked their way. Darby and her mother spun and darted past.

Nina fumbled in her pocket for the map, now rolled into a ball but didn't pull it out. She didn't need to look. She had it memorized. Just confirming it was still there gave her strength.

"Turn...down the alley. Run," shouted Nina as she pushed Darby forward. Now that they'd passed the market place, the crowds thinned to only a few pedestrians who stared as the mother and daughter barreled by. "At the end...right...turn right."

The noise behind them grew louder. Feet pounding, heels banging on the pavement, gaining distance, coming closer. When she cranked her head around she saw Berat. The face of the second man was hidden by a brightly colored shop awning, but Nina recognized his massive body as the tank that had grabbed her in the kitchen.

Darby pitched to the side as her foot twisted in a pothole. Nina reached out and grabbed her daughter's sleeve to stop her from tumbling to the ground. The fabric broke loose in her sweaty hand. Adrenaline flooded her bloodstream. She lifted her daughter by the armpits and propelled her forward. "Behind us. Run, Darby, run."

Nina screamed at two men standing on the street corner, deep in conversation. "Stop them." She slowed her pace, gasped for air, and pointed. "They're going to kill us." The men looked up but made no move to help. They only stared.

Nina surged forward to catch up with her daughter. "Watch for a big flag. American flag...embassy." Sweat ran down Nina's face. Her lungs burned. She didn't think she could run any faster but barreled forward when the Tank yelled in their direction.

"Stop them. Thieves. Stop them."

Bouncing off each other, Darby and Nina scrambled and then ran faster.

"Atatürk..." Nina struggled to pull oxygen into her lungs.

Darby couldn't understand what her mother said but didn't slow her pace. She only raised her hands in a shrug.

"Street...Atatürk...embassy." Nina wheezed in gulps of air.

"Mom, they're gaining."

"Next sign. What is it?" Nina tried to ignore the cramping in her calves, but her pace slowed.

"That's it... Atatürk."

Nina hesitated, put one hand out, and steadied herself against a light pole. "Run, Darby," she gasped. "Run."

"Mom, you okay?"

Nina nodded. Pain ripped up her leg when she repelled off the pole. A few more strides and they were under the street sign. Darby stopped and jerked her head, back and forth from the sign to her mother. "Right or left?"

Both women sucked in air. Darby recovered instantly. Nina's chest heaved. She panted and fought for breath but couldn't inhale enough to answer.

"Quick, Mom. Right or left?"

Nina glanced back. Berat and the Tank were closing in. "The powder. It didn't stop them." The big man ran slower, huffing like a steam engine several paces behind Berat, but they were still coming.

"Hurry, Mom. They're catching us."

Oxygen deficit blurred Nina's vision and addled her thoughts. The picture of the map muddled in her mind. Unsure which way to turn, she dug into her pocket. As she unrolled the map, it caught in her sweaty palm and tore. Nina heaved with exhaustion as she aligned the pieces. "Right, Darby. Go right."

Mother and daughter bounded between two parked cars, then leaped over the curb onto the sidewalk. The path reshaped from straight to curvy. With every step, Nina's legs threatened to give out, but a jolt of energy fired through her when Darby pointed and cried out.

"Mom. Look."

The enormous American flag waving in the breeze, high upon a pole as it reached toward the sky, called them to it. Their bodies lightened. Euphoria over powered the lactic acid burn and their muscles responded.

"Go, Darby. Fast. Don't look back."

But Darby shook her head and seized her mother's hand. "Not leaving you." She hauled her mother forward.

The road appeared deserted. But in the distance, Nina recognized the engine purr of an approaching car. She looked but decided it was useless to ask for help again. As she spun away, her arm slapped against the trunk of a sapling planted near the edge of the sidewalk. Nina ignored the sting and focused on the curve of the sidewalk. But she jerked her head around at the sudden screech and grind of a Turkish police siren. She spun to look, but thoughts of help evaporated as the police car turned onto another street.

Quickly spinning back to run, Nina lost her balance. She wove off course and crashed into an enormous cement pot. A blur of pink and violet flowers blocked her vision as her face ripped down the grain of the cement, shredding skin and bringing blood to the surface. Darby grabbed her mother and lifted her. At the next curve in the path, there it was. A beacon within their reach, the American flag pointed toward safety. It grew larger as they ran. Nina paused at the sight of the freedom symbol flying half-staff, then leapt forward.

Someone must've died today, but it's not going to be us.

Then for only a second, Darby hesitated when they reached the twelve-foot wall of gray cinderblock that surrounded the American Embassy. *The same as my prison.* But the flashback didn't stop her. It moved her toward the flag. Black wrought-iron gates stood at the end of the red trimmed wall. Beyond the intimidating barrier, a massive building, also made of cinderblock, loomed in the distance.

Darby jabbed her arm in the air as a sign of triumph, then screamed with the force of an ocean squall. "Help. Help us."

Shaking from exhaustion, saturated in sweat, Nina and Darby pressed their faces into the bars of the towering wrought-iron gate. They clenched it and shook, rattling the gate on its hinges. "American citizens. Help us."

Darby tugged her mother's arm and spun her around. Lungs burning, she gulped to catch her breath. "They're right there."

Nina followed Darby's outstretched hand toward where Berat and the Tank stood at the curb across the street. Their bodies heaved. Nina whirled back to the guards and shrieked. "They're going to kill us."

Darby's body convulsed to take in air. "Those men...kidnapped us." She spat the words between gasps. "Drugged us. American. We're Americans."

Two armed guards stepped forward while a third remained in the guard house. Nina swayed and folded at the waist. She gripped her knees. She looked up just in time to see the guard lift a black phone to his ear.

"Need your passports."

"Don't have passports," Nina's vision darkened. "Kidnapped…"

Darby understood her mother could no longer speak, so she spoke for her. "We were prisoners. Don't have anything." To keep from falling, she gripped the iron bars until her knuckles bulged. Darby wiped her nose on her torn shirt sleeve. "Asylum. We want asylum. You must protect us." Gasping out her last words, Darby's grip weakened, and she slid down the bars. "Please help us."

The guard who'd been talking on the phone rushed out of the guard house and unlocked the pedestrian gate. He nodded to the other two guards who stood by with rifles drawn. "Bring them in. Quickly."

One guard extended his hand to guide Nina and Darby inside. When the gates closed behind them, Darby's tears turned to wheezing sobs. The second guard stood at attention. He held his rifle across his chest. The concrete shook beneath their feet as the gate scraped and clanked shut. Nina and Darby clung to each other. Shaking and crying, they fell to their knees.

Everyone, except the guard whose glare remained locked on the two men outside the gate, turned toward the roar of an engine. The white SUV parked in front of the embassy's massive glass doors, revved its engine and sped toward the gate. Darby and Nina cringed as the brakes screeched and the car slid to a stop close enough they could reach out and touch it. When the driver, hidden behind blackened windows, jumped out and drew a handgun from inside his jacket, a thick slime burned its way up from Nina's stomach.

Two men dressed in American business suits stepped out of the backseat. The older man reached out, lifted Nina off the ground and pulled her to his burley torso. "I've got you. You're safe."

Nina collapsed against him and held tight. She buried her face in his chest. It was his gentle touch and kindly expression that finally caused her to lose it. When her stomach cramped, Nina retched its contents down his crisp white shirt.

EPILOGUE

In the end, on national TV, Nina heard herself say, "One thinks of human trafficking as a crime against poor defenseless children stolen out of Africa or another underdeveloped country. However, it also thrives in a dark pocket of humanity characterized by extreme wealth and position. People of power inflict cruelty and degradation upon their prey, absent so much as a shred of shame for the harm they inflict."

She slipped off her shoes and watched the TV screen over the backs of the three heads lined up on the couch. Intent on watching her interview, the women did not notice Nina had returned from taking her mother home.

"Victoria, trafficked women are not always poor and uneducated. However, they are taken against their will, drugged, brainwashed, threatened, tortured, and sold to some of the wealthiest and vilest of today's world leaders and influentials. It's an unimaginable underbelly of life that is otherwise invisible."

"Mrs. Richards, most people believe human trafficking exists too far from home to be their concern."

"When in fact, Victoria, no community is untouched. I never would've known such a menace threatens us all, our way of life. Well, in a way *I knew it.* In a way, *we all know it.* We've seen it on CNN, BBC, read of it online. Somehow my subconscious maintained an aloofness, a distance, failing to acknowledge that our young women are forced into slavery. And to accept that it consumed my family? Inconceivable, Victoria. Normal people find it implausible that their family member could be trafficked. I pray to God it never happens, but it can. For me…it did."

Nina cleared her throat to announce she was home. When the women turned to greet her, she said, "Lin Su, please hit the pause button. I want to check on Darby and watch this with you."

Nina's bare feet padded softly as she climbed the stairs. Darby was curled in a ball, gently snoring. She didn't stir when Nina closed the door and headed down the hall. As she passed the guest bedrooms that had become headquarters for her mother's support team, Gaby and Teresa, a smile lit Nina's face. *Who would have thought?*

The solitary action of returning her mother to her condo had brought Nina comfort. *Our world's returning to normal. Our world is, but still so many…* As she descended the stairs, she counted, *three…four…five.* With each step, *six…seven…* she could feel the others. The responsibility weighed heavy across her shoulders. *Bone tired…eight…nine…ten… Need to sleep. But first…*

Nina detoured at the bottom. She selected her largest wine glass from behind the bar and poured a healthy portion of the rich burgundy liquid. She swirled it, inhaled the earthy aroma, then lifted the glass to her lips. *Okay. I'm ready.*

Nina picked up the bottle and walked back to join Amira, Palwasha, and Lin Su. As she sunk into her favorite chair, Lin Su released the pause and the four women watched the recorded interview with Victoria van der Waals.

The camera closed in until the screen filled with Victoria's face. "Mrs. Richards, throughout the continent, mothers, fathers, people in general, stand in awe of the sacrifice you made to rescue your daughter. Many women claim rape is the worst possible crime that could be committed upon them personally. But you set that aside, descended into the darkest segment of society and suffered unspeakable crimes. You entered the world of high stakes prostitution to gain access to your daughter. Tell me how you endured these repeated acts of violation and then rose to do what no one else, not the LAPD, FBI, or even CIA could do...bring your daughter home."

When the cameraman shifted back, the screen filled with the two women sitting in large upholstered chairs, surrounded by artificial plants. A small table between them held steaming mugs. Nina marveled at how normal they must appear, two friends having coffee. *Nothing's ever quite what it seems.*

"Victoria, I researched what would be necessary to save my daughter. I was always the dominant actor. I used those men to gain the information and access I needed to bring Darby home."

"But these men, strangers, you were forced to have sex with them."

"Victoria, please understand, after I made my way to Turkey, I found many victims, but I was not one of them. My daughter's experience..." Nina choked on her words, "very different from mine. Eighteen years old...still a child...drugged, kidnapped, brutalized."

Nina's face flushed as the anger pushed up from her chest. Taking a moment to compose herself, she lifted her coffee mug and sipped. "Victoria, you're correct in that I didn't know the men. However, I did know they were connected to the cartel that kidnapped Darby. I searched for the man who would help me rescue her. And while two attempted, ultimately my help came from two brave women who were also victims of the same cartel. Both trafficked and sold."

"Mrs. Richards, in talking to people, what most feel is admiration."

"Victoria, I want to emphasize that no one forced me to do anything. The LAPD, FBI, and a team of experts provided by my firm's executive kidnapping insurance all worked hard, followed every lead, dug deep into the bowels of the crime world. These professionals opened doors that led me find my daughter. However, after locating her on the dark web, they fell short. Throughout the investigation, I watched plainclothes officers slip out of one world and into the next. After eight days, I knew what I must do. When they failed to go get Darby, I went myself."

Victoria leaned forward in her chair as if to urge Nina to continue.

"The FBI located Darby in Ankara, Turkey. To bring her home, I entered a black market that sells children and women. Victoria, I've watched your show for years. You've covered perfectly vile men who historically enjoyed respect and positions of power, locally and internationally. While at Sugar House, I met shahs, diplomats, entertainers, and politicians, even members of the President's Cabinet."

When Nina's voice caught, Victoria said, "Mrs. Richards, no one wants you to endure additional stress or harm. Please continue at your own pace. If you finish your story today, fine. If not, we'll schedule a second interview as you see fit."

"Thank you, Victoria. Unanticipated memories often disrupt my thoughts. Both my daughter and I were diagnosed with PSDT, but I want to tell you the rest of my story. However, I would appreciate a glass of water." Victoria raised her hand to signal action on the part of her staff as Nina continued. "Some of the news reports are not accurate. So even though it often transports me back to horror I would like to forget, I want people to know the truth regarding what's happening to these women and children."

"Mrs. Richards, no ordinary words exist to describe what you must feel. Nor does the ordinary person understand the atrocities associated with this crime. Currently, sexual exploitation comprises eighty percent of trafficking. The remainder involves forced labor. This is no small violation of human rights."

"Especially for the children, Victoria. Boys are also trafficked, but the cartel that stole my daughter dealt only in girls and women. Trafficking is clandestine. It spans the globe hidden by an intricate web of deceit, abuse, drugs, and death." Nina took a moment to recompose herself. "It's an underground crime that happens within the bowels of the human encounter."

"I believe you would agree, Mrs. Richards, that Angelinos would be shocked to know how many children and women are trafficked within their own city limits. With more than seven hundred this year alone, California reports the highest number of trafficking cases followed by Texas, Florida, Ohio and New York. And let me remind our viewers, these are reported cases. No one knows how many go unreported."

"Victoria, when the CIA raided Sugar House in Turkey, they rescued girls and women from China, Pakistan, Thailand, Moldova, Bulgaria, Afghanistan, Albania, India, Africa, Sweden, France, Russia, Brazil, and Iran."

"Our viewers will be surprised by the countries ranked high as sex trafficking destinations. In addition to Turkey, the names that took me by surprise were Belgium, Germany, Greece, Israel, Italy,

Japan, the Netherlands, and Thailand. Most shocking, however, the U.S. is also identified as a frequent destination. As a country, we should be ashamed."

"Victoria, another unknown fact is that in the U.S., natural born citizens are more likely trafficked than foreign nationalized citizens. Which brings me back to the misconception held by the majority of Americans. Victims are not all from third world countries. The next victim could be your neighbor's child, or yours."

"Mrs. Richards, you and your daughter could have been killed if your captors caught you during your escape. Or if anyone of the women you trusted had betrayed you."

"All risks I had to take to gain access through the same channels Darby was taken. The thing different for me than for my daughter was that I went willingly, thinking if I did, they wouldn't drug me. However, initially I wasn't successful. This cartel uses Devil's Breath on every victim to ensure a quiet, compliant capture and transport."

"Before you and your daughter returned home, Devil's Breath was the topic of my show. Less than one percent of viewers who tweeted reported they knew of the drug prior to my interview with the two detectives. Viewers also commented that learning of this new threat to their safety increased the stress they feel when out in public, in big cities, or traveling internationally."

"Victoria, in my family, of course my daughter feels it most intently. However, both Darby's grandmother and I are unable to leave our homes without a sense of unease."

"Mrs. Richards, will you tell us more?"

Victoria fell silent as Nina told her story, beginning with her first trip to the Belaruse and concluding with the security video from the American Consulate in Turkey. "I couldn't let anyone dissuade me. The stakes were too high. I worked my plan, found my daughter and brought her home."

"Yes, you did, Mrs. Richards, and as far as our research reveals, in a manner no other woman ever has."

"I pray no other woman ever has to. However, while my single act of rescuing my daughter resulted in the demise of one cartel, it will have no tangible impact on this crime. A few CEO's and politicians as well as two members of the President's Cabinet lost their jobs, their careers. Destroyed their lives. However, the effect on human trafficking is equivalent to rescuing a single snowflake from an avalanche."

Victoria faced the camera and spoke directly to her viewers. "We must take action. You may help by rallying your representatives, church and community leaders to demand greater resources be committed to this battle."

Nina nodded in agreement.

"Mrs. Richards, no one before you is known to have done what you did. Personally, my only question is, 'What would I do?'" Nina clenched her fists. Anguish washed across her face. "Mrs. Richards, do you need a moment? We can take a commercial break."

Nina shook her head. "It's difficult for some to understand that sex with a stranger is not the worst a person can experience." She gripped the arms of the chair to control her shaking. "Only a parent who has lost a child knows that intensity of panic and helplessness. The despair I experienced when I thought Darby might be dead is indescribable. When I learned she'd been sold into sexual slavery, I can't begin to explain how I felt. Both Darby and I are in therapy, but honestly Victoria, I don't yet have words to make anyone comprehend my horror."

"Mrs. Richards, your voice is huge right now. I understand you are fundraising for the purpose of increasing awareness and providing services for the victims?"

"Yes, Victoria. Nearly thirty thousand sex trafficking victims die each year from abuse, drug overdoses, and disease. A huge influx of funds is needed, but politicians don't find the topic appropriate on which to build a campaign. Fundraisers don't find the cause fitting for a gala event. Trafficking of women and children for sexual exploitation is the fastest growing criminal enterprise in the world. I can no longer live in my private world and ignore what's happening."

"Mrs. Richards, I understand your house is full of women who befriended you at Sugar House?"

Nina's face lit up. "Marvelously, yes. After I escaped with Darby, CIA raided Sugar House, and all the children and women were repatriated or relocated. Three special women are with me. One is still a child, only seventeen. However, given the life she's lived, it's hard to think of her as so young."

"How long will they stay with you and your daughter?"

"Victoria, one will eventually return to her home county, but the other two will remain in the United States. They will live with me as long as they desire. We are family now."

"Mrs. Richards, studies explain that soldiers, in the heat of battle, fight to the death to save their friends. God, country, or big picture values move to the back, behind the personal bonds formed between soldiers. It is my sense, similar to the soldier who takes all other soldiers as brothers, you have taken all trafficked women and children as family. We would love details of how you are helping these women, such as Lin Su Zhang. I understand she's quite an artist."

Nina admired the oil painting that now filled the screen. "Since coming to live with me and my daughter, Lin Su has been painting up a storm. A friend, a gallery owner, says Lin Su has a career in art, but recommended she train with a particular local artist. Consequently, we've arranged that Lin Su will live with me until she chooses to go out on her own." The cameraman turned back to focus on Nina's face.

"Lin Su's best friend, kind and loving Palwasha, wants to return to her father's farm in Afghanistan. Therefore, we enrolled her in agriculture and farming classes. She'll stay with us a couple of years to complete a degree. Then there is my now second daughter, Amira. Amira Farooqi is from Islamabad, Pakistan, where she took classes in International Studies. She's incredibly smart, speaks several languages, including excellent English. She's inspired by President Alice Brighton and wants to serve her in the Office of Language Services as a translator. As you know, Darby's a freshman at UCLA, therefore, Amira will also attend so the girls will again be…" Nina's voice caught and she could only whisper, "roommates."

"Mrs. Richards, what you're doing speaks to the woman you are."

"It's my pleasure. I'm fortunate to have the resources to help my new international family."

"When do you think you and your daughter will return to your normal lives?"

"There's no going back to normal. Living under the veil of this dark and secret world, eating, sleeping among them, changes you forever. It changes the rest of the world for you. Nothing will ever be quite the same."

As Victoria van der Walls closed her show, the four women said goodnight. Nina refreshed her glass of wine, walked out onto the deck, and reclined in the deckchair. She now found herself so jumpy at sudden movements and unexpected sounds, such moments of inner peace were rare. As her body melted into the cushions, it occurred to her that a dive into ocean depths held much in common with rescuing her daughter.

A journey into a bottomless terrain, ignorant of what lurks below.

For as far as she could see, white capped waves rolled onto the white sandy shoreline, creating a bubbly fluff. *Peace and quiet. In time, we'll all heal. We'll be fine.*

Sinking through a backdrop of marshmallow clouds, the burnt-orange sun would soon disappear. The translucent sea would blacken as the ball of fire extinguished beyond the horizon. Tipping her glass, she toasted the setting sun. *Thankfully, a piece of my life is setting as well. Everyone is safe.* Inhaling deeply, she filled her lungs with salty ocean air, an air that heals all wounds.

Nina leaned her head back and urged her mind to go blank. As her eyelids slid shut, the phone vibrated and noisily quivered across the glass-top table. When it hung half off the edge, close to crashing onto the deck, Nina snatched it back to safety. The screen read, "Unidentified Caller." She sighed. Against her better judgement, Nina touched the screen with her index finger.

"Hello?" She regretted it the instant she heard her own voice.

"Are you Nina Richards?"

"Yes, who is this?"

"My name is Roseanne Cheadle. I saw you on television. I've read everything about you." The caller gulped air. When she spoke again her voice quaked. "My sixteen-year-old daughter has been missing for twenty-three days. Please... Will you help me?"

Why I wrote Story of a Stolen Girl.

I began my professional career in the California Community College system as a cosmetology instructor and retired as a college president. During this time, my primary goal was to develop programs, services, and facilities to improve student opportunities and achievements. In that spirit, I wanted to write a novel that would make a difference.

Every year, 800,000 children, women, and men are trafficked. Human trafficking, as the fastest growing crime in the world, is also the most under-reported. From infant to young adult, children are sold as slaves. To survive, they struggle in untenable conditions to secure the most minimal form of survival. Children work in the sex industry, in mines, in homes cooking and cleaning, in the streets, and on construction sites. They haul rocks, pull heavy carts, and clear land. They slave in sweatshops, kitchens, and assembly lines. Young boys, dressed as girls, are forced to dance and often much more. Parents atone for their sins by selling young girls to religious leaders as "slaves to the gods." From the age of five and into adulthood, should they survive, children make bricks, dig for diamonds, and work on drug and cocoa farms. They die having their organs harvested. They also die in battle when they are turned into killers to fight adults' wars.

Most Americans believe human trafficking is a problem only in poor and underdeveloped countries, too far away to be our concern. However, statistics report over 50,000 slaves in the United States, with another 17,500 being trafficked every year. There has never been a country or time in history when it did not occur. The problem is huge. Resolution requires societal change. If this book stimulates conversation that makes a difference for any of these victims, I am satisfied with its results.

343

Dear Readers,

*Thank you for choosing **STORY OF A STOLEN GIRL**. If you enjoyed it, please submit a review on Amazon, Barnes and Noble, or where ever you made your purchase. I appreciate hearing from you. Please visit me on Facebook or my website. This novel is a researched work of fiction, and you can find my reference materials listed on my website. As well, Questions and Topics for Discussion available at* http://patspencer.net

Sincerely,
Pat Spencer

ACKNOWLEDGEMENTS

A million thanks go to my husband and editor-in-chief, Mike Spencer. I am grateful for his encouragement, love, technical skills, and long hours of proofreading. Without which this novel may never have come to life. A special thank you goes to our son, Sergeant Jeff Spencer, for his expertise in criminal activities, the law, and police procedures. And for keeping my writing authentic by kindly saying, "Mom, you watch too much Bluebloods."

Many thanks go to Vicki Young and the Country Club Book Club for their input and encouragement, and to my longtime friend, Louise Wright, for her suggestions and proofing of the first draft. And finally, thank you to the members of the Carlsbad Writers Bloc who helped me become a better writer.

Dr. Pat Spencer authored a textbook, newspaper and magazine columns, as well as trade and scholarly articles. She received degrees from Riverside Community College, University of La Verne, and University of California, Riverside. She began her academic career as a community college teacher and retired as a college president. She lives in Southern California with her husband, Mike.

23516370R00207

Made in the USA
Columbia, SC
08 August 2018